Richard Hayden has worked in the
theatre and as a scriptwriter. He lives
in London. *The Influencing Engine*
is his first novel.

THE
INFLUENCING
ENGINE

Richard Hayden

BLACK SWAN

THE INFLUENCING ENGINE
A BLACK SWAN BOOK : 0 552 99677 7

First publication in Great Britain

PRINTING HISTORY
Black Swan edition published 1996

Set in 11/12½pt Linotype Melior by Kestrel Data, Exeter

Black Swan Books are published by Transworld Publishers Ltd,
61–63 Uxbridge Road, London W5 5SA,
in Australia by Transworld Publishers (Australia) Pty Ltd,
15–25 Helles Avenue, Moorebank, NSW 2170
and in New Zealand by Transworld Publishers (NZ) Ltd,
3 William Pickering Drive, Albany, Auckland.

Reproduced, printed and bound in Great Britain by
Cox & Wyman Ltd, Reading, Berks.

For Sandra

ACKNOWLEDGEMENTS

I am indebted to Mollie Gillen's *Assassination of the Prime Minister* for the chronology of events and for access to documents I would otherwise have overlooked. John Haslam's *Illustrations of Madness* contains interviews with James Tilly Matthews and a detailed account of Matthews's extraordinary invention – The Influencing Engine. I would like to thank everybody who has helped me with this novel, but above all thanks are due to Bill Scott-Kerr and Jo, Adam Brett, Robert Wilson, Jo Graham and, of course, Sandra Bossy, for their support, advice and unfailing friendship over the years.

And to my parents and family – thank you.

All things are sold: the very light of heaven
Is venal; earth's unsparing gifts of love,
The smallest and most despicable things
That lurk in the abysses of the deep,
All objects of our life, even life itself,
And the poor pittance which the laws allow
Of liberty, the fellowship of man,
Those duties which his heart of human love
Should urge him to perform instinctively,
Are bought and sold as in a public mart
Of undisguising selfishness, that sets
On each its price, the stamp-mark of her reign.
Even love is sold . . .

PERCY BYSSHE SHELLEY, 1812

PROLOGUE

BEDLAM

It was winter. The streets were covered in snow, churned grey and slushy by the traffic of vehicles and pedestrians and, frozen overnight into sharp jagged peaks, dusted by morning with a light coating of ash and soot. Deep snow-drifts filled alleyways and formed slopes against the buildings. Horses slipped on the ice; their handlers trod warily.

The streets around the hospital were daily transformed into an impromptu market composed of makeshift lean-tos and trestle-table stalls. Food, clothes, bedding, shoes and other essential items, second-hand or new, cheap or expensive, buy or sell. Flower-sellers gathered there in large numbers, each competing for the best pitch. Stall-keepers barked their prices at anyone in shouting distance. Hawkers of ballads paraded their latest compositions on long poles, verse after verse after fluttering verse. Packmen weighed down by the weight of linen on their backs picked their way across the icy pavements. Overturned carts blocked the roads, their contents littering the streets and the pavements with fruit and vegetables, pots and pans.

Henry Stillwater, wrapped in a warm cape and muffler, negotiated his way through the commercial pandemonium of the market and passed under an arched gateway into the hospital courtyard. Cobwebs transformed into crystal lattices by the snow and frost of the winter's first, unexpected, snowfall hung in the corners. A narrow path, cut from the ice, led to the entrance to The Bethlem Hospital for Lunatics. The building was impressive. Stillwater recalled that it was modelled on the Tuilleries palace in Paris, a vague insult to the Sun King and his pretensions to greatness.

The door was an enormous wooden affair studded with iron rivets. A grille was set into a man-size door at head height and behind the grille was an inquiring face. Stillwater handed the warden his ticket. The man glanced at it, nodded and opened the door.

Stillwater was surprised to enter a spacious atrium with corridors leading off left and right, a staircase directly in front of him. The warden directed him to a door on the right of the staircase.

The waiting room Stillwater found himself in was suffocatingly warm. He sat in a leather-bound chair in front of the fire and immediately felt drowsy. He shook his head and moved to a seat nearer the window where he could feel a draught on his face.

The hospital was quiet. Nothing he had read about Bedlam led him to expect serenity. He had expected madness in all its frantic forms. Noise especially. He had expected noise: singing, screaming, yelling, banging. Madness, he had been led to believe, was a peculiarly musical, percussive affliction. The very definition of insanity was speaking too loudly, laughing too loudly, behaving in a socially disruptive manner. Why then was Bedlam (bedlam, for heaven's sake) as quiet as the grave?

Stillwater took a piece of paper out of his pocket and read through it for what must have been the hundredth time. He had to be sure his assessment of the situation was accurate. The document he perused was a printed flyer entitled 'A Memorial to the Prince Regent, detailing the hard usage inflicted upon a Sovereign subject by the brutal despotism of Russia'. The petition, which ran to several closely printed pages, was signed John Bellingham. He folded the paper back into his pocket. He was certain. Bellingham was his man.

Someone looked round the door. 'Mr Stillwater? Sorry to keep you waiting.' The man entered. He was in his forties, with receding blond hair, dressed like a City gentleman and carrying a large bundle of papers tied loosely with string. Stillwater had expected a doctor. 'Haslam, John Haslam. I'm the apothecary here.' Haslam extended his hand as he spoke. Stillwater rose from his seat by the window and took Haslam's hand. He squeezed it hard. Haslam looked flustered and turned his body to one side as he said, 'Shall we go? The Committee is waiting for us.'

Stillwater released his grip and gestured towards the door. 'Lead on,' he said. Haslam smiled an uncertain smile.

In front of them a fat turnkey waddled past locked doors. The jingle of the keys dangling from his belt, and the clicking of their heels on the stone floor, reverberated in the long, empty corridors.

'Mr Matthews's case is a curious one,' Haslam was saying as they walked. 'It appears from the records that he was sent here on orders from Parliament.' Haslam laughed, quietly amused. 'It's as if he had been sent to the Tower.' Stillwater did not smile. Haslam changed tack suddenly. 'As far as we can tell, there are no living relatives and, according to the documents submitted on his admission in, um, excuse me a moment—' Haslam rummaged through the papers he carried – '1797, quite some time ago, now. Where was I?' Stillwater reminded him. 'Yes, according to the admission documents, you are to be consulted before any action regarding Mr Matthews is taken. And, well, as it seems that James, I mean Mr Matthews, is, I hesitate to say

11

cured . . . considerably improved, we thought it was time we contacted you, Mr Stillwater.'

The corridor opened out, to Stillwater's left, into a large room separated from the corridor by iron bars. In the centre of the room was a small stove, around which congregated a large number of men. Some were dressed quite normally, others seemed to be clothed in rags, some with blankets draped across their shoulders, others with nothing. The huddled mass was subdued.

'It gets a lot noisier in the summer,' said Haslam matter-of-factly. 'The cold you see. It's very hard to heat a place like this. Are you a relative?'

'No,' said Stillwater, staring at the rolls of fat at the turnkey's collar. His feet throbbed painfully in his boots. He felt the cold keenly now.

The party came to a stairwell that wound up and down. They ascended. At the top of the stairs their progress was barred by a locked door. The turnkey performed his task and Haslam and Stillwater passed through into a narrow corridor. It was noticeably warmer in this administrative part of the building.

'Here we are,' said Haslam, stopping by a door marked 'Committee' in white, painted letters.

The Committee sat round a crescent table. They were an august body composed of doctors pre-eminent in their field. In the chair was Thomas Munro, whose family had run Bethlem Hospital for three generations. To his right was Bryan Crowther, surgeon to Bethlem. To Munro's left sat Haslam, in front of whom was a pile of paper six inches thick.

The remaining members of the Committee radiated outwards in decreasing importance until, on the far left, was a chair set away from the end of the table where Stillwater sat in dismal silence. Munro called the meeting to order. Haslam rose from his chair and began to read from a prepared script.

'On this day, the twentieth of January 1812, the Committee is meeting to judge the mental competency of one James Tilly Matthews, who was admitted to the care of this institution by order of the Privy Council in January 1797. Further to this order was the instruction that any attempt to release Matthews could be authorized only by the Privy Council or its agent. To that end, gentlemen, may I introduce Mr Stillwater, who acts in this capacity? He has been made a member of the Committee for this special session.'

A dozen heads turned and nodded in unison. Stillwater acknowledged their quiet greeting.

Haslam continued. 'I read from notes made by myself and colleagues during the length of Mr Matthews's stay at this hospital.

I pronounce your Lordship to be in every sense of the word a most diabolical traitor . . . you have made yourself a principal in the schemes and treason of the Middle Man found upon the most extensive intrigue.

'I quote from a letter sent by Matthews to Lord Liverpool on sixth December 1796. The author went on to accuse Liverpool of collusion with the revolutionary Government in France and a group of shadowy conspirators called Pneumatic Chemists. Together, asserted the letter, *you did actually effect the murder of that unfortunate monarch, Louis XVI.* In addition, both British and French governments were secretly conspiring to prolong the war for commercial gain and in order to *deprive me of my existence* and *sacrifice me to popular fury.*

'Matthews repeated his allegations from the gallery of the House of Commons. He accosted members of the Government in their homes and at their private clubs and sought to convince them of his claims. He was taken before the Privy Council and declared insane.

'However, confinement served not to dispel the patient's fantasies but merely to confirm them.

13

'The Chemists have me fast. I am in their thrall. The Engine has me and I am devoured. My words and my actions, my very thoughts are not my own. I am penetrated utterly. My most secret thoughts are known to them – everything is laid bare before them through that infernal Engine. I am mined; daily they work the fast depleting seams of my mind.

'Matthews was convinced he was the victim of an elaborate plot devised by magnetic spies, the Pneumatic Chemists, to infiltrate and influence the British government. The Chemists were able to achieve this by means of a machine called an Influencing Engine, which, by manipulating magnetic energy, was capable of influencing the minds of those in the Government.

'When pressed, Matthews was at first unwilling to expand on his theories, but later he described the Pneumatic Chemists as a secret society originating in ancient Egypt. The Great Pyramid, he claimed, was not a mausoleum but rather a gigantic engine room housing an enormous Influencing Engine.

'The Middle Man built the Engine. He is also its most able operator. The machine is worked by a keyboard and foot pedals, resembling an organ. The Middle Man is a master of the Engine. When he sits down at the keyboard you know that you are in for a virtuoso display of magnetic impregnation. Sweat pours from him. His brow furrows. His concentration is absolute. His only aim is to inflict pain on me – the simpler tasks of suggestion and influence he leaves to his junior partners. The Middle Man toys with me. He takes me to the limit of my endurance. I am his gewgaw.

'According to Matthews, he is the principal, possibly the only, recipient of the Chemists' magnetic attentions. They have practised every conceivable form of torture on his body by firing magnetic energy at him from a distance (the gang are purported to operate from a cellar in London Wall). These tortures take various bizarre forms, including Lobster-cracking, Bomb-bursts, Pushing Up the Quicksilver and Apoplexy Working with the Nutmeg-grater. This last, *event working*, is described by the patient as *the forcing of fluids into the head with such violence that pimples, resembling the holes in a nutmeg-grater, break out all over.*

'Again, I read from a transcript of a conversation with Matthews. *The Glove Woman lengthened my brain. I have not undergone this humiliating experience before. In this magnetically induced frame of mind all thoughts are made to assume a grotesque interpretation. At first it was a curious distraction from the Middle Man's more straightforward torture, but it has quickly become unbearable. All good sense appears like insanity, the truth seems like libel and even the Bible is strained into a jest book.*

'*Of all the tortures the Chemists have inflicted on me this is the worst, the most fiendish and destructive. I would give anything, even my life, to be rid of these thoughts. The mental torture of this miserable condition is matched by the physical pain. I can only thank God that I am not yet dead of it.*

'*The Glove Woman is the perfect practitioner of this devilish art. Her hair is red and brittle, sticking out at strange angles from beneath a wide-brimmed hat. She keeps her hands always hidden in cotton mittens. She has never been known to speak, let alone laugh.*

'Matthews's delusions have persisted for fifteen years. However, in the last six months he has made considerable progress and in many ways appears to be restored to his senses.

'The Committee will be aware of the therapeutic successes of Dr Crowther and myself. Now, gentlemen, it is up to you to decide on Mr Matthews's competence. You have heard the extent of his illness. I have described to you the way in which, in the past,

15

he has condemned himself from out of his own mouth. It is for you to judge whether or not he is sufficiently recovered to merit release.'

Haslam returned to his place. The man next to Stillwater whispered confidentially into his ear, 'Haslam wrote a book about Matthews. It's his pet subject. We all had to buy a copy.'

Snow was falling outside. An old man shuffled into the room and lit the candles. The Committee talked among themselves.

The gloom, pushed into the corners by the candle-light, and the low murmuring of the sober gentlemen around him depressed Stillwater. A heaviness settled on him, made him slump in his chair. He should never have come. He should have sent a letter refusing Matthews's release. Nobody would question his judge-ment. Nobody would remember who James Matthews was or what he had done to deserve his lunatic exile.

Stillwater hated hospitals. He never went near them. He could not understand the public fascination with disease and insanity.

The murmurs of the Committee ceased abruptly. The patient was brought into the room, accompanied by two orderlies. Matthews was not bound in a strait-waistcoat. His hair was not wild and long; it was new-cut and neat, though almost completely grey. His clothes were similarly clean and ordered. He wore a threadbare overcoat, beneath it a wool shirt. His trousers were brown moleskin. His feet were shod in boots out at the toes.

He walked calmly, a pace in front of the orderlies. Munro asked Matthews to be seated. He sat on a chair in the centre of the room.

Stillwater could see him well enough. Matthews's attention, however, was focused exclusively on Haslam and Munro. He stared directly ahead; his eyes followed movement, but he did not turn his head. It was as if every movement had been consciously planned before it was executed. Stillwater suspected Haslam had drilled his patient in appropriately rational behaviour.

The Committee took turns in questioning the patient. They asked him about his family and learned that his wife was dead, that he knew nothing of the whereabouts of his two daughters; they would be better off without him. His ambitions for the future were hazy, but he felt inclined to outdoors work, perhaps as a gamekeeper, away from the clamour of the town. He considered himself much improved and wished to express his thanks to the staff of the asylum for their skill and dedication.

Finally came Stillwater's turn. Matthews shifted in his chair to make eye contact with his new interrogator. He shot nervous glances at Haslam. Apparently Stillwater's presence had not been expected; his responses were not rehearsed.

Stillwater did not speak directly. He leaned forward in his seat and stared into Matthews's bloodshot green eyes. He was not convinced by Matthews's answers. They had seemed glib and perfunctory. Neither was he satisfied by the rigour of the Committee's investigation. They had a fierce reputation but no bite. A child could gull them. A stupid child.

Matthews's face was a blank. The man was no longer a lunatic; he had successfully transformed himself into a cipher. Reason and intelligence were there to be found in his measured responses; confidence and tranquillity were evident in his fixed stare; the absense of facial tics and other visible signs of lunacy betokened normality. But if you really looked into the eyes, Stillwater judged, you could find the measure of a man's soul. Stare long enough at a lunatic and, like a dog, he would snap at you.

Stillwater got up from his chair and crossed the room without breaking eye contact with Matthews. He was so close now, he could see the reflection of a dozen candles in his eyes. A dozen points of light, a dozen beacons on his journey to the heart of Matthews and, behind them, something stirring in the darkness of his pupils; Stillwater's own reflection.

It was the chair breaking across his back that knocked him to the ground. It was a jagged chair leg that gashed open his cheek. Matthews stood over him, panting for breath, the bloody piece of furniture in his hand.

The Committee exchanged nods and looks, and each man wrote his own conclusion on the paper in front of him. Haslam tutted loudly. Munro drew a large black cross with his pen. Dr Crowther slumped forward on to the table, a flask of gin in his hand, incapable of speech or any form of muscular activity except breathing.

In the lull that followed his outburst Matthews bent over the prostrate Stillwater. He leant very close and said, 'You shouldn't have come. I know what you're planning. You are the Middle Man. You want me out of the way. I'm just another obstacle to be cleared.' The orderlies grabbed him on either side and forced him into a strait-waistcoat. 'The Engine is running,' he shouted as they pulled him, backwards, through the door, his heels dragging on the stone. 'I can sense it. The Engine is running! The Engine is running!'

ONE

HOME

15th January 1812
9 New Millman Street
Bloomsbury
London

My dearest Mary Ann

My sincerest apologies for not writing earlier. I am at last settled in New Millman Street. The house is clean and my room pleasant. Mrs Roberts, the landlady, is attentive to my every need and a most capable woman. How is Henry? The dear boy was not at his best when I left a fortnight ago. Please write soon and tell me how he goes on.

My business here is taking far longer than I expected and is no nearer a conclusion than when I first arrived. Johnson, my supplier, drags his feet at every stage and can give me no firm date for the arrival of the consignment and refuses to accept a promissory note for the iron. I am afraid I shall be unable to fulfil my commitment to the shipping company and our finances will suffer a further blow as result of the man's incompetence.

How is business? I trust it goes well, though trade is bound to be quiet at this time of year. I called on Phillips and Davison, as you asked. Mr Thompson, the head clerk, was quite adamant that no mistake had been made by him or his colleagues. He showed me the order book and I was forced to agree with him. Thompson was most courteous and I am confident that the matter can be resolved if the area of dispute can be marked out more clearly.

I miss you all and am impatient to return to Liverpool. I have been away too long already. My love to the boys and a kiss to their mother.

Affectionately, your husband John Bellingham.

18th January 1812
46 Duke Street
Liverpool

My dear John

Your letter I received in course and I am glad to relieve your anxiety regarding darling Harry, who is wonderfully recovered and has cut two teeth. I feel most obliged by your attention in regard to our business, but I must request you to call again at Phillips and Davison, as it is their Traveller's mistake and not any fault of ours.

I feel very much surprised at your not mentioning any time for your return, you will be three weeks gone on Thursday, and you know I cannot do anything with regard to settling this Business until your return. We have got in very little money since you left. I think I need not instruct you to act with economy, your feeling for your family will induce you to do it. I request you to write by return of post. The children send dear Papa an affectionate kiss, with one from Mama, and I remain yours very affectionately, Mary Ann Bellingham.

Pray let me know when you intend to return, Miss Stevens desires to be remembered.

February 2nd 1812
9 New Millman Street
London

My dearest Mary Ann

Yours of the 18th was delivered here a little over a week since, forgive me for not replying more promptly. I was glad to hear that Henry is well and has made such a good recovery. I hope that his teething is not causing you too much worry. As for the Business, do not let it trouble you further, everything is well in hand here. I visited Phillips and Davison last week, with some success. They admit the mistake was their traveller's, they asked me to convey their apologies and they themselves will write to you soon. I believe the subject closed. Thank Miss S. for her remembrance and remember me to her also.

I had wished to discuss with you further the education of the boys. With my absence likely to be prolonged by unforeseen difficulties that I shall not enter into here and now, I consider it desirable that you should spend more time with the boys. To this end I ask you to consider relinquishing your share in the Millinery to Miss S. – who, I know, is willing to take everything upon herself except the outstanding debts.

My prospects here are much improved and I am certain that I can conclude my affairs to our complete advantage. This change in outlook has been prompted by a meeting with a remarkable young man – Mr Nettleton. He is a journeyman printer and has become my good friend. He has informed me of his intention to emigrate at the earliest opportunity to New York. Please let me know Eliza's address in New York, as I have mentioned her and assured Mr Nettleton that he might expect at least one friendly welcome in the New World. I am sorry to be away so long, but I beg you to be patient and trust in me.

Your affectionate husband, John Bellingham.

I enclose a receipt for my board and lodging to prove to you my thrift. I can also assure you that every single penny is accounted for and pondered over before it is spent. I have even made a tally of my laundry charges to avoid being overcharged. Believe me, I have only your and the boys' welfare in mind.

10 February 1812
46 Duke Street
Liverpool

My dear John

I was pleased to learn that the unpleasant matter with Phillips and Davison is concluded at last. Miss Stevens and I have heard nothing from them as yet but we trust to your judgement in this matter as in most others.

The boys are well and their education is not suffering through your absence or because of my work in the shop. I cannot see the wisdom in giving up the Business at this time and I find your talk of improved prospects difficult to understand. It was my understanding that your business in London was solely to do with trade and a consignment you expected but which failed to arrive. How long can it take to oversee the delivery of a lot of iron to Liverpool?

Your trade with my father in Dublin is bound to suffer as a result of your long absence and this can do nothing but damage our prospects. Would it not be better for us all if our husband and father was at home with us and not in London?

Have you forgotten about Eliza's mother, my dear Aunt? She passed away in December. I have not heard from Eliza since the funeral, but Uncle James is under the impression she will return to England rather than stay on in a strange city where she has no family and few friends. If she decides otherwise, I will surely let you know where she resides. Until then it is best not to trouble her any further than is necessary. Convey my apologies to Mr Nettleton. I am sorry I could not be of greater assistance in this matter, but I am certain he will find a welcome in New York, as I am assured it is a friendly place.

Our neighbours have been disrupting all our lives again. Mrs H. across the road is now perpetually drunk. She shouts and fights with her husband and her children at all hours. She has been dismissed from her work for stealing. Nobody will do anything about it because they are terrified of her sons, who continue to wreak such havoc in the street that I am afraid to let John out on his own. Mr Allen was very brave to discharge her at all. Somebody had to do something. Her family makes all of our lives a misery.

I expect your prompt reply will answer all my concerns.

Your trusting wife, Mary Ann Bellingham.

February 1812
9 New Millman Street
London

Dearest Mary Ann,

My great concern is for the boys. It is important that their futures be secured by all means in our power. I recall my own experiences as a fatherless young man seeking only to make a way in the world. My late Uncle Daw secured for me a position as jeweller's apprentice with a Mr Love in Whitechapel. If I had shown any aptitude or inclination toward the profession my life might have followed a very different course. I lacked that guidance at an early age which all boys need if they are to take their chances and recognize good fortune when they come across it. Mr Love, a man of excellent character, as my Uncle was at great pains to point out, lost patience with me when, after three years under his careful supervision I was still no further advanced in the trade than when I started. Over those three years I saw apprentices come and go on to become journeymen, whilst I remained a dullard without hope of advancement. If I showed little skill as a watchmaker or jeweller, I did display a keen instinct for invoices, a certain way with a ledger. A life of clerkdom to a young man is like a sentence of death. I sat at my bench, day and night, dreaming of adventure, aching for an opportunity to escape the drudgery of my life, to evade the fate that seemed to await me – a career filled with tedium, uncomfortable stools, cold offices and writer's cramp. I fled the workshop late one night. Runaway apprentices were no novelty then, they littered the streets and gathered in desultory groups at street corners like fallen leaves. A menace to society were these boys who whirled about the streets without money or a guiding hand or a master to chain them to their bench at night. I was fortunate enough to have Uncle Daw, a stern but sympathetic man. He purchased for me, at considerable cost, the position of subaltern on the East Indiaman *Hartwell*.

My chequered past has brought me to this impasse. I have no trade and little education to fall back on. I cannot allow this to happen to my sons. You, Mary, have a head for business. You understand money, you work hard. It is right that you should pass these qualities on to our children. I am a mediocre businessman but I am a caring father. Please do not mistake my absence for indifference.

Mrs Roberts, my landlady, her small son and I attended church together on Sunday. We went to the chapel in the nearby Foundling Hospital. I know you will be surprised by this news and wonder what has happened to your husband to bring about such a change. The chapel itself is quite plain. It is the congregation, composed as it is from a host of children of all ages, parents and foster parents and local people, that attracts me. It is wholly different from any service

I have attended before now. I think I shall go again.

As for Mrs H. and her unruly brood, they must surely get their come-uppance soon. Do not let them worry or bully you. They are nothing but scoundrels and thieves unworthy of anybody's attention excepting only that of the constabulary.

Please think over all that I have written. I do not instruct you to follow any course of action I suggest in these matters, I only ask you to give the matter due consideration.

Your affectionate husband, John Bellingham.

23 February 1812
46 Duke Street
Liverpool

Dear Husband,

You have been evasive and not confided in me the true nature of your Business in London, which I am now certain is the same Affair that we have quarrelled over so often. I am very much hurt to find one of the reasons for your journey, perhaps the sole reason, is to continue your application to the Government for redress. Your pursuit of this matter is contrary to my wishes and the wishes of your friends. Do they not deserve your respect? Am I, your wife, not deserving of respect? If you do not trust my opinion in this matter, at least have the courtesy to be truthful in your dealings with me. To talk of the children's welfare whilst squandering our money in a hopeless search for so-called justice is shameful. What care can you have for them or anyone else when at a moment's notice you drop everything to run away to London? Even if the Business here is not as it could be and money is short – the solution to our difficulties does not lie in London or anywhere except here. I have written to my Uncle James and he is in agreement with me. Do you so easily forget the solemn promise you made me not two years ago to give up wrong thoughts of your wild-goose schemes & expectations? John, you promised me. You even burnt a parcel of papers as proof of your serious intent. You told me they were papers relating to the Affair. Did you lie then, too?

Miss Stevens discovered a copy of a Memorial to the Prince Regent in a drawer. She was looking for the ledgers and found it by mistake. She kept her discovery from me a few days but has lately confessed all – as I believe you should.

I am deeply hurt and affected by this business and wish it to go on no longer. If you can furnish me with an explanation, and persuade me that you have proof of any prospects, then I shall listen. But lying to me is unforgivable. As I have taken you for better or for worse I offer you this chance to explain. I wish you were home to see my anger. I expect your reply by return – do not delay.

Your wife, Mary Ann Bellingham.

27 February 1812
9 New Millman Street
Bloomsbury

My dearest Mary Ann,

I am ashamed of my conduct. I should never have concealed from you the true purpose of my journey. I beg your forgiveness and will try to set your mind at ease regarding my business here. I lately received a letter from Under-Secretary Beckett informing me that my petition has been referred to the Privy Council, which, as you know, is the Prince Regent's private counsel. They shall deliver a sound judgement, I am sure. I delivered the Memorial only a month ago, so as you can see things are moving fast and my hopes rise daily. In addition to the Memorial I have written a petition for distribution to Members of Parliament, the

Treasury and the Chancellor's office. In this way I mean to flood Whitehall with my claim and bring it to the notice of each and every officer of the Government. Do not worry about the cost of this campaign, as my friend Mr Nettleton, the printer whom I mentioned to you before, has agreed to print the petition cheaply – provided his employer allows him.

I need not remind you of my five years of suffering at the hands of the Russian authorities. My imprisonment with common criminals, the fabricated charges made against me, the punishments inflicted on my person and my mind. You know how I suffered. You have seen the evidence written on my body. I was beaten and tortured, bandied from prison to prison, led through the streets of St Petersburg with a common herd of malefactors. And all the while the evidence of my innocence lay gathering dust in the British Embassy.

I plunged from happily married, moderately prosperous man to debased pauper through no fault of my own.

I went to Archangel full of expectation, my only thought was to make a life, a prosperous and happy life, for my family. I left Archangel a bankrupt, the victim of fraud, of vendetta. How did this come about? Why was I singled out for persecution by the Governor of Archangel?

Ever since those years in Russia I have struggled to think of myself as something other than blighted. Physically and emotionally I have very little left to offer except bitterness and a passion for justice. It is my duty to remind Mr Perceval and his Government of my birthright, of the birthright of every citizen, in the strongest possible terms.

I have bored you often enough with my jeremiad. I wish I knew a way of conveying to you my feelings on this matter. Perhaps that is why I am here now, because my story is not wretched enough to provoke sympathy or told simply enough to make the point clearly. I was treated unjustly. I have not received justice. Justice delayed is injustice.

Do you recall the state I was in when I returned from Russia two years ago? You chided me then for staying on in London with Cousin Ann and not returning immediately to my family. But you also know how I fretted over you. I had no idea where you were living or if you were still alive. Do you remember the look on our son's face when he met his father for the first time since infancy? I shall never forget his puzzled, frightened expression. I swore to clear my name, to provide for my family, to make up for the lost years. This is the business I am about. I beg you to try to understand. How could I face my family knowing that I had failed in this matter?

Do you remember how I was that summer? Laid low by colds and fevers. Every minor ailment that passed through the house found its way to me. My child a stranger. My wife, who had coped for so long and so ably on her own, was forced to care for a debilitated and dispirited husband she had not seen nor shared any intimacy with for almost six years. Six years' worth of absence and hardship.

You took in lodgers, you even took in laundry, though I expressly forbade it. You could not understand my stubborn pride even though you matched it with a single-mindedness of your own – a determination to survive. I am seeking only to emulate you.

All our friends tried to dissuade me. Put it all behind you, they said. Remember your family, your loving wife, your children. What chance have you, a private citizen, against the state? The Government will crush you.

For a while I accepted the wisdom and good intention of their remarks and settled again to family life.

And I tried, Mary Ann, I really did try; every day for eighteen months I tried to put it out of my mind, to pretend it never happened. Each time I glanced in a mirror and saw my hair growing back white where it had fallen out, my eyes sunk deep in their sockets surrounded by skin the colour of tallow, the gaps where my teeth had been and the few remaining turning yellow, rotting in the gums – I was so proud of my teeth, my white, healthy teeth – I tried to forget.

When I played with the children I tried not to imagine what your lives had been like without me or whether the elder even recalled his father. When I lay awake at night, you beside me, I fought not to remember those nights in Russia, lonely savage nights. But the more I tried to forget, the clearer my recollection became; the further I tried to get away from those experiences, the closer they seemed to loom. The sharper my memories, the keener my appetite for retribution.

I cannot excuse my lying. I ask only for your forgiveness and your understanding. You know that this affair has always been a matter of dissension between us, but I would be undeserving the name of a parent if I did not endeavour to make some provision for our children. Bear with me a while longer, my dearest Mary Ann, and I promise you shall see more than you dreamed of.

Your loving husband, John Bellingham.

March 1812
46 Duke Street
Liverpool

Dearest John

You are my husband, I must relent. I trust you. You would not pursue this matter without hope of success. However, I wish you to keep me well informed of all that happens in respect of this affair. I will not ask you again to return home to your family. I trust your sense of duty will lead you to do what you must to provide for our well-being. One thing I do ask of you is to commit no rash act from impatience or frustration.

It hurts me that I have to be reminded once again of your sufferings in Russia. No one is more sensible of your distress than I am. But I too have suffered. I was left to fend for myself with an infant son and no means of support for six years. It is right that two people who have shared such great suffering should be honest with each other – do you not think so?

In the meantime be pleased to call on your Cousin Ann Billet, as she is visiting in London at present. She wrote from Southampton to tell me so. She is not aware of your presence in London, and it would be best if you did not mention the real purpose of your visit there. You may tell her that the boys and I are well and that business, if not wonderful, is at least enough to keep us in house and home. I expect to hear from you soon with news from Ann as well as word on other matters.

Your affectionate wife, Mary Ann Bellingham.

I need not remind you to be constantly frugal in your expenditure.

March 10 & 11 1812
Bloomsbury

Dearest Mary Ann

At last, good news. My friend Jack Nettleton has promised to introduce me to an extraordinary individual by the name of Arthur Thistlewood. Jack assures me that Thistlewood has years of experience in politics as well as a whole host of friends and associates in high places. Jack told me that Thistlewood has been eager to meet me ever since Jack spoke to him about my case. I cannot believe my good fortune. It seems that everyone I meet is going out of their way to help me. I have rushed back to my rooms to write to you about it and now think I should wait until I have actually met the man for myself. Everything is arranged for tomorrow evening. I shall complete the letter then.

March 11. Jack came for me earlier this evening at around seven. We travelled across London towards the docks and finally arrived at Limehouse. Our meeting with Thistlewood took place in the back room of a public house near the river. The stink was terrible, so the tide must have been low.

We entered a room at the back of the pub on the first floor. The room was smoky and small, a window at the back looked out over the graveyard of a nearby church. Arthur Thistlewood sat with his back to the window, smoking a briar pipe. Clouds of blue smoke billowed about his face.

Thistlewood greeted me solemnly. Jack had told him about me some weeks previously and he had been looking forward to meeting me and would have done so sooner if other matters did not press so heavily on his time. He sat me down at the opposite end of the table. His face was covered by a coarse, light-brown beard that seemed to hang on his face rather than grow from it. His eyes moved about the room constantly, rarely fixing on me except when he asked a question. This constant motion of his eyes and the heavy atmosphere of the room made me feel a little queasy. I asked for something to drink and he sent Jack down to get us some rum. His choice of refreshment seemed very appropriate for, though it sounds absurd now, he had about him what I can only describe as a piratical air. Then it struck me of whom it was Thistlewood reminded me so strongly – Captain Fiott, master of the *Hartwell* on which I had served briefly as a junior subaltern.

I have spoken to you before about Fiott and my unfortunate adventure at sea, how the crew mutinied and were subdued and how Fiott none the less managed to wreck the ship and send its cargo of gold to the bottom of the ocean within days of our destination. I don't know what it was exactly in Thistlewood's manner that put me in mind of Fiott but once the connection was made I could not put him or the *Hartwell* out of my mind. We were all of us cast adrift, marooned on a barren island for several weeks. I think it was then that I lost any spirit of adventure that lived in my breast. Even now I still fear that condition – I fear being left alone, deserted, stranded. Fiott felt the same way, I am sure. It was his first command after a long time at sea. He was so desperate to assert his authority, to command respect, to protect the people and the goods in his charge, that he forsook sound advice and ended up destroying everything he had fought so hard to preserve. Fiott lost his command and his respect as well as his ship. He was left with nothing. Physically, emotionally, personally marooned with no hope of rescue from any quarter. I wonder what became of him. To look at Thistlewood he could be Fiott – they share a passion and a desperation as well as a similar physiognomy.

Jack Nettleton returned with the rum and I outlined my case for Thistlewood, who expressed great interest in every detail. He questioned me about my sojourn in Russian gaols, how I was treated there, whom I felt was to blame for my predicament. He advised me to direct my actions towards the Treasury and, in particular, the Prime Minister, Perceval. He spoke as if from long experience and warned me that my claim, if pursued through the proper channels, was likely to founder. Either it would be caught up endlessly in legal argument or it would be dismissed out of hand. He was especially worried that the current diplomatic situation between Russia and England would greatly hamper the progress of my case. (He is right. Since diplomatic relations were broken off with Russia every minister has used this as an excuse to dismiss my claim.) Thistlewood counselled me to approach the problem from a different angle. I should look upon my quest for justice as something undertaken on behalf of many others besides myself. Justice, or rather the lack of it, he said, was a universal complaint. I was not exceptional in my failure to gain redress. Where I differed from so many others was in my perseverance, my single-minded pursuit of a just settlement. There have been many, he continued, who have been wrongly accused and falsely imprisoned: thrown into gaol because of their beliefs, because of their desire for a better life or a better wage, because they chose to speak out against corruption and injustice, because they wished to unite together and protect their interests. Even now, he said, scores of men and women rot in gaol or on prison hulks, waiting to be transported or murdered by the state. Simple people, like the weavers, who dared stand up against their employers who sought to rob them of their livelihood and replace them with machines. There were many not at liberty to speak for themselves, for whom I had an opportunity to speak. Many more who had abandoned the struggle, who believed passionately but who were ground down, browbeaten and laughed at; those who, confronted by the implacable, intractable, inhuman face of government went home and forgot about their grievances. I could be an emissary on their behalf as well as my own. I would be doing it all for them, he said.

I was impressed by Thistlewood's speech. He was an articulate man. His words struck a chord in me, remained with me throughout the long journey home, reverberate in my mind even now as I write to you.

One other curious incident. Our room was adjacent to another. The light was on in the room and every now and then I saw the movement of somebody's feet at the foot of the door. No noise of any kind came from that chamber – no sounds of drinking, no laughter, no talk, no whispers, nothing at all. Yet it was obviously occupied. I am profoundly suspicious of Thistlewood. I will question Jack about him later.

I have rambled on and on but still not had time to mention Cousin Ann, who sends her love and best wishes to you and the boys. She was surprised to see me and we spent almost an entire afternoon talking about this and that. Mostly domestic chatter. Her daughters are growing up healthy. Ann is very proud of them. She asked me at some length about my business in London and seemed most solicitous of my welfare. Notwithstanding her kindness she begged me to return to Liverpool, fearing for you and the boys. Does she know something of the affair? I have told her nothing. Please write soon, as I look forward to your letters as only I can.

Your affectionate husband, John Bellingham.

19 March 1812
Liverpool

Dearest John,

I received your last letter only yesterday after what seemed an endless delay. I was worried that this might mean you are in trouble. I am glad to hear that Ann and her family are well. Did she have no other news? The boys are well also, but missing their father whom they ask after every day. What should I tell them? If you are lonely in London, as your letter implied, then perhaps you should return to Liverpool, even if it is only for a short time. We would all be very glad to see you and hear from you in person what goes on in London. I am sure you hear far more than we ever do about the state of the country – which must be a constant topic of conversation in the city. Our many friends also ask after you and desire to know when you will return.

I heard news from my father last week. He urgently requests you let him know the date he can expect the consignment, which he says he never received. I am amazed that you have not written him to tell him of the delays or supplied him with the goods he asked and paid for. I know this is an oversight and no harm is meant by you. Please write and tell him how the business goes, he relies on you so.

I am sorry to gossip again but an extraordinary event took place last Wednesday. Mr Allen's shop burned to the ground during the night. We were woken by the neighbours who shouted and threw stones at the window. We rushed out into the street and watched as the building burned. Fortunately the fire did not spread and the other houses on the street were not affected by the tragedy. Mrs Allen was in the street, screaming hysterically, while her husband tried in vain to comfort her. Mrs H. was there too and when Mrs Allen caught sight of her she charged straight at her yelling the most awful obscenities and knocked Mrs H. to the ground. Everybody is convinced Mrs H.'s sons burnt down the shop but no one can prove anything. It was a terrible incident – though the atmosphere has calmed down since. The Allens have left to live with Mrs Allen's sister in Preston.

Uncle James visited on Sunday. He drove down from Wigan to see the boys. You will be glad to hear that he is in good health. He asked me many questions about your absence, the nature of your business in London, etc., and did not appear satisfied. He was very upset, John, to find us on our own. I did not tell him about the Affair, but I think he guessed. He turned very red and could not speak for several minutes. Then he said that he blamed himself, that he should never have allowed it and other like phrases. He left shortly after

35

and we all of us were shocked by the violence of his reaction. Henry cried; John ran off and did not come back until tea. I was very worried. Do you think this business will be concluded soon so we can all get back to normal? I hope so. Write again soon.

Your affectionate wife, Mary Ann.

26 March
Bloomsbury

Dearest Mary Ann,

I have suffered set-back after set-back. I do not know how to tell you. I am despairing of ever bringing this matter to a satisfactory conclusion. Under-Secretary Beckett wrote to me on the 9th. He told me that his Royal Highness 'was not pleased to signify any commands thereupon'. My petition has been rejected, the Regent will not set it before Parliament. What does he know of hardship and injustice? Again I wrote to Beckett and he replied on the 20th saying that I should address my request to set a petition before the Commons to the Chancellor of the Exchequer. Where am I to go now? Two years ago Perceval rejected my petition, claiming it was 'not of a nature for the consideration of Parliament'. I am come full circle. I am blocked at every twist and turn.

I am not at all surprised at the comments of your Uncle James Neville. He has always borne a grudge against me, for what reason I do not know. He is unable to see beyond the counting house of his own precious business in Wigan, which he believes is at the very hub of commerce, the centre of the world. No doubt he considers me insane and sees my actions as a dereliction of parental duty. How dare he lecture me on the rights and wrongs of my conduct? Rather he should look to his family and give them support, not set out to destroy their faith and trust in each other. Do not tell me any more of James Neville or his opinions.

As for the fire, I am relieved that no one was hurt. I have no doubt as to who caused it – even though I am several hundred miles away. Nothing that family does surprises me in the least. Stay away from them, do not antagonize them and refrain from gossiping about them with the neighbours. Above all keep John away from their influence, which can only be bad.

I have moved off the course I set at the beginning of this letter. It is true that bad news has come thick and fast, but I have responded quickly and, I hope, effectively to open new channels. Today I sent a petition to the Magistrates at Bow Street. I shall have my day in court, I shall argue my case with his Majesty's Attorney General if need be. If this is denied me, then I shall feel justified in executing justice myself. That is what I told them. They have already referred the petition to the Secretary of State. This action was prompted by a meeting I had with Lord Chetwynd and Mr Buller, two clerks of the Privy Council; Mr Litchfield, a solicitor for the Treasury; and Mr Smith from the Secretary of State's office. They told me I had no justifiable reason to expect anything from His Majesty's Government. I asked Mr Smith whether he too thought me out of my senses. Smith replied, 'It is a very delicate question for me to answer, I only know you upon this business, and I can assure you, that you will never have what you are pursuing.' I was forced reluctantly to notice, in a more determined manner, the ill-treatment I had received. And so I have made submission to the courts and the Treasury requesting compensation.

Forgive me, I have run on further than I intended. Despite the disappointments I hold up well. The weather here is very mild for the time of year. We have had very little rain, which is good. You know how the slightest dampness brings on the pain in my back. I have been little afflicted over the past few weeks and have consequently slept well and been able to achieve a great deal. As regards your father, I not only wrote to him some time ago but the shipment itself should have arrived in February. Please inform me if he is still waiting or whether his complaint was not more general – after all, he will go on so.

I remain hopeful about our expectations. All is not lost. Remember Mr Thistlewood? Perhaps now is the time to exploit his generosity. Think of me even as I think of you, John Bellingham.

12th April
Liverpool

Dearest John,

It is now two weeks since I received your last letter, pray forgive me for not writing sooner but I have been very ill. The doctor confined me to my bed and I have been too weak to do anything let alone lift a pen and compose a letter. Do not be concerned as I am now over the worst and growing stronger every day. Henry is staying with a nurse until I feel I can manage him again. She tells me he is happy. However, John is concerned to be separated from his Papa while his Mama is so ill. He is being very brave and is a great comfort to me. I have not been able to attend to any business and Miss Stevens is looking after the Millinery. She does very well at it and bears her additional burden steadfastly. We have more problems with Phillips and Davison, who have again failed to supply us correctly. If it was not for their willingness to extend us credit, I would suggest we change supplier but such a disruption would not be good at this time. I enclose the details left by their Traveller and copies of our requests to them, as you have instructed me to do in the past, and trust you will endeavour to resolve this problem for us once more.

Your news was not to my liking and it seems that your expectations are now further from your grasp than ever before. Please let me know how the Affair goes. I hope to hear good news in your next letter.

Your affectionate wife, Mary Ann.

16th April 1812

My dear Mary Ann

Yours dated the 12th did not reach my hands till yesterday evening – you have acted right in following my instructions and the rest leave to my solicitude and can assure you it is not forgotten. I could have wished you had mentioned where and with whom Harry is and to let me know how the dear boy goes on. Herewith a few lines for Miss S. – for her government in the Business – and which you may consider as the remainder of your letter.

My dear Miss Stevens: As my affairs in London are terminating according to wish, you may easily imagine it's my desire for Mrs B. to quit the Business as soon as possible, and for you to come into full possession of it. The money that has been put in I do not look to, my family having had the benefit of a maintenance, and the outstanding debts I am willing to take upon me. Therefore, when you come to Town, I will accompany you to the respective Trades people for the arrangements so that I do not see any occasion for irksomeness on your part in seeing these folk. Bring the Books and confide in me to do what is right and proper. You will not be deceived. I hope to be informed when you mean to be here that I may attend you at the Coach: and command my services in every respect wherein I can be in any way useful to you.

Yours Truly, John Bellingham.

My dear John

If I could think that the prospects held out in your letter received yesterday were to be realized I would be the happiest creature existing, but I have been so often disappointed that I am hard of belief. With regard to Miss Stevens going to London, before she takes the journey be certain you can make good your intentions, for should you not ultimately be able to fulfil them we would be sunk in ruin from not having sufficient means to meet the Trades people.

I have not shown Miss Stevens your letter, for should you succeed, I mean with your permission to give up my share in the business to dear Eliza, who is in a distressed situation in New York, as her mother did not leave her a farthing, and she will be obliged to return to her family here. How truly delighted I shall be at having any means to return her kindness to me and James.

I cannot help remarking that in writing to Miss Stevens you address her in the same manner as me. 'My dear Miss Stevens' & 'Yours Truly, John Bellingham'. Now I cannot help feeling hurt that there is no distinction made between an indifferent person and an affectionate wife who has suffered so much for you and your children – it appears as if I was no more to you than any woman that you were obliged to write a letter to – I have a delicate & feeling mind: these are insults, more particularly as my indisposition seems to have been forgotten. The change in my appearance will convince you that I have been very ill, as I am now as thin as I ever was.

If I was to follow your example, six lines might fill my letter – but perhaps I am not worthy of more. I shall expect your answer by return of Post, say

Thursday: by that time I hope something will be concluded about your affair.

Yours truly, Mary Ann Bellingham.

24 April
Bloomsbury

My Dearest Mary Ann

I am very sorry to have offended you and will most certainly respect your wishes with regard to the business. If you want Eliza to have it then she must have it. I cannot stand in your way. I am glad to hear that you are better and apologize for my rashly omitting such sentiments in my last letter which, in the circumstances, must have appeared perfunctory at best and cruel at worst. I have been so wrapped up in my Affairs here that I have given too little consideration to my family. I take this opportunity to reaffirm that my family is everything to me, without you and the boys what further reason do I have to carry on with my pursuit of justice? What reason do I have to go on living?

Tomorrow I meet with Arthur Thistlewood again. I am now, more than ever, convinced that he is not motivated by a sense of injustice with regard to my own case. He appears to be pursuing his own ends, but our interests do seem to coincide.

Jack Nettleton, having first introduced me to the man, now advises me to steer clear of Thistlewood. Unfortunately I have no option. I am brought to this impasse by the Government which has chosen to set itself above the law – unreachable, inscrutable, without the slightest care for the torments and sufferings of one of His Majesty's subjects. Their minds are filled with war and trade and they cannot conceive of someone who cares only for his family.

I feel certain that my business here will be brought to a rapid conclusion. What the outcome will be I cannot at this moment even guess. One thing I am sure of and that is my desire to see you all again. I will return home in the very near future – whatever transpires here in London.

Yours truly, your affectionate husband, John Bellingham.

3rd May
Liverpool

Dearest John,

I am overjoyed at your change of heart. We want nothing more than to have you back here with us again. Despite our difficulties and the frustrations of recent months there is nobody who can prevent our happiness as long as we are together. One way or another we shall make ends meet. We shall live contentedly. We shall be together. And we shall raise our boys to provide for us in our old age. If we work hard at it the Millinery will pay its way and we shall achieve again that respect which is our due. I look forward to your next letter and expect to discover from it exactly when you will be with us.

Miss Stevens is about to undertake a journey to London. She will be staying at the home of one Mrs Barker – her cousin – in Kirkby Street. She is there on personal business, but she has brought with her the Books for you to look over, as is your custom. Please do all you can for her, be her servant in all matters. Leave with her a letter and some word about the progress of your claim for compensation. Tell her also when you expect to return.

Yours truly, your wife, happy in expectation of your return, Mary Ann Bellingham.

My dearest wife Mary Ann

I have left this letter with Mary Stevens. She will deliver it into your hands on her return. Bear with me a little longer and I shall be home before you know it, no person is more inclined to be domestically happy than myself.

On account of Miss Stevens's visit I have been rather dilatory this week with regard to my claim but I am determined to set about it vigorously tomorrow. I accompanied Miss Stevens and Mrs Barker to the exhibition at Spring Gardens, near the Admiralty. It is a display of watercolours, most of which are of very questionable quality and far too dear to purchase even if one wished to do so. I looked over the Books and they are in excellent order. I have introduced Miss Stevens to our suppliers and she has agreed to purchase the business. I enclose a letter for Mr Parton, our solicitor, in which I have requested he complete the formalities with you and Miss Stevens. This is for the best, Mary Ann, please trust me and do not quarrel with Miss Stevens or John Parton. It is settled.

My campaign to secure justice and redress has ended in failure at long last. I am now forced to pursue one final course of action in hope of getting my case before the courts and receiving what justice I can. I will bring it into a criminal court. I will compel Perceval to do me justice, as it seems he is the only man who opposes me. His influence is felt in every office, in every ministry, in government. Over the course of the past few months I have travelled from office to office seeking a sponsor for my case. In every instance I have been denied. It seems as though

I have encountered government departments that never before existed, whole layers of bureaucracy invented specifically to thwart me. I have waited in the ante-chamber to the High Court of Procrastination, tried in vain to see members of the Board of Promulgation, been turned away unanswered from the doors of the How-Not-To-Do-It office. Those whom I have managed to see described my claim variously as spurious, vexatious, incomprehensible, flawed, a mountain made of a mole hill, irrelevant, pernicious, a storm in a tea cup, seditious, treasonable, unconscionable, a slur on a great man, libellous, inconsequential, time-wasting, time-consuming, shameful and foolhardy. All have referred me to Mr Perceval. Yet Mr Perceval is un-available for comment on this or any other matter of so little consequence to the Ship of State.

I have taken lately to sitting in the lobby of the House of Commons in an attempt to waylay Perceval as he enters the House for debate or committee. I have sat there on a hard bench, back aching, legs jiggling, hands clutching my petition, seeking an opportunity to speak to the leader of the country, the First Minister. He will not acknowledge me. His secretary, who knows me well, constantly frustrates my attempts to address him. He must know who I am, he must know of my case, and if he knows all this he must know that my claim is a just one deserving at least of a hearing, yet he will not let me approach. He rebuffs me. He ignores me. He insults me, this vaunted statesman. This wretched 'little P.', this under-strapper, the sepulchral Spencer Perceval, always dressed in black, always beyond my grasp. He slips away, time after time. The doors to the Commons swing shut in my face.

Perceval is shorter than I imagined. Short, spare, pale-faced, hard, keen. A sour-looking man with a voice well suited to his appearance, slightly too high-pitched, a little shrill but devoid of emotion. He is obscured by rhetoric. He is a lawyer still. The man who prosecuted Tom Paine and his publishers, who only days ago sent eight weavers to the gallows and transported twenty-four others because they dared to question the march of progress and protest the loss of their livelihoods. Spencer Perceval wishes to make adultery a criminal offence. And, knowing this, I have to ask myself: has it really been worth all the fuss?

You do not know what I have endured the last six months. I would rather commit suicide than undergo it again.

Your affectionate husband, John Bellingham.

TWO

THE CAT AND BAGPIPES

John Bellingham stared at her from across the room. The distance between them was no more than the width of a threadbare rug, but she seemed impossibly far away.

'You cannot mean that, John Bellingham. You should not say such things lightly,' she admonished him, her eyebrows slightly raised in that quizzical manner of hers. She did the same when she disputed figures in the ledgers.

'I repeat, I would rather commit suicide than endure again what I have endured these last six months. I have said as much in my letter. It is the truth.'

She dropped her eyes to the floor. Younger than his wife, Mary Stevens was a pretty woman. Why had she not married? She had not even walked out with a man as far as Bellingham knew. Yet she was undeniably handsome. She looked up and met his gaze. He must have revealed his embarrassment, for she raised her eyebrows again. That, he thought, was a most unappealing habit, the way she creased her forehead and widened her eyes; there was something accusatory about it. Bellingham sipped at his luke-warm tea and trawled through his mind for a subject to change the conversation to. 'What did you make of the exhibition?' he asked, a slight stutter betraying his discomfort.

'I found it most interesting. An inspiration,' she replied without hesitation.

'Really? I found it quite drab. I always find water-colours drab.' He had not meant to sound so pompous.

'Is that so, John?' Miss Stevens inclined her head slightly to one side and smiled. 'And how often do you spend your days gazing at watercolours or any other kind of painting, for that matter?'

'I think I should take the ledgers and go,' he said as firmly as he could. 'I will call on you tomorrow at ten. Will that be convenient?'

'Oh, yes, very convenient.' She stood up quickly, as anxious to be rid of him as he was to leave. 'Goodbye, John.'

'Goodnight, Miss Stevens.'

'Goodnight, Mr Bellingham.' She left the room with a flounce of her skirts. A definite flounce. Bellingham thought her behaviour very trying. The parlourmaid showed him to the street.

The ledgers gripped firmly under his arm, Bellingham strode off quickly down the road. She had not even invited him to stay for dinner. Not that he could have accepted, or would have accepted, but she might at least have offered. He suspected she did not like him very much. Still, she was a businesswoman and a great friend of Mary Ann. He needed her cooperation. He could be civil for just a few hours more.

He arrived at his lodgings shortly after five. Mrs Roberts's son, Edward, sat on the doorstep with a forlorn look on his face. He was always on his own, this boy. He missed his father, who had died at Walcheren. Poor souls, dysentery got to them before they even saw the French. It must have been one of the worst military decisions ever taken, to land them on that tiny island at the height of summer. They were wiped out in a matter of days, not by enemy action but by disease. So much waste, so many fatherless children, for what? For nothing. The boy looked up at him, made him feel guilty.

His room was in shadow. The sun had moved around the house. He locked his door, placed the ledgers on his table and sat back in his chair. Suddenly he felt very tired. He had a headache. His eyes hurt from squinting in the sunshine. His legs were stiff and his feet swollen. He massaged his forehead with his hand and took long, deep breaths. He began to relax.

Mary Stevens, a fine woman, well worth getting between the sheets.

Bellingham shocked himself. He flushed a deep red. He protested to himself: I would never . . . how dare I? Dear God, the very thought. He stood up and looked round, convinced there was someone else in the room watching him. He went to the window. People everywhere, yes, but nobody paying him any attention. He dabbed his forehead with a handkerchief, tried to settle down again, but found himself restless.

Bellingham, uprooter of tyranny. Bellingham the brave.

He felt as though someone were talking to him. The strangest ideas were appearing in his mind like bubbles, rising to the surface and bursting. A momentary sensation as the notion rippled across the surface of his brain, then it was gone, only the faintest trace remaining. It was a fantastically odd feeling, as if someone had reached into his mind and placed a thought there. It had been occurring on and off for almost a month. In fact, ever since he had met with Thistlewood that time in late April. At that very meeting he remembered he had been suddenly struck by the plainly ridiculous notion that Arthur Thistlewood was some kind of a genius. The mere thought of Thistlewood made him shudder.

Bellingham tried to concentrate his mind on the task in hand. He opened the ledgers and began to check the figures. It was slow, laborious work. When he finished he got up, stretched and dressed for dinner.

Jack Nettleton dodged his way along Whitehall against the flow of people and traffic. He was late. He did not have a watch, but he knew he was late.

He could see the sign for the Cat and Bagpipes just ahead. He stepped into the road to avoid a throng of expensively millinered gentlemen swinging their canes like scythes. He choked in the dust kicked up by a passing carriage but continued to stumble towards the tavern. He passed through the black-painted doors of the Cat and Bagpipes.

Inside the tavern was not considerably quieter than outside on the pavement. A large number of men pressed against the bar, swaying and shoving and shouting their orders. A few women sat at or patrolled the tables. Dense smoke filled the air and made the public house seem gloomy despite the evening sun pushing through the dirty windows.

Jack made his way towards the rear where the dining rooms were situated. He passed the stairs, saw a notice pinned to the banister declaring that an inquest was taking place in the upstairs chambers. He heard a loud commotion coming from the upper rooms. He guessed that someone had taken exception to the coroner's verdict. The notice mentioned that drinks were available from the bar. All breakages would have to be paid for. His curiosity piqued, Jack climbed the first few steps before thinking better of the idea and continuing on to keep his appointment with Belling-ham.

Jack spotted Bellingham at a table near the dining rooms. He sat hunched over a pewter tankard of beer. One arm was placed in front of the tankard, while the other supported his head and rested on the table. He looked as if he were guarding his beer, as if he were afraid someone would take it away from him at any moment. His large nose and long face gave him a pinched look. His hair was plastered down over his forehead in Napoleonic style. He stared forlornly at a spot on the floor, midway between his table and the bar, that contained no human feet. Jack smiled, amused by Bellingham's gravitas, made light by his weightiness.

Jack hesitated to join Bellingham. Every week for the last three months, ever since they had first encountered each other at a music recital, the two of them had met for dinner. Every week Nettleton hesitated. Week in, week out, he thought about abandoning his companion. Bellingham, it seemed, never questioned the circumstances surrounding their acquaintance. Jack, however, found it all highly questionable.

Nettleton did not look forward to these rendezvous. The conversation rarely strayed from the subject of Bellingham's struggle for compensation. Bellingham could witter on for hours about his sufferings and his entitlement. If he had a pound for every time he had heard the story of Bellingham's arrest on false charges of fraud, Jack would be as rich as Croesus.

Nettleton was astonished at Bellingham's passion for the past. Bellingham was fuelled by his past. If he ever actually won his case (an unlikely prospect, in Nettleton's estimation) Jack suspected that Bellingham would fall apart. He would no longer have a reason for living. The future was not solid in the way the past was; Bellingham staked his life on the facts – facts were a matter for the past, the future was too uncertain for facts.

It was interesting, Jack thought, that the two most influential men in his life were both obsessed with the past. Bellingham clung to it, he nursed the injuries inflicted on him, never letting them heal over, always picking at the scabs. Thistlewood, on the other hand, wished only to obliterate the past. Root and branch, he would say. Tear it out root and branch.

Bellingham did not notice him, so Jack remained watching the older man a moment or two longer. Bellingham was about forty. His face was not heavily lined, but the lines he did have were deep. His hair was dark brown streaked with white at the temples, thinning on top. His teeth were yellow and several were missing. Bellingham, Jack had observed, very seldom smiled with an open mouth. Many took this as evidence of a humourless disposition. Others saw his tight-lipped smile as arrogant. Jack knew it simply as vanity.

Bellingham's eyes moved quickly around the room, giving the impression of observation, but they flitted too quickly from object to object, unable to take in anything except the most obvious threat. Bellingham's blue eyes were full of a terror that the rest of his body did not display. There was a space all around his table, despite the crush of people. Spaces like that developed around two sorts of people, the dangerous and the scared. Both attracted trouble and nobody wanted any trouble.

Jack thought twice about joining Bellingham but eventually concluded that two frightened people had to be safer than one. He approached and sat down.

Bellingham started and knocked his beer over. He righted his tankard. 'I'd almost given up on you,' he said.

'Sorry I'm late.' Nettleton shrugged. 'Shall we eat? I'm hungry,' he said brusquely. Bellingham nodded, rose to his feet and followed Nettleton.

They were shown into a small alcove at the back of the tavern, separated from the rest of the diners by a ragged, green curtain. A small rectangular table and two chairs filled the alcove. It looked crowded with just the two of them. They sat at opposite ends of the table. Their feet touched in the middle. Jack drew his back sharply, Bellingham more slowly. Both pretended nothing had happened.

Bellingham smiled at Jack; he opened his mouth, exposing his upper teeth. Bellingham felt this showed his trust in and affection for the young man. It was his sincere smile. Nettleton tried very hard not to stare at the yellowed, decaying teeth displayed before him, but he found Bellingham's staring eyes equally discomfiting, so he looked away and made as if he were searching for something in his pocket. Nettleton's ears burned red. He felt his every movement was exaggerated and clumsy. When he finally looked at Bellingham he was glad to see him returned to his habitual morose self. Jack had never known Bellingham to be happy. He was not sure he would care very much for a happy Bellingham.

For his part the older man worried that Jack had found his teeth disgusting. He dropped his smile. He liked Nettleton. He saw in him something of himself as a youth: a certain impetuosity, stubbornness and ambition combined with a dreamy, ill-defined romanticism. Nettleton always accomplished what he set out to do, but he always left it to the last minute. He always postponed a decision in the hope that circumstances or somebody else would make the decision for him. But Bellingham liked Jack.

A music recital. It seemed strange that he had met Jack Nettleton at a recital. The concert (Handel, Bellingham recalled) was given to encourage donations to the Foundling Hospital and the event had taken place in the hospital's chapel. Yet perhaps it was not so odd. Jack was the improving sort, looking to better himself. Why shouldn't a working man attend a concert?

Jack's desire to improve himself was something of which Bellingham heartily approved. He regarded himself as Jack's personal tutor, introducing him to music, painting, the cultured life.

52

It was a self-appointed role but one in which Bellingham took great pride. To act as the young man's mentor, his patron even, the sheer joy of sharing his own delight in the arts with another, gave Bellingham enormous pleasure.

Of course, the fact that Jack was a journeyman printer and thus in a position to be of very practical assistance to him in the pursuit of his prospects was a marvellous coincidence. A hint of fate, or so Bellingham liked to think.

He was lonely. If he was honest with himself, which he was not very often, then the truth of it was he needed a friend desperately. He missed his children. He missed Mary Ann. Nettleton had held out his hand in friendship, Bellingham had clasped it tightly. Too tightly, perhaps. There were times when he felt Nettleton shrink from him. He realized he could be embarrassing, that he talked too loudly in quiet places, that most people thought he had too many airs and graces. People laughed at him. Bellingham was no stranger to mockery; he accepted it as the lot of a just man to be mocked for his principles. Nettleton, however, was less sanguine about other people's opinions. He would never actually do anything about them. He would never provoke a fight or anything like that, anything active. But the taunts did give him pause for thought. And pausing was a kind of inaction with which Jack was very familiar.

Nettleton paused before ordering, waited for Bellingham to give his order and then said he would have the same. Boiled bacon. Nothing extravagant. Jack stretched out in his chair, arms above his head. He yawned. 'I hate this city. I hate this awful, miserable country.'

Bellingham looked at Jack indulgently. He took some bread in his hands and tore it in two, offered half to Nettleton. When Jack wasn't complaining about the state of the nation, he was complaining about the weather. Bellingham smiled, careful not to expose his dental dereliction. He felt indulgent towards this young man and his constant complaints. He resolved that one of the first things he would do when he got his compensation would be to set up Nettleton in the New World. It would be the least he could do for him. The thought alone made him feel warm inside.

Nettleton took the bread and dipped it in his beer. Bellingham cleared his throat. The silence was becoming unbearable, but Jack could think of nothing to say. Bellingham filled the gap. 'I am at my wit's end, Jack,' he said. But he did not relish, as he used to, the prospect of reporting his progress to Nettleton. He spoke because it was necessary, because he was afraid that if he did not say anything, Nettleton would simply get up and leave. 'They have sent me from pillar to post and back again. I am back where I started without having achieved a single, solitary thing.' Jack shifted uncomfortably in his seat which only made Bellingham talk faster. Bellingham leant forward. His face was flushed, not with alcohol blushes but with the effort to communicate, but Nettleton heard nothing. He knew Bellingham's story off by heart.

First the account of the Russian years. His arrest as a suspect in a conspiracy to defraud Lloyds of London. His exoneration and release. Arrested once more, caught up in a bureaucratic net, imprisoned. Bankrupted, his family left to provide for themselves. His efforts to gain help from the British Embassy rebuffed time and again. In and out of prison, vilified, brutalized, near-sodomized.

Bellingham had his story off pat. He had several different versions, of varying detail, depending on whose company he was keeping at the time. The one he told Jack was invariably the most graphic. His account would always conclude with a sarcastic summation of the achievements of Spencer Perceval, as a man, a lawyer, Chancellor of the Exchequer and Prime Minister, delivered like a funeral peroration. As long as Jack nodded and grunted, remembered to add the occasional interjection of support or surprise, he was free to let his mind wander.

It was not that he lacked respect for Bellingham. On the contrary, he had enormous respect for the man. He was fighting a titanic struggle almost single-handedly, a struggle he had no hope of winning, yet he refused to give up. Bellingham was no defeatist – an optimist, perhaps, but not a defeatist. Nettleton admired the way he stuck by his family, the way he seemed motivated by a desire to provide for Mary Ann and the children. Nettleton thought that Bellingham was probably a very good father; he admired him as much as he despised his own father.

A strict disciplinarian, Jack's father had fallen to pieces when his wife had run off with a butcher's apprentice and the contents of the butcher's cash register. He never worked again.

Jack, a bright boy with a string of scholarships, was forced to provide for the deserted family. To this day he handed over almost his entire wage packet to his sister, who ran the household. Jack's father had not lifted a finger in eight years. He sat all day by the fire. He did not even stoke it himself, relying on his daughter to feed the flames and keep him warm. Jack had nothing but scorn for his father. He hated the responsibility foisted upon him at an early age. He yearned for his freedom. He dreamed, day and night, of America. He collected everything he could about the place. He had books and maps, brochures and newspaper clippings. Late at night he used to spread his horde across the kitchen table and linger over the exotic place names with their promise of alien landscapes and red-skinned natives. He read and re-read accounts of the heroic battles for liberty: the Boston Tea Party, Bunker Hill, 'No Taxation without Representation'. Tears welled up in his eyes when he thought about Tom Paine.

There was precious little to hold him in England. Now he had finally left home, only his sense of responsibility, only guilt, held him back.

Bellingham was winding down. He had noticed the glassy, far-off look in Nettleton's eyes. He knew his words went unheeded. He knew also that if he bored his friend with his story, then certainly he wearied the Government too. He pondered for a moment whether he could bore Perceval and the House of Commons into submission. The notion was absurd.

It simply was not working. His paper assault on the Establishment was too easily shuttled, shuffled and filed. His siege on the bastion of bureaucracy was laughably ineffectual. As if David had attempted to turn the Philistines against their giant champion by ridiculing his abnormal height.

'This is my last chance,' Bellingham explained wearily. He no longer cared if Jack heard him or not. It was as if he were talking to himself, working it out. 'Why won't they let the case come to court? Because they know that I'll win. That if it comes before a jury, the justice of my case will be plain to see. A precedent might be set. It all begins to make some sort of sense when you look at it like that: a complex conspiracy to prevent the truth coming to light. Their very silence in the face of my petition (the one you printed for me, remember?) is the most conclusive proof that my case is watertight. What's the solution then, Jack? I'll tell you. Somehow I have to get the case into the courts. It all comes down to that, getting it into court. You see, don't you, Jack?' Bellingham fell silent.

Jack was taken aback by this abrupt end to Bellingham's diatribe. 'Of course you must. It's the only way.

You should do it.' He understood that he'd been asked a question. He just had no idea what the question had been.

Bellingham did not require Nettleton's confirmation. The question had been rhetorical. Bellingham felt that he had resolved something at last. He had decided on a new approach. He needed to find a way of speeding up the process, of expediting his claim. That is what he would concentrate on in the future. He smiled at Jack, who smiled back. It was Jack's turn to speak.

Nettleton was saved by the arrival of the bacon. They talked about domestic matters. Bellingham eulogized his wife, as usual, and Jack vilified his father, as usual. This was safer ground for their friendship – commiseration and gossip.

Jack did not stay for dessert. He was working the late shift at the printworks. He made his excuses and left Bellingham on his own, disappointed. Jack resolved not to go to their meeting the following week. Enough was enough. He walked slowly towards the river and turned to the east, the sunset at his back.

Bellingham sipped at his port wine. The thick, syrupy liquid trickled down the back of his throat, trailing warmth and slight intoxication in its wake. He had sensed Nettleton's disengagement and had expected little else. Certainly he had not expected support or approval from him, but he thought Nettleton had a right to know how he felt. After all, he was involved on a practical level. All those petitions Jack had printed up for him.

The little dining room, which had been cramped a few minutes earlier, seemed empty without Nettleton. Bellingham wondered if there was anything he could do to repair their friendship, but he did not really know what had gone wrong.

He looked at his watch. It was getting late. He should

57

be getting back to his lodgings. He had a long day ahead of him.

Bellingham lay in bed, half asleep. His eyes flickered as sleep subdued his turbulent thoughts. Gradually he found himself becoming conscious of his own breathing: slow and deep. He felt his breath brush past his lips. He felt his pulse throbbing, in his neck, in his legs, in his ears. His heart thumped. A tingling sensation spread through his body and suddenly be became aware of his weight. He felt himself sinking into the mattress, the mattress yielding to his body. He sensed the mattress supported by the bed, the bed standing square on its four legs supported by floorboards, themselves fastened to joists held in place by bricks and mortar. The foundations reaching into the clay earth. The whole edifice, with him inside it, held upright only by gravity. For a moment his safety, the structure of the entire universe, seemed very fragile, fixed in place by a mathematical formula. Then he felt gravity acting on him, a pressure, pushing him down, down, further into the mattress, pinning his legs, restraining his arms, crushing him. He lay perfectly still.

And in the gloom his vision saw further than his eyes ever could in the bright sunlight or the dark night. He saw past the walls and across the alleyways and fields. He saw his neighbours as they pursued the daily business of their lives. He saw them also, dreaming in their beds. All about him, up and down the street, people dreaming their dreams: greengrocer dreams, butcher dreams, parlourmaid dreams, mother dreams, husband dreams, children's dreams. Dreams of love, of wealth, of growing old together and of dying alone. Nightmares, too, that tossed their dreamers like driftwood on the waves. The humdrum dreams of everyday people, the banality of repose, the mundane dreams of the less afflicted. He longed to dream again of heroics and seductions. He wished for sequences of bizarre, unconnected images to flood his consciousness. Yet he would never dream those dreams again, and when his soaring spirit returned at last to his body and, exhausted, he fell asleep, he found himself transported back to St Petersburg, freezing in a filthy cell. Head shaved, skin raw from the cold and the beatings. All around him the snores and sobs of his fellow convicts. He does not sleep well. He cannot afford to. If he does, someone will steal his blanket, threadbare though it is. More than this miserable blanket, the thought of vengeance keeps him warm.

Bellingham woke and turned over. He stretched his legs and pulled the coarse blankets up to his shoulders. A chill in the air. From outside, from far away, a yell, the sound of breaking glass, a woman cried out. He fell back asleep.

THREE

THE CELLAR

As the screams from the cellar faded to a rattle and stopped, Jack Nettleton was gripped by fear. He had always thought he was comfortable with the idea of death. He believed he must regard the possibility of his imminent demise as inescapable. To refuse to countenance any notion of dying was to render death unthinkable and therefore something which could not be faced with dignity or equanimity. However, seated as he was on a rickety old chair, bound securely hand and foot, Jack realized he was deceiving himself. The bruises on his face throbbed. His ribs sang out their pain, intermittently convulsing his torso. His soiled and sodden trousers clung to his legs. His feet were numb. Blood from his mouth trickled down the back of his throat, forcing him to cough, which in turn set off his ribs on their agonizing fugue while his body twitched and danced to the tormenting rhythm. Nausea overwhelmed him. Instead of a peaceful, even vaguely rational, response to his approaching death, Jack was disappointed to discover that panic gripped him, shook him, held him tight.

In an effort to regain control of himself Jack turned his attention to the contraption that filled the rest of the room. It resembled a child's whirligig, built on an enormous scale, protruding through the floor. All that was visible was a pole some eight or nine feet high and the blades of the whirligig attached about halfway up the main shaft. Each of the four blades was about five feet in length, a foot and a half in breadth. The blades rotated slowly, causing the air to circulate gently around the room. If it were not for the dust, stirred and distributed by the breeze, Jack thought the effect might be quite pleasant. The shaft disappeared through the floor and was obviously attached to a device in the cellar. Occasionally Jack heard hushed voices float up from there. The muted conversation was impossible to make out above the creaking of the whirligig as it turned and the continuous low hum of a machine in constant use. Bannister Truelock had called it an Influencing Engine. Jack tried his best not to imagine whom it was intended to influence and how its object was attained, but his thoughts strayed time and again to the topic. In his panicked state he pictured it as some monstrous instrument of torture designed to crack and snap his bones and tear at his skin.

Jack had suffered enough tortures already. Patrick Walsh and his eager colleague had beaten and humiliated him. Bannister Truelock contributed his usual brand of mystic threats and lunatic rantings. And still Arthur Thistlewood had to put in his two penn'orth. The Influencing Engine waited, creaking and humming, gears turning, cogs biting.

Jack tried in vain to dislodge the fear in his mind. He sang quietly to himself, nursery rhymes and heroic ballads. He shouted insults at his absent captors. He even prayed. But he could not shift the panic that settled in his throat, causing him to choke and gag. As his agitation grew, his breathing became more frantic. He gasped and gulped for air. He started to hyper-ventilate. He began to shake, and as he shook he rocked back and forth, back and forth, until finally the chair toppled backwards, sending his head slamming against the floorboards. A crash of pain juddered through his body. He screamed. Nobody came.

Desperate now, Jack forced himself to think of something other than torture and death. He lay on his back staring at the cracked plaster ceiling. He watched the dust, blown on the whirligig wind, swirl in the beams of light that penetrated the window shutters. He thought of the races.

Gambling was not one of Jack's failings. He saw too many men go to the track flush with a week's wages only to return roaring drunk with next to nothing. A family on the brink of survival on pay-day was ruined overnight. The sight of those men, laden down with clothes, furniture, Bibles – anything that could be carried – making that trip to the pawnbroker's with their wife and children hard on their heels, tugging at their sleeves, pleading with them not to pawn the lot, was all too familiar.

Jack felt his responsibilities too keenly to throw away his own wages so casually. Ever since beginning his apprenticeship he had supported his entire family. Every week he had held on to his wages for barely more than a few hours before relinquishing them to his father, who forced him to account for every penny. At first, when he was still a boy, Jack had been proud to be a breadwinner. Now he resented it. How much had he earned over the years? God alone knew, but Jack had not seen any of it. For years his father had not even allowed him the dignity of buying his own clothes.

Leaving home had been the best decision he had ever made. It was more or less the only decision he had made on his own. Three months ago he had vowed it was a new beginning. A new era of decisiveness and action that would see him on his way to the Americas in a matter of months. But the hoped-for changes did not come about. He lay in bed in the mornings waiting for something to happen, but his life resolutely refused to change its pattern of conformity. Then one pay-day he was gripped by recklessness. Just this once he would keep his wages and do something he wanted to do. He went to the races.

Jack's fellow workers at the printworks had been planning the trip for some time. A holiday was coming up. A rare enough occasion to warrant some sort of extravagant outing. As an apprentice Jack was involved in many such debauches. Days spent drinking and boating or simply drinking. Debating societies – approved by the masters, who were either tolerant or gullible – that were poor excuses to sing comic songs, hurl insults at authority and food at one another and drink each other under or over the table. Jack was under no illusion that this trip would be any less enervating than those youthful exploits. In fact, he was counting on it. So he was not in the least bit surprised to find himself supported on either side by two friends as they carried him off to buy another round of beers. Nor was he in the least bit amazed when he was persuaded to place first one bet and then another on the various ropy old nags of his friends' choosing. However, he was shocked to discover that each horse won. He seemed to sober up rapidly after that. The fear of being robbed of all his money displaced all other terrors and emphasized the need for caution. He pocketed his original stake and in a state of cautious euphoria placed his entire winnings on one more horse.

Thinking back on it now, Jack realized that he could not possibly have been sober. For one thing he had con-sumed far too much alcohol; for another he had put a large amount of money on an outside chance because he liked the horse's name: Rebecca's Folly or something similar and equally ominous-sounding. The moment he parted with his tin he regretted it. In order to stem the fast-approaching tide of guilt, he day-dreamed about his possible winnings. He thought of himself *en route* to America, owning his own business, buying a beautiful house, marrying a beautiful woman, but the fantasies failed to dam that rising tide. He turned his attention to the race and made his way over to the finishing post. He closed his eyes as the horses came under starter's orders and opened them again quickly because he felt dizzy. He could not bear to watch the race, but, equally, he was unable to relinquish all hope. He resolved the problem by sitting on the ground and staring at the calves and ankles of his fellow punters. The stench of vomit and urine was very strong at ground level. Jack considered this just punishment for his stupidity. The excretions and rejections of other men's bladders and stomachs formed a suitable backdrop to his penance. He heard the cheers and roars, the shouts of encouragement and the howls of despair as the horses rounded the bend for the final straight. Despite himself Jack stood as the front runners crossed the line. His horse was not among them, neither was it in the rest of the field. He discovered later that it had fallen at the first, broken its leg and been put out of its misery.

Jack thought to himself that he would give anything, do anything, to be out of this situation. He thought, if that damn horse had won instead of being shot in the head, he would not be stuck on his back in an empty room with only a Gargantuan whirligig for company.

The day had started off in a conventional manner. After leaving Bellingham at the Cat and Bagpipes he had gone to work as usual. Jack finished his shift shortly before dawn. He left the printworks quickly in an attempt to evade his colleagues. He was tired. He wanted only one thing, to be home in his bed, asleep. He walked the paved and lamp-lit streets east, towards Shoreditch. He tried to remain alert, despite the lateness of the hour, because to relax his guard for a moment could be disastrous.

In unlit streets he walked in the dirt of the road, avoiding the entrances to alleys and courts. He took the long route home rather than weave through the maze of lanes that made up the rookeries of Holborn and Aldgate.

As dawn approached the lampmen began to extinguish the street lights, market gardeners wheeled their produce in carts and wagons through the suburbs and across the bridges, milk criers worked their rounds. People emerged from cellars, garrets and rough lean-tos, shopkeepers pulled back shutters. The nightly cast of robbers and thieves, burglars and pickpockets, were either still celebrating the night's successes or slinking back to their cellars to mourn its parsimony or lying in the gutter, casualties of an argument or an armed victim chosen in error or too much bad gin laced with turpentine and God knows what else.

A disgusting smell, a reek of rot and decay, hung in the air, not carried on the wind – the night was still – but the stink was concentrated in particular streets. A gut-wrenchingly awful, invisible cloud that lurked around every other corner. The stench grew worse as he approached the river. The Thames at low tide was a foul trickle of ooze and sewage. People kept their windows firmly closed in spite of the heat.

The streets were not crowded but neither were they deserted. Jack walked along an empty street, glanced down a passageway and saw a group of twenty or so men and women throwing dice. One of the men signalled him to join them, but Jack paid no attention – he did not know the man. Everywhere pockets of people skulked in doorways, loitered at coaching inns and outside drinking dens, lurked down side-streets. A few, like Jack, walked to and from work. The occasional carriage or chair jogged past, heading west, the blinds drawn, its half-glimpsed occupants holding handker-chiefs to their noses and mouths.

Jack arrived at his lodgings at about five o'clock. The yard was already bustling; children tumbling out of doors, sitting in the muck and filth, women sweeping steps and scrubbing flagstones, staggering in from a night's washing work, men stumbling to work hurriedly snatching a meagre breakfast.

The door to Jack's house was open. The stairwell was alive with his fellow lodgers. He climbed the stairs wearily, barely acknowledging the nods and murmured greetings of his neighbours. He reached the refuge of his garret and flopped down on to the straw palette.

The room was unfurnished. A trunk, covered in rags and other odds and sods to deter the casual, acquisitive nature of some of his neighbours, was next to the straw mattress under the window. A small bundle of books Jack intended to sell were hidden in the empty grate and shielded from view by a large print of Hogarth's *Gin Lane*. The print, cut in wood and coloured, was the only item of furnishing included in the rent and it had lain face to the wall for the entire three months Jack had lived in the shabby room. The glassless windows, little more than holes in the exterior walls, were still boarded up and stuffed with rags from the winter. They served in some small way to keep the stink out, just as they had almost totally failed to keep the heat in.

Jack lit a greasy tallow candle, set it on the trunk and lay back on his palette. The candle's oily smoke disguised the stench further. He dozed a while, dreamily thinking of a new life in the New World.

He must have fallen asleep. The knock on the door woke him. He waited a minute or two, hoping whoever it was would go away, but the knocking resumed. Jack dragged himself upright and unlocked the door. He saw the face at the door and screamed. Not very loud, abruptly curtailed, more a yelp than a scream. He cut it short to give himself time to curl up into a ball on the floor. He lay there, curled tight, head tucked in, waiting for the blows to rain down. Instead, an arm was shoved under each armpit and Jack was lifted off the floor and down the stairs. He wanted to look but decided against it. He kept his eyes shut and his body closed. He was dumped on the floor of a carriage. The two men who had carried him downstairs climbed in after him. The carriage pulled away. Jack did not move.

'Cover him up, can't you? He looks like a fucking hedgehog.'

Someone covered Jack in a blanket or a coat. It stank. Jack did not move an inch.

When Patrick Walsh did not beat Jack's brains out straight away, Jack thought everything would be all right. If a lunatic like Walsh, a dangerous, violent lunatic who hated you with a passion, did not pummel you to death on sight, then there was hope.

He might be tightly bound to a chair in a room with a miniature windmill in it without any idea as to why he was there, but he was alive and unbruised. Somebody wanted something. And that person could only be Thistlewood, who had been known to kidnap a man just to ask him to look after his dog for a couple of weeks. Thistlewood loved that dog, yet such was his commitment to the revolution that he sent his beloved mutt into a barracks with a bomb attached to its belly. The device failed to go off, but the soldiers beat the dog to death with their rifle butts. Thistlewood stopped at nothing to achieve his aims.

Jack met him first when he was still an apprentice in Lewes. Thistlewood was prowling the south coast attempting to foment mutiny in the fleet. He had introduced Jack to Tom Paine, Thomas Spence and the works of other radical writers. He even took the young printer's apprentice to the house where Paine lived when he was a customs officer in Lewes. The wrong house, as it turned out, but Jack did not discover that until some time later.

Meanwhile Thistlewood put his enthusiastic new recruit to work printing leaflets and flyers. It was difficult and dangerous work. Jack had to wait until he was alone, running off the final ream, and then switch the plates for as long as he dared. Jack was indispensable to Thistlewood, bright and brave and a printer to boot. Thistlewood was careful not to let Jack know he was so important.

Thistlewood moved his operations to London, and Jack went with him, taking the family. But shortly after the move Jack became disillusioned with Thistlewood and his outrageous schemes that always ended in failure and injury to some innocent party or another. Jacobinism had long since run its course, and as he got older Jack could no longer sustain his revolutionary fervour on an exclusive diet of hate. He attempted to break away from Thistlewood and his circle, but this proved difficult to accomplish. Thistlewood was unwilling to let Jack go. Arthur Thistlewood fed on hate and suspicion: he could not allow Jack to roam free. They struck a bargain. Jack would perform the occasional favour for Thistlewood in return for a more or less trouble-free existence.

In Thistlewood's mind Jack was still personally involved in everything he did. Jack could not betray him without betraying himself. Thistlewood considered this an acceptable state of affairs. Jack resolved to leave the country.

Jack knew he would never escape on a journeyman's wage, especially if he kept handing his pay over to his parasitical family. Physically he had escaped them, but the extra rent only exacerbated his financial worries, and no amount of freedom could displace his guilt. He needed a large sum of money to make good his flight. He needed a rich, dead relative, but there were no rich relatives. There was only the race-track. But there was always hope.

Walsh returned to the room after leaving Jack alone for an hour or so. Patrick Walsh, a tall, well-built man had very little conversation. Jack was accustomed to him communicating in grunts and profanities. Whenever he did converse, his lips became flecked with saliva, and little bubbles ballooned and burst as he worked his mouth. Jack was taken aback, then, when Walsh assumed a position behind him, to his left, and began to talk into his ear. Jack was extremely intimidated by this uncharacteristic behaviour.

Walsh was recounting the substance of a dream he had had the night before. Walsh's dream was long, detailed, incredibly violent and shockingly banal. In fact, nothing out of the ordinary.

Walsh's fantasy involved the transplant of various people's brains and intestines. These organs were not surgically removed; the brains were extracted by means of a large brick and a sharp knife, the digestive tract was located with the hands. After Walsh had performed his gruesome task he proceeded to hang and burn the bodies of his victims. Jack wondered if this were fantasy at all – Walsh was certainly capable of mass slaughter – but somehow the pseudo-scientific details were entirely out of place. By the end Jack was convinced Thistlewood had written the whole thing out for Walsh to memorize. Walsh had certainly embellished the gorier parts with a smattering of personal experience, but the whole was simply too demented and Gothic to be true. Not to mention too imaginative. Jack felt he had the measure of the situation. A response was needed. He decided he should burst into tears. He did so. Walsh departed and Jack smiled. Captive he may be, but he was one step ahead of their game.

A minute or two later Walsh came back into the room with a colleague Jack did not recognize. They beat him until he whined, stopped for a breather and started in again. Walsh and his partner were careful not to let Jack slide into unconsciousness. This they achieved by urinating in his face. Through the haze of pain and spray of piss Jack marvelled at their bladder control. They left him lying on his side in a pool of effluent.

He did not have to wait long in that position. Almost immediately he was joined by Bannister Truelock. Jack never thought he would be glad to see Truelock, but he was. Truelock threw a bucket of warm water over him and proceeded to clean the cuts on his face. Truelock said nothing for some time, for which Jack was grateful.

Bannister Truelock had a habit of talking about God (by which he usually meant himself) and the Second Coming (also himself) whenever he opened his mouth (through which, incidentally, the Second Coming would be allowed egress). The thought of being tied up in a room with Truelock for any length of time corroded Jack's soul. However, it would cause him no physical harm. Eventually Truelock spoke. 'Feeling any better, Jack?'

'Not really, Truelock. What about you? Any closer to giving birth?'

Truelock scowled at Jack, his forehead wrinkling with distaste. 'The time approaches, Jack. Yes, it does. I tell you, the appointed time approaches.'

'That must be a relief, Truelock, because you've been pregnant for fourteen years or so now.'

'Well, yes, it is a relief to know that the end of all things is imminent. But one must be patient in the performance of God's work.'

'I was wondering, Truelock,' said Jack, changing the subject while change was possible, 'whether or not you knew why I was here.'

'Patience, Jack. All will be revealed in due course.'

'Am I going to die?'

'Naturally.'

'Today?'

'That is entirely up to you.'

Jack nodded. Truelock's cryptic bent made him a useless source of information. Jack pushed on regardless. 'What is that windmill thing?'

'It's an Influencing Engine,' Truelock said proudly, puffing out his chest. 'Now, you just sit still and listen.'

He stood up, stepped back a few paces and began to declaim the Everlasting Gospel. According to Truelock, God was in all things, but especially God was in Bannister Truelock. In fact, God had been gestating inside Bannister Truelock for some years, but soon God would be born from Truelock's mouth, the Kingdom of God would be established upon the Earth and everybody who had ever lived would at last know that Bannister Truelock, madman, had been right all along.

When he finished his sermon Truelock smiled indulgently at Jack, patted him on the head and left the room. Jack was at a loss to explain why he had been there in the first place. He wondered when Truelock had managed to escape from Bedlam. Truelock seemed to stroll in and out of that place at will. Jack also wondered why Thistlewood would choose to associate himself with someone like Truelock. Admittedly, Bannister Truelock had been closely involved with Hadfield's assassination attempt on George the Third, and that gave him some credibility, but Truelock had not pulled the trigger. Perhaps Thistlewood liked to surround himself with madmen because it made him seem rational by comparison.

Somewhere below him someone began to scream.

Jack lay on his back. Any movement caused him great pain, but the panic had passed. He stared at the

71

whirligig at the other end of the room. An Infuencing Engine. It certainly sounded very sinister. Jack hoped it was not being warmed up ready to influence him. He dismissed the thought. Thistlewood was next. His lieutenants had performed their function. Now it was time for the boss to put in an appearance. If he possessed no other qualities, Arthur Thistlewood certainly possessed stagecraft. His entrance would be well timed and perfectly executed. Jack glanced around for a sign of a trapdoor or other device. He could not see any evidence of false doors, walls or traps, but that did not mean there were none. Thistlewood was a great admirer of Joey Grimaldi. He rarely missed a performance of the great clown's pantomimes. Perhaps Thistlewood was going to dress up as Mother Goose. Jack realized he was a little hysterical.

Feet approached across the floor. When the figure finally entered Jack's field of vision it was not dressed as a goose or any other kind of farmyard animal. Jack's view was limited by his upside-down position, but he recognized the boots, stained with splashes of dark-brown blood, as Arthur Thistlewood's. Jack felt he should struggle to get away. Some sort of response was required, but he was too tired to move or even to speak. He lay very still and watched as Thistlewood circled him very slowly.

Jack could see right up Thistlewood's nose. His nostrils were thick with hair. His neck was red and ragged from a too close shave.

'You have something I want,' said Thistlewood, still pacing in a circle. His voice was deep, reassuringly paternal, daring Jack to defy him.

'I don't have anything, Arthur,' pleaded Nettleton lamely.

'That is not correct,' mused Thistlewood. 'You have a good job, don't you?'

72

'Yes,' said Nettleton meekly.

'Your family are well cared for, aren't they?'

'Yes.'

'Do you know how few people could say the same? Don't you realize that with just these two things, job and family, you are already a wealthy man? Do you know how many people are without work, whose family are dead or, worse, suffering the direst poverty?' Thistlewood stopped pacing and knelt down over Jack's face. 'And are you aware that if a man were to stand up for himself, to try to accumulate some rights, some security, he would be transported or executed?'

'Things are bad,' began Nettleton without knowing what to say.

'They are worse than bad, Jack. But tell me, Mr Nettleton, who is it that got you your job? How is it that you are able to look after your elderly father and those pretty sisters of yours?'

'You got me the job, Arthur. And I am grateful.' Nettleton turned his head. Thistlewood grabbed his chin and forced Jack to face him.

'Will you give me what I want? Will you, Jack?'

'I don't know what you want,' protested Nettleton.

'I want only three things, Jack. Obedience, respect and John Bellingham.' Thistlewood rose to his feet. 'But I don't expect you to do this simply out of friendship, Jack. I would not dream of presuming on you and your good friend Mr Bellingham. I will give you money in return for delivery of Bellingham, and, for the time being, I will take the obedience and the respect on trust.'

'I don't understand,' said Jack. 'What do you want with Bellingham? And surely you could find him yourself, or Walsh could.' Jack was interrupted by a sharp kick to his kidneys.

'Obedience, Jack, and respect. I just felt that

73

you needed a lesson in friendship and a chance to prove yourself. We all need a second chance,' Thistlewood intoned in his paternal voice. 'Don't let me down, Jack. Truelock will tell you the details. Goodbye, Jack.'

Henry Stillwater leaned farther into the doorway as the carriage shuddered to a halt a few feet away on the other side of the street. He watched as Jack Nettleton, dazed and confused, tumbled into the road. Nettleton got to his feet swiftly and started to hobble off. Still- water saw the young man's back disappear into the distance in a cloud of dust and wondered, briefly, how long the drought would last. The carriage pulled away just as Nettleton passed from view.

Stillwater caught sight of a young girl sitting on the doorstep of a house opposite. She played with a stick, drawing patterns in the dirt. Stillwater whistled for her attention and beckoned to her. The girl responded sluggishly. She ambled over to him, trailing her stick behind. Her surliness annoyed Stillwater, but he displayed no outward sign of irritation. Instead, when she finally drew near, he produced a coin and an envelope from his pocket. His gambit did not have the desired effect. In fact, it had no discernible effect at all. The girl took the coin readily enough, but she neither smiled nor dropped her stick. Convinced now that she was a simpleton, Stillwater wondered whether it was worth his while entrusting his letter to her. He scanned the street quickly, but there was no alternative. His impatience grew. His simple idea of a moment ago now seemed like an impossible task. Stillwater sighed and slowly, very deliberately, he told the girl of the errand. She nodded. Heartened by her apparent understanding, Stillwater gave her the letter. The girl nodded again and set off down the street. She did not run. It seemed

to him that she barely moved. Her stick, dragging
behind her, cut a wavy line in the dust as she dawdled
off. Stillwater sighed again and retreated once more
into the shadows.

FOUR

BLOOMSBURY

John Bellingham, down on his knees, faced the window. Early-morning sun in his eyes, hands clasped together, brow wrinkled to a frown, he tried to talk to God. His night-shirt tickled the back of his legs. He attempted to ignore it, to concentrate on his prayer. 'Dear Father,' he muttered. Embarrassed to speak louder in case anyone heard him, but aware that he must speak out loud as proof of his belief in the power of prayer. His eyelids flickered, a slight muscular spasm. He screwed his eyes shut, forced them to obey his will. 'Dear Father God,' he began again. Redoubling his efforts, choosing his words carefully, he continued, 'Protect my family. Keep them safe from harm.'

He thought of Mary Ann in Liverpool. She would be at work already. She would be opening the shop's shutters, checking over the window display. The boys would be playing out back where she could keep an eye on them.

He felt a small ache in his chest, a contraction in his throat, at the merest thought of his family. He could not go back now. He had to see this through to the end, for the children's sake. He would not be able to live with himself if he failed. He had to provide for his children; it was his duty as a parent. Mary Ann could not understand that. She thought his pursuit of compensation foolish, a distraction from the everyday necessity of making a living.

He had promised her in the last letter he sent that he would be home soon. He had no idea what made him add another lie to the catalogue of deceit he had already written. Except that he sensed a finality in the air. The momentum of his actions had brought him thus far, and he just had to take the final step. No matter what he wrote to Mary Ann, he knew he would not be going back to Liverpool, not for some time and perhaps never. He did not want them to worry on his account; that's why he lied.

All the same, though, it would be nice to go home. He could wipe the slate clean, start trading again. It wasn't as if he was a complete failure as a merchant. Mary Ann certainly deserved better: an absentee husband, a business going to rack and ruin, two young children to raise on her own. On the other hand, she did have her family close by. Cousin Eliza on her way back from America. Uncle James in Wigan. Uncle James had always despised John. He refused to visit when John was at home, had nothing to offer but complaints. John would dearly love to prove James Neville wrong.

The smell of breakfast wafted up the stairs, down the hall and under Bellingham's door. He opened one eye, glanced out of the window that looked out on to the backs of the adjoining houses and saw washing lines strung out like cobwebs catching an occasional shirt or blouse. He heard children playing and singing, just as he did most mornings. He would join in sometimes when they sang a song he knew. Bellingham craned his neck, straightened his back and looked out across the backyards and alleys, past the houses, towards Spa Fields. To his right loomed the dark bulk of the House of Correction and further off, glinting in the sunlight, the New River Head and Sadler's Wells. 'God, the

77

Father of Jesus Christ, give me strength to do what is right. Dear God, grant me justice.'

He heard the floorboards creaking in the hall. A chink and a splash as Mrs Roberts's servant girl left a clean pitcher of water outside his door. A shy girl – Catherine, he thought her name was. He had meant to ask but had never got around to it. He had heard her called Catherine, but also Anne and Mary, Fidgeons or Pigeons, that was her surname. Something along those lines. He considered it odd that he could have lived in the house for five months and still not know her name. Then again she was only a servant.

He got up on one knee and was about to retrieve the water from the hallway when he recalled he was at prayer. 'Father, forgive me. I'm rather distracted this morning.' As soon as he said it he regretted his casual familiarity. He was unsure how to retrieve the situation and place his devotion back on the right footing. He resorted to the Lord's Prayer, speaking it slowly and solemnly. Even before he finished he had already decided to try reading his Bible. That would put him in the right frame of mind.

He got off his knees and fetched the pitcher. A wash in cold water would wake him up, shake him out of his distracted mood. Movement made him realize he needed to urinate.

Bellingham poured the water into a bowl. He splashed the water over his face, rubbed his chin. He also needed a shave. He examined himself in the hand-mirror Mary Ann had given him. A haircut would not do any harm either. The thought of a visit to the barber lifted his spirits. The cold, sharp edge of the razor, hot water and soapy, fragrant lather.

He sat down in an old chair with a cane bottom that sagged beneath his weight and took out his Bible. The morning sun burned on to his back as he rooted through the drawer of a small writing table for his prayer book.

He cherished the book's leather binding, the shiny gold edging on the pages. Jack Nettleton had got him a discount on it, trade price. When the time came, he resolved, he would send it to Mary Ann. Taken with that thought, he opened the inside front cover, smoothed down the page and reached out for his pen. He dipped it into a well of black ink. Leaning close to the page, concentrating hard so as not to make a mistake, he carefully inscribed her name. He blotted the page and waited, just to be certain that the ink had dried, before opening the prayer book to the table of lessons.

'May hath XXXI days.' He moved his finger down and read off the previous day's lesson. He had been in church, the chapel of the Foundling Hospital, with Mrs Roberts and her son.

Bellingham did not attend church often. He found no comfort in the ritual, no insight in the sermon. He disliked anyone who claimed to be pious, treated the self-confessedly godly with deep suspicion. He considered himself a believer but had no wish to be addressed as one of the flock. Yet he had attended services at the Foundling Hospital almost every Sunday for the past three months. The hospital had a different atmosphere from that of anywhere else. There they celebrated life noisily and left the dead in their proper place – the cemetery.

Bellingham turned the pages of his Bible to the Second Book of Samuel. He looked at the passage, but it seemed to be about very little. He had hoped it would have some special significance, a hidden meaning, a coded message, a word to the wise. He always approached scripture in this fashion. Like a horoscope. Today he was disappointed. The passage seemed irrelevant, obscure. He recalled that the chaplain had declined to preach on it, taking instead for his sermon the New Testament reading, St John, chapter one, verse twenty-nine. 'Behold the Lamb of God, which taketh away the sin of the world.'

Bellingham's eye wandered across the page. He had some vague thoughts about reading around the text; instead he found himself reading about the first miracle at Cana. Water into wine. He could not help marvelling at the practicality of that first miracle. He imagined the grateful guests at the wedding – how drunk they must have been, how cheap it must have turned out for the bride's family. Bellingham knew the story well. It continued: driving the traders from the temple. 'My Father's House'. Whipping the money-men with a scourge, turning over the tables, scattering money everywhere, setting free the animals. Sheep, oxen, doves, trampling, squawking, flying. Merchants and money-changers scrambling after their lost profits, cursing this lunatic stranger, ignoring the sting of Christ's whip across their shoulders. The priests and the temple guards charging after the violent intruder, muttering about blasphemy and false prophets and madmen. 'Destroy this temple and in three days I will raise it up . . . he spake of the temple of his body.'

And now Bellingham imagined himself in the House of Commons, striding through the lobby with a home-made whip, hurling the mace to the floor, enjoying the spectacle of the Honourable Members fleeing from their benches, cowering beneath the scourge of his vengeance. He saw himself standing on the Speaker's chair denouncing all of them as frauds and war-mongers. 'You have turned the Houses of Parliament into temples of commerce and self-interest,' he shouted. 'You can no longer command the respect of the people you claim to represent. Have you forgotten what our ancestors died for? You have destroyed the House of our fathers.' Dumbstruck, awe-struck, impotent, the politicians would look on as the Sergeant-at-Arms cheered Bellingham. Word would soon spread, and the people of London would crowd into Palace Yard to catch a glimpse of the man of the hour, the courageous Bellingham who, single-handedly had restored liberty to the Commonwealth and brought to an end the tyranny of the aristocrats. Bellingham, the hero of freedom, planting the Tree of Liberty amid the corruption and decay of government. The cheering mob would lift him on to their shoulders and carry him through Whitehall. People yelling and shouting huzzahs from the rooftops as the politicians were led away in chains to stand trial for their crimes against good citizens. 'The zeal of thine house has eaten me up.' His daydream dissolved. Bellingham closed his Bible, angry that he had allowed himself to get carried away again.

Still in his night-shirt, he knelt at his bedside once more and prayed for his family, for himself, for the future. Sunlight shining through the window fell across the unmade bed, fell on Bellingham, cast his shadow on the floor.

He rose to his feet, turned his mind to dressing. His dark-blue, conservative-blue, businessman's jacket hung on the back of the door on the peg below his hat. The suit's style was a little old-fashioned. The hem reached to just below the knee, the cut was wide from the waist down, the collar was high. He examined the thick, unadorned cuffs, button missing. The collar was frayed at the back. A hole in the right-hand pocket. He made a note to be careful of that pocket. The examination depressed him. The jacket was tatty – no two ways about it. Bellingham resolved to visit the tailor again, hurry him up a bit. Taylor owed him a favour. He had paid cash on the nail for a snuff-coloured silk jacket with an extra pocket sewn inside to keep his money and his papers safe. He decided that he must have it today, even if he had to stand over Taylor and watch him finish it. It should have been delivered days ago. He would call in and see the old man on his way to visit Miss Stevens and get Taylor's apprentice to repair the pocket in the blue coat. That should be a simple job. They could manage that while he waited.

Satisfied with his resolution, Bellingham crossed over to the tallboy in the corner and opened the third drawer down. From its bottom he extracted a pair of stripy breeches. Blue stripes to go with his jacket. His favourite pair of breeches. He had thought them a little daring at the time, but the shopkeeper had assured him of their suitability. He checked the breeches for holes and missing buttons.

O God the Father of heaven: have mercy upon us miserable sinners.

Bellingham buttoned up his stripy breeches and then went to the top drawer. It contained a quantity of neatly folded shirts, from among which Bellingham chose a simple white one with no frills or lacy cuffs. Folding the shirt over his arm, he bent down to the bottom drawer and took out a starched collar, three studs, a neckerchief and cameo clasp, a clean pair of white stockings and a pair of garters. Arranging his chosen wardrobe on the bed, he nodded his approval. Taking the shirt, he crossed over to the dresser and disrobed. He scrutinized his tall, bony body, and his vague depression returned. He felt the pressure on his temples building as he looked at the red-and-white weals that covered his chest and curved around to his back. Leather tails had eaten into his torso, snaking under his armpits, always finding new flesh to disfigure. The legacy of his time in Russian gaols. The memory raised goose pimples. The hair on his neck prickled. He shivered.

O God the Son, Redeemer of the world: have mercy upon us miserable sinners.

Bellingham slipped on his clean, crisp shirt, covering

82

the scars of punishment on his back. He looked again at his body, noting the way his sternum dipped inwards and his belly button protruded outwards. He sucked in his stomach so far he imagined he could count his vertebrae.

O God the Holy Ghost, proceeding from the Father and the Son: have mercy upon us miserable sinners.

Bellingham buttoned his shirt to the chest. He pushed his tongue around his mouth, tickling his lower lip, feeling his teeth, counting them. There was a taste of iron in his mouth. His gums were bleeding.

O holy and blessed Trinity, three persons and one God: have mercy upon us miserable sinners.

Spare us, Good Lord.

Bellingham pulled on his stockings, careful not to hole them. He slipped his garters over the top and fastened them above the knee.

Good Lord deliver us.

We beseech thee to hear us, Good Lord.

Bellingham rolled down the legs of his breeches to cover the tops of his stockings and buttoned them.

Grant us thy peace.

O Christ, hear us.

Bellingham found his toothbrush on the dresser and dipped it in the water. He brushed energetically, up and down, back and front. The warm taste of iron again filled his mouth. He swilled and spat into his chamber pot. A pink trail of spittle clung to his lip. He wiped it off.

Lord have mercy upon us.

Christ have mercy upon us.

Lord have mercy upon us.

Bellingham buttoned his shirt to the neck. He attached his collar with three studs. He tied his neckerchief and fastened it with the cameo clasp. He checked himself over and then looked for his boots. He found them under the bed.

O Lord, reward us for cleaning our boots.

Bright, shiny boots with no buckles but with good strong heels. Bellingham sat on the bed and levered them on with his finger.

Good Lord, deliver us from the small vanity of wanting buckles on our boots.

He heard the chambermaid (what was her name again?) creeping around on the landing. He wondered if Mrs Roberts had managed to let that other room yet.

O Lord, arise, help us, deliver us from nosy land-ladies and chattering maids.

The morning was not one for idle gossip. Not today, especially not today. He felt a headache coming on.

Graciously heal us, O Christ. Graciously heal us, O Lord Christ.

A tightness in his bladder.

Let us pee.

He located the chamber pot and carried it to a dark corner, away from prying eyes, and relieved himself.

Amen.

Bellingham took a deep breath and opened his bedroom door. No one was on the landing. After the first short flight of stairs he paused and listened, hoping to hear whether Mrs Roberts had let the spare room. He probably would have known all about it if she had found a tenant, but he listened all the same. The previous lodger had left the month before, heading out for the West Indies. Bellingham had liked the young man but did not rate his chances in the Indies. Then again perhaps his own experiences had prejudiced him against the wan, ambitious youth. But the fact that his own voyage to China (and adventure) on the ill-fated *Hartwell* had ended in disaster had no bearing on the matter at all. How unlucky can you get, though, winced Bellingham to himself, suddenly overcome with self-pity, to sink on your outward journey?

Silence. Bellingham assumed the room to be empty. Several had come to look and be looked over. Few passed Mrs Roberts's eagle eye. Her views on 'suitable young gentlemen' were not renowned for their liberality – though her definition of young, especially in his case, was very generous. Bellingham resigned himself to a lonely breakfast, suffering the sole attentions of his solicitous but overbearing landlady.

The table in the back parlour was set with only one place, further confirmation, if any were needed, of his domestic isolation. Knife, fork, spoon (for the inevitable porridge), side plate, cup and saucer, a small jug of milk all stared up at him in orderly fashion. Bellingham lost his appetite.

Mrs Roberts's pale face peered around the door as soon as he was seated. Her red nose seemed to throb like a beacon, her large hips, swathed in a grey-white apron, swayed as she approached the table to adjust the place setting and inspect the cleanliness of the crockery. Her hands moved constantly to her face to sweep away the straggles of blond hair that escaped from her bonnet.

'Everything all right Mr Bellingham?' she inquired, concerned.

'Yes, fine.'

'What can I get for you then? Nice bit of bread and dripping? Tea, of course. Anything else? I know you have such an appetite.'

'No, thank you, Mrs Roberts. Some dripping and a pot of tea will be sufficient.'

'Not even a bowl of porridge? You always have porridge.'

'No, thank you. I'm really not feeling at my best this morning. So if you wouldn't mind.'

'Very good, Mr Bellingham. Whatever you say.'

'Thank you, Mrs Roberts. There were no letters for me, I take it.'

'No, I'm sorry, there weren't. Anything else?'

'No, no, thank you.' She left tutting loudly, shaking her head.

Bread and dripping arrived in due course accompanied by a pot of tea, delivered by the confusingly named Catherine/Anne/Mary. She smiled testily at Bellingham. He smiled back, the nicest smile he was able to muster.

He ate slowly, spreading the dripping thickly over the slices. All the while he could smell liver and kidneys, bubble and squeak. He felt guilty even though he knew the food would not go to waste. He took a sip of tea. It was strong but not stewed. He contemplated his visit to the barber. Though he looked forward to a cut and shave with uncommon eagerness, he was careful not to rush his food. He thought of his new jacket. He thought of the material, silk. He remembered the touch of it. He considered how much it cost. An extravagance, but why should such a trivial luxury be denied him? Luxury? Was the means to clothe oneself adequately and fashionably to be considered a luxury? He topped up his tea cup from the plain brown teapot, adding a drop more milk.

Soon, when the case was concluded, he would be denied no luxury, no extravagance. Those so-called friends, who had fled at the news of his bankruptcy, would crawl back as word of his new-found wealth spread quickly through the land. Where once only the money-lenders sought him out and the pawnbroker knew him on first-name terms, his victory would bring the trades people flocking to his door. He would have a hundred suits of the finest silk. He would not follow fashion; he would dictate its course.

When his ship came in, he would not have to live down here among the poor and diseased. He would take a suite of rooms somewhere in Belgravia and retain a dozen men and women to care for his needs.

He alone would provide for his family. Mary Ann would never, ever, have to work again. His children would be educated at the best schools, by the best tutors. His sons would be scholars. They would have every opportunity in life. His entire family would be respected. He would be respected. When the case was concluded.

He would set Jack up for life. Even Mrs Roberts could expect a small annuity. Uncle James would be patronized to the limit of Bellingham's ability. Perhaps he would buy him out. An anonymous purchaser. That would be the first thing he would do. That would show Uncle James that he, John Bellingham, was not someone to be judged too hastily. Or maybe he would send Mary Ann some flowers and a new dress, something for the boys also. Maybe he should do that first and deal with Uncle James second.

Mrs Roberts knocked on the door. 'Come in,' he called, startled. Sometimes he thought she must lurk behind doors, peer through keyholes, press glasses to the wall, so perfectly did she time her entrances, so frequently did she surprise him. 'Come in,' he repeated, more or less at his ease.

'A letter for you, Mr Bellingham.'

'Thank you, ma'am. Thank you very much indeed. Who brought it?'

'A little girl.'

'Was there any message with it? Is she waiting for a reply?'

'She ran off straight away. Well, I say ran, ambled really. Sort of skipped and dawdled at the same time. I mean, well, she's gone in any case.'

'Thank you, Mrs Roberts,' said Bellingham, perplexed.

He took the letter from her and thanked her again. He waited until she had left before examining the letter. He turned it over, hoping to find a return address, some clue to the sender. It was certainly not an official document. There was no seal, no insignia printed on the envelope. His name and the address was written in a large, childish hand that he did not recognize. He was suspicious of the package now, reluctant to open it, but curious as to its content. Finally it came to him. The letter was from Taylor telling him his jacket was ready for collection. He opened the envelope and removed a single sheet of grubby, yellowed paper. It was a short missive, written in a mixture of upper and lower case, unsigned. He read it carefully but remained none the wiser and not a little frightened.

Act Now or Lose Everything. Victory to those who Remain True to their convictions. Strike a Blow for Freedom and Remove the Oppressors. Who does not hear the voice of Liberty, let him be Damned. We Will soon bring about the great Revolution then all these great mens heads goes off. A Friend.

Questions filled his mind. What was it he was being urged to do? Why would anyone send him such a foul missive? Did he know anyone who spelt that badly? Perhaps it was all a mistake. It must be a mistake. To say such things was dangerous. It invited the attention of the authorities.

A sense of the implications of the letter built up from his gut. He stared at the crude message for several minutes, paralysed by fear. The door opened, and Bellingham leapt to his feet, grabbing the letter as he went. His cup and saucer tumbled to the floor and broke on the tiles. He turned hurriedly, his face bright red. The maid stared at him. 'I'm sorry, sir. I didn't mean to startle you.' He left the parlour and went upstairs to his rooms, locking the door behind him.

The whole affair was utterly incomprehensible. His

fear subsided only to be replaced by bewilderment. He took out the anonymous letter, together with the envelope, and burned them in the grate. He watched as they turned to ash, made certain there was nothing left before taking a bundle of papers, his petitions and affidavits, out of the tallboy and tying them together. He put the papers in his inside pocket and left the room. From the corner of his eye he noticed that the bed had been made.

'Mrs Roberts,' he shouted as he descended the stairs. 'Mrs Roberts, I have left this week's rent on the breakfast table. Mrs Roberts! If you would be so kind.'

'Thank you, Mr Bellingham. I am obliged.' She emerged from the kitchen at the back of the house rubbing her hands on her apron. 'Good news, I trust.'

'Not at all, Mrs Roberts. I am afraid I shall be unable to accompany you to the Museum of Europe today. I have to attend to business, as a matter of urgency.'

'I understand completely, Mr Bellingham. Perhaps on another occasion?'

'Certainly, Mrs Roberts. Nothing would give me more pleasure. Please convey my apologies to your son.'

'Of course, Mr Bellingham. Good day.'

'Good day, Mrs Roberts.'

Bellingham sighed deeply as he closed the door of Number Nine and turned to walk down New Millman Street. His progress was barred by Mrs Roberts's son, Edward. The boy stared at Bellingham, his eyes narrowed, his lips slightly pursed. 'I'm sorry, Edward. I know I promised. Another day perhaps?' The platitudes did not convince Edward, who continued to stare and look aggrieved. 'You were looking forward to it, I suppose? I really am very sorry.' Bellingham sidestepped the boy and hurried off.

FIVE

THE CELLAR

Thistlewood lit another candle. The room was very dark; the candle was very small, but its meagre light served to illumine his companion's features a little better.

Stillwater, the man who sat across the table from Thistlewood, was in his early forties and, apart from a white cravat, dressed entirely in black. The candle-light showed off a scar on his right cheek to good effect. His eyebrows met in the middle. His permanently frowning forehead had an overhang that plunged his eyes into shadow. Thistlewood found the whole effect quite disconcerting. Not being able to see the man's eyes, Thistlewood had the impression he was under constant scrutiny. He shifted uncomfortably in his chair and worried that Stillwater could hear his stomach rumbling. He ought to say something, but he was afraid of making a fool of himself. Thistlewood had not felt quite so unnerved since he was a boy awaiting his father's admonition. He resented being made to feel so inadequate. On the other hand he, Thistlewood, had requested the meeting. It was up to him to make the running.

'Root and branch,' said Thistlewood rather more loudly than he intended. He waited for a response. None was forthcoming. 'I said, root and branch.'

'Yes,' said Stillwater. His voice was soft and sibilant.

That slight lisp always surprised Thistlewood. Still-water looked like a man with an actor's voice, rich and fruity. This man's sibilant whisper was very much at odds with his outward appearance.

'The past cannot be changed, but evidence of it can be erased. Must be erased. A clean slate. That is what we must start with. Nothing can remain. All must be destroyed. Root and branch. Do you see?'

'Yes.'

The silence returned. The absence of conversation opened up a chasm that engulfed them. Thistlewood thought Stillwater a strangely dispassionate man for a revolutionary. For this reason, Thistlewood trusted him. All those others who espoused the cause did so loudly, with the fervour of converts. Stillwater betrayed no emotion, expressed no opinion. If he disagreed with a course of action, he stated so unequivocally. He also refused to meet Thistlewood in the company of anyone else. Their meetings were always conducted in private, dimly lit rooms with a back door that gave direct access on to the street. His clandestine companion inspired Thistlewood with hope. This was how he always imagined revolutionaries behaving. Of course, Thistlewood had followed him, watched him, made sure of his authenticity. Thistlewood was very conscious of the need for secrecy and discretion. Government agents had infiltrated many like-minded groups. Thistlewood survived because he trusted nobody. Nobody, that is, except Stillwater.

Thistlewood knew remarkably little about his bene-factor; all his attempts to have him investigated had ended in failure. All he knew was that Stillwater lived in moderate lodgings in King's Cross, appeared to pursue no line of work, was quite obviously in-dependently wealthy, unmarried, no children. As far as Thistlewood could be sure, Stillwater never left London, though he was reputed to own a country house in Wiltshire. Yet this man inspired confidence in Thistlewood. He did so because he was serious. He was dedicated to the cause and never flinched from what was necessary. Stillwater was an essential counter-balance to Thistlewood, who was always prone to excess, to extremes, to the extravagant and empty gesture. Stillwater would have no truck with such schemes. Stillwater took the long view. Stillwater was a tactician, a consummate player who understood the game and appreciated its importance. Thistlewood's feelings for this man bordered on admiration. Bordered, but did not touch, for Thistlewood admired no man, especially those with private incomes.

Thistlewood leant back in his chair and lit his pipe. A blue, smoky haze enveloped him. At his back a door opened. Light streamed in. Stillwater leapt backwards into the darkness, sending his chair flying. Thistlewood turned, angry. 'How dare you interrupt us. Why in God's name can't you knock?'

'Sorry,' said the figure framed by the light.

'What is it?' asked Thistlewood impatiently. The corpulent man hesitated. He appeared to shuffle from foot to foot, but Thistlewood got the distinct impression he was trying to make out Stillwater's features. He was pausing until his eyes grew accustomed to the gloom. 'What is it, Truelock?' Thistlewood said firmly. 'What do you want? Can't you see you're disturbing us?' The man in the doorway nodded. 'Well?' Thistlewood got to his feet and deliberately interposed his body between Truelock and Stillwater.

'Should we get the Engine ready? The engineers need to know, to prepare it.'

'Yes, get the machine ready.'

'Right. Fine. Now?'

'Why not?'

'Right. I'll go then. Tell them.'

'Very well, off you go.'

Truelock lingered in the doorway, looking puzzled. Behind him Thistlewood could see the outline of the Influencing Engine. Nine large barrels, brimful of liquid, with wires leading out of them to an enormous construction in the centre of the room. At one end of the machine Thistlewood saw an engineer dressed in a black gown sitting on a stool in front of something that resembled the keyboard of an organ with pedals and stops. The engineer worked the pedals frantically while he manipulated the stops. 'Push off then,' repeated Thistlewood. Truelock closed the door behind him.

'I must apologize, Stillwater, for my colleague's unforgivable rudeness,' said Thistlewood. His apology received no reply, but Stillwater sat down again. 'There is the matter of expenses,' Thistlewood continued.

'Yes.'

'Is there a problem?'

'No.'

'You have the money with you?'

'Yes.'

'Good.'

The monosyllabic answers to his questions made Thistlewood feel ashamed for asking them. How could he doubt Stillwater's continued support for the scheme? Had not Stillwater made the initial approach and agreed to fund the building of the Influencing Engine without so much as looking at the plans? It was the Bellingham development that concerned Thistlewood. Used as he was to clandestine designs and murky conspiracies, he could not see what there was to be gained by persecuting a middle-aged bankrupt like Bellingham. Was it a personal grudge perhaps? But Stillwater was impenetrable; no amount of Thistlewood's much practised guile could draw the smallest scrap of information from him.

Thistlewood found himself in awe of this man. Such

sentiment was out of place. Feelings of admiration and awe did not come naturally to Thistlewood. He began to suspect that something was wrong. He should not feel like this. Arthur Thistlewood could not admire anyone, could not be made to feel wretched by anyone. That was an erosion of his liberty. He could not be beholden to anyone. That was undemocratic. As Thistlewood's resentment of the high-handed treatment meted out by Stillwater developed into hatred, so too an idea for the future grew into a commitment. Come the glorious day, Stillwater would have to die. Sooner, if at all possible.

Thistlewood reclined in his chair and puffed furiously at his pipe. The smoke billowed, obscuring Stillwater. Thistlewood smiled. He no longer felt in awe of this mysterious man. He felt pity for him. How could Stillwater, a man of means, an exploiter, a grubby moneyman, understand the depths of the Thistlewood vision? The notion was ludicrous. A man who lived in half-darkness and spoke only in affirmation or denial could know nothing of the beliefs that drove Thistlewood forward, sustained him after each successive defeat, made even the sweetest moment bitter. Yet he should know. He should be made to see the fruit which he would never, ever taste.

'Root and branch,' said Thistlewood. 'Nothing can survive. Everything must be planted new. To be sure, one day the things of the past will wither on the branch and new growth will replace the dead wood. But "one day" might as well be never to those who live now. Better to destroy all and begin again. Burn off the stubble. Plough up the field. Begin anew. Root and branch.'

Thistlewood stared intently at his companion through the dispersing smoke. Stillwater stared back.

'Yes,' said Stillwater and placed a large bag of coins on the table. 'Root and branch,' said Stillwater as he rose to leave. 'One day,' he said as he crossed the room, opened the door to the street and departed.

Thistlewood was stunned: Stillwater's utterances were tantamount to an outburst. Thistlewood hoped he had not offended the man. He had made up his mind to kill Stillwater, but execution notwithstanding he had no wish to offend him also.

Thistlewood lifted the purse and tested its weight. Everything was in order. He picked up a candle and made his way to a trunk in the far corner of the room. He knelt beside it and unlocked the padlock. Inside the trunk was a jumble of beards, eyepatches, wigs and clothing. He placed the money beneath a crumpled hat and retrieved a bundle of papers from the bottom of the trunk. Returning to the table, he sat down to peruse the manuscript. 'A Vision of Albion' – not a bad title, he mused. He picked up a pen, dipped it in ink, thought for a minute, then crossed out 'Albion' and wrote 'Britain'. 'Begin anew. Look to the future and do not cling to the past,' he muttered as he made the alteration. Thistlewood continued to make corrections to the manuscript until the candle guttered and expired.

SIX

BLOOMSBURY

Bellingham glanced back along New Millman Street. The house where he lodged was a three-storey building in a row of similar three-storey buildings; only the colour of the front doors differed from one to the next. The street petered out into grass and children's games. He turned his back on the verdancy and play. He turned his back on the disappointed boy staring after him reproachfully.

Emerging from between two tall houses, connected at the third storey to form an archway, Bellingham turned left on Guildford Street and approached the Foundling Hospital. The street was only minimally paved. He stepped out into the road to avoid a group of young ladies who considered the walkway their own. The dry weather had left the road a treacherous mountain range of jagged ruts and crevices. Bellingham picked his way across with care, finally arriving at the entrance to the hospital. He carried on past, glimpsing the driveway, the lawns on either side of it and, flanking the lawns, extravagant colonnades. The hospital was bustling with activity. He turned right towards Brunswick Square.

He had left the house with little or no thought as to his final destination. He had an appointment with Miss Stevens in an hour or two. Before that he needed a shave. He was lost in confusion, and his legs took him to the cemetery.

He often came to the small graveyard, reserved exclusively for the dead of Bloomsbury, when he craved peace and quiet, respite from the ceaseless turmoil of landlady, family, correspondence, friends. He could empty his mind here. It is good, he thought, to know exactly where you will come to rest. To be able to point to a specific spot and say, 'It ends right here.' It would be nice to be near the hospital, where life was so abundant and noisy, but the graveyard was so crowded already, there would be little room for anyone else.

He walked slowly among the grey graves, the tombs and monuments, content with the singing of the birds, passing from light to shade through the tree-lined cemetery. Light, shade. Light, shade.

The ground was hard beneath his feet. The brown and withered grass struggled to cover the earth. The cracked dirt gave no spring to his step, yielded nothing. Scorched flowers adorned the freshest graves, their parchment blooms so fragile a single touch could reduce them to powder. The morning sun cast tomb-stone shadows. Silhouetted angels, elongated crosses, shades of arched doorways. Here and there cracked sepulchres and subsiding ground afforded a glimpse of darkness, a hint of nothing, arousing childish fears and promoting disquiet.

Bellingham stood at the base of a fifteen-foot-high obelisk. He peered upwards towards its point. The sun dazzled him. He could find no inscription, no dedication of any kind. The anonymity of such an extravagant monument puzzled and intrigued him. He circled it, looking closely for some trace of its origin, but found none. He walked away frustrated.

From the entrance farthest away from Bellingham a man entered the cemetery. His hands were covered in multicoloured ink stains like tattoos. His clothes were likewise splattered and stained. He was tall and bald. His head darted from side to side as if he were searching for something or someone. Much to Bellingham's relief the inky man disappeared into another part of the graveyard hidden from view by a line of trees and shrubs.

Bellingham came to a halt by a small tomb perhaps four feet high, roofed with black quartz split and splintered from the frosty violence of a hundred winters. A coat of arms, worn nearly smooth by rain, was emblazoned on the side. He crouched down to read the inscription.

ANNA
Daughter of Richard Cromwell
the Protector
and wife of Thomas Gibson
born at Hursley, Hants, 27 March 1659
Died in London 7 Dec 1727

Her quiet tomb, quiet but expensive, seemed to reflect her birth perfectly. Tail-end of the Puritan Revolution, a year before the Restoration, a year before they exhumed her grandfather's body from its Westminster Abbey tomb. The Caroline mob wheeled the regicide's embalmed corpse on a gallows procession to Tyburn. It took them two days to get there. The party stopped off at the Old Red Lion in Holborn at nightfall on the first day. They laid out his corpse on the bar and made a night of it. Bellingham found that part of the tale irresistibly funny. What better way to show disrespect to the Puritan Protector? The following day crowds lined the streets armed with missiles, which they gleefully hurled at Cromwell's cart. The axeman decapitated the corpse that evening. The head was stuck on a spike at the Palace of Westminster, where it remained for thirty years, until a hurricane dislodged it. From there it passed through various private hands until it came to rest in the hands of the Hughes brothers, three Welsh Republicans, who displayed it in a shop in Bond Street some years ago. Bellingham had paid his halfcrown and seen the morbid object. Shrivelled, shiny, leathery and undeniably warty. It might still be there for all Bellingham knew. An ignominious end: head divorced from body, name divorced from meaning.

Cromwell's Commonwealth, associated indelibly with darkness. The dour bearing and sombre clothes of Puritans and Presbyterians. Theatres closed, dancing frowned upon. A decade of dullness, a country stuck in perpetual winter. Until the Restoration – then a fine, warm summer returned to the land, light and colour in abundance. The splendour of the court, its excesses and intrigues, England restored. Politically the obverse seemed to be true. The Revolution groped for the light, struck out on new paths; the Restoration settled for the murky haze that had been before and saw no need to search any further afield than its own self-interest.

Cromwell's granddaughter hidden from sight. Child of a revolution long since dead and buried. An unfinished revolution. Liberty and Property; liberty for Property. Fair exchange is no robbery. Liberty and Property have always walked arm in arm.

He moved on. Passing a ragged hedge, he glimpsed the inky man. He was with a woman, enfolding her in his stained arms. Bellingham watched as they lowered themselves on to a flat tombstone, heard her gasp for breath as he settled his weight on top of her. Bellingham looked away, but their boisterous loving pursued him through the burial ground. He imagined the lovers in their tight embrace; she pushed against the stone, he squirming against her, pushing her into the grave with his passion. Or, later that night, his arm curled around her shoulders, singing together as they staggered home from the pub. For a moment he envied them as he imagined them lying together, spent, on the grass, no words passing between them, no need for words. He could hear them shouting their love to any who listened, as he did. Their joy gave him no pleasure, no voyeuristic thrill, no reassurance of life continuing in the midst of decay. The world they inhabited was self-contained, closed off. Their public love was not an act of generosity, it was a provocation, a yell of individual liberty directed at the collective indifference of their neighbours, of passers-by like Bellingham, who listened because he had to, because there was no alternative.

Through the back gate he skirted around the hospital buildings to emerge near the front lawns, in an avenue of elm trees. Light, shade. Light, shade. The grass, the feel of the earth beneath his feet, the scent of the flowers, the butterflies criss-crossing his path: he thought of his childhood, bright and nameless, a country he would never come upon again.

'Ouch!' He started, rubbed his neck where the missile had hit. Something bounced off his shoulder. Children played among the trees. One, very small, very adventurous child sat at the top of a large berry tree. His friends pelted him from below with sticks and stones. The little boy returned fire with a venomous, deadly accuracy. He noticed Bellingham from his tree-top vantage and let fly a volley of twigs, berries and abuse. 'Little sod,' thought Bellingham. He had half a mind to climb up there after him. Give him a taste of his own medicine. Or find the largest stone he could and land it right on his head. Maybe he would yell and rattle the tree till the boy fell, like an overripe fruit, and squelched to the earth. Serve him right. 'Little sod,' muttered Bellingham beneath his breath.

Shade. Light. Shade. Light. He crossed over the road into Lamb's Conduit Street. The conduit was no longer there but he passed a trough containing a dribble of fetid water. Fetid. London in summer. Fine when it rains. After the rain, the smell of damp soil, wet grass, dust, steam rising from the hot pavement. After the rain London was beautiful and the sewers flowed. After the rain, cool, clear. He wished it were raining now. He would take shelter in a doorway and watch the people running past with their coats pulled over their heads and their clothes clinging to their skin.

Several women, with children in tow, skirts tucked in at the waist, queued at a water pump with buckets, jugs and bowls. Others were washing clothes while children played and furtively pissed in the road. It was so long since it had last rained that the smell was unbearable, except in the open spaces. Sometimes, but not this morning, it got so bad he retched. It would not be the first time he had given up Mrs Roberts's breakfast to the gutter. Embarrassing. It was so hot he wanted to take his jacket off. Sweat rolled down his sides. But it would not be decorous, and besides he did not want to dirty his shirt. He slowed down, expended less effort in an attempt to stem the flow of perspiration.

Theobald's Road.

He slowed down still further. He was sweating like a pig, and his shoes were pinching him again. Just when he wanted everything to be perfect, to be comfortable, just when he needed to be assured in his appearance, his entire body went into revolt. He perspired, his feet swelled, his head ached. What now? His knees. They popped in and out. He could feel them. With every step, each time he bent his leg, he could feel his knees pop. He could hear them now as well. He tried to concentrate on something else. No good. Pop, pop, pop. He thought he must be getting old. Probably going to end up lame, on crutches. Pop. Ugh. It was making him feel sick. Oh, Lord.

He reached High Holborn. The traffic was heavy and

loud. People bustling, vendors shouting, businessmen striding to and fro, their faces set in grim determination; their destination was their fate, the killing ground. Bellingham envied their sense of purpose.

He turned and retraced his steps back towards Theobald's Road, then took a left down an alleyway to Red Lion Square. He came out opposite the Infirmary. Bellingham was amazed at the number of hospitals in the vicinity. The comfort of the sick and dying was obviously a prospering business. Bellingham walked into the grass-and-gravel square and looked for somewhere to sit down. His body seemed to be falling apart, and his nerves were definitely on edge. At this rate he would be in a hospital before he made it to the barber's. He should have stayed in bed.

He sat with evident relief on a wall in the shade of a leafy tree and sighed a sigh that turned into a yawn that made his eyes water. He rubbed his knees vigorously, cursing his luck, cursing his shoes, cursing the weather. He lifted his heels out of his shoes and massaged them. Clouds crossed the sun and a light breeze picked up from the west, bringing unpleasant smells but also some relief from the heat. At last a breeze. The weather was so close it must be coming on to rain. He hoped the weather would break soon. He chose the arrival of the breeze as an appropriate time to resume his walk. He could not waste too much time; he had so much to do today. He crossed the square, walking slowly in the direction of Bloomsbury.

Creak. Thsssp. Creak. Whoosh. The barber, with a genial smile and a polite inquiry, settled Bellingham into the chair and tucked a cloth into his collar, loosening it a little first. He stood beside Bellingham examining the matted, chestnut hair he was about to cut. He lifted a few strands and let them fall, tutting to himself. He fiddled with the hair at the back, making scissor motions with his fingers.

'Very warm for the time of year,' the barber began, with a traditional opening.

'Ummm,' replied Bellingham.

'Just a trim?' A couple of schnicks on the scissors before starting. 'You know, it really is extremely warm. Don't you think? For May? You know, I don't believe it's been as warm as this for years. The last May like this I remember was the time of my Aunt Esther's funeral. That's going back a fair few years now, of course, but it was a day very like today. Warm, sticky. So close you could taste the storm in the air. I remember it because it was so hot you could smell her, my Aunt Esther. A queer old bird she was. Put a little aside all her life, bought herself a plot when prices were cheap. Headstone too, wrote out her own inscription, everything. Very wise woman indeed. I saw the sense in that. I'd always thought it morbid to think about your own death, unhealthy. But I could see her point. Oh, yes, took a leaf out of Esther's book that day. Oh, yes, been putting some aside ever since. Got myself a nice little plot. Under a tree it is. Not exactly in the corner, not what I would call out of the way, more like I've got some breathing space.

'Anyway, she had the works, did Aunt Esther. Oak coffin, silk lining, brass handles. Beautiful piece of craftsmanship, that coffin. Her funeral gown was something special, not the usual paper smock all done up for effect but costing next to nought – no, a cotton gown with Nottingham lace trimmings. Very fine. Believe me, there are few occasions more satisfying than a well-organized, well-attended funeral. Esther's was one of the best. Astonishing to see the turn-out. Who would have thought, I said to the wife, who would have thought that dear old Esther would have so many to pay their respects? We held up the traffic in Holborn

103

for ten minutes. Wonderful to see and richly deserved, especially considering the terrible way she died. Found her in the privy. Ruptured something or other, they said. Awful that. Still, the funeral more than made up for it. There's a lesson there for all of us. It was such a hot day. That's what put me in mind of it.

'Right, how are we getting on? Is that enough off the back? Or a little more? Very good, sir, you just sit back and relax. Tilt your head this way. That's it, lovely.

'There is nothing, and I mean nothing, so comfortable or so secure as a barber's chair. Don't you think so? They are designed that way, of course. It is part of the intense personal experience that is visiting the barber. A qualified barber, of course, from the Guild of Barber-Surgeons. You have to be careful of charlatans in all professions, isn't that right, sir?

'All finished. Want to see? I'll get the mirror. There, what do you think? Thank you, sir. Now, anything else I can do for you? Ah, now I thought you might be wanting a shave, so I took the liberty of heating up the towels ready. Just sit tight there a minute.'

The barber's twittering faded as he turned his attention to another customer. Bellingham relaxed a little, his head against the leather headrest. The warm cloth covering his ears muffled the inanities dribbling anew from the mouth of the conversationally incontinent barber. If only he had kept his mouth shut, the experience might have been a pleasurable one: the cold metal edge of the razor dragging and lifting the rough hair from the back of his neck, moving more smoothly on the second pass over his skin; the sharp point of the scissors snagging on the soft, grey skin of his scalp. Those little nicks sent shivers down his spine. The barber's hands gripping his skull, manipulating it first to the right, then pushing it back slowly to the left, forwards, backwards. Fingertips pressing lightly on his temple, his forehead, his neck. Hands running through his hair. The warmth of the barber's body brushing against his elbows and hands. His hot breath on his scalp as he leant in to tidy his hair. Sensual, pleasing, comforting, a man that close to your body with licence to gently touch, clean and cut. Only his father had been so close before, and that had been a long time ago. He had missed his father all these years. He had not really comprehended that until this moment.

'You still under there, sir? Hold on a mo' and I'll lather you up.' The towel was whipped away and the cold lather applied roughly to his chin and cheeks. The barber hummed as he sharpened the razor, pushing it to and fro over the strop. 'There we are. This will only take a couple of shakes of a lamb's tail. Right you are. You'll feel much better for a shave, I guarantee it. My cousin Bill, he never shaved from one year to the next, had a beard down to his chest. What a fright he was, scared children half to death. And you know what? He was a miserable old bugger into the bargain. Life's too short to grow a beard, that's what I always say. There we go. Lovely. I'll just brush you down. Ah, thank you very much, sir, very generous. I look forward to seeing you tomorrow. Take care now, sir. Cheerio.

'Queer fish, that one. Still, as my old dad used to say, folks is queer and no mistake, except me and thee and thee's a bit odd. Now, what can I do for you, sir?'

The bell on the tailor's door tinkled. The shop was deserted. Bellingham approached the counter. Through a gap in the curtain that separated the workshop from the shop Bellingham could see Skinker, the apprentice, cutting cloth on a bench. The young man paused at his work and lifted a pad of cloth to his neck and pressed it against a suppurating boil. Bellingham wondered whether Skinker had heard the bell. He coughed loudly. Skinker looked up and made his way languorously through to the front. He stopped at the counter and stared sullenly at Bellingham.

'Is Mr Taylor in?' asked Bellingham timorously.

'No,' said Skinker without breaking eye contact with Bellingham.

'Perhaps you can help me, then,' began Bellingham.

'Perhaps I can.'

'I've come for my jacket. It should have been delivered days ago.'

'Have you paid?'

'Yes, I paid up front.'

'Got the ticket?'

'Sorry?'

'Ticket, got the ticket?'

'No, I never had a ticket.'

'Must have a ticket if you paid. Can't do a thing for you without the ticket, see?'

'No. I want my jacket. It's brown. Silk. It was expensive.'

'How do I know that? No ticket, no jacket. I mean, you could be anybody, couldn't you?'

'I have a letter here, with my name and address on it. I've got it somewhere.'

'I need the ticket. If a letter would do, I'd have said ticket *or letter*, wouldn't I? I mean, what is the point in having a system if the system isn't stuck to, rigidly?'

'For God's sake, I only want what is mine, what I've paid for,' shouted Bellingham.

'Hold on. Just hold on a minute. You come in here without a ticket and start shouting. No, I'm sorry, that is not on. I shall have to ask you to leave.'

'Listen to me. Give me my jacket.'

'No,' said Skinker and turned on his heel. He went into the workshop. Bellingham stared after him in disbelief, then climbed over the counter. He started to rifle through the boxes on the shelves underneath the counter. He pulled them out one by one, checked their contents and discarded them. Finally he came across his snuff-coloured silk jacket. He threw aside the crêpe paper and pulled the jacket from the box. He stroked the delicate cloth, examined the stitching carefully, almost purring with pleasure. He clasped the jacket by the collar and shook it to its full length. He eased one arm into a sleeve, gently, then the other, shrugged the jacket over his shoulders. The fit was good, excellent. He clambered back over the counter and stood in front of a full-length mirror. He looked, turned around twice, glancing behind his back, reached into the pockets. Felt for, found, that special pocket concealed inside. The cool silk against the exposed skin of his neck and wrists, the weight and shape of the jacket across his shoulder-blades. He stared at himself in the mirror and sensed himself surrounded by the protective glow of destiny. Nothing, he thought, nothing can go wrong now.

'What do you think you're doing?' Skinker's head poked through the curtain. Bellingham noticed again the boil on Skinker's neck. It oozed pus in a thin trickle. With one hand Skinker pressed a rag to the wound, mopping up the putrescent liquid, with the other he pushed aside the curtain. Bellingham grabbed for his discarded blue jacket and ran for the door. He was at it and through it in a few paces. 'You haven't heard the last of this,' yelled the tailor's apprentice after him from the shop door.

Bellingham made it to the main street quickly, turned the corner on to Southampton Row and wove his way through the traffic and people crowding around him. People pushing, laughing, occasionally apologizing; men tipping their hats to women; women giggling, blushing, some flattered, some angry. Handcarts, carriages and horses trundled haphazardly through the dusty street. Bellingham crossed the road hastening towards Queen's Square and Great Ormond Street, glancing behind him the whole way, every now and then convinced he caught sight of someone following him. Opposite the Foundling Hospital and its green lawns he stopped, breathless. His eyes continued to dart about, desperate to see if he was followed. He saw no one. Gradually he caught his breath, felt his heart beat slow to somewhere near normal, felt the sweat trickle down his sides. After a minute or two more he smiled to himself, relieved, embarrassed and exhilarated. He had the coat, which he had paid for, but he could never go back there again. He made his way home. He needed to calm down a little before his appointment with Miss Stevens. He thought perhaps he had better change his shirt.

SEVEN

COVENT GARDEN

Nobody gives a second thought to a man lying in the
street. Especially not in Drury Lane. The theatres are
dark and quiet, but the gaming houses, unlicensed gin
palaces and brothels thrive. Usually hidden from sight
behind boarded windows, in dark cellars and smoke-
filled back rooms, during the heat-wave they have
thrown open their shutters. Light and the gaze of
passers-by pour in, and the milk-white faces of the
creatures of the night peer out. Prostitutes sit on
the pavement and the steps, in the shade of the
entrances to the courts and alleyways, their skirts
hitched up around their waists, their powdered and
rouged faces almost luminous amid the shadows.
Some, hags with no teeth, bruised and battered; others,
pretty and young, remarkably untouched, girls com-
pleting their apprenticeship beneath the watchful
eyes of their mothers, whose infants hang at their
breasts, crying and mewling. The shouts of men in
despair and joy, drunken brawling and sozzled singing.
And everywhere, drifting up from the slaughterhouses
and the butchers' shops, the smell, the rank smell of
meat and blood and offal. Amid the chaos and the
stink and the sheer need to get past this place as
quickly as possible, few people give a sick man a
second thought.

Gnnghggnnghuggherrghgulpgnngh, pause and gasp

for breath, unnmmmmbleuugrrrh, pant, pant, bile rising, gulp, retch, retch, bleughhh.

Nettleton's stomach spasmed. His muscles contracted and expanded, his throat opened, he gagged and heaved as waves of nausea swept over him. He stumbled in the street and propped himself up against a wall. The city moved around him, assiduously avoiding him, wary of the bruises on his face and the blood on his shirt. The sun drew every drop of moisture from his skin. He felt like a dry husk, desiccated. His knees gave way beneath him, and he slid slowly to the ground. The rough stone of the wall rucked up his shirt and scraped his oyster-white skin. Nettleton lay on his back. He closed his eyes against the sun's glare. He liked it there, on his back. The hems of skirts brushed against his hand, the heels of boots squeezed his fingers. He sensed the shadows of people pass over him, around him. He felt invisible. He felt it was a good way to be.

Someone stopped and helped him to his feet. He opened his eyes and examined his rescuer. He was a young man with long brown hair swept away from a central parting. Green eyes and freckles on his nose gave him a youthful appearance. He was dressed smartly in a light-green jacket, matching trousers and a waistcoat. He said a few words, but their meaning eluded Nettleton. He recognized the accent as Irish. The voice seemed to be asking him something. Directions? Nettleton could make neither head nor tail of it. He shook his head, as much to say no as to clear it of the fog that had settled behind his eyes. He caught a few words now, but the sound faded in and out as if the speaker were running away from him and then rushing right up to his ear and shouting. 'Looking somewhere stay nearby you anywhere can me bother sorry fit state in another on street June cold think sorry what say?' Nettleton pushed himself free of the elliptical Irishman. Wobbling on shaky legs, he sought asylum across the road. At least that side of the street was in shade.

Nettleton aimed for some railings near a theatre. As he slammed into them he grabbed at the thin metal rods and held on tight. He dragged himself along the railings until they ran out. He tried to think where he could go from there. He barely knew where he was. He could not think further than the next step. Anything else made him feel dizzy. Off to the right, about a hundred yards away, he saw the entrance to an alley. Shade, few people, a wall to lean against and help his progress. He focused his mind on his goal, let go of the railings and launched himself forward. Every step was agony, his feet hurt, his knees hurt, his hips, his ribs, his head hurt.

His arms stretched out in front of him, he lurched into the alleyway and collided with a wall. Propping himself up, he paused for breath before groping his way along the wall, supporting his weight with his hands, his legs lagging a little behind the rest. He could not stay still for long. He was haunted by the image of Thistlewood or Walsh coming for him. His body found face down in the mud at low tide, picked over by the young children and old men who found their living in the filth and detritus of the Thames.

He felt terrible, but suddenly it seemed as though he could cope with his injuries. He stopped by a dark shop window to examine himself. Despite his rough handling he was not so badly injured. His upper lip was puffy, a cut across his left cheek, some blood encrusted round his nostrils. He pulled up his shirt. Some abdominal bruising, but it was too soon for most of it to show. Gingerly he pressed his rib-cage, sore but not especially so – nothing broken, he concluded. Worse than anything else was the smell. He stank of sweat and urine. And he was hungry. And thirsty.

111

He looked up. In front of him was Covent Garden. The flower market was busy. Stall upon stall of fresh-cut flowers, doused with water, a whole spectrum of glistening blooms. Makeshift constructions of cloth and tarpaulin tried to shield the delicate flowers from the heat.

Hawkers, baskets overflowing with small bunches of lavender and good-luck charms of heather, wandered about, accosting passers-by, pretending to be gypsies, threatening with their pathetic curses.

Jack spotted a coffee stall a short way off, a lean-to against a shady wall. He bought a cup of the fragrant, exotic liquid in the hope it would settle his stomach. He stood amid the bustle and cries of the market, simply inhaling the delicious, unfamiliar aroma given off by the stall and his own cracked porcelain mug. The first sip burned his tongue and woke him from his reverie. He sat down on a low wall nearby, stretched his legs and his neck. He held the mug in cupped hands, sipping at it slowly, taking deep breaths, feeling his stomach settle. He forgot about Bellingham and Thistlewood for a while. He began to feel better, much better.

A young woman carrying a large wicker basket caught Jack's attention. Her light-brown hair was bunched up on her head and covered with a grey-white bonnet. Her clothes were clean and worn threadbare. He watched the shape of her uncorseted buttocks shift beneath her dress as she passed through the crowd in wide circles. As she moved closer to him on one of her passes round the market, he noticed a large blue bruise at the base of her neck. The sight made him feel angry and a little queasy again. Her face was attractive, and he liked the way a smile seemed to play constantly on her pink lips. It was a while before he realized that she had stopped what she was doing and was staring straight back at him. He snapped his gaze away and pretended to take great interest in his coffee cup, watching the grounds rise to the surface.

The swirling coffee made him feel dizzy. His thoughts swirled too and refused to stay still even for an instant. Images of Walsh and Truelock flashed through his mind, and everywhere he looked were flowers that reminded him of the whirligig, the Influencing Engine.

His situation was hopeless. There was no way out. Whatever way he approached the problem, he could see no solution. He should warn Bellingham about Thistlewood. He should be brave and do the right thing. That was what he should do, but he knew that he would not warn Bellingham. It sickened him to know that Thistlewood's estimation of his character was so accurate.

Thistlewood did not need Jack's assistance to find Bellingham. He could do that himself any time he wished. His relationship with Thistlewood had never been based on need. Initially Jack had considered himself indispensable to the cause, but Thistlewood could find a dozen printers willing to help him. It was the notion of a protégé that motivated Thistlewood. He looked on Nettleton as a son, as a successor. Jack was part of Thistlewood's theatrical sense of self, his picture of himself as a leader-in-waiting, a one-man provisional government. And Jack, wayward Jack, prodigal Jack, was his heir apparent.

The money was Thistlewood's way of letting Jack know who held the whip hand. The mere promise of money was enough to send Jack leaping through hoops, to make him turn cartwheels. The beatings and the subterfuge were, as Thistlewood had said, a lesson in friendship. Something about friendship. The message was clear. Thistlewood could hurt him any time he wished. Thistlewood was proving that the gift of life, the gift of freedom, was his and his alone to give. It

113

was a lesson in power. Jack understood all that, but he still wriggled and squirmed to find a way round Thistlewood's version of the truth.

Bellingham tapped his feet in frustration. Short raps, a rhythm of his own invention, unsyncopated and ugly to listen to, but he liked it. How long would Miss Stevens keep him waiting? He simply could not understand her reluctance to accept his offer. She wanted the Millinery, and here he was handing it to her on a plate. He agreed to take on the shop's debts and to give her all the stock and goodwill. He could not say fairer than that, yet still she hesitated.

He was getting restless. He checked his new jacket over for dirt or creases. It was unblemished. He smiled and then blushed, suddenly self-conscious. He was exhilarated by the recollection of his defiance of the miserable rat Skinker, but he could not mask a certain shame at his own conduct. He was not someone to break the rules. If anything, it was his rigid adherence to, and enormous respect for, the rules that led him into trouble.

The maid walked right past him again. He coughed for her attention, but she paid him none. He caught a glimpse of himself in the mirror opposite, just the top of his head from the eyes upwards. His blue eyes looked up to his bushy eyebrows and his creased forehead. His hairline was still intact. All his hair loss was confined to the crown and, being a tall man, he had no fear of discovery. A loose hair or two stood up on end. He licked his fingers and tried to smooth them back down. As he was engaged in the operation the maid returned.

'You can go in now, sir.'
'Thank you.'
'Door on the left down the hall, sir.'
'Thank you.'

'Hat, sir?'

'You already have it.'

'Cane, sir?'

'No cane.'

'Coat, sir?'

'In this weather?'

'Will there be anything else, sir?'

'No.'

'Much obliged, sir.' She curtsied in a half-hearted way and went upstairs. Halfway up she stopped and leaned over the banister. She saw Miss Stevens's visitor get slowly to his feet. He was, she thought, old-looking. He moved stiffly and took some time to get moving once he had decided to move, like her grandfather. He was going bald, too. From above she could see a circle of grey scalp radiating out from the crown of his head. His beaky nose peaked out from below his thick eyebrows. His clothes were, if she was honest, well worn. He had a slight stoop. Ten years ago he would have been worth another look, but now he was not worth getting a scolding over. She hurried on up to her mistress's bedroom.

Bellingham tidied himself in the mirror and made his way to the door indicated by the maid. He knocked firmly, three raps. He pushed the door and entered the room from which he had been summarily dismissed the previous evening. Miss Stevens stood in front of the fireplace, her back to him, her hands clasped together over her buttocks. He thought her position absurd. Self-consciously male, very aggressive. She was not happy with the ledgers. Clearly, she had a problem with something. She did not turn around when he entered. He sighed quietly. This is precisely what he had hoped to avoid.

'I want you to promise me something, John,' she said, still with her back to him.

'Really, Miss Stevens, if there is something in the

115

arrangement you would like to change, we can, of course, discuss it.' He took a step forward. She flinched. The muscles of her back tightened, her shoulders pushed back and she squeezed her hands tighter.

'John, this has nothing to do with the business matter. We . . . I . . . well, of course it does have something to do with it. John, tell me you're going to give up this foolishness and go home to your family straight away. Give me your solemn oath, John Bellingham, and I will sign the papers. I'm doing this not for you but for Mary Ann and the boys. I know she wants to give up her share of the business to her cousin Eliza. When she finds out what you have done, she'll be very angry. I am willing to face her anger, John, but only if I can be assured that in concluding this matter with you I am making it possible for you to return to your family.' She stopped there and turned around to face Bellingham.

Her face was streaked with tears. She shook with emotion. With anger or with passion he did not know. The sight of her standing there in her best dress, her hair bunched neatly on her head and covered with a crisp white bonnet, weeping silently, moved him. He tried to speak but could not. He thought of moving towards her, to offer her comfort, but was aware of the impropriety of such an action. Instead he did nothing at all but lower his eyes and look at his shoes.

Buckles would make them look lovely. They lack buckles, these shoes.

He could not help the thought. As it was half-formed he tried to abort it to prevent it forcibly from popping into his head, but his best efforts were not equal to the task.

If I had buckles on my shoes, she would desire me. She wouldn't talk to me like this. She would respect me.

'Do I need to repeat everything Mary Ann has told you? Do you know how sick she was? Do I need to remind you that your children's education is suffering because of your prolonged absence? Do you wish them to grow up disadvantaged in life? It is your duty as a husband and a parent to return to your family in Liverpool and resume a normal life. Forget what has happened in the past and work towards a decent future for those you care about. Do you hear me, John? Am I making myself clear?' She was regaining her composure. Her passion, whatever it was, wherever it had sprung from, was resolving itself into simple anger.

'I am aware of all these arguments, Miss Stevens. Do you honestly believe that I have not struggled daily to find an answer to my troubles? But the truth of the matter is that I cannot allow Mary Ann to continue with the Millinery any longer. She is my wife. I should provide for her and I shall.'

She cut him off. 'I suppose nothing further has transpired? I suppose you are no nearer a solution than you were five months ago, when you abandoned your family.'

'I am still anxious to see justice done,' he muttered.

'Of course you are. I do not doubt your integrity, John. I am even convinced of your cause, and there are precious few who could say that. However, I am also of the opinion that you are going about this the wrong way. If you wish to obtain justice, then obtain a lawyer. In the meantime, if you wish to provide for your family, think on your responsibilities. The best possible means of providing for your family would be to return home to your business and work hard, very hard.' She raised her eyebrows and widened her eyes. 'I need you to swear to me, John. Swear it. Swear you'll go home. Swear it.'

Bellingham, the people's hero, will never admit defeat.

'Mary.' He lifted his head and looked her straight in the eye. 'Mary, I swear.'

Someone was shaking Nettleton's shoulder. He turned his head and squinted at the person in front of him. The face was very close. He could see the dirt clogged in the pores round about the nose. The rough, whiskery beard, a mixture of blond, brown and red hairs, bristled close to his own cheeks. He could smell the beer on its breath, the cheese and the onions. All this he could see, but he did not recognize the face.

'I seen you with him, haven't I?' the face said. It smiled. Its mouth was barren of teeth. It looked like an idiot's. 'It is you, isn't it?'

'What?' Jack found his mouth was dry. 'Can I help you?'

'I thought so. I thought it was you. Me and my friend, we had a bet. I said it was and he said it wasn't and it was, isn't it?' The face pushed closer. The eyes were black and bloodshot-white.

'I don't think so.' Jack felt intimidated.

'The fancy bloke with the stripy trousers. Always hanging around Parliament. We seen you last night.' An eye winked.

'You couldn't be more wrong.'

'Ah, now, you don't have to say anything. We know. We see everything, me and my friend.' The face looked crestfallen at the suggestion that it could be mistaken.

'Who is your friend?'

'He's that one over there.'

Nettleton changed his focus. An arm, attached to a shoulder, came into view. It was extended behind and pointed in the general direction of a large group of people gathered by a stall selling liquor. 'Which one?'

'The one with the hands.' The face's own hands were held in front of Nettleton's eyes in illustration and emphasis.

'I see.'

'I can tell him I won the bet then?'

'Tell him whatever you wish.'

'Ta. I will. See you around.'

'I doubt it.'

'Oh, I will, no fear.' The face receded towards the group of men it had pointed out earlier, and as it moved backwards, facing Nettleton the whole time, he saw that the face belonged to the body of a man who might have been a porter in the market. His limbs were brown, and his shirt was open to the waist. His knee-breeches were undone at the knee, his shoes worn and faded. As Nettleton watched the stranger merge with the crowd, he thought he saw someone else, someone he recognized. Arthur Thistlewood waving at him from the midst of the crowd. Then in an instant he was gone, lost to sight.

Jack was still disoriented. He shook his head. He got to his feet and scanned the market for any sign of the strange man or Thistlewood. Nothing. Nausea stole over him once more. He had to get out of this situation. He had to do something.

He felt a little dizzy. He closed his eyes and took a deep breath. He swayed a little, but the world did not spin any faster than usual.

Thistlewood was playing with him, letting him know he would not forget their bargain. Jack sighed. He needed to make a decision, but the mere thought made him sick to the pit of his stomach.

Bellingham handed the maid a letter to pass on to Miss Stevens; it was addressed to his wife. In the letter Bellingham looked forward to returning soon to the bosom of his family. He held out the promise of his homecoming while trying, one last time, to make his wife understand why he was in London. He wanted Mary Ann to appreciate his situation, the impossibility

119

of his living a normal life until this affair was concluded, one way or another.

Inwardly, he despaired of Mary Ann or anybody else fully sympathizing with his position. Everybody, it seemed, wanted to dismiss what happened to him, to sweep it out of sight. Why did they find it so difficult to comprehend the importance of those events?

The years he spent in Russia were crucial to him, they defined him, they gave his life shape and significance. Without those injustices to fight against he would have given up the ghost of his miserable existence long ago. He was not doing this for his children, no matter how much he protested the opposite, nor for his wife, nor for revenge, nor for politics, nor for the money. He was doing it because it was the only thing that made him feel alive. It was impossible for him to imagine his life without Perceval. When he thought of their lives he saw them as parallel lines that gradually became intertwined or as converging lines moving closer and closer together until finally bisecting and . . . He had not thought that far ahead. What would he say when he saw him at last, face to face? Who would speak first? He thought that he Bellingham would speak first. He would ask the Prime Minister, 'Why have you ignored me for so long? I am your destiny.' He liked it. 'I am your destiny.' There was weight and importance in a phrase like that.

'Shall I bring you your hat, sir?' The maid peered up into his face. She looked concerned.

'Yes, please. My hat, yes,' he could feel himself blushing. She brought him his hat. 'Please do not forget to give Miss Stevens the letter. It is extremely important.'

'I shan't forget it, sir. Good day, sir.' She smiled warmly.

He could feel her smile on his back all the way down the steps and on to the street. He turned to smile back, but the door was already closing. 'Good day,' he called. He was very cheerful all of a sudden. Everything was taken care of, the business was in good hands, and it would thrive under the husbandry of Mary Stevens.

Suddenly he felt light-headed and fleet-footed. He was free of the ties that had held him to the ground. If he launched himself from the heights, he would not fall. He would soar.

Nettleton blamed Bellingham for everything. Bellingham and his unreasonable demands for compensation had made Jack's life intolerable. If Nettleton was forced to accept Thistlewood's money and betray Bellingham, then Bellingham only had himself to blame for being so stubborn and pig-headed. It was resolved, then. He would take the money. He would say nothing to Bellingham.

Jack staggered away from Covent Garden. He did not look back, though he was certain he was being watched.

Jack's progress to Bloomsbury was fitful. He was forced to sit down every few minutes to combat the dizziness and nausea. It was as if his very body was revolted by his cowardice, disgusted by his treachery. But somehow he managed to place one foot in front of another. By grace or by luck he avoided carriages and thieves and stumbled at last into Red Lion Square.

He sat for a moment on the steps of the Infirmary. He noticed that a small crowd had gathered in the square. A man, on a box or a stool, stood head and shoulders above the rest. Jack saw that people were watching from the windows.

From the opposite corner of the square John Bellingham approached the gathering. Like everybody else, he was curious. From his clothing and his demeanour Bellingham could not deduce the speaker's profession, whether he was an artisan, shopkeeper or mendicant preacher. He did not look like a preacher. He did not carry a Bible. He seemed too agitated, too worried, to be a professional public speaker. As Bellingham got closer he was struck by the man's eyes, a pale, almost transparent, blue.

Nettleton saw Bellingham and retched.

'We struggle, brothers and sisters, after centuries of oppression we struggle still. We struggle to make ends meet and raise our children in safety. We strive, we reach out, those of us who have not lost hope, we fight for the future,' the speaker declaimed. He did not shout. His voice was barely raised at all. His audience turned their heads to hear and craned their necks.

Bellingham caught sight of Nettleton and waved.

'We do not know what the future may hold, but still we strive to reach it. Our instinct tells us it must be better than this. It must be. If there's no hope of anything better, why bother at all? Why show any restraint? Why not just grab what you want? Why hold back? What is the point of compassion, of mercy, of freedom if our present actions can have no effect on future events?'

The crowd began to drift away, suddenly losing interest. The man was no blasphemer. He was not going to make fun of the royal family or hurl bloodcurdling threats against the rich. He had just got up in the morning with an idea in his head that he could not shake. Some Utopian notion that made sense only to himself.

Nettleton flinched. He checked to see if there was some way of evading the meeting. Open ground on both sides. Bellingham was heading straight for him, calling out his name. Collision was inevitable.

'Jack!' shouted Bellingham, waving his arms. 'Jack, it's me. Over here.' There was obviously something the matter with Nettleton. Even from a distance he looked decidedly peaky. He appeared to be twitching.

Nettleton moaned. He rolled his eyes heavenwards. Why did it have to be now? Why today?

Bellingham bounded over to Jack. There was a spring in his step. A jauntiness that he was at a loss to explain. He was unaccountably pleased to meet his friend. He wanted to talk to him about the note he had received, about his encounter with Miss Stevens and, most important, his triumph over Skinker.

'We are born to a kind of paradise on this earth,' the speaker yelled desperately from his podium. He was deserted, alone in the middle of the square.

Bellingham and Nettleton both looked at him, struck for a moment by this final statement flung into the empty air, before turning aside.

'Dinner?' asked Bellingham.

'Why not?' Nettleton shrugged.

EIGHT

THE HAM AND WINDMILL

A small wooden sign, its paint peeling, marks the location of the Ham and Windmill.

A scrubbed wooden floor, covered in a thick layer of fresh sawdust, stretches from the front doors to the bar itself, situated at the back of the taproom and made up of a series of trestle tables laid end to end with barrels resting on top in wooden brackets.

Tables and benches are grouped near the bar, and towards the door is a series of snugs, high-backed wooden benches, some with curtains pulled across to form private cubicles.

To the left, as Bellingham and Nettleton enter, is a door that leads into a parlour. Posted to it is a handwritten sign that reads 'Available for Functions'. The alehouse is not full, but it is doing brisk trade. People stand, sit, eating and drinking. Windows are blacked out or else heavily curtained.

Set in the wall is a peephole to warn of approaching Bow Street Runners, beadles and press gangs. A boy sits on a stool looking through the peephole. At first glance he looks brightly awake, alert to the potential dangers, but closer inspection reveals he has drawn wide-open eyes on his closed eyelids and he is fast asleep. Thankfully it is too early in the day to worry unduly about the intrusion of the state or for the smell of vomit to replace the sweet, bready smell of the beer and porter. People sit around singly drinking seriously or in groups talking spiritedly. Nettleton and Bellingham choose a snug near the door and settle themselves on the hard wooden seats.

They talk animatedly for a while, Bellingham mostly. He seems enlivened by something. He gestures with his hands as he talks, wide, sweeping gestures that seem to encompass the whole room. Circles shaped in the air by his hands moving from the wrists, by his arms moving from the shoulder. He looks up. He looks down. It is as if nothing is hidden from him, as if he sees everything clearly. Nettleton shrinks before this awesome display of magisterial self-confidence. He hunches his shoulders up round his ears and draws them forward, closing up his chest. He keeps his head lowered and looks up with his eyes, cowed and cornered. He crosses his legs beneath the table and shields his abdomen with his elbows.

All thoughts of food have disappeared from Bellingham's mind. He is engrossed in his own world, a world which does not include this present moment but is composed solely of future events. A world where he alone is the protagonist, where it is his decisions that decide the fate of the world. The mundanities of everyday life, such as food, are an unwanted distraction from the essential task of shaping the future.

Nettleton, meanwhile, is wholly concerned with the present and the demands of his stomach. At every pause for breath in Bellingham's speech he tries to interject. 'Mutton pie.' He throws it out like a challenge. Bellingham ignores him or else does not hear. 'Beef,' tries Nettleton, but he is unable to deflect Bellingham from his visionary task. Nettleton admits defeat. He turns his attention to a conversation drifting across the divide from the snug behind him, where a group of three young people are discussing revolution as if one were imminent.

They talk loudly of acts of terrorism and violence; they express openly their admiration for the heroes of the struggle, of Emmet, of Despard, of Robespierre, knowing that if their casual talk is overheard, it will be given tavern-grace. Such talk costs little and can never be believed.

Margaret, the only woman in this small group, speaks in terms of acceptable losses and unavoidable casualties, and her ability to reduce matters of life and death to statistics, to facts and figures scrawled on the back of a crumpled and torn flyer, secretly impresses her comrades, who, despite their bravura performance, have too great a power of imagination to talk of death without envisaging ripping flesh, scorching skin and flying limbs. For them (they are young still and will have many more conversations like this one to become better acquainted with the idea) the blood-drenched streets are palpable with smell and colour, slippery too, and covered with strips of torn clothing, and the gutters are clogged with shoes. Shoes everywhere and nobody left to fill them. They avoid each other's eyes, they sip at their beer. They have another jug or two, and their ability to imagine is dulled as their anger grows and they mistake this drunken gravity and the pounding of their blood in their veins for passion.

'I have a list.' Matthew, the youngest, pulls a scrap of paper from his trouser pocket. 'A list of those who must die if the revolution is to succeed.'

'I have a list too,' chimes in Peter as he searches through his jacket and his trousers and feels in his boots. 'But I think I've left it at home. Don't worry, though, I remember it.'

'First,' Margaret says softly, 'I'll read my list. Number one, all Catholics.'

'That was on my list,' whispers Peter.

'I have it too.' Matthew holds his list out. 'Look there, see: "Catholics".'

126

'Number two, Reverend Monkton.'

'Who?' Matthew queries.

'Monkton.' Margaret repeats his name.

'Never heard of him.' Peter shakes his head. 'What did he do?'

'He put the constable on to my brother. Accused him of receiving stolen goods.'

'He was the biggest fence in Whitechapel, your brother, wasn't he?' Peter leans across the table.

'He was, but what right did Monkton have to turn him over to the hangman?'

'Fair enough,' Peter acquiesces. 'Parson Monkton makes it to the list along with all sneaks and tell-tales.'

'Thank you, Peter. Shall I continue?'

'Please go on,' says Matthew.

'Next, Andrew Puddephat.'

'From St Giles's?' Peter asks.

'The very one. He is a pig and a corrupt individual who should, along with all lecherous, treacherous males, be culled for the greater good of humanity.'

'Because?' Matthew fails, again, to grasp the connection with the revolution.

'Because he led me up the garden path and took my virtue, almost.'

'I see.' Matthew nods but his brow is furrowed, and he looks very puzzled.

Margaret's list continues in similar vein, and eventually Peter and Matthew stop questioning her choice of individuals worthy of execution. After the unfortunate Puddephat, Margaret lists a whole host of people who have crossed her. From tradesmen who have overcharged to shopkeepers who have been rude, women who are prettier and neighbours who are wealthier and, finally, her parents who failed her. As she folds her list and replaces it in her pocket book Matthew and Peter glance at each other apprehensively. Secretly both are pleased that Margaret's list bears such a close resemblance to their own. Peter nods at Matthew, who nods back, and Peter begins by clearing his throat.

'Catholics,' he says from memory. 'All other clergymen excepting only those who are known genuinely to support the cause of reform or who have sworn oaths against the Government. The Government, of course.'

'Of course,' says Margaret. 'I didn't include the Government only because it seemed so obvious.'

'Ah, but it needed stating.' Matthew raises a finger, a new confidence coming over him when he sees Margaret on the defensive.

'Agreed,' says Margaret through almost clenched teeth.

Peter's list of death is not long. He claims to have forgotten a substantial portion of it. He includes in his list all masters and most 'journeymen of the arrogant sort such as Mr Thomas of Clerkenwell, who so egregiously wounded and defamed me with my employers, leading to my dismissal and blacklisting among all watchmakers. In retaliation for depriving me of my livelihood I shall deprive Mr Thomas of his life.'

'Strong words, Peter.'

'Strong reasons, Matthew.'

'Matthew's list,' says Margaret.

'My list – obviously leaving out all those groups otherwise covered by you, my colleagues – begins with customs officers. They are corrupt, and their activities run contrariwise to the working people's enjoyment of the fruits of the earth.'

'Tom Paine was a customs man.' Margaret smiles wickedly at her dropping of this piece of information.

'But he ain't one now,' Matthew retorts. 'I continue, customs officers, press gangs.'

'Hear, hear.' Peter claps.

Matthew also has particular grievances with butchers who, he claims, are disreputable and very often sell gamy or rotten meat to the working people while reserving the best and freshest cuts for their aristocratic clients. On top of this they discharge their waste very often into the streets, which promotes foul smells and disease. In the absence of regulation of the trade all butchers should be served notice of execution if they do not look to their filthy habits and bad practices and clean up their act. Matthew's tirade shocks his comrades. He has, it seems, kept his hatred of butchers very well hidden until this moment. Hardly have they recovered from his assault on the meat merchants than he is launching an offensive against cab drivers. Not only do they frequently overcharge their clients and cravenly toady to the well-heeled, but – and here Matthew adduces personal evidence (dates and times and places) – they shower the humble working man and pedestrian with a combination of mud, water and abuse, either singly or ofttimes together. Matthew has a plan to make an example of cab drivers while employing them in the service of the revolution. He suggests hijacking them and forcing the cabbies to act as get-away drivers and suicide bombers. On this point Peter and Margaret wholeheartedly concur.

They order another jug of beer. They toast each other and wipe the froth from their lips. In unison they sit back in their seats and close their eyes. Peter opens his first. He tears off a strip of peeling wallpaper and starts to scribble furiously on the back of it. When he finishes he grabs the attention of his friends.

'Comrades, it occurs to me that if there is one fault with our list of post-revolutionary assassinations, it is this. Most of the people on all of our lists have done us a wrong. If we are not to be accused of revenge and of pursuing our own personal vendettas under the banner of the revolution . . .'

'God forbid,' the other two mutter, interrupting him.

'Then we have only one option,' he continues.

'Which is?' they ask eagerly.

'To swap lists with each other.'

'It's so simple,' cries Margaret.

'Let's do it,' agrees Matthew.

Quickly they hand each other their lists, but it is only when they get home that they realize that they have not been entirely honest with each other. Margaret, when she looks at Matthew's list, sees at the bottom Peter's name. Similarly Matthew, when he looks at Peter's, sees Margaret's name. And Peter is quite unperturbed to see Matthew's name appended to Margaret's. They are not surprised, nor do they suspect. They choose not to say anything further about the lists, and whenever they meet there is a curious triangular conspiracy between them that everyone else assumes is of a sexual rather than a revolutionary nature.

Bellingham, his excitement spent, makes his way over to the bar, where a raucous group of young men are holding court. Their eyes are already bleary, their bodies swaying as if blown in a light breeze.

One man, considerably worse off than the others, stands facing the barrels. His whole weight is supported from a single point as he leans backwards. His trouser belt hooked over a nail is all that spares him from the effects of gravity and a bump on the head. His eyes are half closed and a slack-mouthed gin-grin besets his face.

Bellingham pushes his way to the bar. A man next to him engages him in conversation. 'You cannot stand in the way of Progress. Science is changing our lives. We are at the beginning of the Machine Age.' He struggles to focus on Bellingham's face.

'Yes,' says Bellingham, trying to catch the barman's eye.

'These machine wreckers, these Luddites, they're fools. In the long run we shall all benefit. When we have all been replaced by machines we shall have more time for leisure. Don't you think?' The man cocks his head to one side inquisitively, but the weight of his head pulls him down, and he falls to the floor.

Bellingham holds up two fingers and his beer is slopped into two tankards.

An old man approaches Bellingham. He is stooped and shrivelled. His wrinkled skin lies in folds on his face and arms, barely connected to muscle and sinew any more. His eyes move alertly, and while he could not be described as lithe, there is a sort of suppleness about his movements as he infiltrates the people crowded around the bar. He insinuates himself towards Bellingham. He has him in his sights. The old man cuts off his victim's escape and traps Bellingham against the bar.

'Oi! Oi, you! Yes, you. I'm talking to you.' He shoves a bony finger into Bellingham's chest. 'Show me some respect. No respect from you young people any more. You hear me? I said young people have no respect for the elderly. When I was young we venerated our old folk. We cared for them and gave them pride of place in the community. We did things for them. We ran errands for them. We called on them. But me, I don't see my neighbours' faces from one month to the next. I bang on their ceiling and they bang back, and that's about it. When I see them I shout at them, and do they reply? No, they barely give me the time of day. Is that civil? Is that respectful?

'Yes, thank you, I will have a jar with you. I can see you're different. I know who I like.' The old man pauses to gulp at his drink, but his eyes never leave his captive. He holds Bellingham squirming, wriggling, bored, pinned to the bar by the force of his gigantic and aggressive will. Slamming his empty beer mug down on the bar, he says, 'Do you know what this is for?' He points to a medal on his chest. Bellingham looks and, though he does not say so, it seems to him to be a copper coin attached to a grubby strip of ribbon by

131

a piece of string. 'This is for marksmanship. There, you didn't know I was in the army, did you? You would never have guessed that, am I right? I could shoot a parting in your hair from a hundred feet away. I can blast the cork from a bottle from one hundred and fifty feet. I can kill a man with a shot clean between the eyes. Have you ever seen a man die?' Bellingham nods. The old man eyes him suspiciously. 'Violently, I mean. Bloodily.' Bellingham shakes his head. 'I have. A thousand times. I've seen heads explode and legs carry on walking with no torso on top. That's what war is. But what do you lot know of war, you namby-pampy, mollycoddled, feather-bedded, skirt-shielded mother's boys?'

He gobs the words out, and his anger takes even him a little by surprise. He raises his voice to address a wider audience. 'They call me Billy Patriot because I am a patriot and I don't care who knows it. Patriotism is little valued in this day and age, but let me tell you I am for Church and King, and I will not take any more of this Republican cock-and-bull.' People clap and cheer wildly. Billy gets another drink and somebody gives up their seat for England's last patriot while Bellingham staggers back to his snug, chastened by his fragrant encounter with one of the great unwashed.

Jack bites into a pie he has bought from a man hawking his wares in the pub. His cheeks bulge out. There is so much food in his mouth, and he has to work his jaw so hard to chew it down, that he barely has space or time to breathe. 'God, I'm starved.' Crumbs of pie crust fly from Nettleton's mouth. 'This is good, really good,' he enthuses as he swallows and takes another huge mouthful. 'You should try it.'

Bellingham puts his elbows on the table and cradles his head in his hands. He appears to deflate suddenly, his shoulders drop and his chest sags. The noise and chaos depress him. The alcohol-flushed faces and gaping, gasping mouths suck the energy from his limbs. Even his hair, newly cut and neat, looks as if it is draped over his skull rather than growing there. He lifts his head and glances lethargically about the tavern. Bellingham thinks he recognizes the man across the room whose hands and arms are tattooed with ink stains. He watches the inky man's public display with no interest.

The inky man has her jammed between his body and the wall. She sits, legs astride the crude wooden bench. Her skirts are hitched over her knees so she can span the bench's width. Their faces are pressed together, their eyes tight closed. His ink-smeared arms and hands enfold her, caress her. His fingers run up and down the length of her spine while hers massage his bald head and thick neck. She presses so hard with her fingertips that his skin is streaked with red marks as she raises the blood to the surface. They are blissful and oblivious (kiss, kiss).

The lovers move apart from each other with an audible squelch (heads turn quickly away, everybody drinks). He holds his stained hand to her white cheek and gently strokes her smooth skin. She rests her hand on his shoulder. They stare at each other a while without moving. For the first time her eyes move from contemplating the features of her lover and she notices someone across the room. She points with her free hand and asks, 'Isn't that the man from the cemetery this morning?'

Her lover turns his head and peers at Bellingham. 'Yes.' And he does not give Bellingham a second thought. He takes her face in his hands. She pulls him closer. They kiss ever more passionately, and as they come apart to breathe a thread of spittle connects them chin to chin.

A large group, composed mostly of men, also watches but with active disapproval. They turn and stand on their benches to get a better look. They shake their heads and tut loudly. A man with enormous white sideburns calls the meeting to order by banging his beer mug on the table. 'Brothers and sisters, I should like to point out that we were definitely right in our decision to expel the two members whose names are best left unsaid but whose licentious activities are openly displayed for all to see. There is no place within our Church for such flagrant and vulgar disregard for simple decency. In the words of St Paul, and I quote, "If any man that is called a brother be a fornicator, do not keep company with such an one, no, not to eat." ' Finishing, he sits down at the head of the table. A younger man gets to his feet slowly, cautiously. 'While I am in total agreement with Brother Elihu on the vulgarity of their behaviour, I am confused as to the condemnation of their activities on other grounds. Do we or do we not believe in free grace, justification not by deeds but by faith? Is it not our contention that the Gospel of forgiveness and love takes precedence over, is perhaps even opposed to, the oppressive moral laws of Moses? Why, then, is their public display of amorousness any more to be condemned than our own public display of drinking?' The words tumble out in a bit of a rush. The young man stares at the table and rubs his hands together throughout his speech. 'That's all. I was just wondering.' He sits down beneath the withering glares of his fellows.

Elihu looks round, expecting someone to get up and counter the young man's argument. He looks in vain. As his ancient gaze falls on his congregation, one by one they look away or shuffle papers or stare at the bottom of their mugs. Elihu sighs and rises to his feet. 'There are at least two sins here. The sin of adultery; this woman is not his wife and therefore has no claim to conjugal affections. And the sin of calling attention to oneself, which those of us who follow this outlawed

134

faith know all too well to be the most arrogant and damaging of all sins.' Elihu pauses. 'It has been one hundred and fifty years since anybody really cared about what we thought or how our behaviour might influence the general populace. We are tolerated, it is true, but why should we provide the scandals that enable them to dismiss us as eccentric lunatics and advocates of free love? The Antinomian path is an exciting route to understanding and salvation, not an excuse to behave just as you please. Now, if that has answered Brother James's question, I think we should turn our attention to the real purpose of this meeting, which is to take ideas for the new hymnal. Who would like to begin? Sister Helen, why don't you stand and share your inspiration with us?' Helen stands reluctantly. She is hesitant and scans the faces of her fellow worshippers looking for help. 'Come along, Sister,' Elihu is getting impatient.

Helen unfolds a piece of paper and starts to sing very quietly.

'I can't hear her,' someone says from the far end of the table. 'Get her to speak up.'

'Put a bit of effort in, Sister,' says someone at her elbow, trying to be encouraging. Helen's voice lifts a little, but she is wildly off-key. In fact, each sequence of notes could be in a different key. She sings.

Joshua and Samuel wait by the entrance to the tavern. Joshua keeps his eye on a handcart parked outside. Samuel is watching a middle-aged woman who appears to be singing. She is bright-red. Even her ears are red. Her nose glows red. Samuel is fascinated by the sight. Joshua is worried. He glances nervously at the cart. A dog wanders up to it and starts to sniff. Another joins the first. Then another. Joshua rushes from the tavern, waving his arms and shouting, 'Shoo! Shoo!' The dogs turn and stare at the ragged figure running towards them. They look at each other, then back at the cart, and then wander off in different directions. Joshua returns to the tavern. Samuel's attention is still directed elsewhere.

'Dogs again,' says Joshua. 'Bloody dogs, eh? Bloody dogs.'

'Umm,' Samuel responds.

'It'll start to smell soon,' Joshua confides enthusiastically.

'Can't deliver it smelly, Joshua. Must be fresh,' his attention returning to his colleague. 'Extraordinary. She can't sing at all. Not one note. Why would she do that if she can't sing? What is it that makes someone humiliate themselves like that?'

'What?'

'Can't be smelly, Joshua. Must be fresh.'

'Right. How much do you reckon we'll get for it?'

'You can never be certain. There is no set price. There may have been a surfeit of corpses today. Or perhaps there wasn't. Ours is young. They like them young. Not too damaged. Should get a reasonable price. Enough to buy you some new clothes, Joshua.'

'What's wrong with these?' Joshua gets defensive. He fingers his tatty clothes with affection. 'They're comfortable these. I've had them ages.'

'Drink up, Joshua. Got to get going.'

'Where's this one going, Sammy?'

'Bart's. St Bartholomew's.'

'In this heat?'

'You push and I'll carry the umbrella.' Samuel finishes his drink, picks up a large umbrella propped against a wall and leaves the tavern.

Joshua gulps down his beer and hurries after him. 'Can't I carry the umbrella?'

'You're the apprentice. You have to push the cart.' Samuel does not even turn round.

'All the way?' asks Joshua, clearly disappointed.

'We'll see.'

He is about twenty years old. A rough beard adorns his face. A floppy black hat is pulled down over his eyes. He checks to see if he is observed. He knocks on the cellar door. Rat-a-tat-tat-tat. An eye appears at a tiny hole in the centre of the door. The bolts are pulled back and the man is admitted. The cellar is dimly lit. It's dank and cool down here, out of the sun. Despite the musty smell and the rustle of the rats scurrying around behind the barrels, doing whatever it is rats do, it is very pleasant in the cellar. The coolness alone might explain the presence of fifteen or so men. That or the cards on the makeshift table. A man approaches the new arrival and grasps him firmly by the hand. The handshake lasts some time as each struggles to manipulate the other's knuckles and joints of the finger while they exchange a number of words.

'Unity.'

'Truth.'

'Liberty.'

'Death.'

'Brotherhood.'

'Integrity.'

'Welcome to the meeting. We thought you weren't coming.'

'I had to make sure I wasn't followed.'

As one the group turn and ask in a simultaneous whisper, 'You were followed?'

'No, no. I had to make sure I wasn't.'

The group seem pacified by the response. The young man takes his place among his comrades.

'We have a new member,' announces the hand-shaker, who is deferred to by everyone and is probably a leader. 'We must swear him into the division. Are we all agreed? May he join?' There is a general murmuring of assent. The hand-shaker motions to someone nearby, who retreats into the shadows at the back of the cellar and returns with a man wearing a blindfold. His ears

137

appear to be stuffed with wax, and his hands are tied behind his back. The blindfold and the ear plugs are removed.

'Step forward,' says the hand-shaker. The recruit steps forward. 'Answer me this. Do you desire a root-and-branch change of social and political system?'

'I do.'

'Are you willing to risk everything you have, even your life, in the struggle to leave our posterity free?'

'I am.'

'Are you willing to do all in your power to create the spirit of love, brotherhood and affection among the friends of freedom and omit no opportunity of getting all the political information you can to further the cause?'

'I am so willing.'

'Swear it.'

'I swear.'

'Untie his hands, please. Welcome, comrade, to the United Englishmen. You are part of an organization with a glorious history. No other clandestine society has recruited so many members, attempted so many *coups d'état* or held so many midnight meetings as ours. And now we shall take a moment to honour the memory of the glorious Colonel Despard, executed as a traitor by the forces of reaction and long remembered as the greatest United Englishman. Citizens, I give you the toast: Colonel Despard.'

'Colonel Despard,' they repeat and drain their glasses.

'Despard was an oaf.' The old man delivers his judgement emphatically. 'He did more damage to the cause than anyone apart from that lunatic Hadfield.' His friends nod their heads in agreement. They sit in comparative comfort in the parlour. The chairs have some padding. The floor is cleaner, and the noise is not as intrusive. The old men around this table value their privacy as if it were their liberty. They are of more or less similar ages. Artisans and professionals united by their memories and their activism.

'When Despard was arrested I thought that would be it. I thought they'd come for everybody. I even packed a bag ready to leave.' Henson laughs at his own comment. 'They were scared to death though, the aristocrats, the politicians and their lackeys. One newspaper – I shan't forget it, it conjured up such a picture – said, "Shall Despard's headless corpse walk into every taproom to make proselytes an hundredfold?"'

'When was that? I should know, shouldn't I? But I've forogtten. Ten years ago?' Watson asks the company in general. He is frail. His hands are covered in liver spots. His voice is quiet.

'Nine: in 1803 they chopped his head off.' It is his son who answers. Grey himself, tired-looking.

'Barbaric, when you think about it. "Behold the head of a traitor." Makes my blood run cold.' Galloway gives a shudder and shakes his head.

'But if Despard had succeeded, would you have joined his rebellion?' The questioner is younger. The older men gang up against his naïveté. He had not been there. They respect his intelligence but enjoy wrecking his theories on the practical reefs of their experience.

'Of course. But that's a big "if",' continues Henson. 'Despard did not really have anything. It's doubtful that he was seriously planning a coup. The prosecution never produced any direct evidence of the conspiracy, never proved he was at the head of the conspiracy, even if it did exist. Despard kept his mouth shut, and he died for it. But I ask you, a *coup d'état*? The only result of all that plotting and frenzied oath-swearing was the destruction of the old Painite correspondence societies. We used to correspond with groups in Halifax, Sheffield and Edinburgh. We sent delegates to Paris to talk to the Jacobins and exchange ideas and see

139

the revolution at first hand. We were serious about our agitation. We didn't make wild plans to murder the Government and the rest of that hopeless, desperate nonsense. Despard was a passionate man. I met him once. He had charisma by the bucketful. That charming Irish lilt of his. Yet, really, he had very little political commitment. He was obsessed not with Ireland's freedom or the people's freedom but with his own failed career. He'd been a heroic and brilliant soldier. Nelson spoke up for him at his trial. Did you know that?'

'I read the transcripts.'

'Brilliance does not guarantee promotion, however. You need money and family to achieve that. I mean, his failure as a career soldier made him see the corruption at the heart of English politics. But if he'd got his promotion, do you think for a minute he would have plotted a tea party without the permission of the Ministry? Of course not. He would've been on the other side of the barricade, come the day.'

'What does that have to do with anything? Luck or fate?'

'I'm saying he acted out of personal grievance, not from a deep-seated belief in the need for fundamental change. The real point is, he destroyed the underground that people like us had spent so many years building up.' Henson stops there, exhausted. Watson's son takes over.

'We used to travel the country organizing demonstrations, making contact with local organizations, setting up correspondence societies. I remember Dad tramping the country lanes round Sussex with a wheelbarrow full of copies of *The Rights of Man* and pamphlet summaries of Paine's ideas.

'Henson printed them on the sly, and me and Dad delivered them wherever and whenever we could. And people were glad of it. Most of them couldn't read, but they all knew someone who could. People who can't read have incredible memories. If they want to memorize something, they can do it like that.' He snaps his fingers. 'I knew this man. Just a farm labourer. Hardly any learning at all but an intelligent, quick-witted man none the less. He knew *The Rights of Man*, Parts One and Two, virtually word for word. And he understood it too. Incredible. Put us all to shame. They sent him for transportation in the end. Fell foul of the Combination Acts and the Seditious Meetings Act. Who doesn't? We're all breaking the law just by sitting here together.'

'It all changed when Bonaparte crowned himself emperor,' Galloway chips in. 'Napoleon betrayed what little there was left of the revolution. It's his war the French are fighting now. How can it be a war of liberation when he calls himself emperor and hands out crowns to his brothers like they're going out of fashion? It's just a territorial war, a bloody waste. We should be fighting him.'

'God forbid I should climb into bed with the Tories, but Galloway is right. Napoleon is a tyrant. I opposed Pitt for his tyrannies. I would be a hypocrite, unworthy to call myself a republican, if I didn't oppose Bonaparte and his monarchical ambitions.' Henson has a second wind. The others are glad to let him speak on their behalf, just like the old days. 'These people today who get all puffed up about armed rebellion and send letters to Paris begging the French to invade on behalf of the citizens of England – they are traitors. I remember when they caught that priest, Father O'Coigly. He had a letter on him giving the terms on which he would allow the French to invade. Something about Britain remaining an autonomous republic and levying taxes only to cover the invasion costs. I liked that bit.' Henson laughs. A big guffaw. 'Ridiculous. No, I tell you it's all fallen apart. We used to wear our masks and shout out our slogans in midnight meetings in fields. What was it we used to say?'

'We are the Sovereignty. You are the Sovereignty.' Old Watson speaks up, a smile on his face. 'I remember that!'

'There was another as well. We used to put it across the top of the leaflets. It was, let me see now . . . "Shake the Earth to its Centre." That was it.'

The questioner is in awe of these men. He is ashamed to be born in a time of apathy and reaction, when it is fashionable to be anti-French and extol the virtues of constitutional change. He wishes with all his heart he had been of an age during the Great Agitation. He hopes and prays (though he is a staunch atheist, having read and reread Paine's *Age of Reason*) that he will be alive and fit when the next period of activism comes around. 'Do you think we'll ever see its like again?'

'Of course we will. The struggle has only just begun. For the moment the extremists and the informers have the upper hand, but it won't always be like that.' Henson yawns. Watson sets up the chequerboard on the table, and the old men's interest is diverted. The younger man takes his leave and slips quietly away. The old men's heads turn briefly as he opens the door, and the noise from the taproom surges momentarily into the calm and quiet of their parlour.

The tavern is bustling with midday diners and drinkers. A large number throng round the barrels, calling for more jugs. Pot boys scurry to and fro collecting empties and rinsing them hurriedly in a scummy-looking trough of water before filling and delivering them afresh. The young man is about to leave when a man climbs on to the table to his right and shouts for silence.

The man on the table is in his thirties. He is impeccably dressed. Not the kind of gentleman usually found in a public bar, and certainly not the kind to be found standing on tables addressing the masses, he attracts everyone's attention.

'Unaccustomed as I am . . .' he begins falteringly.

'Get on with it,' an impatient punter yells.

'My name is John Williams. I have come from Cornwall because I had a dream.' He is shaking with nerves. 'I had a dream that I was in the lobby of the House of Commons. A place well known to me. A small man dressed in a blue coat and white waistcoat entered, and immediately I saw a person whom I had observed in the first instance, dressed in a snuff-coloured coat and yellow, metal buttons, take a pistol from under his coat and present it at the little man above-mentioned. The pistol was discharged, and the ball entered under the left breast of the person at whom it was directed. I saw the blood issue from the place where the ball had struck him. His countenance instantly altered, and he fell to the ground. Upon inquiry who the sufferer might be, I was informed he was the Chancellor of the Exchequer. I further saw the murderer laid hold of by several gentlemen in the room.'

'Rubbish!'

'Get off!'

'I've heard better stories in church!'

John Williams steps down from the table. He nods politely to the young man next to him, puts on his hat and strides out of the public house in high dudgeon. There is a split second of absolute silence as his back disappears through the door and into the bright sunlight, then the hubbub begins anew.

Nettleton looks at Bellingham in his snuff-coloured coat, throws back his head and drains his mug. He wipes the froth from his upper lip with his sleeve. Bellingham is looking at a rather vile, sickly young man standing at the bar, holding a piece of lint to his neck. Nettleton follows Bellingham's gaze. When the young man removes the lint from his neck Nettleton can see the boil and the pus oozing from it. 'Skinker,' Bellingham says, almost to himself. As they both gawp the man turns round, seeming to sense their attention. When he catches sight of Bellingham he points and yells at the top of his lungs, 'Stop, thief!'

Nettleton is completely overawed by the sight. Before he knows it Bellingham is scrabbling over the table and heading for the exit. Nettleton follows as swiftly as his full stomach will allow. He can offer Bellingham refuge from his accusers.

NINE

THE CELLAR

It was a grandfather clock. It had belonged to his grandfather. It was made in 1688, the year of his grandfather's birth, the year of the Glorious Revolution, the year that saw the defeat of Catholicism and the ascent of the House of Orange. His father had always taught him that the Glorious Revolution would be the last revolution Great Britain would ever see. His grandfather and his father had dedicated their lives to that belief. They had lied and cheated and even killed to ensure that everything, as far as the mass of the population were concerned, remained exactly the same. Henry Stillwater watched the clock's pendulum swing back and forth. He wondered what his ancestors would have made of his current activities. The world had changed out of all recognition since his father's death in 1774, before the loss of the colonies, before the revolution in France, before Tom Paine, before Napoleon, before Pitt the Younger, before Perceval. What would Henry Stillwater senior have had to say about the Luddites, for instance? Would he have condemned them, knowing, as his son did, that each machine could at a stroke throw hundreds of individual weavers out of a job that had been at best seasonal and at worst downright dangerous in the first place? Stillwater wished his father was there to advise him. His father would tell him if he was doing the right thing.

He had never sought approval or justification, yet at this moment Stillwater would have given anything for a ten-minute conversation with his father. The whole business had reached a crucial stage. Stillwater could not decide whether or not to intervene. He watched the pendulum swing. Its ineluctable motion held him spellbound. Everything hung in the balance.

The chair was made of light oak darkened with age. Its arm rests were thick and worn smooth. They abutted the back upright at right angles, made other right angles at the opposite end with a strut connected to the seat and ended in rather handsome scrolls. The legs were square and solid, strengthened by two crosspieces that met at a point a foot below the exact centre of the chair seat. The back was straight and carved from a single piece of wood. Roses in bas-relief ran along the curve at its top. It was, or rather it had been, the work of a master craftsman, but at some point in its existence the chair had been manhandled and broken. From the rear one could see that the wood of the backrest was splitting. The arms were fixed in place by two or three nails whose heads were bent over into the wood. Underneath the seat was shored up by a couple of planks also crudely attached with inexpertly driven-in nails. The chair was, in fact, a ramshackle, shoddy affair. It was suspended ten feet from the floor by four chains that converged to a single point, an iron ring. The ring was attached to a hemp line that ran across two pulleys before descending to the ground. The line was tied off to a cleat bolted to the wall. The chair swayed gently back and forth as Bellingham, himself securely fastened to the chair, shifted his weight from one side to the other.

Below him, his feet seemed to dangle mere inches above their heads, people passed to and fro, going about their work. All their efforts were directed towards the machine that filled most of the cellar. The main body of the machine was composed of something that resembled a very large, square chest of drawers, roughly twelve feet by twelve feet wide and six feet high. To the right of the chest of drawers were nine large barrels filled with foul-smelling substances. Each barrel was connected by a long hose to the chest of drawers. Four metal poles rose from the centre of the chest of drawers to the ceiling. A single wooden shank ran up from the machine and passed through a hole in the ceiling. A small shaft of sunlight entered the cellar from that hole. Otherwise the room was lit only by a number of lanterns hung round the walls. Also on top of the machine was a tray, connected with wires and pipes, of what appeared to be up-turned glasses. In front of the chest of drawers, a little to Bellingham's left, was a table with two square boxes on it. A man sat at the table, staring at the boxes and making notes in a book. To Bellingham's right, also in front of the machine, a man sat at a table poring over an enormous book filled with hieroglyphics and other strange symbols that Bellingham could not quite make out. Finally, facing Bellingham and sitting behind the machine was a man who could only be the operator. On either side of him were two enormous paddles. Bellingham could not see exactly what was going on, but from the way the man moved he could have been playing the organ.

Men in overalls scurried about, tending to the machine's needs. Wearing face masks, they filled the barrels from brimful leather buckets. The liquid in the barrels bubbled and belched foul-smelling gasses. If any of the liquid was spilt, someone would shout a warning and a team of men would arrive to spray the spillage with water and cover it in sawdust before removing the refuse in metal tins. Mechanics adjusted things with spanners and hit things with hammers. They crawled under and over the machine.

They listened to its workings, their ears pressed to its side. They pulled things and pushed things. They got out rulers and set squares and books of tables and measured things.

And the whole time, above their heads, just beyond reach, Bellingham sat in his chair and swayed as if in a breeze. They ignored him of course. Their energies were focused on the machine, and not one of them gave any thought to its end-use. They were skilled engineers, experts in a particular area; they were not contracted to consider the ethics of their toil. Bellingham, on the other hand, was forced to consider his position and left to ponder the possible practical applications of the engineers' labour.

Hanging there in the near darkness, helpless, alone, Bellingham began to cry. Quiet tears squeezed from the side of his eyes and trickled slowly down his cheeks. His nose started running. He opened his mouth to breathe and a sob escaped. He struggled to free his hands. The chair began to swing violently and then to turn. First anti-clockwise until the chains were all entangled and then, unravelling, he spun clockwise back again. The chains clanked and the rope creaked as Bellingham's demented maypole dance became more and more desperate.

The metal flap slammed shut with a clang. Thistlewood shook his head. 'What does he think he's doing?' He lifted the rectangular flap in the door and peered through into the engine room. Bellingham was still flinging himself round and round in circles.

For a fraction of a second Thistlewood felt sorry for his victim. He put himself in Bellingham's position and found it extremely uncomfortable. With a shrug of his shoulders Thistlewood dismissed the sentiment. He thought of his new boots, ruined. Those blood stains would never come out. His attitude hardened.

'Truelock?' He called out the name, unsure if he would receive a response. 'Are you still there, Bannister Truelock?'

A man dressed entirely in black except for a thin strip of white at his collar emerged from the shadows.

'Yes, I'm here.'

'I thought you'd gone.'

'I have nowhere to go,' said Truelock.

'I thought you'd gone to get a drink,' explained Thistlewood, a little testily.

'You shouldn't drink when you're pregnant. Especially not when your foetus is the Son of Man.'

Thistlewood could not find an adequate reply to Truelock. He looked at him and realized he had absolutely no faith whatsoever in this individual, which was unfortunate because the entire strategy rested on Truelock's information. 'Sit down, Bannister.' Thistlewood motioned to the chair opposite. Truelock lowered his considerable body on to the frail-looking seat. 'Explain to me how the machine works. One more time.'

Truelock took a deep breath and began.

Bellingham stopped struggling. The creaking of the rope and the violence of his motion made him afraid he would fall. His heart was beating very fast. His breath came in short gasps. He felt overwhelmed by terror. The sensation was far from unfamiliar. He recognized it immediately. He had felt it every night for years, all through his time in prison and under house arrest in Moscow and even since his return. The terror was a survival mechanism. No matter how physically tired the body was, the terror kept it tense and alert. Anything could happen in a prison during the long hours of darkness. Even in the supposed castle of your own home you were not safe from the intervention of the state. Three in the morning, and the sound of a boot kicking in your door wakes you from a deep and peaceful sleep. Dreams of wealth and happiness still fresh in your mind as you are hauled into the icy street and shoved into a cart.

He had learnt how to cope with that fear, even how to sleep with it. The fear of never knowing if you will live to see the following day, the fear that your life will be over before you have achieved anything with it, the prolonged agony of regret, the leisurely night-long contemplation of wasted opportunity. Bellingham was familiar with these sweaty activities, familiar to the point of tedium. In the midst of his terror he was detached from it; he could assess it and compare it to other instances of terror.

It was not fear that caused Bellingham's bitter tears to trickle but rather frustration. Every which way he turned, he was thwarted by this or that individual who either sought to impose his or her own demands and morality on him or else tried to make the execution of even his simplest plan impossible. Take the boy in the tailor's, for instance, the way he had obstructed and obfuscated, quarrelled and quibbled over a mere slip of paper. It drove Bellingham to distraction. Even Mary Stevens had attached moral strings to their business transaction. Washerwomen tried to rob him of pennies. His landlady wanted him to be a surrogate father to her little boy. Jack Nettleton seemed the only one to act in plain good faith without thought of reward or judgement. He wondered what had happened to Jack. He hoped the young man was safe. He would hate anybody to be hurt on his account.

The spinning was starting to make him feel queasy. He wished it would stop. His fear of what would happen to him was gradually being replaced by a profound sense of the absurdity of his position. He felt very foolish, tied to a chair dangling ten feet above the ground, hovering over what appeared to be an oversized piece of bedroom furniture pumped full of the shit from nine lavatories.

They had left the Ham and Windmill shortly after half past one. Bellingham remembered checking his watch as they stepped into a cab. The journey across to Jack's lodgings in Shoreditch was surprisingly swift, if very bumpy, and they arrived around two o'clock. Bellingham paid for the cab. Nettleton did not even offer. He seemed to have something else on his mind.

Bellingham hurried after Nettleton and climbed the stairs to the garret. Sparsely furnished with a palette bed and a wooden trunk. Bellingham marvelled at his young companion's ability to live with next to nothing. It came home to him then that they came from very different backgrounds.

Bellingham had grown up with a certain financial security. He had not been spoilt or particularly privileged, but he had had access to toys and books. There had never been any doubt that a healthy meal would appear on the table at least three times a day. He had been brought up to take a certain place in society. He had been educated to have expectations of society. He had been taught that if you obeyed the rules, then society would reward you. Prosperity was as much a question of conduct as it was of opportunity and hard work.

Nettleton, though, had seen the world from a different perspective. For Jack virtue brought nothing but its own reward, and propriety was the ruination of family. Children were not for educating but a means of support for their parents. The more children the greater the potential income to the household. Nettleton had lived on the verge of disaster all his life. For years he had gone hungry if it was necessary. For years his sacrifices had been unheeded, unacknowledged. For

151

Jack, Bellingham thought, the world must seem a thankless and grasping place.

From different positions they had arrived at similar conclusions, but where Jack had grown pessimistic and almost cynical, Bellingham had remained optimistic. There was a higher justice. Good and right and decency would prevail against the monsters of indifference and the tyrants of corruption and the villainy of class.

Nettleton went over to the trunk and, without saying a word, changed out of his filthy clothes. He wiped down his body and face and rinsed his hair through. He put on clean clothes and sat down on top of the trunk. Bellingham could not think of anything to say, so he said nothing.

After a while Jack stood and began to pace up and down. It was clear to Bellingham that something was troubling him. Bellingham lowered himself on to the bed. His knees ached with all the walking. He winced as they bent.

The air in the room was stifling. The windows were nailed shut. A smell of candle grease pervaded everywhere and behind it, just a hint of boiled meat and cabbage.

Bellingham wanted to help Jack, but he found himself at a loss to understand the man's behaviour. Also he felt slightly uncomfortable in Jack's room. It was not as if the usual niceties would suffice. There was no decor to compliment, no comfort to admire. There was nothing or next to nothing. It left Bellingham embarrassed for conversation. He felt like an intruder on someone's very private grief, as if he had arrived at a housewarming only to discover the house had been burgled. He wondered if Jack was angry with him.

For the first time Bellingham noticed the bruises and lesions on Nettleton's face. He had been so absorbed in his own troubles he had failed to remark Nettleton's problems. Why hadn't he said anything? Bellingham stood up. He reached out his hand to stop Nettleton. 'Jack,' he said gently. 'Jack, are you all right? Those bruises—' but he did not get to finish his sentence. Nettleton looked him straight in the eye. Bellingham stopped talking, his mouth stayed open. 'I have to go,' said Nettleton and he left.

'Jack!' Bellingham shouted down the stairs, but Nettleton was flying down them two at a time.

Bellingham sat back down on the bed. He sighed heavily and rubbed his eyes with his fingertips. He thought he should probably stay and wait for Nettleton to come back, but he had other business to attend to. He might even find the time to take Mrs Roberts and Edward to the exhibition after all. The idea of giving the little boy something to smile about for once appealed greatly to Bellingham. He would do it. On behalf of his own son, about Edward's age, he would go to the museum. Bellingham felt good about his decision. It was positive, life-affirming, and though the actual trip might be a bit dull, it would be no less edifying for it. His mind made up, Bellingham got to his feet and approached the door just as it was pushed open from the other side. He expected to see Jack Nettleton, but he did not see what he expected.

For one thing the man at the door was much taller than Jack. To be sure, the door was only five feet eight or so high. In order to see under the lintel Bellingham had to bend his knees. The caller was so tall and stood so close to the low doorway that only the lower half of his head was visible. The jaw was square, thin lips slightly pursed, nostrils spread flat across the width of the upper lip, skin potato-pale. The man ducked down and stepped into the room, pushing Bellingham backwards as he came. 'Excuse me,' said Bellingham, raising his voice an octave or so involuntarily. 'What do you think you're doing?'

'You Bellingham?'

'What's that got to do with you, may I ask?'

'You're Bellingham. Come with me.' The man reached out and took hold of Bellingham by his jacket lapels. The fist was huge. The skin was off the knuckles.

'Watch the jacket. Please. It's new.' He could not help it. The jacket meant a lot to him.

A second man appeared behind the first. He was smaller and rounder. He wore a black cassock and a clerical collar. He smiled and waved. 'Don't mind Walsh,' said the man in black. 'He gets over-zealous. Put him down, Walsh, there's a good chap.' Walsh let go of Bellingham and retreated a step a two. The man in black wiped his hand on his cassock and extended it towards Bellingham. 'I'm Truelock, Mr Bellingham, Bannister Truelock.'

'John Bellingham,' said Bellingham, taking Truelock's hand cautiously, 'but you already seem to know that.'

'Oh, yes, we're terribly well informed. Anyway, I don't see why we should delay this any longer. Shall we be off?'

'Off? Where are we going?'

'I'm afraid I can't divulge that information.'

'Are you from the magistrates?'

'Oh, dear me, no. Nothing of the sort. Don't you know? Thistlewood sent us. He wants to see you.'

'How did you know I was here?'

Truelock smiled again. He had a pleasant smile. Sincere. When his mouth smiled his whole face smiled with it, even his eyes.

'What about Jack?' asked Bellingham.

'Don't worry about Jack. We'll sort him out later.' Truelock winked.

At the time Bellingham thought that an odd choice of words; now he found it positively menacing. He felt guilty too. He seemed to attract trouble like a cesspool did flies. He should not have gone with them, but what choice did he have? Truelock made it seem so gentlemanly and natural, but Walsh was hovering in the background, threatening violence, waiting for violence, desiring violence. And if this is what they had planned for him, a supposed ally in the fight against tyranny, what did they have in mind for Jack, who by his own account had abandoned the fight? No doubt he was in possession of sensitive information that they had no wish to see passed into the hands of the authorities. To be honest, it did not require much imagination to envisage Jack's fate. Bellingham had read about people like this; Jacobins, insurrectionists, plotters. He had no idea they actually existed, let alone actually carried out plots and *coups d'état*. And to think Thistlewood was such a man. Jack had told him about Thistlewood and about his politics, but Bellingham had assumed it was all more or less innocent; words and pamphlets, an anti-establishment game, an angry yell of protest, but not this. Not actually bloody dangerous. When he thought about it, all this was Nettleton's fault anyway for introducing him to Thistlewood in the first place. Then again, Nettleton had tried to warn him later on and he had ignored that warning, but Jack had been far from ingenuous about the real nature of Thistlewood's political ideas and aspirations. To be fair, perhaps Jack did not know them. Perhaps he had been deceived too.

Truelock led the way down the stairs, Bellingham was second, Walsh followed behind. They emerged into the sunlight still in single file, passed through the entrance to the court and climbed into a waiting carriage. Bellingham was sandwiched between the two men. They were both large in their own way: Truelock fat and Walsh bulky with muscle. Bellingham found himself perched on the front of the seat, squeezed forward as the other two leant backward. The curtains were drawn across the carriage windows. Bellingham felt nervous. He was wringing his hands and breathing deeply. His anxiety was obvious. Truelock drew something from his pocket and passed it to Bellingham. Bellingham took the piece of paper and unfolded it. It was a printed leaflet coloured by hand. It read:

Three hundred years ago a PHILOSOPHER sayed, that the stars give the day-light.

One hundred years ago, a PHILOSOPHER proves to the publick that the SUN give the day-light, and without the rise of the SUN there was no day-light.

One thousand eight hundred and twelve years ago, the PROPHITS rote the LAW, which was the Gospel and said, that Christ was born of the Virgin Mary and walked on the face of the earth that groes weat, oats, beens and barley.

Now, a PROPHIT rises, and says he will prove to the publick that Christ will appear out of the dark soul of the PROPHIT, ware in he stands to give light and be delivered out of the PROPHIT'S mouth.

The same is the two-edged SWORD which is Christ; the same is the Son of God, the same is the TRUTH, the same is a new dockterin, the same is a new revelation, for all the world; the same is Christ and his true and living PROPHIT Saturn, in him, whom, Christ is well pleased,

Bannister Truelock
Mad Man

Truelock watched Bellingham intently as he read the pamphlet. He reacted to Bellingham's every movement. A raising of the eyebrows and Truelock held his breath. A frown and Truelock's mouth drooped.

Bellingham finished and turned to Truelock. He was surprised to see Truelock staring wide-eyed at him. He did not know what to say. 'What did you think?' asked Truelock breathlessly. 'Did you like it?'

'I've never seen anything quite like it before,' said Bellingham tentatively.

'If you're interested in my life's work, I've got lots more,' Truelock's beady eyes began to blaze with passion. 'The time is fast approaching when all these things will be fulfilled: the flaming lions of Judah will be seen on Mount Sion and the angels will open the gates of Jerusalem. Albion's days are numbered and the two-edged sword will lead the hosts of Virgins against the Antichrists of Popery and Monarchy.

'Do you like the way it's coloured? I mean, can you understand the scheme – why it is that the prophet is blue and the law is red – or not? Is it clear, do you think? I'd value your opinion.

'I have been with child for twenty-five years,' said Truelock, switching back to his declamatory style. He puffed his chest out as if to show his importance and his pregnancy. 'The Messiah will soon be born from my mouth, and all things will come to pass. In your history, the Bible, it is mentioned that a prophet will rise. Now, I am that prophet spoken of; the Messiah will be produced from my mouth in spirit, not in fleshly substance, as was the case with Christ Jesus.'

'You're shouting, Truelock,' said Walsh. 'Don't shout.'

'Forgive me, Walsh. I was getting carried away.' Truelock made a face and leant close to Bellingham. He whispered, 'Would you like to see my proofs? I'll show them to you later if we get the chance. There are seventy-eight signs in all, and my comments on them. When they are published they will bring people to the light. They were to be published once, but the authorities censored my opus – indeed, in the commentary on the thirty-seventh sign, I predicted that they would. But soon the light will shine forth from my mouth and the scales shall fall from their blind eyes. The rich shall be laid low and the poor raised up. Antichrist will be destroyed and will perish in the lake of fire, and Albion shall be no more.' Truelock winked at Bellingham. Bellingham smiled. Truelock nudged him. Bellingham smiled.

'I know what you're thinking,' said Truelock. 'You're thinking, what about the New Testament, the new revelation of God's will, aren't you?' Bellingham nodded, happy not to have to contribute any further to this extremely confusing conversation. He looked at Walsh, but Walsh was staring straight ahead. He looked back at Truelock.

'The Bible is a vulgar and indecent history. It does not contain one solid or sensible argument. As for the New Testament itself, it is merely a falsehood and a deception devised by the Pope and his Cardinals to achieve their material and wicked aims. I mean, what price is celibacy to pay for wealth and power beyond your wildest dreams? I take no notice of the Bible except, perhaps, to revel in its glorious absurdity or laugh at the scale of the hoax. I ask you, what good has the Church ever done for anyone? Protestants and Catholics alike, centuries of oppression, blood-letting, and still, fundamentally, for most of us nothing has ever changed. We must be patient. The day is approaching. It will come soon. It will come soon.' Truelock sat back in his seat. Bellingham leant forward. At the beginning he had thought he was meant to participate in the conversation, but now, much to his relief, he realized that he had merely been a captive audience. The carriage rumbled along rutted roads.

Walsh and Truelock made a great show of blind-folding him when they arrived at their destination, but the cloth they used was thin, and Bellingham could see through it darkly. From the smell he knew they must be close to the river. The building was a derelict warehouse, set apart from surrounding buildings and accessible only from a narrow side-street. They had not travelled far. Bellingham guessed they were in Wapping.

Thistlewood eyed Truelock warily. Truelock was bent over the table studying a large drawing. He bit nervously at the tip of his left index finger. His brow was creased. He looked worried. So did Thistlewood. Worry, anxiety and strained silence prevailed. Thistlewood sighed loudly. Truelock shot him a glance. Thistlewood shrugged and Truelock returned to his contemplation. After a while Truelock said, 'I think it's this way up.' He oriented the map through one hundred and eighty degrees.

'I know which way up it should be,' said Thistlewood through clenched teeth. 'The long poles on top? They're on top.' Truelock failed to respond to Thistlewood's heavy sarcasm. Thistlewood was tired of Truelock's pretence. 'You don't know how it works, do you?' Truelock did not respond. 'Do you?' He shouted. Truelock jumped.

'No,' said Truelock. He hung his head, shamefaced.

'Do they?' asked Thistlewood, pointing towards the engine room.

'They built it, so I suppose they know how to use it,' Truelock said doubtfully.

'Get one of them in here,' barked Thistlewood. 'I want to hear it from the horse's mouth.'

Truelock nodded and hurried off to find someone. Thistlewood sat down and put his head in his hands. He was struck by the fact that he had absolutely no control over the situation. He did not know why they had built the machine. He did not understand how it worked. He did not know *if* it worked. The entire strategy seemed unconnected with reality. He tried to remember whose idea it had been, but he could not recall who first mentioned the Influencing Engine. He was gripped by an almost overwhelming urge to leave, to walk away from this hellish mess. Either that or hurt someone. Hurting someone would probably do the trick. Hitting them in the face with a stick or maybe just humiliating them in some way. The mere thought of unprovoked violence perked Thistlewood up considerably.

Truelock returned and ushered someone into the room. Thistlewood recognized him; he had seen him round about the place. He was one of the senior engineers, an operator. Truelock did not wait to be dismissed before he pulled the door shut behind him. The engineer stood by the door. He was dressed all in black. His clothes seemed to be in tatters, but on closer inspection it could be seen that he was wearing a pleated academic gown on top of black trousers and black coat. His chest was bare.

'You wanted to see me, sir.' The engineer shuffled, unsure of himself. He was a young man. He hardly seemed old enough for such a responsible position. Thistlewood did not remember hiring him. He would not have employed someone so young.

'Yes, I did want to see someone. What's your name?'

'They call me the Rook, sir, or the Don.'

'Very well, Don, tell me about this machine we've spent so much time, effort and money building. Tell me how it works. Tell me what it can do.' Thistlewood leant forward expectantly.

The Don was an enthusiastic speaker. He started nervously but quickly found his feet. He moved about the room, eventually arriving at the table and using the drawing to illustrate his lecture.

He began, obscurely enough, by recounting the

strange tale of a group of priests in ancient Egypt and their struggle to wrest control of the state from the Pharoahs. After physical insurrection ended in disaster and mass executions they took their struggle underground and formed a secret society dedicated to the promotion of their ideas and with the aim of placing its members at the heart of government unbeknownst to their enemies. The strategy was only partially successful, and the society was in danger of discovery on many occasions. Until, that is, the arrival of one particular priest, a master of mathematics recently humiliated and removed from his post as chief astrologer to the pharaoh. This priest had an idea, a bold idea, a dangerous idea, a magnificent idea. Within a few short months, he promised his co-conspirators, they would occupy the seat of power, without opposition or excessive bloodshed. History recorded that, before the year was out, the faction of the Lower Nile had swept to power. History, however, does not record how this coup was achieved. In order to be in possession of such privileged information one needed to be a member of that secret society, a society that still exists: the Pneumatic Chemists.

Thistlewood watched the Don carefully. The tale was quite fantastic already, and it was clear the narrator was only warming up. Thistlewood considered whether this man was an out-and-out lunatic or simply a gullible twit who liked good stories. On the other hand, it did no harm to listen, and eventually he would explain the function of the engine. Thistlewood fidgeted with the papers on the desk. The Don noted his employer's impatience and hurried quickly on.

In spite of its public success the society remained secret, its ceremonies and rituals known only to the few who had access to its inner circles. Its structure and hierarchy were hidden and its secrets jealously guarded, so that situation obtained for century after century.

The vaguest rumours leaked to the outside world of a powerful sect that secretly controlled the actions of every government, that subverted the right of citizens and nations to any form of self-determination and turned even the strongest empire's policies to serve its own ends. And then suddenly, without warning, the Pneumatic Chemists began to break cover. Perhaps they saw in the revolutions and wars that were shaking Europe to its core an opportunity to tighten their grip and consolidate their power. Perhaps, after all these centuries, their influence had waned and they sought to rebuild their power base. Whatever the reason, all over Europe drawings like the one on Thistlewood's table had started to appear about two decades ago. The sketches were far from complete, and the mysteries of the machine contained in books full of arcane symbols and hieroglyphics were for those with the scholarship, the hunger and the patience, merely games to be solved. There was a world to win.

The Don was quite flushed by now. He was smiling broadly and looked for all the world like a Methodist convert sworn off the drink and proclaiming the Gospel on a street corner. Such was the Don's fervour and, Thistlewood felt, his distance from the earth.

Catching the look in Thistlewood's eye, the Don changed his tone and adopted a more technical approach to the subject. He explained that the Influencing Engine was more properly known by its ancient name, the Air Loom. Its function was twofold: to make its victim, through manipulation of the body's fluids and its natural magnetic properties, receptive to the power of the Engine. These twin aims were achieved by the vibration of magnetic impregnations and could be conducted by skilled operators close up or at a distance of several hundred yards.

The Engine was powered by a powerful combination of electricity and natural products: male and female seminal fluid, effluvia of copper and sulphur, vapours of vitriol and aqua fortis, deadly nightshade and garlic in equal parts, the effluvia of dogs and, most important, the essence of putrid effluvia and of mortification and plague, the refined stench of a cesspool, preferably piped directly into the mixture and allowed to percolate through, gas from the anus of a stallion and human gas, Egyptian snuff, which was absolutely essential, arsenic vapour and effluvia, the poison from a poisonous toad and the crushed petals of white roses and red carnations. Naturally the mixing and brewing of this heady cocktail – quite apart from procuring the ingredients – was an expert job and had been the most difficult part of the process to master. Too much of one ingredient or too little of another and the engine would not function. Worse still, the concoction would ferment and the barrel explode with such violence, and releasing such an overwhelming stench, that anybody within fifty feet was overcome immediately and died drowning in the filthy gases. They had been forced to dump many thousands of pints into the Thames over the past two years, and surgeons still argued over the cause of death of the bloated, green-tinged corpses discovered along the riverbank during the same period.

However, the Don assured Thistlewood, the Engine was ready to test on a human subject. Tests conducted on animals had proved inconclusive, and they were not at all sure the Engine was designed to be used on any creature except human beings.

The procedure was simple in theory and uniquely complex in reality. The first stage, the most essential to the whole operation, was to attune the machine to the wavelength of the test subject's brain. This was achieved through a sequence of test bursts, the results of which were compiled and recorded by the terminal operators in front of the Engine. By firing bursts across a spectrum of wavelengths a mean could be calculated and the Engine fine-tuned to its victim. This increased the chances of a successful inpregnation and, though laborious, was well worth the effort.

Once the subject had been isolated, the next operation was to cut the soul from sense – in other words, to place a block between the emotions and the rational functions, to prevent the heart from communicating with the intellect. At this point the operator could begin the process of suggestion. The technique was called kiting and involved lifting into the brain the same idea time after time. The idea floated around the consciousness, virtually undetected, for hours on end, like a kite undulating in the currents of the intellect. Whatever the victim thought of, he was led invariably back to this one kited thought. The victim was always aware that the thought was extraneous to his thought process, and this made the idea more forceful, appealing with the power of a vision or a sudden insight.

These two functions formed the day-to-day operations of the Engine as it quietly worked away to serve the interests of the operator. In the unlikely event of discovery or, more commonly, when a secret assassination was required, the operator had a variety of techniques available to him. He could choose to elongate the brain and thus render the victim insane by making all serious matters ridiculous or lock the victim's fluids and thus impede his speech by building up fibre at the root of the tongue. If more extreme measures were called for, Lobster-cracking or Bomb-bursting were the favoured techniques. The first was a manipulation of the external pressure of the magnetic atmosphere, and its horrendous effects were akin to the cracking of a lobster's shell: circulation stagnated and the body's vital motions were arrested. Death was the inevitable result. Bomb-bursting achieved a similar result through opposite means. The internal gases and fluids of the body were rarefied and refined until they became inflammable, causing the victim to combust spontaneously or explode internally. A horrid crash was heard in the head and blood poured from every orifice. The practice was usually fatal.

The Don finished. He looked drained. Thistlewood, on the other hand, was stunned and not a little incredulous. He pondered the engineer's words for a moment or two before making any kind of reply.

He had had no idea the machine was quite so powerful or that its uses were so varied. Then it struck him that perhaps they were not the only people in possession of such a device. The Don confirmed that many rival gangs had acquired the technology and the plans, which had been widely distributed. It was possible others either had the secret or were close. The news was bad. Thistlewood had long been concerned at the sheer number of revolutionary groups competing for recruits, striving to outdo each other in the ambitiousness of their plans. If the Engine were to remain Thistlewood's weapon, his advantage over his rivals, he must make use of it almost immediately. The possibilities, of course, were limitless – the opportunity to control any group or individual within his sphere of influence not just with the fact of the machine but with the mere suggestion of its existence and its terrible capabilities. The engineers themselves would have to be tightly controlled and extremely well paid. If they became over-ambitious, the situation could quickly turn against Thistlewood, and he could find himself cracked open like a lobster. He fixed the young engineer with his fiercest eye. 'And you can guarantee me that it will work exactly as you've explained?' The engineer squirmed beneath Thistlewood's gaze. Suddenly lost for words, the loquacious man could only nod his head. 'One other thing,' said Thistlewood.

'Where did you come across the plans for the Influencing Engine?'

'I was given them,' said the Don evasively.

'Where? By whom?'

'It happened like this,' began the Don.

'No more stories, thank you,' said Thistlewood sharply. He was fed up with tales of secret societies and ancient books. 'Just the facts, please.'

'My cousin's friend's sister's fiancé introduced me to a man. He would not give his name, but he told me he was a Pneumatic Chemist. He told me all I've told you and he gave me a copy of the drawing and the books of instructions. When we'd got it to a viable stage, we contacted you through Bannister, and that's it.' The Don stopped rather abruptly, afraid he had already said far too much.

'You met a man who gave no name, introduced to you by a total stranger?'

'Yes.'

'What did he look like?'

'It was dark.'

'I see.' Thistlewood remained silent for some time.

The young man did not know what to do, whether to leave or stay. He waited a moment or two longer. 'Is it off?' asked the Don. 'Is it cancelled?'

Thistlewood lifted his head, leant on the table and placed his fingertips together. 'Of course it's not cancelled. We might as well see if it works. What have we got to lose?'

Bellingham's oscillating had all but ceased. He and the chair swayed back and forth gently. Below him there was a flurry of activity that absorbed his attention. A chain of men ferried buckets of slop to the barrels. Another group was huddled over the table of figures. They looked from their arcane symbols to Bellingham. They pointed and discussed matters in hushed voices. They disputed and argued, they made calculations and measured distances and angles. The barrels began to bubble; lids were quickly placed on them and the foul fumes were sealed off. The machine itself began to rattle and shake. The drawers opened and closed of their own volition, releasing steam and noxious-smelling gases. A breeze from somewhere dispersed the gases. A slight hum started and grew louder and louder until it filled the entire room and vibrated everything and everyone in it.

A young man, a black gown flapping about him in the breeze, approached the operator's seat. He pushed the gown behind him and sat on the stool. He placed his feet on the pedals and took a firm grip on the two paddles either side of him.

Two other men, in white overalls, took up positions in front of the Engine, one at the screens, the other at the table with the books. Meanwhile, behind the Engine other people took up positions lying down on the floor to the right and left, holding bags of tools and spare parts.

The noise and the wind increased, and as they seemed to reach their peak the man at the machine began to operate the paddles. He pushed them up and down alternately; when one was up, the other was down. He started slowly but quickly picked up speed. The sweat stood out on his forehead, ran down his nose and neck. Great damp patches formed under his armpits. He pumped faster and faster and faster, all the while working the pedals with his feet. Gradually the humming changed pitch. It rose higher and higher. A new sound joined the whining of the Engine. Barely discernible at first amid the clanging and clanking of the machinery, the hissing of the gas and the bubbling liquid, after a while it rang out confidently. A sweet counter-tenor voice. The man at the machine sang as he worked.

'As through Moorfields I walked one evening in the
    spring,
I heard a maid in Bedlam, most sweetly she did sing.
She wrung her hands and tore her hair and thus
    exclaimèd she,
I love my love because I know my love loves me.
If I was a swallow I'd lie upon his breast,
Or if I was a nightingale I'd sing my love to rest.'

Bellingham did not feel foolish any more, and his
fear had shrunk to easily manageable proportions.
His main reaction now was curiosity. From his position
in the sky he felt as if he were observing some strange
play performed solely for his benefit. He tried to
find meaning in the actions of the people below him
but could not. Their movements were mysterious
and ritualistic. Their sense of expectation created a
dynamic and exciting tension in the room. Bellingham
was amazed but could not get away from the thought
that they really believed the contraption was going to
do something, that their labour would bear fruit. Their
behaviour went beyond irrationality and bordered on
the mystical. The only experience that was in any sense
comparable was the time he had attended an Orthodox
Catholic mass in St Petersburg. The simplicity of faith
and superstition combined, the ritual, the stink, the
singing even – everything reminded him of that mass.
He had felt similarly aloof and observant then too.

He had wandered into the church to give thanks for
his release after two years of gaol and house arrest. His
movements no longer restricted. Free to go wherever
he pleased, the charges dismissed. The ceremony was
completely alien to him: The priests' enormous beards,
uniformly streaked black and grey it seemed to him,
the lavish decorations, the extravagant gestures of the
congregation as they crossed themselves time and again
and intoned the declarations of their faith and their

contrition. Bellingham gave thanks to God because, in truth, he did not know whom else to thank, but even this small celebration was misplaced. Within a few months he was in gaol once more and stayed there a further three and a half years.

He wondered whether it was that incident that had destroyed what little faith he had in prayer or divinity. Certainly until very recently he had not been near a church or thought once to pray. Back then it had been a powerful sense of being there, of being alive, that had prompted his thoughts to turn towards the Almighty; now it was a sense of mortality and impending doom that directed his mind to a contemplation of eternity. Now, as then, he was not able to muster much enthusiasm or concentration. He was inclined to believe, with Tom Paine, that his mind was his only church. Practically the only thing that Bellingham retained from his church-bound youth (his mother had been a committed churchgoer, his father, alas, simply committed) was a profound sense of his own guilt and the Almighty's omniscience. In his young mind life was reduced to a series of trade-offs and calculated risks. If he was good, his life would proceed untrammelled by tragedy or disfigured by failure, but the more evil deeds he perpetrated, the worse it would be for him later on. If he lied to his mother or to a friend, he could expect swift retribution. Every mishap, every accident that befell him he could attribute to this or that sin committed earlier that day or the day before. Lying was bad; skipping his chores was bad but not as bad as lying. But the worst sin of all was masturbation. If he took any pleasure in himself, while not actually anticipating being hit by a thunderbolt he could expect disaster to strike. The sin of Onan was a calculated risk. If he needed good luck on a particular day, if he had a favour to ask of his mother or even if he just wanted the weather to stay fine, he had to restrain his hands and curb his lusts. In the same way that he read the Bible, looking for hidden predictions of the future, he saw his own fate as directly linked to his moral conduct. He hated himself for such irrational beliefs but found them difficult to reject.

As he watched from his vaulted position Bellingham saw that the room was emptying and those remaining who were not directly involved in the machine's functions were hiding themselves behind makeshift metal screens. They peered through tiny slits, eager to see what would happen next.

The man at the paddles was singing an aria from Handel's *Messiah*, his treble voice wobbling and failing as his physical exertions increased. He was pumping the paddles furiously now. Up, down. Up, down. Up, down.

Jack Nettleton could hear singing. Even above the whining of the windmill and the loud humming that seemed to fill the air he could distinctly hear singing. A high voice, like a choir boy's, only strained and eerie-sounding. It gave him the shivers. Not that he had been at his ease beforehand, being back in the room where Thistlewood had compelled him to strike the bargain. The same room, still smelling of sweat and urine. The battered and broken chair still in the corner. His own blood, dried dark brown, stained the dirty floor. And that giant windmill turning and turning.

They were keeping him waiting. Why did betrayal have to be so inconvenient? Why couldn't he just take the money and run? As much as anything else he was afraid of being double-crossed. On top of that he was afraid he would find out what they were doing to Bellingham. That was the last thing he wanted, to see the results of his treachery.

Treachery. It sounded so melodramatic, so final, a judgement. Yet Jack did not feel like a traitor. He was not proud of his behaviour. He was disgusted with himself, but he did not hate himself so much as that. He did not feel he deserved all the blame. The circumstances were difficult; the situation was complex. The only outcome that was certain was his death or mutilation if he failed to come through with the goods. He would challenge anybody to act any different. The money was neither here nor there. It was a sweetener, an inducement, but it had not been a deciding factor in the decision. On the other hand, it would be nice to have the money. It would be nice to get out of that hellish place with its odd noises and phantasmal singing. Apart from anything else Jack needed to relieve himself. He had consumed far too much Dutch courage waiting for Walsh and Truelock to turn up. By the time they did he was practically on his knees. He had thought he might have to go and point Bellingham out, kiss him on the cheek or something equally biblical, but apparently it was all over and they had come to take him to his reward.

He had sobered up considerably waiting in the room, but he was desperate. If they did not come soon, he would have to piss up the wall. For some reason Jack thought he was better than that. He realized the singing had stopped.

Stillwater was restless. Not that anybody who happened to pass his window and look in would have known. They would have seen a grey, featureless man standing perfectly still and staring out into the street. The unobservant might have mistaken him for a tailor's dummy. Those inclined to pity might have taken him for a melancholic; others, of more romantic bent, for a poet engaged in some meditation of love won and lost. Anyone who knew Stillwater, and there were precious few cunning or deceitful enough to do that, would have been amazed at his agitated state. His fingers drummed against his thigh. His eyes blinked. His cheek twitched. Stillwater, they might conclude, was very disturbed. Indeed he was. For that day was the first time his father had spoken to him in twenty years.

As Stillwater watched, the blue skies began to cloud over. The clouds approached from the west and the grey sky, spread like a cloth behind the buildings, gave the scene a two-dimensional look. It was as if he were looking at a painted backdrop. A light breeze stirred the treetops. A storm was coming.

'Remember this,' his father had said, just as if he were standing next to him. A quiet voice, deep and un-wavering, an authoritative voice.

Stillwater turned from the window to contemplate his father's portrait on the wall above the fireplace. It showed the old boy impassive and controlled as always, standing stiff-backed, his arm leaning on the very mantelpiece above which his likeness was now hung. He thought about his father's injunction to remember.

A paternal arm around his shoulder, the smell of new-cut grass, the sun on his back. Founder's Day, Stillwater recalled. He was fourteen years old. Almost a man. His father would not touch him like that again. He remembered the weight of his arm and the scent of his father's sweat. Hot and close, musty, acrid. He had been startled by the strength of that smell, startled by its manliness, by its sexuality.

'Henry, my boy, I want you to remember this.' His father did not look at him. He addressed the horizon, and Stillwater looked up into his father's face, dazzled by the sunshine. 'There are only two things worth fighting for in this world. Family and king. To fight for your family is an animal instinct. Anyone would fight for their family, it's natural. But it takes something very special to fight for the king. Now, I don't mean the king himself. I don't mean George the Third or the

Fourth or whoever follows him. Without the House of Hanover there would still be a monarchy. Without the monarchy there would not be an England. At least, not our England. Do you understand, Henry?'

The boy did not understand but was too ashamed to admit the fact. He could not disappoint his father. He remained silent and listened as the lecture continued. 'The job of protecting England and her empire from those who would destroy her ancient values, who would subvert her way of life, is a difficult one. Subversion is not just a matter of bearing arms against the sovereign. Treachery and subversion, while they are similar, are not the same, though, it must be said, one does lead quite naturally to the other.

'Subversion is a matter of loyalty, a matter of the heart. People who show any affinity towards the republican movement or Catholicism – these people are suspect. That's just plain common sense. Their aspirations are not the State's aspirations. Their religion is not the State's religion. Their values are different. By the same token, all those who decry marriage and family life, those who try to destroy the fabric of our society – squatters, the able-bodied poor, those who advocate homosexuality, indiscipline in schools or those who oppose capital punishment, anyone who encourages the education of working people and universal male suffrage – these and a whole gamut of people and attitudes like them are pecking away at the foundations of our society and weakening it.

'It is right that these people should come under our scrutiny; that the State should, for the good of the vast peaceful, normal majority, make sure that these people never gain influence over our way of life, over our lawmakers or over our children. In order to do this the State must exert a greater, more powerful influence. And that is my job, son. I influence people. Remember this, Henry. Let it guide you.'

173

The idea for the Influencing Engine had taken root in his child's mind that very day. He imagined his father striding the land, buffeting people with his Influence, bringing them roughly, rudely, against their will, to heel. England's saviour. A kind of Excalibur and King Arthur in a tricorn hat. A part of him still responded to that image of untarnished heroism. Recalling it could still make him proud of what his father had achieved.

Stillwater could sense his father's disappointment from beyond the grave. It was true, he had failed to fulfil expectations; he had never succeeded the way his father had succeeded.

The world, however, was a very different place. His father had been slow to see the consequences of industrialization, of mechanization. The old certainties of class and title, the strict divisions that kept society so neatly ordered, no longer applied. Society had become fluid and mobile. People no longer remained in the parish of their birth until their death. A peasant no longer saw any reason why he should not be as rich as a lord. Belief in God and the Church and the rewards of the afterlife were no longer enough to hold people back; they clamoured for education and opportunity. They demanded their say in the running of the country. Democracy was coming. Its arrival might be delayed, but it could not be stopped. Like a creeping paralysis, like a draft of hemlock, it impinged first on the edges, spreading towards the centre, and when it reached the heart . . .

The Influencing Engine was supposed to have delayed that gradual erosion of privilege. He and James Tilly Matthews had devised it as a preventive measure. Stillwater explained its action as akin to a sponge's. The Influencing Engine, the idea of it, placed in a revolutionary or insurrectionary group, would soak up every last resource of energy, imagination and

174

money. In return it would provide them with nothing, except perhaps death.

Matthews and he had attempted to create something incredible that was just the right side of believable. They hoped it would attract revolutionaries the same way alchemy attracted scientists. The Influencing Engine was a short-cut to power, guaranteed to turn base radicals into governments.

Stillwater had been proud of their scheme. It was extravagant and audacious, the culmination of his childhood fantasies, the ultimate counter-revolutionary tool. His father, he knew, would not have approved.

It had been Tilly's idea to create the Pneumatic Chemists, a fictional secret society that would provide the fictional Engine with an ancient provenance. He combined elements from a whole host of other societies: the Knights Templar, the Carbonari, the Russian Castrators and the Freemasons. He based the scientific aspects of the Engine's function on mesmerism (a popular 'science' based on the manipulation and control of man's inate animal magnetism). A heady mixture of Egyptian mythology and pre-Newtonian science. Tilly wrote reams about the Pneumatic Chemists.

Stillwater, meanwhile, expanded the scope of his idea. He planned to disseminate his false propaganda across the whole of continental Europe. Using Paris as a base, he could saturate the myriad radical groups spawned by the revolution in France with information about the Pneumatic Chemists and the Influencing Engine. He wanted to engage every insurrectionary group, every secret society and religious sect, every ideologue and power-seeker, in the race to build the Engine. In the pursuit of the chimerical Engine they would dissipate their energy, discredit their intellect and, finally, be destroyed.

Matthews, disguised as an emissary of the Pneumatic

Chemists, set off for Paris. He spent many years under cover as a tea merchant, infiltrating radical groups and establishing the credibility of Pneumatic Chemistry.

Ironically Matthews survived the most turbulent years of the revolution without coming to much harm. He was imprisoned by the Jacobins for his adherence to mesmerism, condemned as an aristocratic, pre-revolutionary indulgence, but beyond that he emerged unscathed. Stillwater struggled to persuade Matthews to stay in England – they could complete their plan by correspondence, he argued – but Matthews disagreed. He needed to be in Paris; without his presence the scheme had no hope. Reluctantly, Stillwater let Matthews go back.

Stillwater never discovered the truth of what happened to Matthews on his final trip to Paris, but the James Matthews whom Stillwater had known since schooldays, the dashing, brave young Tilly, never returned home. In his place came a mad man, raving about betrayal and secret pacts, about Pneumatic Chemists and traitors in the highest places. Matthews had become uncontrollable. The scene he made at the club was unforgettable.

Wild-eyed and ragged, Matthews had burst into the dining room shrieking at the top of his lungs. Dinner suits had scattered and Brown Windsor splattered as Matthews launched himself on to the table. He walked its entire length, kicking aside candlesticks, tureens and glasses until he stood above Stillwater. He levelled his finger at his former schoolfriend and associate and shouted, 'You! You are the Middle Man. You are a traitor!'

Stillwater took it all very calmly. He tried to placate Matthews, but there was nothing to be done. The man was a lunatic, plain and simple. Over the following weeks he repeated his accusations in Parliament, yelling them from the Strangers' Gallery. He accused

Stillwater of the foulest acts. It was unbearable. Matthews had to be stopped. By rights he should have disposed of him, but Stillwater could not bring himself to sanction the assassination. Instead Matthews was incarcerated in Bedlam, and, as Stillwater knew to his cost, he was still there and still as mad and bitter as the day he came back from France.

Tilly's wife died shortly after his committal to Bedlam. The cause of death was registered officially as a broken heart. Stillwater thought it possible. She left her two infant children in the care of their godfather, Stillwater. He made sure they were well cared and provided for, and despite himself and the distance he endeavoured to maintain, he had grown very fond of Elizabeth and Caroline.

It had ended in disaster, then, the great enterprise that Matthews and Stillwater had begun.

Sixteen years had passed since Matthews's return from Paris. Sixteen years, during which hardly a day went by when Stillwater did not blame Matthews for the collapse of their plan. Stillwater fingered the scar on his cheek.

It had destroyed Stillwater's career, of course. He had been moved from a window desk to a room without natural light. He was isolated from the real centre of things, cut off from power, condemned as a maverick and a failure.

He was charged with creating a network of informers and infiltrators, but he was not trusted with running them. He had devised a system of recruiting *agents provocateurs* and informers from among convicts and debtors that proved so successful he was in danger of becoming redundant. He was old and slow. He was forgotten by his colleagues. He was marginalized and ignored. But Stillwater was far from defeated.

He may have been pushed to the sidelines, but that only worked in his favour. His colleagues were less discreet in his presence; he was able to gather information without trying.

Thistlewood had come to his attention in just such a way. He was working late one night (sorting through the Prime Minister's post, looking for potential subversives and threatening letters) when a young man came into his room and perched on the edge of the desk. 'Just thought you'd like to know, old boy,' the young man began, smirking, 'that your conspiracy has finally started to pay off.'

Stillwater was amazed that anybody remembered. The young man handed him a note from one of his informers. Thistlewood, an agitator and known subversive, was in possession of the plans to a fantastic and dangerous machine called an Influencing Engine. Stillwater smiled. 'What do you intend to do about it?' he asked the young man.

'Absolutely nothing. We thought you might like to handle it,' the young man said as he left.

Stillwater rose from his seat, and as he did so he heard guffaws of laughter from the other office. He crumpled the note in his hand, but he did not forget it.

Stillwater funded Thistlewood's construction of the Influencing Engine from government funds. Apart from anything else he was curious to see what would happen when Thistlewood tried to make it work.

He noticed that his grandfather's clock had stopped.

Bellingham was overcome by the most extraordinary sensation. It began with fear. He was enveloped in a cloud of steam and gas. It smelt dreadful but very familiar; it smelt like the Thames.

The gas poured into his lungs. It was warm. He felt as if he were drowning. He struggled and gulped for air. He tried to free his hands. He rocked and squirmed and struggled in the chair, which twisted and turned in response. Suddenly he realized that he was not suffocating. A strange feeling developed in the pit of his stomach. An expansiveness, not unlike very bad wind, but changing into a massive adrenaline rush that accelerated through his body. Dizzy, disoriented, elated, he imagined he was flying. And as he looked down between his dangling feet the clouds of smoke dispersed and he saw the ground rushing past him. Green meadows and yellow wheat fields, forests and woods, mountains and hills, rivers twisting and converging. He felt the wind against his face and the moisture of the clouds as he was carried at tremendous speed over the landscape of England. Before he could grasp what was happening, as his vision adjusted to his flight, the cloud smothered him once more and he found himself swinging, confined to his chair.

A few seconds later and his eyelids were heavy. A profound tiredness swept over him and he closed his eyes. When he opened them he found himself back at his first school in the postmaster's house, watching his friend Thomas read haltingly from the Bible. The boy's grazed knees shook in his short pants and he looked round in panic. Thomas saw a big word approaching, perhaps several big words in a row. He was desperate and afraid. The postmaster's instrument of learning, a long hazel switch, whistled in the air as it anticipated a lesson. Thomas was struggling to continue and hold back his tears. His classmates looked at each other with a mixture of relief and glee, but none of them would meet his eye. Then a miracle. The postmaster stopped Thomas before he got to the difficult passage. His duty fulfilled, Thomas beamed with delight. The remainder of the class cowered and stared at the floor, each one expecting and dreading the light tap on the shoulder that would seal their fate.

The tap fell on a young boy sitting near the back and staring out of the window. He was pale and distracted.

His blue eyes shone light and clear. The boy moved to the centre of the room and picked up the Bible. The postmaster indicated for him to carry on where Thomas had left off. 'And then shall the end come. When ye therefore shall see the abomination of desolation . . .' The boy read with confidence, but the words did not emerge from his mouth the way he intended. A pained and puzzled expression crept over his face as he realized that the way he heard the words in his head was not the way anybody else heard them. The switch whistled through the air and the boy yelped. His classmates laughed, nervous and above all else thankful it was not them this time.

He had not thought about that incident for decades. What made it invade his consciousness at this moment? He remembered his humiliation, the sheer injustice of it all. He was a good student. He always found time to con his lessons. Yet he was an unpopular boy. The postmaster disliked him. His fellow pupils were merely indifferent to his presence in the classroom and actively hostile to his participation in their games. He and Thomas had usually ended up together plotting their revenge on their persecutors.

The clouds obscured his view of the weeping boy and his jeering classmates. The rope that held him suspended began to creak as the chair spun round and round.

They had made the boat together, he and his father. He could not remember very much that they did do together, but the boat was a triumph. A tiny craft carved from an old chair leg. Its bottom was flat, the front end pointed and the rear end square. Bow and stern were terms he learned later during his less than illustrious naval career. For now it was enough that the piece of wood in some way resembled a boat. A rounded piece of wood was jammed into a hole gouged out of the boat's centre. A triangle of paper served as a sail. They

180

were proud of their handiwork, father and son. They took the boat in to show Mother. She nodded her approval. The boy's heart was bursting with pride. The pair of them set off to sail the boat on a nearby pond. The boy was dying for his neighbours and classmates to see him now, walking hand in hand with his father, the boat held proudly in front, its white sail snapping in the breeze.

He placed the boat on the still, dark water of the pond. It wobbled a little and then righted itself, its mast sticking straight up towards the blue sky. Father and son leant over the water, and together they gave the boat a little shove and launched it across the pond. To the little boy it might just as well have been the other side of the world, the other side of the pond seemed so far away. He set off in pursuit of his boat as fast as he could go. He circumnavigated bushes and trees, leapt over clumps of grass and mounds of earth, never taking his eyes off the boat, which continued on its precarious maiden voyage.

He seemed to lead a charmed existence. Instinctively his feet found firm ground when they needed it and carried him into the air to clear obstacles. The boy chortled with delight. His father watched, all worries and pressures for the time being forgotten. The sunlight on the water reflected in ripples on the green foliage. The boy careered on his way until the boat was in sight. It was becalmed, bobbing up and down a few feet from the shore. The boy looked for a stick but could not find one long enough. He threw pebbles to try to edge it nearer to his grasp. He stretched out, straining. He heard his father call out, and as he looked up he fell.

He slid into the water and as he dropped he saw a wave crash over the boat's bow and pull it, with him, down into the murky depths. He saw his breath leave his lungs in huge bubbles that rose quickly towards the sunlight. He saw plants and felt them brush against his skin and curl round his ankles. His breath was escaping in smaller and smaller bubbles and now the bubbles all but ceased. He did not struggle or flap his arms or legs. He had not the first notion of what to do in water or how one existed in the water. It was cold he thought, very cold. Then suddenly he felt his direction being reversed. A hand on his collar pulling him up and up until his head burst through the water and his grateful mouth opened to receive the air, and he coughed and spluttered and cried in his father's arms for their lost boat.

He was desperate. It was unbearable. He could not hold on any longer. It was impossible. He had to relieve himself. Jack stood in the corner and sighed as he emptied his bladder. The urine ran down the wall and trickled through his legs. Pale yellow and frothy with alcohol, it flowed copiously. The breeze generated by the nearby whirligig was pleasant against the back of his neck. He shuddered as a shiver went down his spine. His tensions drained away as his bladder drained. At last the final drops dripped to the floor, splashed on his boots and he tucked himself away inside his trousers. He turned in time to see the first trickle of his urine fall over the edge of the hole through which the whirligig protruded. There was a blue flash like lightning and an explosion that hurled Nettleton back against the wall and blew the doors off their hinges.

He was flying again. He felt the air rush against his cheeks. He was exhilarated as he plunged downwards. He barely had time to register that this time his flight was for real before he crashed on to the table below and came to rest on top of Patrick Walsh. A cushioned landing. The chair shattered on impact and Bellingham found himself sprawled on the floor, bruised but essentially unhurt.

All around him lay the wreckage of the machine and its operators. The floor of the cellar was covered in a thin film of viscous, foul-smelling fluid that stung the flesh, mingled with a light dusting of plaster from the cracked ceiling. In the middle, where the main body of the Engine had been, was a burnt-out, smouldering pile of wood, pipes and twisted metal topped by a kind of windmill with all four blades broken in two. As the clouds and dust began to clear he saw a face peering through a hole in the ceiling. It was Jack Nettleton. Despite the carnage and the extraordinary circumstances Bellingham was glad to see the young man was alive. He tried to call out but found his voice choked with the dust. He could only cough and splutter. And once he started coughing he found it difficult to stop. There was an acrid smell in the air, and his throat burned whenever he breathed in. Bellingham dragged himself to his feet. He caught a glimpse of daylight from across the cellar and staggered towards it. He passed three other bodies: two crushed by falling masonry and pierced by flying metal, the third unrecognizable, a bloody, battered corpse, the clothes torn from its back, which had clearly taken the full force of the explosion. Bellingham gritted his teeth and made straight for the light. There was a door, or what remained of a door, and behind it a room filled with pieces of paper blown about by the blast. Despite his anxiety to get away Bellingham stooped and picked up one of the pieces of paper. It was torn and singed and much of the writing was illegible, but some of it was readable.

We will build a society where all are free, where none are bound by chains to factories or ploughs, where all will work willingly for the greater glory of mankind and the state. There will be no crime, for none will go begging; none will starve, for all will provide. We will be free at last from the tyrannies of monarchy, aristocracy and industrialists. There will be no religion, for we shall have forged a paradise on earth. There will be no masters and slaves, no moneylenders, no lords and barons, no rich and poor. Such notions belong to the past. They are diseases that must be cut out, gaping wounds that must be cauterized. We will bleed this country until it is free of corruption. In order to build we must first destroy, and in order to destroy we must have faith in the vision that sustains us.

He crumpled the paper into a ball and threw it over his shoulder. He swept the chalky dust from his snuff-coloured coat and wiped the filth from his blue-striped breeches and his white stockings with the paper that lay strewn about him. He ran his hand through his hair, adjusted his cravat, took his watch from his waistcoat pocket and checked the time. Three o'clock.

In front of him was a door hanging from a single hinge. Beyond the door the daylight and steps leading up to the street. He saw something lying at his feet, covered in dust and partially hidden beneath sheets of paper and splinters of wood. He bent down and picked the object up. It was a pistol. He blew the dust off. It was new. The barrel glinted as it caught the sunlight. Gunmetal, cold and hard, there was nothing quite like it.

He heard footsteps behind him, someone panting for breath. The panting formed into a word. His name. He put the pistol in his coat pocket before he turned to see Nettleton clambering over the ruins towards him. Bellingham paused and let the young man catch up. As soon as Nettleton drew level Bellingham set off without saying a word. He strode purposefully forward and ascended the steps to street level two at a time. Nettleton almost had to jog to keep up with him.

They emerged into the sun-drenched city. A number of people had gathered on the street corner opposite the site of the explosion, but nobody did anything, nobody made any attempt to stop them or help them. They simply stood and watched as if they were waiting for someone to tell them what to do, as if independent action were impossible and collective inaction the only possible alternative. Bellingham ignored the helpless crowd and headed for the river.

Glittering in the afternoon sun, the Thames wove into view, twisting away east and west. For a time the river seemed to elude them, a sight of it tempting them down this or that dead-end street, winking at them for a second, then disappearing behind a warehouse. At last they found a route that took them riverside.

Nettleton always found the sight of the river breath-taking. Even now, dirty and stinking, a death river carrying disease as well as ships on its filthy waters, the mere sight of it filled him with awe. It was approaching low tide, and the stench was awful. A nearby jetty stretched out across the mud and just reached the water. A wherryman sat on the end of the pier, his feet dangling over the edge. He agreed to take them west.

Jack sat in the stern, facing the oarsman. Bellingham sat next to him and looked out over the water. Nettleton took Bellingham's silence for hatred. The stark facts of his betrayal shamed him. He craved absolution, but at the same time he was convinced it was not his fault. In any case it had all turned out all right. Bellingham was alive and largely unhurt, and he had escaped intact also. True, he did not have his money, but Nettleton regarded that as positive, as proof that he had not really betrayed his friend. The oarsman caught a crab and tumbled backwards. The wherry swayed and Jack clasped the sides tightly. The boat moved out further into the centre of the river, where the water was deeper, and turned towards Westminster. Bellingham did not speak.

TEN

PRIMROSE HILL

The sky darkened steadily from the west. Clouds moved swiftly over the face of the sun, bringing intermittent gloom. Bellingham hardly noticed. He lifted his gaze to stare out across the rooftops of London, and it struck him that the city was much smaller than he had imagined. From the top of Primrose Hill he could see where it began and where it ended. He could see that there were some places where it was not. Green spaces in its centre, like gaping holes in its heart. And at its fringes, though roads stretched out like grasping fingers, yet the city was bounded, circumscribed, limited. And he, Bellingham, stood outside its borders, beyond its reach. He could take it all in from the hill. By turning his head slowly from side to side he could see it all in panorama. Down there, in its streets, hemmed in by wood and stone, he sometimes felt there was no escape, that London was so vast, so powerful, it would devour him before a single scream could pass his lips. But standing in front of it now he realized that all he had to do was raise his hands in front of his eyes and London would disappear. He tried it. He blotted out the city with a single movement of his hand.

He kicked at the dirt. They say this is where they came to bury the victims of the Black Death. People gathered here to watch the Great Fire – standing on a mound of corpses, watching the city consume itself, watching the flames mount towards the skies and scythe through the buildings, leaving only smouldering desolation in their wake. Watching the streets fill with goods as people, astonished and scared out of their wits, desperately tried to save their chattels and their lives. Lavish furnishings and great paintings lying side by side in the road with crude tapestries and embroidered homilies, Persian rugs and singed rush mats. Everything burning, without discrimination: Mansion with slum and library with tavern. The king and his noblemen riding through the streets of their devastated city, unable to act, unable to offer the least relief or respite from the merciless flames and the air filled with smoke, the sun shining through it, a bloody, mocking red.

The weight of the pistol in his pocket stretched his jacket tight over his shoulders and tugged at the seams. He traced the route he had taken from the river and his eyes came to rest finally on Jack Nettleton as he toiled up the slope to join him.

'What kept you?' Bellingham asked Jack. 'A man your age should leap up here. You should take more exercise, Jack.'

'Is that some sort of joke?' Jack replied, panting, bent double to catch his breath. 'Have I been beaten, blown up and dragged halfway across London only to be accused of being lazy? Is that it?'

Bellingham did not reply. He turned his head away from Nettleton's red face and looked towards the city. Steeples pierced the horizon, the dome of St Paul's, the wedding-cake spire of St Bride's, the towers of Westminster, and, far beyond the shimmering Thames and its thumbnail traffic of ships and barges, the hills of Surrey almost lost in the heat haze. And ringing the city round, the black smoke belched from the brick kilns, drifting skywards, scarring the horizon.

The brickmakers, aiding and abetting the city in its ceaseless expansion.

'Beautiful,' gasped Nettleton, breath almost caught, as he joined Bellingham.

'Yes,' murmured Bellingham, his gaze fixed on the Palace of Westminster.

Not far below them, at the foot of the hill, carriages juddered silently along rutted tracks. A team of navvies dug trenches in a seemingly haphazard pattern. The musical clink of metal striking stone carried up to them on their lofty vantage.

'It'll be here soon, the city,' Bellingham said. 'It will blast and hack a road right through here. It'll cover the fields with its houses and fill the streams with its sewage. It'll chop down the trees to feed its fires and cover the earth with cobbles. It will take it all away.'

Nettleton said nothing. Bellingham turned away from the scene and walked to a sheltered spot near the brow of the hill. He sat on a tree stump and took the pistol out of his pocket. It was a neat fit in the inner pocket designed for valuables and papers. It slipped in there nicely, as if the pocket were tailor-made for it. He took the pistol out and weighed it in his right hand. The grip fitted snugly in his palm. He formed a fist round the handle and squeezed the pistol tight. He lifted the weapon to shoulder height and took aim, sighting down the barrel with his right eye. He extended his index finger and looped it round the trigger. 'Bang,' he said.

Nettleton sat on the dry, cracked earth and watched closely as Bellingham toyed with the pistol.

'How can you tell if it's loaded or not?' asked Bellingham. Jack shrugged his shoulders. Bellingham turned the gun round and squinted down the barrel. He tried to turn it into the light and still get a glimpse, but he could not manage it. He sniffed at the mouth of the barrel.

'I wouldn't do that if I were you,' said Nettleton.

Bellingham again raised the gun to shoulder height, clasped his left hand around his chest and under his armpit, as he had seen his father do once, to steady his aim. 'Bang,' he said.

Nettleton was gripped by a sudden anxiety that formed itself into a question: when you fire a bullet straight up into the air, where does it go? It had to come down somewhere. What if it got caught in a crosswind and blew over someone's head? If it dropped on them, would it kill them? Accelerating towards them at a rate of, say, sixty feet per second? From a height of what? Thirty feet? Further? There must be cases of people killed during victory celebrations when pistols were fired in the air, mustn't there?

The question obsessed him for a few minutes. His palms started sweating. He felt very peculiar, dizzy almost. He watched Bellingham fiddle with his pistol. He had never seen Bellingham with a weapon before, yet he handled it with confidence. With purpose.

'Bang! Bang!' shouted Bellingham. He wanted to pull the trigger. He wanted to know what it felt like to shoot a gun. His eagerness to fire the pistol shocked him. He was a man of principle. He believed passionately in the principle of justice. Yet here he was with a gun in his hand, itching to use it. Something had changed.

The internal debate he had conducted with himself on a daily basis for two years was over. Even the sound of his own voice in his head had fallen silent. There was a smell in the air. A charge. Like electricity. The sky darkened. Something was different.

The world around him appeared unchanged; the trees remained rooted to the earth, birds sat in their branches, grass fringed their roots, clouds crossed the sky above them and the sunlight pierced their leaves. His perception of the world had altered. The gun in his hand had become a prop, the landscape a backdrop. Perceval was transformed into a minor character in a wider drama.

Something had changed.

He caught a glimpse of Nettleton from the corner of his eye. Jack was sitting on the ground, his knees drawn up to his chin. He looked thoroughly miserable. He felt sorry for the young man. Nettleton was trapped in a predicament what was, entirely, not of his own making. Bellingham knew what it was to be robbed of choice. He had tried to extricate Nettleton.

After his first meeting with Thistlewood at the Shin and Bladebone in Limehouse, Bellingham had been filled with doubt. His misgivings stemmed entirely from his assessment of Thistlewood's character.

Thistlewood's brand of rigid, dogmatic certainty had its place, and Bellingham had thought at one point it might be useful to him in the pursuit of his claim. However, there was a wildness about Thistlewood that made Bellingham distrust the man. Even at his most desperate, when all avenues seemed closed to him, when he had tried every approach he could think of, he never seriously contemplated throwing in his lot with Thistlewood.

However, when Thistlewood wrote to him requesting a second meeting, Bellingham felt obliged to attend. He would take the opportunity to decline, politely, Thistlewood's services. He did not tell Jack about the meeting because he thought that he had involved Nettleton too deeply already and, more important, he had an idea that he could be of service to his friend.

Thistlewood requested an outdoor meeting in Holborn. Bellingham arrived at the appointed time and was kept waiting for twenty minutes before Thistlewood emerged from an alleyway opposite.

Thistlewood was in buoyant mood. Loquacious and full of bonhomie. He took Bellingham to a nearby shop where he bought twopennyworth of plum-batter pudding studded with raisins. He chose his portions carefully, making sure they were thoroughly hot and recently up from the oven. Bellingham accepted his share of the sweet. It tasted very good. He was surprised. 'The best,' said Thistlewood, beaming. Bellingham realized that Thistlewood looked extremely smart. He wore a snuff-coloured jacket with a green collar, white breeches and high, soft leather boots. His hat was green also. Bellingham liked the colour of the jacket. He thought about getting one himself.

They walked towards Lincoln's Inn Fields eating the pudding, enjoying the early spring evening. It was starting to get dark. The lamplighters were out with their carts and their ladders. Barristers bustled past them, their gowns fluttering like tattered flags behind them, wigs grasped in their hands. The clerks followed, weighed down by books of precedent and overflowing files of paper and parchment. 'The business of the law,' commented Thistlewood, watching them hurry past, 'is extremely lucrative to those people who practise it and impoverishing to those who seek to use it.' Bellingham looked at him. Thistlewood was staring at him, one eyebrow raised, the other lowered. 'Know what I mean?' asked Thistlewood. Bellingham nodded.

They stopped near the entrance to the Inns of Court. Thistlewood motioned to Bellingham to sit down on a bench. Thistlewood sat next to him. 'Have you thought any more about my offer?' inquired Thistlewood, running his finger around his gums to remove any raisins or bits of pudding that might have lodged there.

Bellingham was glad they had got to the point at last. 'Yes, I have thought about your offer. I've thought about it long and hard, and I'm afraid the answer must be no.

I shall not require your assistance. I shall continue with my aim of bringing the matter to court, no matter how long it takes.'

'That is your final word? That is your decision?'

'Yes. I have decided. It's not that I'm ungrateful, it's just that I feel I should do this my way or not at all. This is not about anybody else. It's about me and my family. It's about how I was treated. Nobody else.' Bellingham was relieved to get it off his chest. He found Thistlewood unpredictable and thought his reaction might be extreme, but he took it well. He expressed his admiration for Bellingham, for a man who stuck to his principles despite their evident flaws and inherent contradictions. Bellingham felt faintly damned by this praise, but, encouraged by Thistlewood's moderation, he continued.

Jack Nettleton, explained Bellingham, was a problem. A problem that needed to be eliminated. That got Thistlewood's attention straight away. Bellingham grew more courageous. Nettleton had to be taken out of the picture, removed. Thistlewood nodded enthusiastically. If the Nettleton problem could be dealt with, then he might be willing to throw in his lot with Thistlewood. Without Nettleton perhaps a deal could be struck. Bellingham had him. Thistlewood agreed and expressed his surprise. He was genuinely astonished, he said. Rarely had he so badly misread a situation. Of course Nettleton was a problem. Of course he could be 'solved'. The solution of problems, Thistlewood explained, was a speciality of a friend of his called Patrick Walsh.

'Is he an agent for a shipping company?' asked Bellingham.

'No,' replied Thistlewood.

'A sailor then?'

'Not a sailor, no.'

'Something generally to do with the United States?'

'Nothing whatsoever to do with the United States.'

'How then, may I ask, will he be of any use to us?'

'How, may I ask, would a sailor or a shipping agent be of any use to us?'

'Because,' said Bellingham, unable to comprehend the obtuseness of Thistlewood, 'America is across the ocean and you need to sail on a boat to get there.'

'You mean you wish me to arrange for Nettleton to leave the country and set himself up in America, and then you might consider allowing me to help you?'

'Precisely,' said Bellingham, happy that at long last he had made himself understood. 'Jack's done enough for me already, and for you. It seems unnecessary to expose him to any further risk.'

Thistlewood held up his hand. 'Don't say another word,' he gasped. His face was purple. The veins on his forehead and neck stood out. They throbbed visibly. Bellingham bit his lip, but too late. Far too late. Thistlewood flew into the most terrific rage. He stamped his feet and yelled at the top of his lungs. He foamed at the mouth a little. He was so angry a blood vessel burst and his nose started to bleed. The blood flowed over his lips and down his chin and dripped on to his beautiful jacket, splashed on to his white, white breeches and stained the soft, light brown leather of his new boots.

Bellingham's mouth dropped open. He dropped his plum-batter pudding. The extremity of Thistlewood's reaction left him paralysed with fear. He thought about trying to shrug it all off as a bad joke. If he prostrated himself at Thistlewood's feet and begged his help, pledged himself to Thistlewood's service, perhaps he would get away with it. On the other hand he could just turn and run.

In his moment of indecisiveness Thistlewood reached out and grasped Bellingham's arm. 'How stupid are you?' Thistlewood asked the question slowly, forming each word with careful deliberation. When he had put his question he left his lips pursed interrogatively. Bellingham looked at Thistlewood and tried to tug himself free without replying. Thistlewood continued, 'Why do you want to protect him? Don't you realize that without me you and Nettleton would never have met? Did you think it was all a coincidence?' He spat blood. 'Poor Jack.' Thistlewood spat again. 'Poor Jack. He just wants to get along. Poor put-upon Jackie-boy. Jack has aspirations. Jack wants to better himself. Jack wants to ditch his family and wriggle out of his responsibilities. Jack would betray his friends for sixpence ha'penny. But Jack only wants to make something of himself. Jack only wants to crawl out of the gutter. So everything is all right. Poor Jack. He'll be poor when I get my hands on his filthy carcase. He'll wish he was in America then. He'll wish . . .' Thistlewood's diatribe tailed off in a coughing fit. He let go of Bellingham's arm. Bellingham needed no prompting. He fled.

For weeks afterwards he had expected Thistlewood to come looking for him. The slightest creak of the stairs, the merest noise, was enough to wake him from his sleep. But Thistlewood never came and eventually the memory of the meeting faded, until all that remained was a longing for a snuff-coloured coat and the realization that he would never get satisfaction from the courts – the Bow Street magistrates confirmed this when they threw out his case. A different approach was needed.

Nettleton knew nothing about that meeting. Bellingham wondered whether he should tell him what had happened, but he thought it more prudent to let it lie. What difference would it make now? Jack would be angry that Bellingham had even gone to another meeting with Thistlewood after he had warned him against it. Jack had been right, of course. It had been a bad idea. Apart from anything else Bellingham was embarrassed by his own foolishness.

Sitting there on top of the hill, Jack looked sunk in misery. Long face, mouth drooped at the corners, eyes staring at the ground. A wind that seemed to blow up from nowhere ruffled his untidy brown hair and pulled at his trousers. Bellingham felt a distance between them that he had not felt before. It had been the same in Jack's lodgings. He just could not reach him. Nettleton was closed off to him. He was stung by the sensation. He felt cut off. He felt alone. Yet it suited him to be solitary. It was all for the best.

Bellingham turned his attention back to the pistol. If he was going to succeed, he needed a radically different approach. 'I am your destiny,' he murmured. 'You are my destiny,' he said to the pistol.

Jack could not work it out. How had things become so complicated? What was it that attracted him to this man, that led him to befriend him and then betray him? How could he allow himself to be in the presence of this man, the only man who bore him no ill will, who did not seek to manipulate or harm him and whom he had sold for five pounds? Admittedly the victim did not know he was a victim, and the supposed 'price' of Jack's betrayal had never been paid. Somehow, though, Jack did not think this qualified him for redemption. Guilt and money aside he needed to understand what was happening to him. He needed to find a way out of all this chaos.

Everything was a lie. It was all a sham. His great friend John Bellingham was nothing of the sort. Jack had attended the recital because Thistlewood had told him to go, and for the same reason he had gone out of his way to make the acquaintance of the man who had lingered at the exit, smiling diffidently at the other members of the audience as they filed out. Bellingham had received a few nods of the head in return, but nobody stopped to talk and it was plain he was as much a stranger, as isolated and alone, as Nettleton.

Amid all the intrigue Nettleton had forgotten his role as deceiver. He had come to like Bellingham. He had tried to warn Bellingham. He was not blameless, but he had done his best to rescue the situation. He was as much a victim as Bellingham.

He felt cold and exposed on the hill. He sensed Bellingham staring at him. He wished he would go away and leave him alone. He wished he had never got involved in any of this ridiculous escapade. He wished his entire life away, from the moment he had been introduced to Thistlewood by the Fish, a celebrated drunkard who worked at the printer's where Jack had done his apprenticeship, right up to the present day. All of it. Wipe it away. Start clean. The proverbial fresh start. If he could have unravelled the thread of his life he would have. He felt sorry for himself. He was drowning in the blue shallows of self-pity. His whole, miserable, underachieved life dragged out of him as the breath escaped from his lungs.

Jack had always assumed that it was he who controlled the direction of his life. His concerns, his needs, his desires shaped the choices before him and the decisions he made. As he sat in the cold wind on Primrose Hill he came to realize that this was far from the truth. His entire existence was conditional on other people's behaviour, on their expectations and wants: his father, who expected him to provide for the family, and his family who were happy to endorse their father's view of Jack's role in life; Thistlewood, who regarded him as a wayward adopted son, a kind of political prodigal who would one day return to the bosom and, in the meantime, was a useful little Judas; Bellingham, who without even trying exerted a powerful influence on him, who forced him to examine himself and revealed, by his own almost saintly glow, the glaring faults in Nettleton's character.

Perhaps he had been looking for a surrogate father all along. That would certainly explain the ease with which he had fallen under Thistlewood's influence. To think he had willingly, even gleefully, engaged in talking about murder and execution, revolution, hardships to be suffered for the sake of future generations, as if all of these were quantifiable elements in a balanced equation. They had calculated acceptable losses as they ate their dinner. Willing to sacrifice, willing to lay down lives, in the name of peace and the quality of life. Not just their own lives, but the lives of countless others. Now? Now it was abhorrent, unthinkable, to show such inhumanity. What does it take to do that? Not very much, he knew that. Far less effort to contemplate mass destruction than to strive to prevent it. To prevent even a single death. That was a goal worth fighting for.

He watched Bellingham put his pistol in the inner pocket of his snuff-coloured jacket. He thought about the petition he had printed for Bellingham. He had risked a lot to do that. He had done it on the sly, late at night, covering his tracks diligently. Discovery would have meant instant dismissal and the end of his dreams of escape. Despite the risks he went ahead anyway. He felt a need to seek Bellingham's approval, to earn his favour and trust. Even though the thought of betrayal had never been far from Jack's mind, he wanted, more than anything else, Bellingham to like him. Nobody, not Jack's father, not even Thistlewood, had aroused such feelings in him, but then neither man was given to displays of affection, neither was a man whose sanction would be sought, let alone given. Both had ultimately proven themselves failures.

His father had given up, preferring to condemn his

son to a life of slavery rather than cope with his own problems.

Thistlewood, although without doubt a strong man, single-minded and capable, a leader, was, in the final analysis, unsound.

Bellingham, in a way, had been Nettleton's rock. A virtuous man of undeniable strength, devoted to his family. A rock of moral certitude to which Nettleton could tie his leaky boat of moral irresolution. He had come to believe that if Bellingham succeeded, then he would succeed, and failure likewise would bring failure.

However, Jack no longer saw things the same way. He could no longer pin his hopes on somebody else. He could not allow himself to be manipulated or used by anybody. He had to take responsibility for himself. He had to make his own decisions.

John Bellingham too was deep in thought. More morbid in his frame of mind, his thoughts more inclined to revolve around questions of misfortune and fate. What course of action was left to him when his pleas for justice went unheeded and the world seemed to have forgotten him? Retribution. Not for him thoughts of love for mankind, nor simple-minded sanctity, but rather hate and anger hardening into resolve. No place for sentiment any more. If he was to act at all, he must act quickly. He pulled the pistol from his jacket pocket. Felt its weight in his hand.

Something had changed.

John Bellingham had never thought of himself as a violent man. Though images of destruction had filled his head since childhood, he had not once in his life committed an act of violence. But, he thought, as he took aim, stiffened his arm and locked his elbow, some things could not be helped.

The gathering clouds finally fulfilled their gloomy

promise. Moving in from the west, a rainstorm collided angrily with the heat, sparked in sheets of lightning, thundered its discontent, forced its way forward. Large drops of rain fell almost lazily from the dark sky. Bellingham and Nettleton headed for the shelter of a nearby horse-chestnut tree. The two men turned their collars up, pulled their coats across their throats against the pouring rain and sudden drop in temperature. The lightning illuminated the skyline in blue-white flashes; the thunder rolled as the storm moved over their heads. The smell of the sodden earth rose, welcome, in their nostrils.

Jack watched as Bellingham placed his pistol again inside that inner pocket. His brow creased. He shifted uneasily from foot to foot. 'What are you going to do with the pistol?' he asked eventually. Bellingham shrugged. 'Don't do anything hasty, will you?'

'No,' said Bellingham. 'Nothing hasty. Something I've been thinking about for years. You see, Jack, I will have my day in court. No matter what it takes, I will have it.'

'I don't understand.' Jack shook his head.

'They gave me a sort of *carte blanche* to seek redress. I told them. I warned them. I said I would take matters into my own hands. What else can I do? They've backed me into a corner. This is the only way I can state my case. No jury in England would convict me if they knew the truth. How else can I make my voice heard? It is essential that I act, if only to get the opportunity to state my case. Only people like Perceval, who have spent their lives in the Establishment, or like Thistlewood, who are prepared to go to any lengths to attain their goals, achieve anything in this world. The rest of us are simply left to bicker among ourselves and divide the few scraps they throw down to us as unfairly as possible.'

'John.' Nettleton tried to sound soothing. 'Don't do

anything you'll regret. Think about Mary Ann and the children. Don't make them suffer for your principles.'

'They'll cope. Mary Ann will cope. She's a survivor. She understands. She knows I must do it.' Bellingham shrugged again. 'She could marry again. I don't care what she does. She must do what she has to do, just as I must.'

'Don't use the pistol, John. Don't kill anyone, I beg you. Give it up. Go home. Can it really be worth dying for?'

'You've changed your tune, Jack.'

'I never asked to become involved in any of this. None of it was my choice. I've acted out of friendship and landed up to my neck in it.' Jack blushed at his lie.

'I'm sorry, Jack. Dear Jack. Perhaps you'd better go now.'

'I'll stay.' But he knew it was too late.

'As you wish, but you'll not persuade me otherwise, so why don't you just leave me alone to get on with it? Though there is one thing I've been meaning to ask you.'

'What's that?' said Jack, dreading the question.

'How did Thistlewood know I was at your lodgings? Do you think someone told him, Jack?'

'I don't know, John.' Nettleton gulped. 'Maybe he had us followed.'

'You're probably right.' Bellingham turned to face Nettleton. 'Are you off then?'

'It's raining.' Jack was ashamed that he could not think of anything else to say.

'It'll blow over. The storm's moved on already. Go. Go now.'

They shook hands. Stiffly, formally. Nettleton, collar up, disappeared over the brow of Primrose Hill, and John Bellingham leant back against the trunk of the horse-chestnut and closed his eyes.

Nettleton stumbled and slid down the hill, tripping over, dripping wet, splattered with mud, grass stains on his trousers. He outran the storm, but he did not stop running.

Bellingham folded his arms tight about his waist to keep the water off his pistol. He flattened himself further to the tree trunk, looking for a dry spot beneath the canopy, and waited for the rain to stop, for the storm to rumble its way eastward. He shivered. Drops of water dripped from the leaves and landed on his head and shoulders, finding their way down the back of his neck.

He moved out eventually into the sunlight that followed the downpour and descended the hill. The rain trapped in the long grass soaked his shoes and stockings, but as he made his way along more established paths the sunshine began to dry his clothes. He passed the navvies at the bottom of the hill just as they emerged from cover to resume their work. They nodded in his direction as he went by. He raised a hand in salute.

He turned to the right and made his way towards Marylebone, hoping to avoid the crowds of people and the traffic in the city and approach Westminster from the more affluent, less densely populated side.

He picked his way across the muddy ruts in the road, keeping to the grassy verge wherever possible, stopping now and then to wipe the dirt from his shoes with a handful of grass or a large leaf. The creaks and bangs of an occasional carriage shuddering along the makeshift road sent birds and quietude flying. Bellingham whistled as he proceeded, leisurely, in a westerly direction.

ELEVEN

WESTMINSTER

Like a mere bagatelle glancing off the pins rolling down the board, the man collided with people on the pavement, each collision sending him careering off in a new direction to a new collision. He bounced off the belly of a fat man, rebounded on to the rump of a plump woman, sent a thin man flying. His course diverted by a wall, he lurched into a man carrying apples on his head. The apples and their bearer tumbled to the earth; children appeared as if from nowhere to scoop them up. In this fashion the man progressed down the street, not by his own volition but taking his direction and even his speed from those he chanced to bump into. A man, seeing the lunatic coming straight for his wife, swiftly stepped out to intercept the madman with his cane. He sent him wildly off course and into the road, where, miraculously, he bounced from the side of one cart to the side of another, from the flanks of one horse to another, until finally he came to rest in the middle of the road.

Without anything to hit him, to push him, to direct him, he seemed incapable of movement. After a short while his legs gave way beneath him and he sat in the dirt of the road, his back straight, his legs stretched out in front of him. A cloud of dust settled around him, on him. His gaunt face was fixed in a glum expression. His long, sparse hair fell over his eyes. His clothes were muddy and torn. He wore no boots; his feet were bound in cloth and string. The traffic avoided him, but he could not evade the kicks and the whips of the drivers. Children danced around him, skipping deftly through the traffic. They taunted him with names and threw anything they could find at the sitting target. Apples, rotten vegetables, discarded food, horse dung, dead cats, stones, pieces of metal and glass. The missiles bounced off him, some without causing injury, others drawing blood or knocking him sideways. Whenever a child got too close or scored a hit, the man lashed out with his arm, as if at a wasp, and then lapsed again into his motionless trance. This curious response drove the children wild. It exasperated them. They could not believe an adult was staying still long enough to be pelted by them. Nobody else would put up with it, so, they reasoned, he could not be an adult, which meant he must be fair game.

The poor unfortunate's torture continued until the constable and the beadle arrived to remove the obstruction. At the first touch of their hands on his arms he flew into a rage. He screamed and shouted, he kicked out with his feet and struggled maniacally to escape their hold. The children withdrew immediately at the appearance of authority, but they watched from shop doorways and peered around corners as the object of their curiosity was dragged away.

Nettleton watched too. His clothes also were muddy and torn. He too felt lost and abandoned in the city. He hoped he was not on the verge of arrest, but he feared that perhaps he was. His friend Bellingham was about to do something he himself and everyone else would probably live to regret. Jack was not sure what it was, but he felt sure it would be an arrestable offence. The madman in the street was likely to end up in a lunatic asylum. He would probably die there at the hands of a seriously disturbed inmate, by his own hand or aided by the medical profession. Yet to Nettleton the man had not seemed mad. Melancholy, certainly, but not mad. Like most of the city's inhabitants, he was dispossessed, not just of the means of making a living, or of a comfortable habitation, or of that vaguest of things, political rights, but also of spirit and will. His impotent anger was pathetic to behold. He had seemed to react because a reaction was what everybody desired, not because he cared in the least about the missiles hurled at him or the cruel taunts of the children. Jack thought he understood the poor man's insensibility to his own fate; he had lost his will to act. He would accept the actions of others because he no longer possessed the energy or saw the necessity for his own action. Jack felt similarly paralysed. Poised between temerity and inertia. Earlier, on Primrose Hill, he had felt emboldened by his decision to take charge of his own destiny. Now he found that he hadn't the faintest notion of what that destiny might be, let alone how to take hold of it and bend it to his own will.

For as long as he could remember, his only ambition had been this: to make a difference. Jack was aware that this was about as vague an ambition as it was possible to have. It did not necessarily involve the pursuit of power, influence or wealth, and yet neither were any of these things precluded. Sometimes he imagined his name above the entrance to a grand building of some sort or another, a library perhaps. On other occasions he daydreamed about people discovering his grave and an earnest father explaining to his wide-eyed son or daughter what a great man Jack Nettleton had been and how he would live in the memory . . . The paean would usually fade away as tears welled up in Nettleton's eyes at both the prospect of his greatness and his death. Much of what he had done in his short life had been aimed at making a difference. Foolishly he had believed that Thistlewood offered him the chance to make a spectacular impact on the world. Disabused of that notion, Nettleton none the less continued with his vainglorious dreaming. The trouble was that he had no conception of how to achieve his ambition or what achieving it actually meant.

He had looked around for guidance in the matter. He read books and listened to preachers. He had attended lectures on everything from self-improvement to personal hygiene. He had been swept along by anyone who spoke with passion about the future. When the gales of persuasion blew, Jack had no real moral ballast to hold him steady. Now that he thought about it, he could not recall ever having made a moral decision, a decision based on ethics as well as self-interest. Throughout most of his life his decisions had been made for him by men who believed they knew better or thought they had a prior claim on his obedience. His father, his master in the printshop, Thistlewood. And all that time he had been happy to let them make his decisions. He wondered if anyone would ever allow him the space and time to make his own sense of the world.

He had been standing near the corner of Tottenham Court Road for almost half an hour. Somebody had even thrown a penny at his feet. He thought, if he could persuade his legs to function, that it was time to move on before he attracted too much attention to himself. He shuffled off and turned down a side-street, away from the main concourse, its traffic and noise. The smell of fresh coffee floated under his nose, tempting him, tantalizing him. Just around the corner into Soho Square – a coffee-house. He turned towards the square almost in a trance, the turmoil in his mind suddenly displaced by the wonderful aroma of roasting coffee beans. His entire being focused on one aim, the purchase of a cup of dark, thick, sweet coffee. Just around the corner. A few more stumbling steps.

Jack occupied a snug towards the back of the small coffee-house. Again the smell absorbed him for a moment, allowed him to relax. He sat back on the bench, stretched his legs out underneath the table. The hum of conversation surrounded him and made him feel secure. There was something very substantial about a coffee-house. It was a place for serious conversation, not for idle discussions about the weather. There was something exclusive and slightly dangerous about coffee-houses. They were filled with hushed talk of politics and not the bravura cries of conquests, real and imagined, inviting respect or ridicule, which filled the taverns. Jack knew instinctively that this was a place that would not betray him. It was filled with people like himself. Artisans and journeymen seeking to better themselves by avoiding alcohol and taking the opportunity to read the newspapers, magazines and periodicals provided by the proprietor. Their discussions were well informed and lively. Here and nowhere else was where Thistlewood's precious revolution would start, not in the taprooms or the rookeries, not among the thieves and the drunkards but here among sober people seeking answers to the questions that perplexed them.

He realized with a start that he was being stared at. He looked around and caught a glimpse, out of the corner of his eye, of dozens of heads turning away. He was quite a sight. For the first time he registered fully how filthy he was, covered head to toe in mud and grass, his clothes ripped, burn holes in his trousers. Talking to himself. Hardly inconspicuous. He shrugged and tried to ignore the unwanted attention.

From a booth behind him he heard talk of trade and

war. The progress of the Peninsular War against France and the threat of hostilities with America. He turned to listen to the conversation. He could see only one of the participants. Not the main speaker, a listener. He was tall, several inches taller than anybody else around him. His hair was black, flecked with white. His face was long, his cheekbones high, his expression impassive, inscrutable. He did not react to anything he was told. If he responded, it was with a monosyllable. A yes or a no. There was something familiar about him, but Nettleton was too interested in the conversation to pursue the likeness.

'The Orders in Council,' Nettleton heard, 'are possibly the most damaging piece of legislation to be passed in the last two decades. It's tearing the heart out of Britain's industrial capability.' Nobody in the speaker's company demurred. 'It is simply imperative that it is repealed before it's too late.'

'I couldn't agree more.' Somebody else spoke. Nettleton could not see him. 'First Napoleon tries to snuff out our export markets, and, fine, you can understand it, we are at war with him after all. But when your own Government joins in the carnage and starts closing down all the areas of trade unaffected by your enemy, that is a different matter altogether. We all accept that war can bring hardship as well as make fortunes, but we aren't at war with the USA, so why should their markets be closed to us? Perceval has a great deal to answer for. He's ruining all of us. Not to mention the Americans. There's talk of war. Not just talk, if you ask my opinion.'

'In the West Riding, over a third of textile businesses closed down in the first few months of last year,' said another, a Yorkshireman. 'We'll all of us have starved to death by the time they sort this bloody mess out. Something has to be done.'

'Yes,' said the tall man Nettleton could see. A short

silence followed as if his companions thought he might elaborate, but he said nothing further.

'Over eleven million in exports two years ago – that's what trade with the States was worth to us. Last year, under two million pounds. That is disastrous. How can anyone deny the fact, the plan fact, that the Orders in Council are destroying this country. We've got expensive machines lying idle, we've got warehouses full of wool and cotton we can't sell. On top of all that the workforce is being thrown out of work, and who do they blame? Us. Us and our bloody machines. If we don't watch out, we'll have our own revolution to deal with – and, believe me, it won't start in London. It'll be in Manchester, or Nottingham, or Halifax. And we, poor sods, we're the ones who'll cop it. Mark my words.' A hush followed the Yorkshireman's speech. Nobody was going to disagree with his assessment.

'So what's to be done?' The original speaker took up again. 'The man who invented the Orders in Council, who pushed them into law, is now the Prime Minister. We're not going to get far with Perceval in power, that's plain as day. Admittedly, this inquiry into the Orders in Council is a start, but Perceval didn't even turn up to Friday's session. Brougham was furious, absolutely livid. He's someone who gives me hope, Brougham. He may be an ugly, ambitious sod, but there's no doubting his brilliance. He's worked hard to get this inquiry off the ground, and so far things have gone well. The committee's received thousands of petitions against the Orders in Council. I mean, the public pressure is building, but nothing is going to change with Perceval sat there like patience on a bloody monument, sticking to his high principles.'

'Perceval is the problem.'

'Absolutely.'

'Got to get rid of him.'

'How did we get stuck with him in the first place?'

The conversation shifted to an analysis of Whig and Tory politics that left Nettleton cold. Addington, Portland, Liverpool. Names that meant little to him. The conversation, though, disturbed him. War with the United States imminent? Had he left it too late? Was escape impossible? He had known nothing except war his whole life. Ever since he could remember, Britain had been at war with someone. War in the colonies. War in Europe. What would he do if there was a war with the United States? He had to leave quickly. Now was the time. He simply had to make up his mind and go. The prospects in America were good for someone like him, reasonably educated – at least he could read and write. Obviously the situation was deteriorating rapidly. Common sense told him he should leave immediately. If he waited until everything had blown over, he ran the risk of being arrested or, worse, back in Thistlewood's clutches. That is, if Thistlewood had survived the explosion. Jack had few doubts about that; anything else was wishful thinking. He was out there somewhere, licking his wounds. If there was one thing Thistlewood had, it was patience.

So he should go. With what, though? He had no money. He might not even have a job to go back to any more. There were plenty of journeyman printers looking for work. If he missed a day, he had no right to expect the benefit of the doubt. In any case, Thistlewood knew where he worked and where he lived. This whole business was sending him spinning. He could not hold on to it all any longer. He had to get out of there.

Jack passed through the narrow streets of Soho. Barefoot and ragged, grubby children of indeterminate age scrabbled among the rubbish and played with mangy dogs which licked their faces with rough tongues. Older boys and girls pushed off the dogs, fought with them for the best scraps; they retrieved rags, broken pots, china, shoes and bones. Irate restaurateurs and shopkeepers threw sticks and stones as well as names, clearing the scavengers away like flies and, with the flies, the scavengers scattered and then swarmed back to settle once again on the city's rotting waste. Distressing to the observer, offensive to the righteous, a problem for the constabulary, these carrion children were a symptom of decay dissonant with the public's preferred image of a Christian society prospering amid industrialization. They exposed the myth of wealth creation; they served as an unhappy reminder to the thriving few of the many not blessed with this world's providence. A reminder of their jaundiced Utopia thinly made over with a godly paternalism, of their failure to build Jerusalem, to bring Heaven to Earth, these mudlarks, bone-grubbers and sewer-hunters left to wander the remnants of the discarded dream ragged and barefoot, distressing and offensive.

Jack moved on, and they disappeared – until he glanced down the next alleyway. It was easier to forget. To shift the burden. Easier still to rationalize coldly. They have to learn to stand on their own two feet in the school of hard knocks. Nature will cast aside those who cannot or will not fend for themselves. Nettleton had enough trouble keeping body and soul together to worry overly about the scavengers. They were as common as the cobbles. But all the same he felt some sense of shame, some pity. What was to be done? There were charities, of course. Homes for lost children. Yet it was not the misery of their condition that moved him but their animal-like existence. There was no dignity in their foraging. But what price commiseration? What price fine sentiments? Action was required. But whose? His? He was caught, confronted with his own failure, his own responsibility, his own opportunity to do something. But Jack retreated into words and excuses, into his soul, because his own body was well enough looked after.

He passed through into the main street. The thoroughfares were clogged. Men and women barged and pushed, children swarmed, horses trotted and cantered, dogs barked and ran between the wheels of carts and trolleys, drays and carriages. Hawkers hawked, ballad-singers caterwauled and generally made life much more miserable than it should have been. Jack thought someone should pass a law against ballad-singers. Lock them all up together in a small, lightless cell with those bloody dancing sailors from across the road, throw in the stilt-dancers, pig-faced women, the owners and trainers of six-legged cows and two-headed horses, sapient pigs, dancing dogs, bears and camels. Cram them all in, force them to live in their own self-made hell of so-called entertainment.

He pushed through the crowd. There was no escaping them near the market. He was battered with their singing and their barking. Too many people with a living to make, and they all came there to do it – to the gold-paved streets.

Covent Garden was superabundant with pedlars and buyers, flowergirls and newsboys, whores and soldiers, swells and commoners.

A nearby stall caught his attention. 'Fish and bread a penny,' the stall-keeper shouted as he fried the fish in a skillet on top of his portable stove. The fish, shapeless, brown and sprinkled with parsley, came served on a thick slice of bread. For all its unappetizing looks, it tasted good.

As he leant against a wall eating his fried fish, he saw that the market was in a process of transition as the costermongers who had been there since dawn began to pack their wares for the long trek home

212

before the evening pedlars arrived and the whore-houses opened for the night trade.

All around him the shutters were being thrown back in the houses and taverns. Women sat in the windows at street level or leaned out of upper windows. They called out for custom, though their trade needed no advertising. The character of Covent Garden was undergoing its daily transformation from market in legitimate trade to the illegitimacy of brothels, wine cellars and gaming houses, the trade in pleasure. The clientele changed also. Though no one was excluded from these pursuits, the maids and housekeepers, the labourers and the simple purchasers were by and large leaving to make way for the dandified gentry, clouded by scent and powder, stepping cautiously through the debris of the day's trade as they made their way to a pre-theatre dinner, or a pre-dinner drink, or a game of cards. They eyed the flesh displayed around them with lazy glances, looking for the face or the body or the attitude that was capable of arousing their pampered and spoilt meat. How incongruous these fantastically rich men were amid the appalling poverty of the place.

Jack finished his fried fish and wiped the crumbs from his mouth. Despite the distaste he felt for what he saw, Jack could not help feeling excited by this trade. There were a great number of prostitutes, and while he might not like the way the trade advertised itself, he was completely ambivalent towards it. He could not deny that though he considered it ethically undesirable, prostitution was certainly a practical way for a man to indulge his lusts without complication or recrimination (as long as one did not count the pox as a recrimination). At the same time he viewed the use of a prostitute as the sexual betrayal of a wife or lover, even of a future wife or lover (the pox again). Somehow he was able to feel both guilty and innocent at the same time.

As he was staring at the whores setting up shop, Jack caught sight of the man from the coffee-house. The tall, dark-haired man. He was talking to a woman whom Jack also recognized as the uncorseted flower-seller he had so admired earlier in the day. In such a large city to see the same man twice in the space of a couple of hours, to hear him discuss matters of direct interest to Nettleton, to see him talk to someone Jack had noticed – Jack's curiosity was piqued. He wanted to know more about this gentleman.

Jack followed Stillwater out of the market and into the dark alleyways and backstreets where the afternoon sun could not penetrate. All around them miserable urchins played together among the rubbish, loitered on corners or in doorways. Men and women gossiped, blathered, blustered and yelled in the streets, in the yards, through the windows at their neighbours (whose hands they could almost touch across the narrow passages), at their relatives, at anyone who passed by. Pedlars and costers sold the cheapest goods on every corner: scraps of tobacco, gathered from discarded cigars and knocked-out pipes, rolled together and sold by the quarter-ounce, the proceeds of a day's dredging through the mud-flats of the Thames at low tide were here proudly displayed on makeshift stalls. Also, here and there, upmarket costers were selling at discounted prices goods they had failed to offload during the day. Tailors, pawnbrokers, vittlers and landlords touted for custom. Charity workers and clergymen extolled the virtues of hard work, family life, temperance and Christianity. Lay preachers offered tracts and sang hymns. Millenarians warned of the end of the world. Prostitutes hurried to and from the main drag. Promises, promises everywhere: the best beer, the best sex, the best prices, eternal life, everlasting damnation, plum pudding, top-quality rags, odds and ends.

Nettleton struggled to keep Stillwater in sight. He was tall and stood out in a crowd, but he was fast and moved with great determination and purpose. It was not long before Jack was lost in the labyrinth of alleys and lanes. They might have been going in circles or have doubled back in various combinations of directions, but he had no idea where he was being led. Also he was disappointed. He had never followed anyone before and had been looking forward to the adventure, but this man just seemed to walk for the sake of it.

As Jack despaired, however, Stillwater stopped suddenly in front of a rag merchant's. The wares were piled in baskets outside the shop, brightly coloured scraps of cloth – that was it, just scraps of cloth. Inside were box after box of buttons. You could search for a day without finding two that matched. Stillwater was not interested in rags or buttons. He beckoned to someone in the shop. Whoever it was inside was reluctant to come out and Stillwater was forced to gesture again. If that irritated him, he showed no sign of it. Finally a man came out of the shop. He looked around furtively all the time Stillwater talked to him. He was very jittery and nervous. Stillwater gave him a small purse. The man nodded as he was given his instructions. He was a curious fellow. Middle-aged, his back very hunched. He wore a stripy hat like a nightcap with a long tassel on the top that dangled down the side of his head. He had a peculiar squinting look and blinked almost constantly. Stillwater's transaction concluded, the hunched man scurried back into the shop and Stillwater moved on.

The next stop was outside a tavern. Here Stillwater talked to a group of men who, Nettleton thought, all looked ridiculously sinister. One was enormous, as tall as Stillwater and broad with it. A huge bull of a man. Completely bald with scars all over his face and scalp. Another had a peg-leg. Yet another wore an eyepatch.

Two of the others, who might have been brothers, had only two arms between them, one the right, the other the left. If he had seen it in a burlesque, he would have laughed like a drain, but Nettleton had a feeling laughter would be inappropriate here.

Stillwater entered a large building. The gloom outside in the street was as nothing to the nearly total darkness within. Jack hid at the bottom of the stairwell as Stillwater conducted his business on the landing above him. He could hear the voices but not the words. Stillwater's now familiar sibilant whisper was joined by a woman's voice. A gummy voice of an old woman without any teeth. The chink of coin. Nettleton could see nothing, but he heard Stillwater descend the stairs.

The pattern was repeated several times. Jack followed Stillwater as he liaised with a great variety of villainous-looking characters in graveyards and slaughterhouses, in cellars and garrets, in backroom distilleries and backstage at theatres. Jack was amazed at what he saw, but he never managed to get close enough to hear what the deal was. He was still completely in the dark. He imagined that Stillwater was some kind of criminal mastermind, gathering together a fearsome gang. But that was thinking the worst. He might just as well have been a philanthropist distributing his wealth to the poor and needy. The group of amputees might have been ex-soldiers, the rag merchant nursing a sick wife, the old hag caring for orphans. Just because they looked ugly, grotesque and frightening it did not mean they were murderous cut-throats. On the other hand, Jack was not so sure. There was something he did not trust about this shadowy man who seemed to mix as easily with industrialists and politicians as he did with thugs and criminals.

By the time they returned to Covent Garden Jack was none the wiser. He was racking his brains to remember where he had seen the man before. He was sure he had, but where? With Thistlewood? It seemed the obvious answer, but Jack was convinced he had never seen him with Thistlewood. He would have remembered that. An instinct for self-preservation made him remember people he had met with Thistlewood. Perhaps it was years ago, in Lewes. But, no, he recognized him as he was now: the flecks of white in the hair, the dark clothes, the impassiveness of his long face, the look in his eyes that might have been sadness or complete indifference.

Stillwater went into the Covent Garden bath-house. Jack thought about following him in. He paused on the steps for a moment or two.

She approached him from behind and tapped him on the shoulder. He leaped into the air in fright. He turned to face his accuser and was surprised to see someone he did not know. She smiled at him, and he noticed a bruise on her neck. He thought he recognized her too, and he was thrown into confusion. He smiled and opened his mouth to speak, but nothing intelligible came out. He stepped towards the bath-house entrance and then stepped back towards her again. He repeated the movement two or three times, his mouth opening and closing silently the whole time. 'Hello,' he managed to squeeze it out. He *did* recognize her. She was the woman he had seen talking to the tall man, the woman he had noticed in the market that morning.

'Come with me,' she said. He dithered. 'Come with me,' she repeated, reaching out for his hand. He went.

She drew him by the hand. He needed to be led. He was not at all sure about this. They walked only a few hundred yards. She let go of his hand and climbed a set of stairs that rose from the street to a balcony on the second floor of a tenement building. He mounted the rickety wooden stairs after her. She opened a door at the top and ushered him in.

217

The room was small and cramped. A tiny window opened on to the street. A piece of patterned cloth nailed to the frame served as a curtain. A low, wood-framed cot placed under the window stretched almost the entire width of the room, leaving just enough space for a chair at its foot. At the head of the bed a small cabinet was set to one side. It was covered with a cloth and littered with the ends of candles, scraps of material and a comb with several teeth missing. Against the wall opposite the window, to Jack's right as he came in, was a rail with one dress and a few other tattered items of clothing hanging on it. The centre of the room was occupied by a large tin bath. The fireplace was surrounded by pictures cut from newspapers or handed out as flyers. In the hearth were four large pots of steaming water. Two other pots were suspended above the fire.

As Jack stood in the doorway the woman poured hot water into the bath. Jack closed the door behind him. She looked at him standing there by the door and sighed. 'Take your clothes off,' she commanded.

Stillwater entered the lobby of the House of Commons through the St Stephen's entrance in Palace Yard. He took his watch from his fob pocket and glanced at it. Five o'clock. He knew it must be fast because he could not hear the chimes of the nearby churches or the watches of those around him. He waited for the tintinnabulation of the hour and adjusted his silent watch accordingly.

The lobby was quiet. Not at all so busy as he had expected. He made his way across the lobby to the entrance to the Chamber and took up a position to the right of the large closed doors. He was an impress-ive figure. Tall, with a military bearing, a horseman's straight back and a long neck, he could see most of what was happening around him.

Small cabals of politicians stood near the fireplace or grouped around the four columns in the centre of the room, conspiring, laughing. Whigs mingled with Tories, parliamentary animosities temporarily forgotten, hostilities temporarily suspended.

Stillwater, as usual, found himself sickened by the sight of these gentlemen of importance who conducted themselves as if they were in a club. A genial smile here, a promise of supper there, a shared joke with an old friend, an introduction to a helpful acquaintance. Stillwater had nothing but scorn for the light-heartedness of the British attitude to government and war, the bungling dilettante spirit that was nothing but that – an amateurish groping for resolution. They relied on people like Nelson and Wellesley, professionals despised by the ruling class for their upbringing or their seriousness, the very qualities those self-same rulers relied upon for salvation – people like himself who saw the bigger picture, who took the long view, who were willing to bend the rules to get the job done and willing to take the blame when things went awry. The fact that there were only twenty or thirty people present in total only went to show how lightly they took the whole issue of the Orders in Council. The inquiry continued in the House and these men ignored it as if it were of no significance.

Stillwater spotted Bellingham sitting on a bench to his left, facing the lobby entrance.

Nettleton reclined in his hot bath. He slid down until his head was immersed and his feet stuck out over the end. He ran his hand through his hair, matted with mud. He smoothed out the tangles and rubbed the dirt away. He enjoyed the submarine booming his hands made as they struck the sides of the tub. He emerged cleaner, fresher, and submitted himself willingly to her hands as she scrubbed and scraped at the flesh of his back, of his chest, with a wash-cloth. She soaped and rinsed his armpits. The soap was fragranced, a delightful smell. Carefully, she picked away the dirt from underneath his fingernails. She lifted his legs from the water and washed his thighs, his calves, his ankles, his feet, in between his toes. She had him sit up and bend over and washed his buttocks. She put her hand through his legs and washed his genitals.

He lay back in the bath, a little stunned. More than anything else he was reminded of his mother. He had not thought about her for twelve years, not since she absconded with the butcher's boy. He closed his eyes and tried to consign his childhood memories to a different part of his mind. He could wallow in nostalgia later. For the moment he wanted to wallow in the bath, surrounded by the warmth of the water and the heat of his desire.

He considered his body. He found it pleasing for the most part, but he had always been dismayed by the failure of anything but the minutest tufts of hair to grow on his chest. Most men, it seemed to him, had carpets on their chests. Tufts of thick, black hair sprouted from underneath their collars, from between the buttons of their shirts. They even had hair on their backs. Yet all he was endowed with were a few pathetic patches of long, wiry hair. These tufts, separated by a tract of white skin, formed a fascinating triangle: a clump at the base of his neck and a curious fairy ring of hair round each of his large, pink nipples. Recently too he had developed a slight paunch. An incipient pot-belly.

The bath water was by now a murky grey colour, covered in flakes of soap, grass and other bodily bilge. He thought it was time to get out. He lifted himself to his feet. The heat of the bath and the sudden exertion made him feel faint.

* * *

Bellingham twitched and fidgeted. He held in his hand a large bundle of papers which he referred to now and then, as if he were trying to memorize parts of what was written there. Every so often his hand would reach into his jacket and touch something concealed inside. He kept his gaze, when he was not reading his papers, fixed on the entrance. Each time the tall folding doors opened he jerked forward expectantly; each time someone he did not recognize entered he relaxed back on to the bench. Because someone entered and left the lobby every few seconds, this movement had the appearance of a rocking motion. His behaviour was attracting some curious glances, but he was oblivious to everything except the opening and closing of that door.

A young clerk tumbled into the lobby and pushed his way through to a door on the other side of the room. As he shoved the Honourable Members to one side he countered their stern looks with the phrase 'the Prime Minister'. All eyes turned to the door, and an expectant hush fell over the assembly. A number of petitioners jostled for position by the entrance, grabbing at each other's coat-tails and pulling their rivals back so they could take their place in the front line of worthy causes.

A minute or two elapsed before Perceval made his entrance. Already the noise had risen once more to the level of hubbub, and as the petitioners clamoured for the Minister's attention it became uproarious as suits were pressed and petitions thrust into the little man's hands. But Perceval was in a hurry, already late for the inquiry into the Orders in Council. He pushed aside the various petitioners and made straight for the entrance to the House.

As Perceval strode as quickly and manfully across the lobby as his short legs would carry him, Stillwater saw Bellingham rock forward on to his feet and, with the more leisurely stride of a much taller man, intercept Perceval midway. The few Members in the lobby paid no attention to this collision. The two men were pressed close together. Stillwater approached stealthily. Bellingham was talking to the Prime Minister, showing him his petition. Perceval shook his head, a hand raised to indicate his desire to get past Bellingham and on with his business. Bellingham took Perceval's hand, drew the Prime Minister even closer to him and whispered something in his ear.

Stillwater lurched towards Perceval. He saw Bellingham produce a pistol from his coat pocket. He saw Bellingham place the barrel against Perceval's chest. He saw Bellingham squeeze the trigger. Nothing happened. Nothing happened. No deafening gunshot. No heads quickly turning. Stillwater looked at Bellingham's pistol and realized it was not cocked. He took a pistol from his own pocket, cocked it and, holding it by the barrel, offered the handle to Bellingham.

Bellingham and Perceval turned to look at Stillwater. In the midst of the crowded lobby they seemed to hold each other's gaze for minutes on end. They looked from one to the other in amazement.

The late-afternoon sun faintly penetrated the ragged curtain. She rubbed Nettleton dry with a clean cloth. He abandoned himself to her care. He allowed her to manipulate him however she wished. She lifted his arms above his head and dried his armpits. He left them there until she lowered them to his sides. She pushed him this way and that, turned him round, bent him over, lifted his feet into her lap. She was thorough and silent. He respected that silence. He welcomed it.

His thoughts drifted back to Bellingham but would not stay with him. He was ashamed of himself for not being capable of thinking about his friend, for finding deep within him an empty space where his affection for the man should be. It was as if the hot water had rinsed him of his guilt, dissolved it, as if his immersion had cleansed him of sin, as if his selfishness and his betrayal floated like scum on the surface of the water.

She finished towelling Nettleton and stepped back from him a pace or two. Casually she undid her blouse and stepped out of her skirt. She wore no corsetry. She was naked. Jack gulped. She was not a great beauty. Her body was rounded, a little flabby in places. Her breasts, while nowhere near pendulous, sagged somewhat. The hair under her armpits bushed out from between her arms and the sides of her chest like grass poking up in the cracks between paving stones. Nettleton lowered his gaze. Her triangle of hair reminded him of his own. She did not let him look for very long before she moved over to the cot and lay down on top of the coarse blanket. Jack followed and knelt beside her. He was uncertain how to proceed. He simply did not know what to do next. She pulled his shoulders towards her and he did not resist. He smelt her flesh, a strange commingling of sweat, perfumed powder and bread. The smell was sweet and overpowering. He shifted so that he lay on top of her. He was surprised how easily the contours of their bodies fitted together.

She reached down and grabbed hold of him. Nettleton gasped in surprise but yielded to her manipulations. He lay on top of her, inside her, without moving, enjoying the unfamiliar but pleasant sensations of warmth and enclosure, the tingling of pleasure, pure pleasure, that travelled through his groin and shivered up his spine. She raised and lowered her buttocks in an attempt to get him moving. He imitated her movement and eventually engaged in a counter-rhythmic activity that served to heighten his pleasure and brought into use certain muscle groups whose existence he had been previously unaware of. He bent his neck and tried to lick and bite at her nipples. It seemed the right thing to do, but the operation was difficult and he soon gave up. She took his head in her hand and pushed it firmly into the blanket by her ear. With her free arm she held him close to her body. The musty smell of the blanket, the strength of her embrace, the tightness of her arm lock squeezed from his mind all thoughts of Bellingham, betrayal, Thistlewood, pistols, petitions, government, Influencing Engines, whirligigs, Bannister Truelock, Patrick Walsh, politics, secret societies, public houses, Covent Garden, flowers, strange men, nausea, beatings, money, America, the races, mother, father, squeezed them right out through the top of his head, replaced them with thoughts of warmth, intimacy, lust, affection and gratification.

She made no sign that she heard or acknowledged his muffled groans and gasps for breath. Her brow was furrowed to a frown as Nettleton wriggled around on her belly and did not smooth over until he gave a series of little jerks, said, 'Ugh,' and was still. She released his head, pushed his shoulders down until he left her and rolled over on to his back, the ughs fainter and still audible. She left her cot, stepped into the cooling bath and bathed herself quickly and efficiently.

Bellingham turned away from Stillwater, looked down at his pistol and calmly cocked it. At the click of the wheel Perceval too turned from Stillwater and stared at the pistol, its muzzle pointing directly at his heart. Bellingham looked up from the gun in his trembling hand. Perceval lifted his eyes to meet Bellingham's. Bellingham squeezed the trigger gently. The hammer fell and the gun discharged with a muffled crack.

Stillwater put his own pistol back in his jacket and stepped forward to try to catch Perceval as he staggered backwards, his head turning from side to side, and fell.

'Oh! I am murdered.' Perceval breathed it out, like a death rattle, his expiration, his valediction.

Nobody moved. It was as if they were models posing in a portrait. A clatter of footsteps from the gallery stairs, from the House itself. The doors thrown open. 'Shut the doors,' someone shouted, suddenly shattering the silence, animating the stillness. 'Let no-one escape.'

Stillwater knelt down next to the stricken Perceval. Blood issued in leisurely trickles from both corners of his mouth. Blood gurgled up from his destroyed lungs and frothed on his lips. It spread in a dark, reflecting pool across the cold stone floor.

The Sergeant-at-Arms pulled Stillwater to one side as four of his men lifted Perceval by his legs and arms and took him away. Stillwater took a handkerchief from his pocket and wiped the Prime Minister's blood from his hands. He surveyed the scene.

The urbane and cultured members of the country's most exclusive club were shocked to their core. The unthinkable had happened. Not only had their sanctum been breached, it had been most disgustingly violated. Their reactions were equally extreme. Some fumed and talked already of hangings. Others stood, mouths agape, seemingly unable to comprehend the nature of the events. Others, who had missed the actual shot or been late in arriving because of gout or infirmity, shook people by the shoulders and inquired urgently what had taken place, though the blood on the tiles left little room for doubt. 'Who?' they asked. 'Who?'

Stillwater caught sight of Bellingham, who sat quietly on the bench, the discharged pistol held limply in his hand. Stillwater was amazed. Bellingham had made no effort to escape. None whatsoever. It was incredible.

Somebody tugged at Stillwater's arm. He turned to see an industrialist of his acquaintance from Yorkshire. The businessman whispered confidentially, 'The finger of benevolent Providence is visible in this horrible event.' Stillwater merely nodded.

Jack lingered by the door, adjusting his clothes. He cleared his throat. She turned to face him. Her look was questioning. Nettleton did not know how to broach the subject. He blushed a deep red. 'I think I . . .' he mumbled. 'Well, I mean . . . don't I . . . you know?' He looked at her with a pleading look, but she did not even blink. 'Don't I owe you any money? How much was all that?'

'You don't owe me anything.'

'I don't? You mean . . . ?' Nettleton brightened. He felt a little light-headed. Proud.

'Your friend already paid. Close the door on your way out.' She turned away to face the wall and curled up like a question mark on the dirty blanket.

Jack pulled the door shut quietly. He stood there on the balcony for a minute or two. It was still bright there where the sun could reach him. Below, the streets were silent and dark. The silence was eerie, more like a hush, the conscious withholding of noise, than its absence, the moment between the benediction and the rising of the congregation.

The quiet lasted a meagre few seconds before a shout and a dog barking brought the whole city cacophony to his ears. He descended the stairs. The street was deserted. The clamour he heard was from farther away. It was a noise like that of a large crowd. The babble of voices getting louder and louder, dying away suddenly only to return, louder than ever, following, as if on cue, a loud banging of metal on metal, a whistle, the pounding of drums or the crash of windows smashing. He could not pinpoint the location of the crowd. The noise seemed to surround him. He tried to retrace his steps to Covent Garden market but soon lost his way. The streets were almost empty. A few old men and women, beggars and cripples loitered still in doorways and leant out of windows. Jack stopped to ask a woman seated on a doorstep what was happening. She took the long clay pipe out of her mouth. 'Got a penny?'

'I just wanted to know where everyone was,' said Jack very slowly, suspecting that she had not heard him the first time.

'Ha'penny then? For tobacco.' Jack handed over the ha'penny. 'You haven't heard then?'

'No,' said Jack, exasperated. 'Just tell me where everybody is. Please.'

'Over there.' She pointed at the building about four paces in front of her. She lowered her arm and filled the bowl of her pipe with tobacco from her apron pocket. 'Got a light?'

'No,' said Nettleton, reaching into his pocket for another coin. 'But I have a farthing.'

'Farthing'll do,' she said, putting the coin in a pouch, pulling the pouch down in to her skirt. 'Shot the Prime Minister, aint they? It's the signal, ain't it? The Regent and his loony father are next. Long live the republic,' she muttered, suddenly lowering her voice.

The news took him by surprise. Bellingham had shot and killed the Prime Minister. Not just anybody. Not a policeman. Not a civil servant or a diplomat. He had killed Perceval. He had murdered the Government.

Nettleton set off in the direction he faced. His mind was filled with the terrible news. He rapidly came to the conclusion that the hag was lying in order to extort as much money from him as possible. Yet the intelligence was so remarkable that he could find no reason why it should not be true. Nobody would make up a lie like that, not even a crafty old witch like her. He had half a mind to go back and double-check the facts, but he was not sure he could afford to.

He attempted to proceed in the direction the old woman had indicated. The sounds of riot grew louder.

Encouraged, he pressed on. The roaring of the rabble was deafening, and as he turned a corner he emerged near the church of St Martin-in-the-Fields and Charing Cross.

The crowd moved through the streets in orderly fashion. There was not the usual brandishing of guns, knives and swords, though every so often the familiar cry of the mob rose above the general hullabaloo, 'Light your windows. Light your candles for John Bellingham.' If the windows did not open or if candles were not lit, a hail of stones would shatter the panes. The cry was infrequent, however, it still being light outside, and it was directed only at the largest private dwelling places on the Strand and beyond. By and large the crowd was in a mood of celebration. It was like a promenade. People wore their Sunday-best and strolled leisurely, arm in arm, talking and laughing, towards Westminster.

Jack joined the festive mob as it meandered its way along the Strand and rambled into Whitehall.

'God bless you, John Bellingham, God bless you,' shouted an old woman standing on a post, yelling Bellingham's praises to the world. Elsewhere, in the doorways of taverns and coffee-houses, industrious ballad-singers, poets and entertainers were busy extemporizing odes, epitaphs and songs to the courage and heroism of John Bellingham. People told jokes about Perceval, speculated on the course of events, placed bets on the outcome. The young and the idealistic saw the killing as a spark that would ignite the revolution, the kindling for a conflagration that would engulf the country. 'Rescue Bellingham or Die,' read several hand-painted placards. The humid night swam with talk of the assassination. 'More of these damned scoundrels must go the same way, and then poor people may live,' Jack overheard as he passed a group of old men smoking their pipes, ambling in the direction of

Parliament. He did not catch the reply but knew the speaker's companions would nod sagely and mutter, 'Aye.'

A man ran down the middle of the street, skittering through the crowd, leaping into the air and shouting with almost frantic joy, 'Perceval is shot! Hurrah! Perceval is shot!'

Jack dodged this way and that, weaving his way through the good-natured mob as it followed its course lazily but implacably towards Parliament. He did not know if going there was a good idea, but he had to see it. He had to witness the conclusion of it all. He wanted to see it through to the end.

The power and enthusiasm of the crowd were a joy to behold. A sight he had long wished to see. It invigorated him, it empowered him, it drew him to its heart and promised him safety as long as he did not stray, as long as he was prepared to act. The mob was a collective entity acting as an individual. If it acted, then you had to act or cease to be a part of the mob. And a mob could do only two things: act or disperse. Jack submitted to this silent compact, readying himself for the inevitable assaults by the forces of law and order, Church and King.

Every street was stiff with people, and the going was very slow, but gradually he pushed his way into the main body of the mob and was sucked along by its fitful, peristaltic surges until he was deposited in a wedge of people stuck opposite the Banqueting House on Whitehall. As he waited for an opportunity to move forward there came a shout from the right and a sudden scattering of people in all directions. The road had seemed packed a moment before, movement forward or backward had appeared impossible, but now the crowd was parting. Jack turned to look as the gates to the nearby barracks swung open. A fully armed mounted troop, swords drawn, trotted towards them.

Suddenly all movement stopped. Silence descended amid the part of the crowd that could see what was happening. Jack was taken aback by the sight of armed men, of frothing-at-the-mouth, smelly horses. Riflemen moved out to flank the Horse Guards. The few seconds of silence were broken by the officers' barked orders. Without a moment's hesitation the cavalrymen charged the crowd, which attempted to scatter even further than it already had. It strained and screamed and pushed, but there was nowhere else to go.

Some climbed up poles and statues and scaled fences and buildings. They tore down flags and hurled pieces of wood, food, bottles and stones. Others were slashed by gallantly flashing sabres. He saw yet others, trampled, clubbed and stabbed, fall helpless beneath the hooves of the frightened horses.

In front of him, towards the river, he could see the brave cavalrymen ploughing through the field of peaceful people and he could see those once peaceful citizens emerge in the wake of horses, batons and glistening steel as extremely angry people.

When Jack moved forward the increasingly mob-like mob parted before him as if knowing and respecting his more prominent role in the unfolding story. Nettleton plunged on. Near Palace Yard he managed to squeeze himself on to a small, grassy knoll close to the St Stephen's entrance to the House of Commons.

The cavalry were making slow and painful progress towards Parliament, though now its progress was painful to both sides. Someone near the river started jumping up and down and yelling, waving what appeared to be a helmet high above the heads of the crowd. Before very long the nearly naked and trussed body of one of His Majesty's celebrated Horse Guards was passed, wriggling and squirming and shouting, over the heads of the cheering mob and dumped into the river with a splash. It took the soldiers more than

230

half an hour to reach Palace Yard and dismount, during which time the mood of the mob had grown ever more violent and murderous.

They packed the square in front of the Houses of Parliament, overflowed down Whitehall, bridged the Thames at Westminster. They chanted Bellingham's name. Their huzzahs and drum rolls filled the evening air. It was a heady mixture. The humid heat, the masses collected together, the struggles and violence of the Horse Guards, the closed immobility of the carriage waiting to begin its journey to Newgate and the cold, insensibility of the Palace of Westminster, where Bellingham sat, expressionless, waiting for his moment, knowing his time had come. The danger was palpable. It did not need to be imagined. Everybody saw it, from the greenest army recruit to the most seasoned rioter – the possibility of extreme violence, of savagery, of unleashing something that perhaps could not be stopped. The crowd, the soldiers, every-one poised on the edge.

Jack surveyed the crowd from his vantage point on the grassy knoll. He thought he saw some of his workmates in a group near the bridge. He wished he were with them, oblivious to the importance of the events, enjoying a night out. The printworks would be closed. They would be in buoyant mood.

His eye caught a group closer to him. They were among the most vociferous. They yelled bloodcurdling threats and imprecations. They set an example for those around them, who, by joining in, thought they were following the mood of the meeting. The curious thing about this small knot of riot captains was that they all, to a man, had something missing. An arm, a leg, an eye.

A little way off a group of men were burning the Prince Regent in effigy, egged on by a small man with a hunchback. Further away shops were being looted and windows smashed by a renegade section of the crowd. In each of these disturbances Nettleton saw, or thought he saw, a hidden hand. The hand of the man he had followed earlier. He had paid each and every one of these rioters.

Jack's heart quailed as he realized that what he looked at was no more a spontaneous expression of the people's will than a whipped horse's gallop is an expression of its own desire to move quickly. The mob's will, whether it fully appreciated it or not, was Stillwater's will. The people did his bidding, though they would never know who he was. The whole farrago had been reduced from a life-and-death struggle, from an act of revolutionary defiance or supreme idiocy, to a series of transactions in a complicated system of barter and exchange, to a business deal – to money.

Nettleton was filled with loathing. Their smell, the ignorance of their conversation, their clothes, their sullen, stupid-looking faces, their dull, twitted eyes – everything about the mob repulsed him. He was closed in, trapped. He looked for a way to make his escape, to leave the grotesque farce behind him, but he was hemmed in on all sides. The more he looked, the more faces he picked out from the crowd. That bunch of apprentices throwing sticks and tearing up the cobbles, the tall man had recruited them behind the Drury Lane Theatre. The motley collection of youths and vicious old women near the front who were surging forward, spooking the horses, spitting and yelling and throwing missiles, Jack had seen them all take the mysterious man's money. He was suddenly struck by the thought that everyone in the mob was related, however remotely, to one of these ringleaders. Far from balancing on a knife edge, law and order was firmly in the pocket. There would be no revolution; there wouldn't even be a riot. This was the endgame of some match, some machination, of which he had chanced to glimpse only a few moves. It was all influenced, all engineered, designed and built for some hidden purpose beyond the grasp of any of its protagonists.

Suddenly the mob surged. A massive movement towards Westminster Bridge. Shouts and yells drifted across the square. They were trying to take Bellingham away by boat. Just as the entire crowd shifted riverwards, the small door of the St Stephen's entrance opened and John Bellingham was bundled out between five burly dragoons. As they dragged him towards a waiting carriage, the guards parted for a moment and Bellingham was afforded a glimpse of the crowd. He stopped dead, his mouth open in amazement. A cheer rose from the portion of the crowd able to see him.

Jack looked at the tiny figure in the distance. He squinted to try to get a better look at his face. One of the guards shoved Bellingham from behind. He tripped and fell, bloodying his nose. He was hauled back to his feet by the ropes that bound his hands behind his back and manhandled into the carriage.

From the midst of the crowd Jack saw a fat man trundle forward. He recognized Bannister Truelock instantly. Truelock ran through the soldiers, knocking them aside almost casually. He leaped into the carriage, shouting something that Jack could not quite make out, but it raised a huge cheer from the crowd nearest the incident. Just as the cheers faded a Horse Guard grabbed Truelock by the hem of his cassock and yanked him out of the carriage. The door was slammed shut and the blinds drawn. And as Truelock tumbled to the ground the driver lashed at his team of horses. They pulled away quickly. Truelock screamed as the wheels passed over him, his howls of agony replacing the sound of drums, drowning out the huzzahs, audible above the snorting of the horses and the clanking of the carriage.

TWELVE

OLD BAILEY

Tuesday Morning, Old Bailey

Dear Mrs Roberts

Yesterday midnight I was escorted to this neighbourhood by a noble troop of Light Horse and delivered into the care of Mr Newman (by Mr Taylor, the magistrate and MP) as a State Prisoner of the first class. For eight years I have never found my mind so tranquil as since this melancholy but necessary catastrophe: as the merits or demerits of my peculiar case must be regularly unfolded in a Criminal Court of Justice to ascertain the guilty party, by a jury of my country, I have to request of you the favour of sending me three or four shirts, some cravats, handkerchiefs, nightcaps, stockings, &c., out of my drawers, together with comb, soap, toothbrush, with any other trifle that presents itself which you think I may have occasion for, and enclosing them in my leather trunk, and the key, please, to send sealed, per bearer; also my greatcoat, flannel gown and black waistcoat, which will much oblige, Dear Madam, your very obedient servant, John Bellingham

To the above please to add the prayerbook.

*   *   *

A True Account of the trial and defence of John Bellingham, horrid assassin of the Right Honourable Spencer Perceval, at the Old Bailey, Friday the 15th May, 1812.

The Prisoner at the bar was of tall stature, thin in person, his face oval, his nose aquiline and prominent, his eyes convex and a dark blue in colour. He was dressed in a brown greatcoat, yellow waistcoat with small black stripes, and nankeen trousers. The Prisoner looked terrified at first and gave the appearance of being quite overcome by the occasion. However, he recovered himself momentarily and stepped forward to the dock and bowed deeply to the Court.

The Defence (Chief Counsel Mr Peter Alley) rose at once to ask the Court for an adjournment in order to show that the Prisoner could be proved to be insane if sufficient time were allowed for witnesses to appear in his favour. Mr Alley was ruled out of order. The Prisoner must first make a plea to the charges before the Court. Mr Alley argued that his defence rested on the presumption that Bellingham was insane and therefore unfit to plead. The prosecution, led by the Attorney-General Sir Vicary Gibbs, intervened to make known its opposition to an adjournment. Sir Vicary: 'It is necessary that the Prisoner should be called upon in the first place to say whether he be Guilty or Not Guilty. When he has done so, then his Counsel may be called upon to help him.' Chief Justice Mansfield (Judge Presiding): 'I cannot hear any person as Counsel for the Prisoner until he has pleaded. We are not to know at present that the Prisoner has any Counsel. Nor even that the Prisoner is the man referred to in the indictments.'

The two indictments were read by the Clerk of the Arraigns, and the Prisoner was called upon to plead.

'My lords, before I can plead to this indictment I must state, in justice to myself, that by hurrying on of my trial I am placed in a most remarkable situation. It so happens that my prosecutors are actually the witnesses against me. All the documents on which alone I could rest my defence have been taken from me and are now in the possession of the Crown. It is only two days since I was told by Mr Litchfield, the Solicitor of the Treasury, to prepare for my trial; and when I asked him for my papers, he told me that they would not be given up to me. It is, therefore, my lords, rendered utterly impossible for me to go into my justification; and in the circumstances in which I find myself, a trial is absolutely useless. The papers are to be given to me after the trial, but how can that avail me for my defence? I am, therefore, not ready for my trial.'

The Attorney-General jumped immediately to his feet, eager to proffer his explanations, but the Chief Justice silenced him and brought the Court back to the matter in hand. The Prisoner had not yet pleaded. Bellingham replied again that he did not wish to plead at this point. The Court insisted and prevailed. Bellingham said, in a subdued voice, 'Not guilty. I put myself upon God and my country.'

Mr Alley then presented to the Court two sworn affidavits, one from Ann Billet of Southampton, the other from Mrs Mary Clarke of Bagnio Court, Newgate Street. Each stated her belief that Bellingham had earlier exhibited many signs of madness.

Sir Vicary Gibbs, in the acerbic manner that has become his trademark as Attorney-General, replied: 'It appears that this is clearly a contrivance to delay the administration of justice. Where has the Prisoner been for the four months preceding this act for which he is this day called upon to answer? He has been resident in this town, in the midst of a family, known to multitudes of persons in this town, transacting business in this town, and with as much sagacity and as perfect and masculine an understanding as any man who now hears me.'

The Chief Justice, after hearing that two doctors, whose attendance had been requested by Mr Alley, had both refused to appear, ruled that there were no proper grounds for postponement.

The prosecution opened with a long address by Sir Vicary Gibbs to the jury, in which he reiterated the charges made against the Prisoner and explained the difference between civil and criminal incapacity. 'A man, though incapable of conducting his civil affairs, is criminally liable, provided he has a mind capable of distinguishing between right and wrong.'

Bellingham listened with the utmost serenity. He frequently looked round and appeared to contemplate the crowd with a curious eye. He took from his pocket an orange, which he peeled and ate. Amongst the spectators was the Marquis Wellesley and other distinguished gentlemen. The Prisoner asked for a chair, which was brought immediately. Seated, he looked entirely composed and listened attentively to the Attorney-General.

A procession of witnesses followed the opening address and testified to the events of Monday the eleventh. The Prisoner was identified as the perpetrator of the heinous crime. One James Taylor, a tailor, identified a coat he had made as a special commission for the Prisoner. The coat itself was identified by John Newman, the Newgate Keeper, as the one in which Bellingham had arrived at Newgate. His assistant further identified the item of clothing. 'I was in the room when the Prisoner acknowledged this coat to be his coat; he said that in the scuffle in the House of Commons the coat was torn, and that he wished to have it mended; there was a man in the chapel yard in the room under the Prisoner's room that was a tailor and the coat was lowered down to him, by a string to the window, to be mended.'

The case for the Crown concluded with the identification of the pistol as the instrument of murder and the further identification by Mr Dowling that it was the pistol he found in Bellingham's hand after the assassination.

'Prisoner, the evidence being gone through on the part of the prosecution, now is the time for you to make any defence you have to offer or to produce any witnesses whom you wish to be examined.'

The Prisoner got to his feet and replied: 'I leave it to my Counsel, my lord.'

'Counsel is allowed only to examine witnesses and advise the Prisoner on points of law. Otherwise your defence is in your own hands.'

The Prisoner, after some moments looking through his documents, which had been returned to him, began his defence by thanking the Attorney-General for his animated opposition to the possibility of his insanity. He admitted the act: justification for it was what he set out to prove. Bellingham's address lasted two hours.

'Gentlemen, I beg your pardon for thus detaining you, but I am wholly unaccustomed to situations like the present, and this is the first time I have addressed a public audience. I therefore hope to receive your candid indulgence, and trust that you will pay more attention to the matter detailed than to the manner in which it is delivered.

'Do you suppose me the man to go with a deliberate design, without cause or provocation, with a pistol to put an end to the life of Mr Perceval? No, gentlemen! Far otherwise. I have strong reasons for my conduct, however extraordinary, reasons which, when I have concluded, you will acknowledge to have justified me fully in this fatal fact. Had I not possessed these imperious excitements, and had I murdered him in cold blood, I should consider myself a monster, not only unfit to live in this world, but too wicked for all the torments that may be inflicted in the next.'

Bellingham read to the jury the petitions he had sent to Parliament and, one by one, their formal rejections. He was, on occasion, overcome by emotion. His hands were seen to tremble, and once he burst into tears. For the most part, however, he was firm, level and composed. He was, he asserted, falsely imprisoned in Russia: 'Think, gentlemen, what I endured – and what was my offence? Nothing: there was not the shadow of proof against me. It was falsehood from beginning to end; yet this they called giving me justice. This, thank God, is not the way it is administered in this happy country.'

At this point he was overcome with emotion and wept quietly for some moments. Chief Justice Mansfield was compelled to call on him to continue.

'Gentlemen, thus was I again thrown into a dungeon. I was dragged about the streets with offenders who had been guilty of the most atrocious crimes. Of what must my heart have been composed, that was the sufferer of this indignity, and this torture, to the eternal disgrace of both nations? I applied to Sir Stephen Shairpe again without success – I was not listened to – I could obtain no redress there. I sought it here in my native country. I was again refused! My fortune and my character have been ruined, and I stand here alone and unprotected by all but the laws of my country. They, I trust, will afford me that which all others have denied.'

The Prisoner paused again, twisting in his fingers a sprig of rue. 'I have admitted the fact. Again I admit it, but I must state something further in my justification. I have been denied the redress of my Government. I have been ill-treated. I was accused most wrongfully by a Governor-General in Russia and have sought redress in vain. I am a most unfortunate man and feel in my heart sufficient justification for what I have done.' Here the Prisoner touched his breast. 'For eight years I have been persecuted on account of circumstances that were mere invention for my ruin: I was driven almost to despair, and I had even a *carte blanche* from the British government to right myself in any way I might discover. I have done so.

'I am now unexpectedly called to judgement, though for the last eight years I have sought judgement and justice from the Government in vain. For six long years I was confined to Russian gaols. For six years I suffered that miserable condition, bandied from prison to prison, from torture to torture, made a public spectacle of, led through the streets of St Petersburg with a common herd of malefactors. I saw myself reduced to utter ruin. I was involved in debt without any means of extrication. I was sinking under the pressure of accumulated miseries – miseries brought on not by my own indiscretion, but by the injustice of others. The Attorney-General has told you, and he has told you truly, that till this period my name, my character, were without blemish, till this melancholy, this deplorable transaction, which no man, I can solemnly assure you, laments more deeply than I do. Till this fatal moment, my life was without reproach.' At this point his voice wavered and he broke down weeping once again. 'That my arm destroyed him, I allow; that he perished by my hand, I admit; but to constitute felony there must be *malice prepense*, there must be the wilful intention, and I deny that it has been proved. Unless proved, the felony cannot be made out – this you will shortly hear from the Bench – and in that case you must acquit me.'

He sat down, exhausted from his great exertion, and asked for a glass of water. His face was flushed and his hair damp with perspiration.

After consultation with Counsel the witnesses for the defence were called. Ann Billet, cousin of the accused, came to the stand. She testified to their shared childhood, the death of the accused's father from insanity. His constant brooding on his sufferings had worried her. He dreamed of wealth of estates in the country. His obsession had reached a point where the merest mention of Russia threw him into a passion. His anger and grievances were well known and the topic had long been avoided by any who called themselves friends. The witness, however, was unable to adduce anything but hearsay evidence of the accused's insanity. Rebecca Roberts, the Prisoner's landlady, was excused attendance on the grounds of ill-health. In her stead her housemaid gave evidence. She confirmed that Mr Bellingham was a quiet gentleman but often seemed confused and nervous. He appeared to write a good many letters.

'On the Monday, before you went out, had you noticed anything particular?'

'I noticed a word and his actions. I thought he was not so well as he had been for some time past.'

Shortly after the evidence of the maid a commotion broke out at the back of the courtroom. Sheriff Heygate informed the Bench that two men had just arrived from Liverpool in a post-chaise and four, to speak on the Prisoner's behalf. The news caused a considerable stir, and Chief Justice Mansfield was forced to bring the Court to order. The two men were brought in and sworn to the stand. However, when they saw the Prisoner, they both declared that 'He is not the person we had supposed him to be. We had supposed him to be another person, bearing his description, in whose conduct we had frequently seen marks of derangement.'

The Lord Chief Justice moved swiftly to his summing up. His was an emotional summation. At every mention of the late Prime Minister, Mr Perceval, he burst into tears. The spectators joined in the weeping, and the whole was a most pathetic spectacle that deeply affected this reporter for one.

The jury retired to consider their verdict, which they reached in fifteen minutes. The foreman, in a faltering voice, announced the verdict: Guilty.

When asked if he had anything to say why sentence of death should not be passed upon him, the Prisoner replied: 'I would ask you to recollect that my family was ruined and myself destroyed by these miseries merely because it was Mr Perceval and his Ambassador's pleasure that justice should not be served; sheltering himself behind the imagined security of his station and trampling law and right in the belief that no retribution could reach him. When a Minister sets himself above the law, he does so at his own risk. If this were not so, the mere will of a Minister would become the law, and what would then become of your beloved liberties?

'A man who robs for a few shillings is deprived of life. I have been robbed of everything. I have been imprisoned for years; my wife, my family, have been ruined; and I am now called to answer for my life simply because Mr Perceval chose to patronize iniquity.

'I hope, I pray, that my actions will be a warning to future Ministers to attend to the applications and prayers of those who suffer by oppression.

'And now, as it seems that I am destined to sacrifice my life, I shall meet my doom with conscious tranquillity. I shall look forward to it as the weary traveller looks for the promised Inn, where he may repose his weary frame, after enduring the pelting of the pitiless storm.

'I have said enough.'

*   *   *

Sentence of Death, 15th May, 1812.

Prisoner at the bar:

You have been convicted by a most attentive and merciful jury of the most flagitious crime human nature can perpetrate, wilful and deliberate Murder, a crime which in all ages, and throughout all Nations, has justly been held in the highest detestation.

Odious and abominable as it is in the eyes of God and man, it presents itself in your case with every possible feature of aggravation. The object of your bloodthirsty vengeance was endowed with every virtue that can adorn Public and Private life, whose suavity of manners and gentleness of deportment disarmed hostility of its rancour and violence of its asperity. By his Death you have deprived charity of one of its most sincere and active Friends, religion of one of its firmest supports, domestic society of one of its happiest examples of Endearment and felicity, and the country of one of its brightest ornaments. A man whose Ability and whose worth would probably have produced lasting benefits to the Empire and ultimate advantage to the World. Every part of your iniquitous conduct is strangely impressed with the foulest character of atrocious guilt. When he was in the midst of unarmed friends, defenceless, except in the consciousness of virtue, and confiding in that security which ought to surround every man in this Christian Country, on the very point of fulfilling his public duty to his Country, nay, at the very threshold of the sanctuary of its Laws, your infuriate hand committed this impious deed.

To indulge in any conjectures as to your motives for this horrid act would lead me into an investigation of all that is base and perfidious in the Human Heart.

The more this dreadfully diabolical transaction is contemplated, the more does the mind recoil from it with repulsive Horror. For the sanguinary Nature of assassination is most abhorrent to man, inasmuch as it is calculated to render Bravery useless and Cowardice predominant. Justly does your crime merit the excoriation of mankind. And the voice of God has declared that 'He who sheddeth Man's blood, by Man shall his blood be shed.' Publicly, therefore, must you expiate that crime, whereby you have so much afflicted and disgraced your indignant country: and, I trust that the example of your ignominious fate may duly operate to deter all others from the repetition of a crime which must infallibly attract the vengeance of a justly offended Deity.

A very short time indeed remains for you to supplicate the Throne of Grace, for that Mercy which Public Justice forbids you to expect in this world. I sincerely hope that the interval which has passed between the perpetration of your horrid Crime and the present moment has not been unemployed in imploring pardon of the Almighty, and it is my most fervent wish that your Prayers may, through the merits of our Redeemer, find acceptance.

It only remains for me to pass upon you the dreadful Sentence of the Law, which is that you, John Bellingham, be taken to the Place from whence you came, and that on the Monday next you be conveyed to a Place of Execution and there be Hanged by the Neck until you be dead and that your Body be afterwards Dissected and Anatomized. And may God have mercy on your soul.

THIRTEEN

NEWGATE

The Reverend Daniel Wilson checked his appearance in the vestry mirror. He liked what he saw. The puffy, gossamer sleeves tied tightly to the wrist with black silk ribbon looked spectacular. His black mantle hung in voluptuous folds around his neck, contrasting dazzlingly with the bright whiteness of his shirt and the thin strip of black silk round his collar. The hair was looking good today also. Curly and swept back from the forehead and over the ears, cut short, but with a luxurious thickness. He crossed himself surreptitiously and knelt before the mirror to pray before making his entrance into the chapel.

As he opened the connecting door he was struck by the familiar smell of the burning candles, the faintest hint of incense, the warmth of a full chapel. It was so quiet that he could hear the breathing of a hundred souls. The smells, the sounds, were comforting and welcoming to him. There were some among the clergy who dreaded the Sunday service and the address to the congregation. They hid behind the order of service as if it were a mask. Wilson was different; he ached for Sunday and the opportunity it afforded him to share his learning and reading, his ideas and his personal vision of salvation, with a willing, participating, critical audience.

He took a deep breath and passed through the door.

He nodded to the verger, who closed it behind him. Wilson walked out directly to the altar. He eschewed the practice of processing into the service, proceeded by choirboys and swinging censers. In any case the chapel was too small for such elaborate ceremonies. Wilson regarded the chapel as his private lecture theatre. The congregation were welcome, but they were expected to make use of their minds and not sit back and doze off. If Wilson had something to say, he demanded that they listen. And Daniel Wilson always had something to say.

That particular Whit Sunday, May 17th, Wilson took as his text not the usual passage from Romans about the Holy Spirit, for he knew that in almost every church in all corners of the kingdom that sermon would be preached – even the Nonconformists would preach from that text. Instead he concentrated on the words of the Psalmist in Psalm 68. 'The rebellious dwell in a dry land.' That was his keynote, but the remainder of the psalm was equally applicable, with its talk of widows and the fatherless, its images of drought and rain, the notion of God delivering the righteous from their enemies. The imagery was a peculiar mixture of the savage and the poetic. The dogs lapping at the blood of thine enemies. The wings of a dove covered with silver and her feathers with yellow gold. This was a deep seam to be mined.

The larger-than-usual numbers, the haste with which even the oldest, goutiest and shortest of breath dropped to their knees, Wilson knew the signs. The fear of his congregation was palpable. These were evil times. The church filled up like this only when people felt their lives touched directly by events. Times of war, of riot and unrest – they brought out the faithful in large numbers.

' "The rebellious dwell in a dry land." ' Wilson left the phrase echoing round the chapel as he adjusted his notes and made himself comfortable in the pulpit. He followed this pregnant pause by leaning forward and taking off his spectacles. ' "The rebellious dwell . . ." ' He looked about him. In the front row, a wealthy family in their own pew, mother and father, three daughters and a son all avoiding his probing gaze. Wilson waited until he had made eye contact with every single one of them, even the eight-year-old, who shifted uncomfortably and sat on her hands; he waited until he was sure that they could bear it no longer, until they salivated with expectation. ' " . . . in a dry land." ' He replaced his spectacles and relaxed into his introductory remarks.

Not one single worshipper was in any doubt about the subject of Wilson's homily. The week's events had left their scars. Reports of riot and wrecking from the north brought with them the spectre of violence and insurrection. Men lifted their hands to their necks involuntarily and rubbed where the spectral noose chafed. Women held their children tight to their skirts and would not let them out of their sight. The gaming houses and brothels were nearly empty. The streets were deserted from lamplighting to dawn. People kept their distance. Social divisions translated into physical barriers. Barred doors, closed carriages. It was as if everybody was waiting for somebody else to put up the barricades, to throw the first stone, to fire the first shot.

Wilson understood the mood of his audience. He knew most of them personally and dined with the most prestigious on a near-rota basis. Apart from anything else, he was an eligible bachelor who would need a suitable bride when his elevation to bishop was finally confirmed. He knew what they wanted to hear. He knew what they did not want to hear. For them, to know that God's justice was a higher justice, that His laws were not their laws, was worse than useless: it was damnably close to treacherous. They needed to

247

know that God was on their side, the side of commerce and civilization, that He would not countenance the triumph of the lower sorts, the inferior set of people, that, at least in Great Britain, the universe would remain ordered as He had ordained it from the beginning. They wanted to know that although it was harder for a rich man to enter the Kingdom of Heaven than for a camel to pass through the eye of a needle, the 'eye of a needle' was, in fact, a comparatively large gate into the city of Jerusalem. And because he knew them, because he knew that they were all, by and large, good people, Wilson had no qualms about assuring them that their wealth was a sign of God's blessing and their place in the choir of angels was as safe as their gold in the Bank of England.

'The rebellious,' said Wilson solemnly, 'need no long introduction from me, though perhaps it would be wise to clarify that term, to expound on that expression, to speak a little of rebellion.' There was a general rustling of muslin and crêpe, creaking of leather shoes and deflating of lungs as the congregation settled down into their pews. 'When we speak of the rebellious, what exactly is it that we mean? When the Psalmist chose that word, what was he trying to convey? Was it meant to refer only to those who take up arms against the legally constituted Government? Those who organize resistance to authority? I do not believe so. King David knew something of rebellion. His own kingdom was torn apart with civil strife. His own son turned against him, Absalom, slain as he hung suspended by his hair from a tree.' Wilson threw back his head and drew a deep breath. He faced his audience with a look of immense grief that shocked those who were paying attention and who had never before witnessed the histrionics for which Daniel Wilson was justly famous. ' "Absalom, O Absalom, would God I had died for thee! O Absalom, my son, my son!" ' Wilson wailed. He let his chin drop to his chest and spoke very quietly. 'David knew the pain that only a parent can know at the waywardness of a child. And it is this second kind of rebelliousness of which the Psalmist sings also. You have taught your son to walk, to talk, you have given him everything – food, shelter, clothing, love – and you are repaid with calumny and detestation. Wilfully your offspring go against your will. They test you to the limits of your endurance.

'Rebellion, then, need not be a matter only of armed struggle. It can be the pushing away of a parent, the scorning of good advice and right conduct. Rebellion is not just a matter of defiance of man's laws; it is an opposition to the will of God, our spiritual Parent.

'Who would deny that God has a plan for mankind? Who would presume to know what that plan is? Yet we can feel assured there is such a plan. Those who seek to defy that plan, the divinely ordained progress of History, seek to defy God. They are of the Devil, and they do the Devil's work.

'The smashing of a loom is the Devil's work. The destruction of an engine is the Devil's work. The sending of anonymous letters, the writing of seditious pamphlets, the reviling of the King in the agony of his affliction, republicanism – the Devil's work.' Wilson was red in the face. He was pounding his fist on the pulpit. His audience, who to a man, woman and child believed him, even they were a little frightened by his tremendous zeal. Wilson sipped from a glass of water. It was not fresh, and he shot a punishing glance in the verger's direction. The verger shrank into his seat and covered his eyes with his hand. Wilson gulped the stale water down and turned his attention once more to the congregation, who sat on the edge of their seats, unsure whether to make a run for it before the fire and brimstone descended or to stay where they were, beneath the vaulted ceiling's sacred protection.

' "In a dry land." A dry land,' he mused. He pushed the phrase round his mouth with his tongue. 'Why should the rebellious live in a dry land when the rain falls on the just and the unjust alike? What is the nature of their drought? The love of God is to the righteous as the rain to a dry land. It lets them flourish and blossom anew. The enemies of the Lord do not have His love, they live in a perpetual drought, tormented by thirst, railing against their parched land, their parched throats, cursing God as if He and not they themselves were responsible for their condition. They need only turn to Him and He would give them water to drink and manna to eat, but they will not turn. They are stubborn, and they turn their backs on Him. And where there is not God's love there is too the absence of morality. Men and women lie together outside matrimony, they gamble and drink, they neglect their children, they neglect their work, they look enviously at their hard-working, God-fearing neighbour and they see his plenty and they would kill him for his bounty. But before long they have turned that poor soul's husbandry into dust and ashes blown on the scorching wind of their Godless immorality.'

Wilson had them in his thrall. He always knew how to get to them, how to lead them to draw their own conclusions, to infer the deeper meaning from his essentially theological address. Wilson himself was not a reactionary; he saw himself as a liberal conservative. He read the pamphlets he so roundly condemned. He kept abreast of politics from both Whig and Tory perspectives. He had read Thomas Paine and even approved of one or two ideas in *The Rights of Man* (though he knew for a fact that *The Age of Reason* was a poorly researched piece of anti-clerical propaganda). He was widely read in the arts and sciences. Byron, Wordsworth, Coleridge were all known to him. He had dined with the Lambs on one occasion.

Wilson understood that he lived in a time of change. The machine was changing the pace of life. The world no longer travelled on country time – the cities led the pace. If more goods could be produced, then more goods would have to be sold. The hissing and clanking, the relentless pushing forward, pushing forward, of the machine drove them all onwards, propelled them into the future. Wilson appreciated that this sudden change of pace created uncertainty and anxiety in his congregation, in the country as a whole. Nobody knew exactly where they stood any more, nobody could explain exactly what it all meant. There was chaos all around, and it was the Church's special function to provide stability and unchanging moral certitude. Therefore Wilson applied himself to the task of shoring up the values of the old world in the face of the pressure from the new, the different, the unknown. He kept his liberal opinions for the dinner table and his notebooks. There were plenty of young tyros preaching up a storm about the need for change, for equality, for the abolition of this and the protection of that. As a priest he felt it incumbent on him to provide the faithful with the reassurance they craved.

Daniel Wilson finished his address with an appeal for calm, for common sense, and bowed his head in prayer. He offered up prayers for the dead and for those about to die. He prayed that the Lord would do His will and he hoped that they, His servants, would be able to follow that will and restore order and good government to the people in the trying times that lay ahead. He mentioned no names, though all knew of whom he spoke. The prisoner in the condemned cell, his victim in the cold earth.

He left his curate to shake the hands of the departing congregation while he dressed in the vestry. He had an appointment for dinner with James Stephen, MP. He was eager to make a good impression on Stephen.

He did not want to be late and he did not want to rush. Appearance and demeanour were qualities that very few clergymen considered adequately. It was all well and good for a country parson to wander around the fields and the hedgerows with sweat dripping into his eyes and his shirt-tails hanging out, but a cultured, educated urban minister needed gravitas and cultivation in order to move in the right circles, in order to get the job done properly. Wilson considered it his duty to move among the wealthy and powerful, reminding them of their immortal souls and the wider ethical considerations of Christian tenets. Curates were ordained to deal with the sick and the poor. If they did not get their hands dirty when they were young, they would never develop the requisite humble bearing of a true servant of God.

Wilson slipped his dark frock coat over his shoulders, plunged his feet into his spotless black boots. His man had done a marvellous job; he would tip him something extra for that in this week's wages. He picked up his umbrella and left by the rear entrance. He walked across Gray's Inn Fields and climbed into his carriage on High Holborn.

James Stephen was one of those gentlemen whose white hair grew upwards from the crown of his head. Silhouetted or seen only by his shadow, he always looked as if he was wearing a hat. The phenomenon was not extraordinary and would not in itself have caused the youngest of his domestics to run out of the room laughing. Rather, what caused these frequent and, to James Stephen quite perplexing, outbursts of giggling was his habit of having his hair tightly curled and waved into the appearance of a beehive. Stephen was proud of his coiffure and was universally praised for it. He never suspected for a moment that his flatterers possessed a stronger grasp of human vanity and frailty than he himself.

Daniel Wilson did not comment directly on Stephen's hair, which he had specially curled and preened for Perceval's funeral the day before, but Wilson did give it what he considered to be a longing glance. That seemed to satisfy Stephen, who welcomed the minister warmly and bade him sit down.

'Drink?' asked Stephen, his hand poised on the bell cord.

'A sherry would be very welcome on such a frightful day,' said Wilson, looking over his shoulder out of the window. The rain was pouring down. The wind slammed the rain drops against the pane and rattled the frame.

'Perfectly dreadful,' said Stephen, his hand reaching to smooth back a curl that had dropped on to his forehead. Wilson pretended not to notice.

A servant arrived and Stephen ordered two sherries. The servant crossed over to a cabinet three paces behind Stephen's chair and prepared the drinks. He delivered them on a silver platter, avoiding eye contact with both men. Stephen dismissed the man and waited until the room was clear before continuing.

'Been with me ten years,' he said, leaning forward and lowering his voice. 'Never seen anything like it. Did you take note of his attitude? How could you fail to? I am told it's the same everywhere. Some people – good people, mind – have dismissed all but the most loyal family retainers. The fear, you see. It pervades everything. It seeps into your bones like the cold and damp. It makes you cough and choke like a consumptive. Tomorrow is not soon enough. It would have been better for all of us if he had died resisting arrest or done away with himself.'

Wilson raised his eyebrows at this remark. He understood the gentleman's position, but there was, after all, such a thing as Christian charity.

'Forgive me, Reverend,' said Stephen, sitting back in his chair and slurping noisily at the sherry. 'Spencer and I, we were very close. It's all been such a shock. For me, for Jane and the children, for everyone. Even the Opposition, even the Whigs, were upset. Forgive me. Of course, the foulest murderer should be allowed the time to contemplate his immortal soul. Who are we to deny him the very thing he denied poor old Spencer. But . . . but . . .' He faltered, produced a handkerchief from his coat pocket and dabbed delicately at his eyes. 'He is such an inhuman monster,' shrieked Stephen.

The outburst took Wilson aback. He jumped in his seat and almost spilt his drink.

'I'm sorry, I'm so sorry,' blubbered James Stephen, quite overcome with emotion. 'You see, I went to visit him this morning. Oh, I should never have done it, not in the state I'm in. But it was Jane, you understand, she wanted me to visit, to tell him that she would pray for him. Can you believe that? Can you comprehend the goodness of this woman? Her husband is violently murdered by a lunatic, and she prays for the murderer, she forgives him. Do you think, perhaps, that she might be some sort of saint? Of course not. I didn't mean that seriously, but her fortitude, her will-power, is astonishing. You can see that I admire her, but do not misunderstand. I have known Jane Perceval for many years and, though I regret to say it, there could never be anything more between us than the deep, deep friendship that already exists.' James Stephen stopped his inadvertent confession abruptly. He looked Wilson in the eye and smiled. 'I trust your discretion, Daniel. Tell me, what is it about a man of the cloth that prompts a person to unburden his soul the minute he is alone with him?'

Stephen then laughed, rather too loudly. 'You were saying,' prompted Wilson, 'that you visited Newgate this morning.'

'Was I? Oh, yes, I was. I did. I went there early this morning. Have you ever been?' Wilson shook his head. 'Dreadful place. The stench! Awful.' Stephen shuddered. 'Are you cold? Suddenly I'm cold.'

'About this morning?' Wilson interjected before Stephen could veer any further from the point.

'I saw him this morning. I saw him. We are taught the Devil comes in many guises. This morning he appeared to me in a snuff-coloured silk jacket, a black waistcoat and a flannel gown. It was a sight worthy of the most atrocious Gothic romance. The villain in all his finery, greeting his visitors with the urbanity of a society host, his doleful, cold eyes glinting, his brow creased with worry, inquiring after my health, apologizing for the less than salubrious surroundings. He stood there, looking down on me as I sat on the edge of his bed, the fetters round his ankles, his hands clasped behind his back, and I felt as if he knew some terrible secret, that he had glimpsed something hidden from the rest of us, that he had some insight that gave him such confidence, such assurance, in the face of his certain destruction and the horror of his crimes.

' "Are you a lawyer?" he asked me. I was so astonished at his appearance, at his calm, that I could say nothing. "The hangman, perhaps?" I expect he was trying to shock me. I can tell you that he succeeded. I shook my head, like an idiot, as if his questions had been legitimate. He did not smile. I explained that I was the Member of Parliament for Grinstead and a personal friend of Perceval and his family. He said nothing, but he nodded. I continued and expressed my hope that I could carry word of his contrition to the grieving widow and, for myself, a retraction of those defamatory remarks he made at the trial about the late and very much lamented First Minister. I finished almost breathless. He stared at me intently throughout

255

my short speech, don't you know. He barely even blinked. When I had concluded he remained silent and quite, quite still for several seconds. Then he moved towards me, his chains dragging on the flagstones. He sat next to me and said, he said: "The Government think to intimidate me, but they are mistaken. I have been guilty of no offence, having only done an act of public justice." ' Stephen gasped, as if stunned afresh by the audacity of the remark. Wilson sighed. An expression that he hoped showed sufficient solidarity. 'Naturally, I left straightaway rather than give the man an audience for his lunatic ravings. But even as the door closed behind me, I heard him laughing.' Stephen gulped down the dregs of his sherry. 'To protest his innocence knowing that he has been convicted by a God-fearing jury. To claim innocence when he does not even bother to deny that he killed Perceval. Is he insane, do you think? Can these be the acts of a rational human being? I confess I do not know. When asked if he had shot over somebody's shoulder, because the ball had taken a downward path when it entered Perceval's breast, he was shocked. He never would have dreamed of firing thus and endangering the life of another. His aim, he said, was unobstructed. He says this to a journalist and to me he claims to be innocent of all offence. How can it be? What is happening to the world, Daniel?' Stephen leant back in his chair and closed his eyes.

'What is it I can do for you, Mr Stephen?' inquired Wilson when he thought the silence had gone on long enough. 'Do you wish me to tell you this man is mad? I am not qualified to make such a judgement. You should speak to a doctor if that is what you want. I am a man of God. The most I can do is encourage him to look into his heart, into his soul, and acknowledge the sin that lies therein. If he is possessed of the Devil, I will gladly engage in a struggle for what is left of the unfortunate Bellingham's soul. I cannot promise you anything more than this.'

'I have arranged for you to visit the prison tonight,' said James Stephen, without opening his eyes. 'I would be grateful if you would try to complete the mission with which Jane Perceval entrusted me and which I have failed so pathetically to fulfil. Bring us news of his sincere repentance, Reverend Wilson. Bring us this news, and we will be eternally grateful.'

'Of course,' said Wilson. 'I will do what I can.'

'Thank you,' said Stephen, and his mood brightened as he was unburdened. 'You're staying for dinner, aren't you?'

'Thank you. I would be happy to sit at your table.'

'Perhaps you could say grace for us?' asked Stephen jovially.

'Certainly. It is my job, after all.' Wilson smiled.

Stephen laughed and called for another sherry.

It was only on the journey through the muddy, Sunday-deserted streets of Mayfair and Holborn that the idea of publishing an account of his forthcoming battle with the Evil One popped into Daniel Wilson's head. He turned the idea over in his mind as the carriage jolted him along and the rain beat on the roof. It appealed to him. He liked the idea of being published. He imagined looking up from his desk and seeing his own name on the spine of a book on the shelf. The thought gave him goose-bumps. That his personal intervention, and the subsequent account of his struggle with the Devil (to be published at a modest cost to himself), would place him in front of his rivals in the race for the bishopric did not even occur to him until much later. No, when he examined his conscience, he found it clear and uncorrupted.

As he stepped gingerly from his sodden transport, cloak pulled firmly across his throat, water bouncing from the rim of his hat, Daniel Wilson noticed another gentleman in sombre black hurrying towards the doors of Newgate Prison. He gave him no further thought, preferring to concentrate on executing his journey without slipping on the slimy cobbles of the prison yard.

Wilson was shown into the Turnkey's Lodge to wait for Mr Newman, the prisoner's Keeper. He found the stale-tobacco atmosphere oppressive and at first did not notice the damp gentleman he had seen earlier warming himself by the fire, steaming away gently, but as his attention was drawn to the warmth of the fire he could not fail to see the young clergyman standing, legs apart, in the hearth. Wilson nodded genially in his direction. The young man grinned nervously. Wilson politely inquired after his business.

'I came in the hope of visiting John Bellingham,' said the young priest, falteringly.

Wilson leaned back in his chair and slowly placed his finger tips together in front of his chin. 'Umm?' he said. 'Tell me more.'

The young man sat down next to Wilson and began his story. Wilson remarked during the course of their conversation that his companion was very much his junior and extremely pale, blanched even. Wilson interrupted the young man and inquired after his health, involuntarily bringing his handkerchief to cover his mouth. The young man replied that he was, on the whole, quite well, but that the atmosphere of the prison was having a detrimental effect on his constitution. Wilson agreed that prisons were, in general, unwholesome places and regretted the necessity for such institutions in a land of plenty. He reflected, briefly, on what their mere existence revealed about the fallen nature of humankind and man's need for Divine grace. His companion agreed and went on to explain that he could find transport only on the outside of a carriage and had thus been exposed to the elements for the length of his journey.

Had he come far?

From Whitechapel. Wilson ventured to suggest that he share his cab home and thereby help to prevent the onset of illness. The young man thanked Wilson for his generous offer.

As they spoke Wilson could not help his gaze wandering to the rather shabby appearance of his fellow minister, in particular the muddy boots and coarse trousers hidden underneath his greatcoat. A bushy, ungroomed moustache squatted uneasily on his upper lip. Wilson could not help thinking that it looked rather out of place, not to mention extremely unfashionable, but he shrugged this thought away. He was clearly a dedicated man with a strong sense of vocation. He asked his companion's name.

'Nettles, sir, William Nettles,' replied the young man. 'I've come from Liverpool, sir, to see Mr Bellingham on behalf of his wife. She has asked me to visit and provide what comfort I can on his last night. He has refused to see his wife, sir. Did you know that?'

'No, I did not. Why would he refuse this final comfort?'

'I am sure I do not know. The problem is that I have been denied permission to see the prisoner. I have lost my letter of introduction from Mrs Bellingham, and I have no other means of identifying myself.'

'That is unfortunate,' mused Wilson. 'Perhaps I could help. You could come with me as my assistant, if you wished. I shall be going up to see the prisoner in a little while.'

'That is very kind of you, sir,' said Nettles admiringly.

'Not at all. I am simply impressed by your dedication. You have come a long way to fulfil your commission to Mrs Bellingham. It would be a dreadful waste if your time were wasted. Yours is an example that should be cherished.'

'Thank you, sir.'

They lapsed into silence. Wilson turned his attention to the fire and asked one of the warders to stoke it up a little. The weather, he commented to nobody in particular, was most unseasonable. Nettles made no reply. The warder only grunted as he shoved the poker lethargically around the grate to very little effect.

After a brief interval Keeper Newman came into the lodge and announced that he would show Reverend Wilson to Bellingham's cell. Nettles fell in behind Wilson, and no questions were asked about the second clergyman.

As they crossed the yard Newman intimated that for a small fee he might be able to procure some food and port wine. Wilson, mindful of his own thirst as well as the malnourished look of his chance companion, agreed to the purchase and handed over the required sum. The small party re-entered the prison building by a small door in the corner of the yard. They passed through corridor after corridor of cells, open and closed, on their way to the condemned block, which was situated towards the rear, on the Newgate Street side of the prison. As they approached Bellingham's cell they saw that it was already open. Newman stopped short of the door and ushered them forward. Wilson hesitated a moment before stepping into the open doorway.

Reverend Wilson was struck first by the sight of John Bellingham, the horrid assassin. He was tall, towering several inches above Wilson and Nettles. His brow was permanently creased, his eyes large and watery blue. The nose was especially prominent, roman. His eyes focused, along that nose, on his visitors. He wore a blue flannel gown over a crisp white shirt. A cravat fluffed at his throat. A smart, snuff-coloured jacket and a black waistcoat hung on the door. Bellingham was getting to his feet as Wilson entered, an operation made difficult by the shackles that weighed him down and restricted his movement. The fearsome Bellingham, Devil incarnate, seemed to Wilson to be quite amiable in spite of the circumstances.

It was only after he had taken in Bellingham, the larger-than-life occupant of the cell, that he noticed the cell itself. Eight feet long by six wide. The bed ran along one wall and was made to face a tiny barred window set about ten feet up, just below the ceiling. The narrow width, combined with the height, gave Wilson the impression that he was looking down a tunnel with a glint of light at the end. In the far corner, opposite the bed, was a small ledge surrounded by a metal grille in which was set a large candle that cast a thin light over the cell but did not reach the corners. In one of those corners, directly beneath the candle, was an empty chamber pot covered with a filthy rag. A single chair was beside the bed, but just as Wilson registered the fact, Newman offered another. The prisoner evinced great surprise and pleasure at his visit. He seemed particularly happy to see Nettles. Wilson thought he saw Nettles wink at the condemned man, but dismissed the observation as a trick of the flickering light.

Keeper Newman closed the door on them. Bellingham approached his visitors and shook them by the hand. Wilson took the opportunity to speak first. He wished to assert himself, to stamp his own personality on the meeting, before he, like James Stephen, was overwhelmed by Bellingham's beguiling cheerfulness.

'Mr Bellingham, let me first say that I come to you with no motive other than your own very real benefit. You are within a few hours of an eternal state and I feel it is right that we should talk fully and frankly about this state of affairs.'

'Undoubtedly,' said Bellingham. His voice was

confident, a gentle tenor. 'No topic could be more interesting to me.' Wilson was glad to have begun. The conversation was off to a good start. He was on top of the situation. 'Reverend Nettles has travelled from Liverpool also with this intention. Perhaps together we can make some progress towards your salvation.'

'Indeed, indeed, it is to be hoped so.' Bellingham beamed with delight. 'Please be seated, both of you. Reverend Nettles, perhaps you would like to sit here by the door. Reverend Wilson, opposite me. Gentlemen, I only wish I had the means to entertain you after your journeys.'

'Mr Bellingham,' said Wilson, sitting down, 'as I feel sure this will be a protracted visit, I have taken the liberty of ordering some refreshments to be delivered.'

'Really, Reverend, this is most kind. In other circumstances I would insist that, as your host, it is my duty to provide the vittles, but I am in no position to argue.'

'If I may say so,' ventured Nettles, speaking for the first time, 'it is the least we could do.'

'To be sure, I agree,' said Bellingham, sitting on the edge of the bed. 'You will forgive me, gentlemen, if I occasionally lie down. The weight of the fetters, you see. So unnecessary, but I accept them in the spirit in which they are meant.'

Wilson, desiring urgently to get to the heart of the matter, waved this excessive politeness aside and addressed Bellingham in soothing, pastoral tones until the prisoner was comfortable, at which point he started out on his mission of salvation by opening up to Bellingham the great, fundamental truths of the Scriptures generally. He explained mankind's position as sinners before God; the evil nature of sin; the purity and excellence of God's Holy Law. Wilson opined that as God sees all our sins and transgressions, from the impure thought to the full horror of a violent deed, the burden of our sins was far, far heavier than we could ever conceive. Therefore a right view of our character and situation before God and a genuine abhorrence of sin as committed against Him were essential to repentance. 'I hope I make myself understood,' said Wilson severely.

'Perfectly,' replied Bellingham civilly and with the wisp of a smile at the corner of his mouth. 'I know myself to be a sinner. We come into the world sinners.'

This seemingly mock-serious reply gave Wilson pause to recall the comments of James Stephen. He looked briefly to Reverend Nettles for support on this vital, preliminary issue, but the young man cast his eyes down, turned red and made a great show of coughing. Seeing no help forthcoming from that quarter, the good and kind reverend pressed on alone with his task.

He launched into a marvellous and powerful offensive, describing the stupendous love of God for Man, proved for eternity by the sacrifice of His only begotten Son on the cross in order to deliver humanity from the wrath of Judgement Day. The learned Wilson described the pain and fear of Christ in the Garden of Gethsemane as he awaited betrayal at the hand of one of his friends; the terrible torture of the scourge, opening horrific wounds that would have no time to heal; the thorns digging deep into his flesh as the soldiers, crowning him in mockery, pressed the coronet on to his head; the nails driven into his hands and feet; the final humiliation and suffocating distress of death by crucifixion.

'All this and more,' stressed Wilson, growing impassioned, 'to save you, Mr Bellingham, to save Mr Nettles and myself. The way of mercy is thus opened. God is, in Christ, reconciling the world unto Himself. Pardon and justification are offered freely to every penitent, and the sanctifying influences of the Holy Spirit are promised to all that duly seek them, to enlighten, renew and purify the heart.' He waved his arm around to indicate the three of them, the entire world. 'This being, then, the perilous state of Man as transgressor and this the mercy of God in Jesus Christ, let me beseech you to confess and forsake your sins and seek salvation humbly from God.' Wilson fell back in his chair, red-faced and exhausted, already struggling to commit his turn of phrase to memory, filing away for future use, and possible publication, his extraordinary revelation of grace.

'Reverend Wilson,' spoke Bellingham, 'this pardon, this grace you speak of, is indeed a great and wonderful thing. Tell me, how is it that I obtain it?'

Wilson recovered himself. He was encouraged by this display of curiosity. It showed a humility previously lacking. He explained in a quiet voice that Bellingham must have true contrition to be pardoned. 'A broken and contrite heart He will not despise.'

Bellingham nodded. 'I have confessed my sins before God, and I hope in his mercy.'

The glibness of Bellingham's remark, his coolness, worked as spurs against the reverend's mental fatigue. He had already preached once today, and dinner had been long and heavy on the stomach. None the less he sprang to the attack. 'This is not true repentance,' he fumed. 'This is a mere cursory acknowledgement of wrongdoing. There must be hungering and thirsting after salvation.'

'Hungering and thirsting,' repeated Reverend Nettles feebly, wagging his finger sententiously but unconvincingly and using his other hand to press his moustache to his lip. Wilson and Bellingham looked at him with surprise.

A knock on the door echoed around the cell, announcing the arrival of a large bottle of port, some cold beef and mutton, bread and three mugs. The laden tray was set down on the bed, and the Keeper retreated. The interruption deflated somewhat the heated discussion, and the lean Reverend Wilson implored his hungry and thirsty companions to 'tuck in' while he poured himself a mug of port.

There was silence for several minutes as Bellingham and Nettles engaged their mouths in eating. After a sufficiently long pause Nettles asked after Bellingham's health.

'Well enough, as well as a man's can be who is subsisting on bread and water,' he replied. 'But tell me, how is my family?'

'They are well too, considering,' said Nettles with a melancholy look.

'You think I should have seen my wife?'

'It's probably for the best this way.'

'Yes, without doubt, I feel sure.' Bellingham paused, then added, 'Mr . . . er . . . um . . . Nettles? Your moustache suits you very well. New, isn't it?'

'Thank you, John. Yes, it's a recent addition,' said Nettles.

During this short exchange of pleasantries Wilson himself tucked in to the meats and bread. His long discourse had left him hungering and thirsting.

'Mr Bellingham,' Wilson began again when he was certain Nettles had concluded his conversation and he had finished his light supper, 'do you feel this earnest desire for grace and pardon and this sense of a Saviour that I have tried to point out to you?'

'I confess my sins,' said Bellingham, his mouth still full of beef and bread, 'but I cannot say I feel that sorrow you describe, nor that earnest hungering of mind after salvation.'

'Mr Bellingham, please understand that I can go no further until there be some impression on your heart, some relenting, some desire after a Saviour. Until then all I can say will be in vain. Will you permit me, before I proceed, to implore that grace of the Holy Spirit which alone can soften and renew the human mind?'

'I am certain it would help,' interposed Mr Nettles. 'You must prepare yourself to become a vessel for the Spirit.'

'Yes, I agree,' said Bellingham.

Wilson, feeling that he had at last managed to penetrate Bellingham's defences, placed his mug on the tray and composed his features in a semblance of sobriety and meditation. He leaned close to Bellingham and covered the prisoner's supplicating hands with his own. 'Let us pray,' he intoned in a fine Anglican *sotto voce* that it had taken him many years to perfect. 'Dear, Gracious Lord, Saviour of the World, we beseech Thee to hear this our prayer and look kindly on our humble, sin-filled souls. Just as Thou, in Thy infinite and glorious wisdom, sent Thy only begotten son to die for us on Calvary, to take upon his shoulders the sins of the world, send to us now Thy Holy Spirit so that, as St Paul had the scales lifted from his unbelieving eyes on the Damascus Road, Thou may soften and renew the hearts and minds of us, Thy humble servants. Take from John his hardness of heart, open his eyes to Thy benevolent glory, let him look upon Thy loving face and open his heart to Thee. In a spirit of humility let him seek forgiveness, and we pray Thee, Lord, grant him that peace of mind as he prepares to meet Thee in eternal grace and bliss. Amen.'

'Amen,' chimed in Bellingham.

Wilson opened his left eye and peered at Bellingham suspiciously. The prisoner's eyes were screwed tight shut. Wilson closed his own eyes and in a determined but reverent voice asked Nettles to lead them in the next prayer. Nettles hesitated.

'Reverend Nettles,' said Bellingham, his eyes still closed, 'I would be so grateful if you could intercede on my behalf. My tongue is still tied. Please, I beg you, ask the Spirit to release it.'

Nettles cleared his throat and began, in a rough voice that fluctuated wildly in volume and pitch, to pray.

'Lord Father, who art in Heaven above and in our, er, hearts too . . . umm . . . Lord Father, who sees all our wrongdoings, please, er, please listen to this prayer. Our brother sinner, John, who sits before you in chains, is hard of heart. We implore you – yes, implore you – to send down from up there in the, er, heavens, the fire of your Spirit to ease his troubled mind, to allow him to unburden the sins of his soul.'

'Yes, God, grant me the grace to unburden my sin.'

'Um . . . I'm sorry.' Nettles lost his train of thought following Bellingham's interjection. 'Yes, er, God grant this sincere and humble request because this man is so full of sin' – he was warming to his theme now – 'that his soul is poisoned, overflowing with putrid, disgusting, decaying, festering sores of sin, polluting his mind. He brims over like a cup with diseased ideas and horrible delusions, so send him Your Spirit to release him from his bondage and open his heart. Yes, that's it. Amen.'

'Amen,' said Bellingham.

'Amen,' said Wilson, releasing Bellingham's hands, his eyes wide with incredulity. He thanked Reverend Nettles in a strained voice for his unorthodox but no doubt effective prayer and was privately amazed at how badly he had misjudged the young man. Gathering himself together once more, Reverend Wilson decided to change his tack and attempted to convey to Bellingham the eternity of bliss that awaited the saints, an eternity of wonderful and beautiful things without number and without time, nameless and unimaginable, but very, very nice. Nicer than anything else and, of course, eternal. He then moved, with some skill and poignancy, to the subject of damnation. It was a topic on which he was able to be quite specific in naming some of the revolting tortures that awaited the un-repentant sinner, and he was emphatic about the extraordinary length of time over which these horrors would be performed because they were also infinite in number and duration. He spoke eloquently of con-suming fires, of boiling seas and lakes of blood and degradation and screaming and pleading without end as the damned were hurled forever downward into the abyss of Hell without hope of mercy or remorse, for they had shown none.

Wilson was breathless and parched. He reached for his port. Nobody spoke. He had succeeded in introducing a more serious, contemplative note into the proceedings. He had made his point lucidly and dramatically.

'True, sir, we none of us know what will take place after death,' Bellingham said calmly, following a pause in which the only sound to be heard was Wilson slurping his port.

'On the contrary,' roared Wilson, his blood suddenly boiling, seething with rage. 'We know very well what will happen after death! Hell and damnation for you, sir! Hell and damnation! Unless you repent. Repent, sir, repent or be damned! Repent!' He repeated his demand for contrition as he stamped his boot on the floor. 'Repent, I tell you, or Hell and damnation will follow as surely as night follows day. While for me, sir, for me, eternal salvation, the resurrection of the body, Heaven on Earth. Let me assure you, Mr Bellingham, when we meet our Maker I shall make a good account of my life, whereas you will be cast from his sight. The wheat and the chaff, sir!' He almost spat it out. 'The sheep and the goats, sir, divided. Sheep and goats,' he bleated. 'I can only conclude from your obduracy that you labour under an evil heart of un-belief.'

Bellingham, to Wilson's further annoyance, remained calm in the face of the assault. 'It is my profound belief, Reverend Wilson, that all good men shall be saved. Be they Christian or Jew, Muslim or pagan. Even the Catholics and Nonconformists will be saved.'

'Preposterous! Absolute rubbish!' guffawed Wilson, unable to believe his ears, unable to contain his anger. 'Heathens saved? Why bother to convert them, sir? Why waste our time in the spread of civilization? Why not let them run around stark-naked, howling at the moon?'

'Why not indeed, sir? I believe this with all my heart.'

'Prove it, Bellingham. Give me proof.'

'It is not a matter of proof, Reverend Wilson. As with most matters of religion, it is a matter of faith, a part of the conscience that you wish to awaken in me.'

'Faith? Rot. Don't talk to me about faith. There is nobody more faithful than I.' Wilson faltered. He realized he was being drawn into something dangerous. He switched back. 'But tell me, Mr Bellingham, who are the good?'

'Ah, an excellent question, Mr Wilson. I refer you to the fifteenth psalm of David. "Lord, who shall dwell in thy tabernacle: or who shall rest upon thy Holy hill? Even he that leadeth an uncorrupt life: and doeth the thing which is right, and speaketh the truth from his heart."'

'Surely you would not dare to presume that you have abided by the ethics of the psalm?' said Wilson as he hurriedly thumbed through his Bible and glanced down at the relevant passage. He poked his finger at the page. 'If any man could be described as doing evil to his neighbour, that person is you!'

'Please, I never claimed that I was a good man, or that I embody all the virtues of the psalm. But the Psalmist draws no distinction between those of

269

different race or creed, philosophy or politics. He simply assures us that the good will dwell with the Lord forever, in the same way as Christ assured us that the meek will inherit the earth.'

'To dispute this fully would take much more time than we have available to us and reference to many revered and godly sources who would wholeheartedly, and to a man, refute your argument.'

'I take it, then, that you cannot.'

'At this present moment I choose not to engage you in debate, yes.'

'The next moment will be too late, I fear.'

'Then we should return to the pressing matter of your soul and refrain from specious theological discussions.'

'Perhaps,' said Bellingham. He sat back on his bed and placed his prayerbook beside him.

Daniel Wilson shook his head in exasperation. He unclenched his fists and wiped his sweaty palms on his coat. 'I have tried to avoid any discussion of the direct reason for your present predicament, but I can do so no longer. You seem to have no clear idea of what you have done. If you did, you would shed bitter tears. It is my duty to impress on you the enormity of your crime.'

'I have taken a life and now I freely give my own in recompense. An eye for an eye. What more is there?'

'To begin with,' urged Wilson, verging on despair, 'we are not talking of an abstract, a commodity or even a limb of the body. We are talking about a life, a very real, human life. A life that contributed to society, a human being who was loved by his family and devoted friends. A man well known for his compassionate deeds. In addition this was a man who had given you no personal offence. It is probable he knew nothing of your distress.'

'Oh, Mr Wilson,' Bellingham interrupted, 'he must have known about it.'

'Perhaps, then, he was perfectly within his rights to refuse your claim for compensation?'

Bellingham made no reply except to fold his hands in his lap and watch Wilson with increased, sullen attention as Wilson reached into his coat pocket and drew out a letter.

'This document will prove my point, Mr Bellingham. Without a doubt it will reveal to you the atrocity of your crime, the evil you have done to Perceval and the country. This letter is from the late Mr Perceval to a certain journeyman printer whom he had come into contact with. Mr Perceval, at his own behest, undertook to pay for the schooling of this poor journeyman's youngest child and provide a quarterly allowance for the child's board and clothing. It is important, Belling- ham, that you hear the contents of this letter.

' "Sir, I send you a draft to discharge the following items:

Bill for boy's schooling	£1 2/- 6d
Quarterly allowance	£5
Extra payment on account of wife's illness &c and toward defraying any debts thereby incurred	£5
	£11 2/- 6d

' "I received your letter to which you refer, and if I had found any means of complying with the request contained in it, I would have answered it; but that was not the case. I should hope that if I do not comply with any such request you have sufficient proof that my non-compliance is not owing to a disinclination to serve you. I am, sir, your humble servant, Sp. Perceval. Downing Street

April 27th, 1812. To Mr Dickinson, No. 3 Princes Court, Drury Lane." '

There was a triumphal air in the cadence of his voice

as Wilson finished the letter and folded it away. Stephen had been right to give it to him. It had proved an invaluable weapon.

'This was very kind to be sure,' said Bellingham quietly. 'An extraordinary man, on the one hand to display such simple Christian virtue, while on the other to display such callousness by signing the death warrants of a hundred weavers equally concerned for their jobs, their wives and their children's schooling. Truly a remarkable gentleman.'

'How dare you, sir? How dare you impugn the name of one so generous of spirit, so godly and Christian in his behaviour? Let me tell you that this man's wife prayed for you at his funeral. Yes, sir! Prayed for you! Thus, while you, on a mere presumption of injury in your own mind, have assassinated a man who had never personally injured you, and whose amiable and benevolent character you cannot but acknowledge, his widowed partner, whose injuries from you are incalculably greater than any you can even pretend to have received from Mr Perceval, has, in all the poignancy of her anguish, been offering up prayers to God on your behalf.' Wilson choked with fury and tears as he spluttered out his indignation.

'This was a Christian spirit!' Bellingham agreed. For once he appeared to be genuinely moved. He lowered his head, breaking eye contact with Wilson for the first time in the interview. 'She must be a good woman. Her conduct was more like a Christian's than my own, certainly.'

'If I were to allow you all you wish,' pursued Wilson, rising from his chair, scenting victory, 'that you were injured in the most aggravated manner, yet can that warrant, in any degree, an act of blood? Can that justify you in taking what you are pleased to call justice into your own hands, and to hurry, without judge, jury or law, a fellow creature, without a moment's time for reflection or prayer, into eternity by the treacherous blow of an assassin?'

'Yes.' Bellingham regained his composure. 'He lived but a few minutes.'

'Can your opinion of justice being refused warrant your becoming the judge and executioner in your own case?' Wilson leaned over the prisoner, brought his face close to his. 'Was your view of your own case so infallible?'

Wilson touched a nerve. He heard Bellingham draw in his breath sharply. Wilson sank back into his chair and bowed his head to his knees, exhausted. Bellingham's chains clanked. 'I have confessed my sins before God and trust to a general amnesty of them,' Bellingham said weakly.

Wilson raised his head at Bellingham's quiet declaration and spoke slowly, more from fatigue than a careful choice of words. 'When David, the Psalmist whom you so admire, committed the dreadful crimes of adultery and murder, was he satisfied with a cursory confession of sin and a trust in what you call a general amnesty?' Wilson could no longer disguise the disgust, even hatred, in his voice, nor did he care to. 'Was not his whole heart transfixed with sorrow? Did he not make every reparation to society in his power? And yet, did not the judgements of God continue to pursue him to the very borders of the grave?'

'And yet, David, King David, was not called upon to pay the price that I must pay. His reward was to be the ancestor of God on earth, of Jesus Christ.'

'Yes, yes,' said Wilson testily, ignoring the first part of the statement. 'But this was after David had repented and forsaken his sin and arose purely from the mercy of God in order to show that Christ was to be the saviour of sinners by springing from sinners.'

'Ah, but no man can know all his sins, as you so

rightly pointed out earlier, therefore a general confession is all that one can make.'

'Mr Bellingham, can you now possibly imagine that you are justified in the sight of God in this act?'

'To stand before God is a very different thing from standing before men; and the scripture says, "Thou shall do no murder." '

'How infatuated you must be that, acknowledging as you do that your act is a crime in the sight of God, you are not yet sensible of its atrocity and are practically justifying yourself on account of it.'

'The Lord makes no distinction between one crime and another; all are heinous in his sight. But as we are all creatures of God's own creation, we can only live our lives His wonders to perform. "What shall we say then? Shall we continue in sin that grace may abound?" '

'That is a despicable blasphemy! I regret that I can do nothing for you at this moment.'

'The next might be too late, Mr Wilson.'

'I think perhaps I weary you too much by our long conversation. It would be best if I retired.'

'By no means,' cried Bellingham. 'What could be more agreeable to me than to spend the remaining hours of my life in speculation of the hereafter? I should be glad if you could stay the whole night.'

'I think not, Mr Bellingham, though if I can be of any service, do not hesitate to send for me, no matter the hour. Mr Nettles, we must take our leave.'

'Very kind of you, Mr Wilson,' said the taciturn young clergyman, 'but I think I should stay a while. As the sole representative of the family, I feel it is proper.'

'Very well, I shall not argue with you. I fervently pray that you will prevail upon Mr Bellingham to come to a right consideration of his position before God. Mr Bellingham, I will pray for you.'

'Most kind, Reverend Wilson. I have appreciated our

discussion. I would ask you to come again, but I fear we will not have the chance to speak again. Before you leave, however, I would like to say one thing for Mrs Perceval's benefit. My action, sir, was performed with neither haste nor levity.'

'Goodbye, Mr Bellingham. Turnkey!' The door opened and Reverend Wilson's mission to save the soul of the despicable Bellingham ended in failure. As he was escorted down the corridor he was sure he heard the sound of laughter coming from Bellingham's cell. He knew there was something funny about the Reverend Nettles.

Wilson shivered as he sipped at his brandy and stared out of the window, deep into the darkness beyond his own reflection. The image of that man sitting in his cell not more than half a mile away, feasting on the food and wine that he, Wilson, had provided, tormented him. He was filled with a profound loathing, not just for Bellingham, but for all those who had gathered to cheer his name. A man had been arrested and charged with crying out, in public, 'Oh! I will fire my gun tomorrow: I did not think there was an Englishman left that had such a great heart. He could not have shot a greater rascal!' How could the common people think like that? Their animosity was dreadful to behold. He began to think that Edmund Burke had been right after all when he referred to them as 'the swinish multitude'.

The rain was still falling hard. His man Johnson came into the parlour. 'Someone to see you, Reverend Wilson. Are you receiving?'

'Who is it, Johnson?'

'He would not give his name, sir.'

'Show him in just the same,' said Wilson, coming away from the window and approaching the door. In the shadowy hallway he could see a tall figure hand his cloak and hat to Johnson. Wilson smiled as he recognized an old friend. 'Henry!' he called out. 'Why didn't you give your name, you old rogue?'

'I thought I'd surprise you, Daniel,' said Henry Stillwater. He did not quite smile, but the corners of his mouth twitched perceptibly.

Wilson ushered him into the easy chair near the fire and called for Johnson to replenish his drink and pour a stiff one for Stillwater. 'You went to see the infamous prisoner, I hear,' Stillwater said. Wilson smiled again. It was just like Henry to hear about his encounter in Newgate before even he himself had told anyone. He had been the same at school. An invaluable source of information about the masters and pupils. He always knew more about everything than anybody else. They said his father was some sort of spy during the Thirty Years War, but nobody was certain. Rumours like that circulated through a public school like – what was it they used to say? – syphilis through a convent. Foul saying, but school was the place for that sort of thing.

Wilson gave Stillwater a full account of his struggle with the Devil's agent. Stillwater let Wilson finish before passing any comment. He cocked his head to one side, as if he were deaf in one ear, and drank his brandy slowly, savouring it. 'Nettles?' he asked when Wilson had concluded. 'Are you certain about that? Nettles?' 'Oh, yes, Henry, quite certain. The Reverend Nettles. Said he was from Liverpool, down on behalf of the man's wife. Poor woman. What must it be like for her and the children? They'll have to change their name, of course.'

'I've never come across a Reverend Nettles before,' said Stillwater, puzzled.

'There are a good many clergymen in the country, Henry. That you've not come across one particular youthful, rather incompetent parish curate before is hardly a surprise. Believe me, they're two a penny. I have one here,' Wilson laughed. His old schoolfriend's visit had rather cheered him up. He did not see Stillwater very often. He always popped up at the oddest moments.

Stillwater's face clouded over. His eyes narrowed and seemed to darken. 'Not to worry, though,' he said, suddenly in a different mood. Brighter, more cheerful. 'I've come to make you a proposition, Daniel.'

Wilson lifted his eyebrows. He tried to remain calm and collected, but inside his chest his heart was pounding. Henry Stillwater was going to include him in something. The most secretive man in the kingdom was going to ask a favour of Daniel Wilson. His face froze in anticipation.

Stillwater continued, 'I am confident that in the next few weeks we shall see a change in the fortunes of this country. I need not tell you that the war in Spain progresses well. What you may not know, however, is that word has reached us that the Tsar is on the brink of reneging on his treaty with Bonaparte. We can expect war in the east before the end of the year. All this means only one thing. Victory is, at last, within our grasp. And yet all is not well. We are about – and this is completely confidential, Daniel, it must not leave this room – we are about to open hostilities with the United States.' Wilson reeled. He had heard the rumours. Who had not? 'I tell you all this to explain in some small degree my absence for the next few months from England. And now I come to the reason for my visit. I need someone to look after some of my business interests and be guardian of my affairs until my return. Will you do me that honour, Daniel?'

Wilson struggled hard to conceal his disappointment. He swallowed hard. 'Of course, Henry. How may I be of service?'

When Stillwater had left Wilson returned to the

window. He was amazed at the breadth of Stillwater's business interests. A textile mill in Lancashire, an import/export company bringing spice and tea from India, sugar from the West Indies, cotton from Virginia, sending out finished textiles, clothing, uniforms for the colonial armies, luxuries for the plantation owners. Wilson found it hard to believe that he could have time for such a diversity of interests along with his work for the Government. Then, again, perhaps it was just a sinecure that Stillwater deliberately cloaked in mystery, and all he really had to do was sit at home and collect five hundred a year.

Suddenly it struck him that everything was dangerously off-kilter; that society, possibly even civilization itself, was at fault. He considered his own position. His easy life, looked after and pampered by servants. A wet nurse had given him the very milk from her breasts, had kept him strong and healthy at the expense of her own child; a nanny had given him the affection his parents felt unable to give; a boy, whose name he had long forgotten, had dressed him, grown up with him, had known him more intimately than any other human being. As children they had played together; as men they had never exchanged a non-sartorial word. The very security of his position, the knowledge that if talent failed him, then money in the right hands would surely never leave him unrewarded – all this had obscured from him the truth about the society he kept. So different from the society that inhabited the streets and houses in Holborn and Bloomsbury mere yards from his front door. He had been blind – until now. Where before he had seen civilization and progress, now he saw corruption and depravity, a society where everything was a commodity, where everyone and everything had its price, where the rich were applauded for the simple fact of their riches, where the behaviour of the wealthy was tolerated because it could be set against a wider context of education and breeding. What did it matter if Squire Jones raped his housemaid and beat his groom to death with a walking stick when you considered that he owned half the county and employed a thousand men in his fields? How far was this habit of turning a blind eye from the old habit of selling indulgences? The world had been turned upside down for less.

These reflections transfixed Wilson. He thought he saw movements in the bushes. Torchlight in the road. He heard shouts near Theobald's Road. Bellingham himself had only lived a few hundred yards away. He extinguished all the candles and turned the lamp down low. The dying fire threw his shadow against the far wall, framed him in red. And suddenly he knew what had to be done. They had to call out the militia. They needed to round up a few more of these scoundrels, these republican troublemakers. They needed to make a few examples. Otherwise the whole tottering edifice would come crashing down around their ears. And that – that really would be intolerable.

FOURTEEN

ISLINGTON

Stillwater scrutinized his face in the mirror. He considered the implausibility of his life and the impossibility of his remaining any longer in the country in whose service he had foregone so much.

With most of his business affairs passed into the hands of Daniel Wilson, Stillwater was no longer required to exist. In time all trace of the man would disappear and the process of eliminating him would finally be complete. Stillwater would at last be free to emerge from the shadows, to embrace the world.

The sound of laughter reached him from the drawing room. The sound echoed in the hallway, as if it were trapped. The house seemed unfamiliar to him. Many years had passed since female voices, let alone laughter, had been heard in its cold, panelled rooms.

Stillwater entered the drawing room. At the creak of the door hinges the room's three occupants turned to face him. The ladies curtsied politely. Stillwater nodded at each in turn.

The room was sparsely furnished and very large. The rugs and carpets were rolled back against the walls, creating a dance floor. Stillwater sat in a comfortable chair near the fire. He was silhouetted by the bright suffusion of early-morning light through the windows at his back.

The eldest of the three women, Mrs Botham, took a

seat next to Stillwater. She eyed her two young charges maternally. She perched on the edge of her seat as if on the verge of leaping up and scolding the two young women, but every time she leaned forward and opened her mouth she thought better of it and turned back, smiling to her host.

Stillwater watched as the two women, shyly at first but with increasing confidence, danced in the silent room. The steps were executed charmingly, at times with grace, at times with a girlish giggle. They were a boisterous pair, all too aware of the absurdity of the situation but trying very hard to behave themselves.

These visits only occurred once or twice a year. The occasions were not looked forward to by the ladies. Yet he was their benefactor. A kind, generous man who asked for nothing in return for his money except these odd visits, the courtesy, the opportunity to share, no matter how briefly, in their youth.

'Elizabeth, Caroline, why don't you come and sit down?' Mrs Botham called. The young women stopped dancing abruptly.

'You dance very well, both of you,' said Stillwater.

'Thank you, sir. We should dance well, for we are taught little else,' said Caroline.

Stillwater nodded. Elizabeth Matthews resembled her mother. She wore a pale-blue bodice and a long white skirt that reached to her ankles. Her feet were enclosed in delicate pink satin slippers. Her dark hair was braided and coiled into a bun on the crown of her head. She looked, he thought, very elegant. Very lady-like. Very much like her mother. Her sister, Caroline, on the other hand, took after her father. Impetuous, intelligent, a little wild. She would probably remain a spinster.

'Really, Caroline,' chided Mrs Botham. 'You should be grateful for any kind of education. When I was a girl we counted ourselves fortunate to be taught how to dance. You have been schooled in French, geography and a little history. More than you shall ever need, my dear. Besides, it is not proper for a young girl's mind to be cluttered with all manner of useless information.' Mrs Botham looked to Stillwater for support.

Stillwater was not listening to Mrs Botham. He was considering the possibility of adopting the two young women. He wanted to confess all – all his weakness, his grief, his loneliness. He wanted them to fall to their knees and praise Heaven for the miracle that moved so kind a man to welcome them into his home. He would take them in his arms and cradle them as they cried and laughed. He would touch them, and their confusion would disappear. He would speak, and his heart would again be filled with tenderness and compassion.

He had left it too late. He sighed inwardly. Had it really taken him sixteen years to admit his loneliness? Was he that cold-blooded? He knew that he was.

'May I ask, sir,' Elizabeth ventured to say to her patron, 'why you have asked us here? We see you so rarely.'

A single tear rolled, unnoticed, from the corner of his eye and slid slowly down the side of his nose. Her voice was sweet and gentle. Her eyes, which did not waver from contact with his own, were sparkling brown pools. Brave, brave girl, he thought.

'Miss Matthews!' exclaimed Mrs Botham, rising from her seat.

Stillwater waved her back down. 'Elizabeth, Caroline, my dears,' he said, his voice hoarse with emotion, a sentimental lump in his throat. 'It is my great privilege to be your guardian.' The word came only with a visible effort. 'It is I who pay for your schooling at this good lady's academy.' The women nodded, encouraging him to continue. He was a taciturn man by nature. They understood that this did not come easily. 'For some time now I have been contemplating a journey abroad. I wish to tell you, in person, that I am about to begin that journey and that' – he paused, longing for eloquence – 'I shall be away for some considerable time. I want to assure you both that my financial support will continue. If you will allow me, I aim to help you make your entrance into society.'

'Where are you going?' asked Caroline.

'Caroline Matthews!' censured Mrs Botham.

'I am afraid I cannot say, Miss Matthews. It is a highly confidential matter.'

'They say, Mr Stillwater . . .' Elizabeth glanced at her sister conspiratorially. 'They say you are a spy. Is that true?'

'That is enough, ladies,' said Mrs Botham very sternly, but her admonition went unheeded.

'That is not very kind of them, whoever *they* are,' said Stillwater, secretly amused and flattered. The same rumours had circulated about his father when he was at school. 'Spies and informers are usually inferior people, a ragged debtors' army. They inhabit public bars and gambling dens. Do I strike you as someone of that inferior sort?'

'I have read that the Prince Regent himself is no stranger to gambling or drinking,' countered Caroline Matthews.

'It is not a question of whether or not one drinks and gambles but of where one indulges these vices,' quipped Mrs Botham.

'Rest assured, ladies, I am no more a spy than the Prince Regent is a miser,' smiled Stillwater. He was enjoying their company, their directness. 'Now, do you accept my offer? Remember, I do this because it pleases me to do it – you are not indebted to me. I ask for nothing in return except, perhaps, the opportunity to visit and hear about the course of your lives. Are we agreed?' Elizabeth and Caroline assented. Stillwater, heartened, rang for some breakfast.

Stillwater sat back in his chair. He was alone once more. The house was empty, but conversation trilled in his ears. The sound of their voices thrilled him. For the first time he found himself regretting the life he led. He pictured himself getting dressed for work in the morning, coming down to breakfast and hearing about the latest society gossip: who had proposed to whom, whose fortune had been gambled and lost on the Stock Exchange and whose newly made at the gaming tables. Elizabeth and Caroline serving him tea and hot, buttered toast as they chattered. A hard day's work in the City would follow, sitting in a warm office surrounded by good furniture and tasteful paintings, to be crowned by a jubilant welcome home from his adopted daughters, who would pester and fuss over him until bedtime.

Stillwater had never tortured himself with such exquisite sentimentality before. This normal, idyllic life was not difficult to imagine. For a man of wealth it was achievable. But Stillwater had made his choices many years ago and his life, as he had shaped it, was incapable of containing such a dream.

His role, if he was forced to describe it, was analogous to that of a priest, but instead of being dedicated to the service of God, his life was dedicated to the State. He had chosen to sacrifice himself on the altar of England's need, like his father before him and *his* father before that.

He got to his feet and crossed over to the grandfather clock near the door. He reached up to open the casing and wind the mechanism. He hesitated, thought better of it and left the room.

He took the key from its hiding place on the lintel above the door and unlocked his father's bedroom. A damp, musty smell wafted out as he opened the door. His feet left trails in the dust as he crossed over to the windows and pulled back the shutters.

The Influencing Engine sat on a table in the middle of the room. He bent over it and blew across the paper blades of the whirligig. Dust swirled and the tiny windmill turned.

The model was ancient. A construction of paper and card. He and Tilly had toiled over it for days, pasting and painting. He thought of poor old Tilly and what he had sacrificed for their great plan.

Stillwater opened a drawer in the table. It was filled with thick, yellowed pieces of paper. They looked quite ancient. He took a sheet out. It was covered in hieroglyphs and Latin, but the majority of the page was taken up by a drawing of the Influencing Engine. Stillwater remembered sitting up late into the night holding the sheets of vellum over a candle flame to try to achieve the aged effect, while Tilly created more and more bizarre hieroglyphics to adorn the edges and came up with the incredible list of ingredients that would fuel the Engine. Stillwater recalled editing that list of some of its more esoteric substances, such as *witch's hellebore* and the *gas of a horse's greasy heels.*

Stillwater had given his life for his country. He had worked diligently, barely surfacing from the shadowy world he occupied to brief, or be debriefed by, those whose interests he so zealously guarded. Colleagues, whose names he hardly had time to put to their faces, came and went, some disillusioned, others dead, married or pensioned off. All those years he tried to do the decent thing. Britannia became his wife, his mistress, his daughter. He gave so much to her that nothing remained for anyone else.

'Remember this,' his father had said. An injunction to obedience, a life of service. But Stillwater was unable to equate his father's easy patriotism and simple faith

285

in the essential decency of the State with the grubby reality of his own profession; reduced, as he had intimated to the young ladies, to a refuge for rogues and thieves.

He would have resigned, if they had given him the opportunity, but they did not. He had been summoned early one January morning to an office in the roof of the building to be told by a civil servant that his position would be terminated.

Of course he was humiliated. His political masters had used him and discarded him. They had absolutely no idea who he was, what he had achieved, what he had abjured in order to preserve their rotten boroughs and their sinecures. He was a faceless name on a bureaucrat's list. The civil servant had not even looked up from his desk as he handed him the letter of dismissal.

Stillwater had been so shocked that he had not left his house for a week. His father's portrait had stared sternly down on his disgraced son for seven days. At the end of the week Stillwater determined to make a new life for himself. He was not a young man, but he still had an opportunity to live life. He came to see his divorce from Britannia as a blessing.

However, when he turned his attention to business affairs Stillwater discovered that the most serious barrier to peace and prosperity, the biggest obstruction to trade was his former employer, His Majesty's Government.

The Orders in Council were bringing merchants and industrialists everywhere to their knees and Britain to the brink of war with the USA. The Orders banned trade with all French ports and with any country who traded with the French. This effectively banned all trade with any country which was not part of the British Empire.

For someone like Stillwater, whose family business

was based on cotton and textiles, that was an absolute disaster. When he investigated his business interests, neglected for almost two decades, he found them in a parlous state. Not because of maladministration, but because of the trade restrictions. He had given his all for his country. He had foregone family and friends. He had eschewed society in order to maintain it for the rest. Did he not deserve some recompense? Was he not entitled to some form of reparation for all his hard work? For his sacrifice? He felt that he was so entitled.

At first he agonized over the irony, but eventually he resolved to do his duty. 'Remember this,' his father had said. Remember that without Perceval, England would survive; with Perceval, England (and with her Stillwater) was threatened by war and by bankruptcy.

Stillwater was not alone in his anger and bewilderment. Potters, millers, manufacturers of all sizes and hues were clamouring for something to be done. It had not been hard to persuade a group of them that he, Stillwater, was the man to do it. All he asked in exchange was a small share in their profits. If he was successful, they would thrive. If he failed, then he himself would gain nothing.

The means to accomplish his plan had presented itself five months ago in the form of a petition to the Prince Regent from one John Bellingham, a merchant from Liverpool. As a matter of course Bellingham's persistent correspondence had been passed on to Stillwater. Checking the post was all they had considered him fit for by the end.

However, Bellingham, he knew immediately, was the perfect dupe. Stillwater actually believed that, given time and the opportunity, Bellingham would have killed Perceval without his intervention, but time was not on Stillwater's side.

Stillwater wrote regularly to Bellingham. He pretended to be from the Prime Minister's office or from the Treasury. He encouraged Bellingham to pursue his claim and just as Bellingham felt he was getting close, just as he thought he was making progress, Stillwater ceased to intervene and left Bellingham to run up hard against the brick walls of bureaucracy.

As Bellingham's frustrations mounted and Stillwater pondered how to effect his desired, deadly aim, something else happened. Stillwater was astonished to discover that plans for an Influencing Engine had turned up in the hands of Arthur Thistlewood, a maverick radical well known to Stillwater from the Spithead naval mutinies. Thistlewood, he knew, was stupid, vicious and inordinately pretentious.

Thistlewood was also a wonderful smoke-screen. Stillwater made sure that Thistlewood made contact with Bellingham. If anyone ever investigated, they would get as far as Arthur Thistlewood and give up – he was Stillwater's front, behind which he was free to act without fear of discovery.

Everything had worked out excellently. Stillwater's swan-song had achieved more than he could ever have hoped. Perceval was dead, and the Orders in Council were soon to be repealed by an administration friendlier to the needs of industry. Thistlewood was out of commission for a while. The Influencing Engine was destroyed. And Bellingham?

Stillwater crossed over to the window. The day had turned to drizzle. He pulled out his fob watch. Almost eight o'clock. Bellingham would hang soon. He was an unfortunate man. Stillwater shrugged. He took the whirligig from the middle of the model and broke it in half. He put the Influencing Engine on the floor and stamped it flat before placing it in the fireplace and setting light to it. He thought of Elizabeth and Caroline dancing.

As of tomorrow Stillwater would cease to exist. He would assume another identity and begin a new life in

America. Elizabeth and Caroline would be looked after by Wilson, who had control over some of Stillwater's financial affairs (as well as strict instructions never to reveal the true source of the young women's good fortune).

It hurt him to think he would never see them again, that the house and all its contents would be sold, that all trace of his previous existence would be expunged. He thought also of Tilly languishing in Bedlam. In any campaign some losses were inevitable.

FIFTEEN

CATO STREET

A dim grey light struggled over the rooftops and spilled
into the streets around Newgate Prison, and with the
dawn came the spectators with picnic baskets and
blankets. They did the same for royal visits and pro-
cessions, arriving early to lay claim to the best
spots, using their children as fence posts to denote
their territory. Others, wealthier or better connected,
occupied rooms and rooftops in the vicinity, over-
looking the place of execution. A light shower fell at
around four-thirty. The wise raised their umbrellas,
the reckless got wet. Soldiers and militia took up
discreet positions nearby, garrisoned in courtyards and
alleys.

Arthur Thistlewood peered out from behind a pair
of heavy, red curtains. The light hurt his eyes. He
fingered the dirty bandage round his head. The wound
was itching like the devil. A good sign, a sign of
healing. He wished he could say the same for his
leg, set in a rough splint and agony to move. He
manoeuvered himself away from the window on his
crutches and sat down heavily on the edge of the bed.
'God,' he said out loud, 'let his death be prolonged and
miserable. Let the hangman be an incompetent wretch.'

Thinking of Bellingham led him to Nettleton. 'Ungrateful bastard!' he shouted at the top of his voice.
There was a banging on the floor from the room

below. Thistlewood hammered the floorboards with his crutch. 'Bastard!'

Exhausted, he lifted his broken leg gingerly on to the bed and lay down. He could not get it out of his mind. The explosion. Whenever he closed his eyes he saw again the brilliant blue flash, the door flying off its hinges, the plaster raining down on his head. He smelt the charge, the iron in the air, and then the stench of all that shit from the barrels. He saw Bellingham, the conniving sod, falling from the roof and landing on Walsh. The memory of the sight still retained the power to nauseate him. He reached frantically for the chamber pot beneath his bed. He found it and his fingers plunged into a cold liquid. It was full. The sensation passed. He wiped his hand on the sheet.

How had they managed it? That's what really got his goat. It galled him to think he had been outwitted by a pimply boy and a sad old fool like Bellingham. If the police had raided or the army surrounded the building, there would have been honour in that. A fight. But this? The whole thing was wrong. From the start he'd had his misgivings. Alarm bells ding-donging in his head when Truelock approached him with the scheme. Influencing Engine? It couldn't have influenced a dog to piss up a tree.

Outside his window the noise was increasing. Vendors shouting, selling umbrellas, pies, blankets, cushions. Thistlewood moaned. He was still in the clamour and dust of the explosion. Truelock had managed to haul him to safety. They saw Bellingham and Nettleton leave. If his leg had not been broken he would have followed and done for them. He watched as the remains of the building sagged and tumbled down into the basement, burying the Influencing Engine, or what was left of it, beneath tons of rubble.

He must have fainted at some point, from loss of blood or pain. He woke in a bed. A clean bed. The smell of soap gradually replaced with the stronger scent of sweat and bodily function. He looked around and realized he was on a ward somewhere. He could not move his leg. He panicked. He assumed they had amputated it. He pulled frantically at the bed clothes. He had to see for himself, he had to see it. To touch it, to know it was still there. It was. He fell back on the bed and slept the clock round.

When he woke for the second time Stillwater was standing over him. Stillwater put his finger to his lips and handed Thistlewood a thick envelope. Thistlewood pushed himself to a sitting position, but Stillwater was already leaving the dormitory.

'Morning,' a voice said. 'Feeling better?' A female voice. Thistlewood turned his head. He winced. 'I expect you're feeling a bit sore still. From what I hear you're lucky to be alive.' She was a nurse. He guessed that because she wore a white dress and a head scarf. Why else would a woman be in that place unless she was a nurse.

'Are you a nurse?' he croaked hoarsely.

'After a fashion. I visit people. I try to make them more comfortable.' She was a large woman, matronly. Wide hips, large bosom, strong arms. Her face was pale, her eyes green. Her hair, a deep orange, was beautiful against the white of her scarf, her light skin. Not just her hair. Everything about her was beautiful. Her voice was soothing and gentle. There was no coarseness, only a faint hint of an accent. Scottish, he thought. He forgot about the pain in his leg and watched her closely as she smoothed his blankets and generally tidied around his bed. When she moved on to the next bed he was consumed with jealousy and misery. He felt as if he would never see her again. If only he could get out of bed and chase after her, prove to her he was a man and not just a patient. Oh, the cruelty of fate, he moaned to himself. He did not even know her name.

'Jane,' she answered. 'And you're Arthur. The gentleman who visited yesterday told me.' Thistlewood stared into her eyes, a pained expression on his face. 'What can I do to make your stay more comfortable, Arthur?'

'Visit me more often,' he said with candour and a shy smile. She squeezed his hand as it lay on the coverlet. His heart stopped beating for a second. She left him there, impotent, on his bed. He interpreted that squeeze in a hundred different ways. The first thing he thought was: she feels something for me. The next was that squeezing hands was probably an everyday aspect of her charitable work. She squeezed the hands of dying men whose names she did not know, the hands of consumptive children and people like himself. His last thought was that she cared about him. It was not just that she had squeezed his hand. It was the way she had squeezed it, the lingering touch, the bashful glance to the floor, the slight flush on her cheek.

The next day she arrived as usual after dinner. 'You were asleep through it all,' she said. 'It only occurred to me this morning.' Ah, he thought, so she was thinking about me this morning. 'Did you know that the Prime Minister had been shot? Killed. What was his name?' She paused, thinking. 'You know, I've completely forgotten his name. Isn't that awful?' Thistlewood opened his mouth and found he was not in control of it, 'He was, er, his name, er, was, er . . . I don't really follow politics,' he said. Her face brightened, 'Neither do I.'

But she did like a good hanging. So much so that she paid a guinea to rent the room for the night prior to the execution. Thistlewood was staying there. She would come later. His heart pitter-pattered at the thought.

Thistlewood had never been in love before. The sensations were totally new and unexpected. On his own he was not convinced it was a good thing, to be governed by emotion instead of reason. However, when he was with Jane he felt very differently about emotions. He was glad, in a way, that Walsh and Truelock had perished. He would never have met Jane otherwise. In some obscure way he should, perhaps, thank Nettleton and Bellingham also. But this he could not bring himself to do. Nettleton was a traitor and Bellingham was an ingrate. He was glad he was here to cheer him into eternity. And for once Thistlewood was not with the crowd, shivering and wet. For once he was with the swells, dry and warm with an excellent view of the scaffold.

A thought struck him. He groaned and beat the bed with his fists. 'Damn!' His manuscript. Destroyed, buried along with all the rest. His vision of Britain, his manifesto. He would never remember it all. The salient facts, of course, he could remember those. He had copied most of them directly out of the works of Paine, Spence and Godwin. It was that occasional prose flourish that he lamented, the turn of phrase that had given him so much pleasure. It was another good reason to welcome Bellingham's death. Not that he needed any further reasons.

He had lost friends, credibility, hopes and dreams, all up in smoke. Crushed to death. But Arthur Thistlewood was not a man to be defeated so easily. His spirit was not so lightly daunted. He recalled the time during the naval mutinies when his entire team of agitators had been whisked away overnight. Had he let that get him down? Had the fact of their deaths discouraged him? He knew them all. He had recruited them all personally. Yet he had not allowed their fates to move him, to budge him an inch. He was unswerving in his devotion to the revolution.

His head suddenly filled with a vision of Jane's red hair tumbling to her shoulders as she took off her bonnet and unbraided her plaits. He imagined the warmth of her body. The strength of her embrace.

Nothing could distract him from the cause. He was unwavering. Immovable. A fixed point by which others could navigate. Are you lost? Lacking political direction? Then fasten your eyes upon Thistlewood and set your course by the fixity of his beliefs. He was a beacon shining through the darkness of injustice, inequality and poverty. He was a . . . he was . . .

The image of her naked body, as yet unseen but discernible through the petticoats and skirts, flashed into his mind. Her hips, wide, fleshy, curving gracefully into her thighs. Her legs tapering to the most elegant ankles. The roundness of her belly. Her breasts soft mounds. Broad shoulders. Her white skin soft beneath the touch of his fingers, the gentle scratch of his nails.

Thistlewood sat upright with a start. What was he doing there, wasting his time on daydreams, romantic daydreams at that? This was not the Arthur Thistlewood he thought he was. Had his brains been jumbled by a blow to the head? He did feel strange. Absent, that was it, as if he was not wholly in the present, as if a part of him was permanently elsewhere. Was that love? It did not seem very practical. How could one concentrate on one's job, one's career, if these thoughts continued to invade your mind? There had to be a way to control this emotion, to bring it under the sovereignty of the rational mind. Thistlewood began to understand the genius of a celibate priesthood. But what if he was unable to control himself? His options were limited. When he was in her company his mind was capable of considering nothing except her. When he was deprived of her company he mourned for her, mooned over her, grew melancholy and poetic. He had even purchased a volume of poetry. He wished he had more experience in these matters, perhaps then his course of action would be clear. How could he have come thus far in life without gaining any experience of love or the opposite sex? He was dumbfounded at this elementary flaw in his otherwise perfectly executed (Acts of God and other chance elements excluded) life.

He pushed aside these thoughts for the moment and determined to deal with them later. He reached over to the bedside cabinet and picked up the envelope Stillwater had left for him. He had been waiting for the right moment to open it. When he felt safe and secure. It would not do to let this communication fall into the wrong hands.

The envelope bulged. Thistlewood broke the plain wax seal and extracted a thick bundle of vellum paper documents. He opened them out on the bed. They were title deeds to a property. A letter was attached.

'T. Commiserations on your unfortunate condition.'

Thistlewood smiled to himself. Looked at a certain way, the Influencing Engine project had been successful. Perceval was dead. What more could he ask for? The general uprising that should have been coincident with the assassination did not take place, but that was due to his lack of involvement. If only Bellingham had confided in him, who knows what might have happened? Stillwater seemed to regard the operation as a success too. He was an extraordinary man, this Stillwater. Thistlewood wondered if Perceval's death had been Stillwater's aim from the very beginning.

'I regret that our other ambitions were not fulfilled. To other matters: our association must end. I am leaving the country at the first opportunity. Do not try to reach me by any means. Should we meet again it would be by chance. As a reward for your achievements I would be obliged if you would accept the enclosed deeds to a property of mine. The deeds have been made over to you. May you continue successful in all your endeavours. S.'

Thistlewood examined the documents. The deeds to Number One, Cato Street. A stable and upper room in a quiet mews near Paddington. Thistlewood was touched and suspicious in equal measure. Such generosity. He folded the documents away and ate the note.

The door to Thistlewood's room opened and Jane peered inside. Thistlewood beamed with delight as he swallowed the last piece of Stillwater's missive. Jane wore a black cape, the hood over her head. She was carrying a picnic hamper. 'Arthur? Are you awake, Arthur? I can't see a thing, it's so dark in here.' Thistlewood swivelled where he sat and dangled his legs over the edge of the bed. He reached for his crutches and launched himself to his feet ready to greet her. 'Arthur! So there you are.' She held out her hand to be kissed.

'Jane,' he enthused. 'Jane, you came at last! How I've missed you.'

'Arty-warty, did you miss me?' She puckered her lips and took his face in her large hands. She shook his head from side to side. 'Arthur, where have you been hiding all these years?'

'Oh, here and there.' He shrugged.

'You are so mysterious sometimes. It's very sweet of you. I could eat you when you get all shy and secretive.' She kissed him on the forehead and helped him back on to the bed. 'You just put your feet up and relax. It's still an hour or so to the off.' She pulled back the curtains. The morning gloom was turning to drizzle. Below, in the streets, a sea of umbrellas. She unpacked breakfast from the hamper. A tablecloth that smelled of soap, clean. Meats and bread. Conserves, pickles, fruit. Crockery and glistening cutlery. Napkins rolled in little wooden rings. Salt and pepper in little pewter shakers with the word 'Salt' or 'Pepper' inscribed on the relevant vessel. The plates were decorated with

297

crudely drawn hearts. Around the rim of each was written 'Thomas & Elizabeth, 1784'.

She served the food using a fork, knife or, where appropriate, a spoon. She ate with a knife and fork. She did not speak with her mouth full and kept it closed when she chewed. She must breathe through her nose, Thistlewood found himself observing with surprise, as if the possibility of breathing through nostrils had never occurred to him before. Her napkin was folded across her lap. He removed his from its position tucked into his shirt collar and mimicked her behaviour. She did not seem to notice the social gulf that lay between them. She was looking out of the window.

'Not a bad crowd, given the weather,' she commented. 'I was here for the Haggerty and Holloway offing. Years ago now, but what a sight. Awful, the panic, people trampled to death, suffocating beneath piles of people. How many? Thirty deaths! I thought they would ban public hangings after that. Good job they didn't. Nothing like a hanging in the morning.'

Thistlewood did not respond. His mouth was full of bread and last year's gooseberry jam. He never thought he would find someone so well suited to himself. He had never looked, but that was because he thought the effort would be futile. And here he was, looking at a beautiful woman with ample domestic skills, independent means, as eager as he to watch the hanging. He never knew that life could be so sweet.

SIXTEEN

AMERICA

The old man did not react initially. The women's quiet weeping did not seem to move him, emotionally or physically. The thought crossed Jack's mind that he was dead. He leaned in closer to the old man's box chair. His pipe was smoking. His nostrils were quivering with each breath. Not dead then, not in the way the word is usually meant. But alive? He was not alive either. He was poised somewhere between absolute immobility and twitching life. He was in a state of suspension. His progress, if progress it could be called, to that state of conscious inaction, had been long and irremediable. It began shortly after his wife had run off with the butcher's apprentice.

First he had given up on his business. Debts, which he had never known before, swallowed him whole. The business of business, which had for so many years fascinated him, became dull and futile. He stopped filling in the ledgers. He stopped writing altogether. The feel of a pen in his hand filled him with revulsion. Books, his whole life had been books, the kind he read and the kind he sold, pages covered with words or numbers. When he looked at them he could not make them out. The shapes of the letters were unfamiliar, their meanings treacherous and uncertain. The world, a place he had always regarded as solid, fixed and dependable was suddenly dangerously ambiguous. Every action acquired a significance beyond itself, contained within it a secret code that others understood but he could not decipher. In the face of his incomprehension he absented himself from the world and began to view it from a remove.

He refused to leave the house. The Chapel sent a delegation to inquire after the health of one of their elders. They knew the story of his wife's abscondment (everybody knew the story except for him, he refused to listen, he would not hear it) and sympathized. They prayed over him and for him. The minister laid on hands and bade him have courage and think of his children. But their attempt at healing failed and he withdrew further and further into himself until even the Church was obliged to abandon him to his indolent misery.

As his children grew up he passed every responsibility on to them. Jack, as the eldest, assumed the mantle of wage-earner. His younger brother would join him before very long. Rachel and Susan, still very young girls, learned to wash and cook and clean. They managed the household expenses between them and dealt with all the trades people. Their father intervened less and less. When he judged that his family was capable of functioning without him he retreated to his box chair in front of the fire and sat down and did nothing for the rest of his life.

Jack did not hate his father. He despised him. Not only for giving up, but for his willingness to place his children in front of him as a human shield. And as his father's own humanity seemed to ebb from him Jack came to despise him more. 'Why won't he just die?' he used to ask Rachel, but the man never did. Not even now. He would simply sit and stare. He was staring now, staring directly at his daughters who wept because their brother was leaving them for good and because, as a parting gift, they had given him their hair.

Then it started to happen. Imperceptibly at first. A tiny quivering round his shoulders as if he were shivering from the cold. Jack did not notice. He was trying to placate his sisters, to tell them how grateful he was for their gift. He would write, he said. He would never lose touch. The old man's quivering developed into a shake. His shoulders rose and fell. His hands held the chair with a white-knuckled grip. And the shaking spread to his chest, his abdomen, his thighs, his calves and his feet. His feet began to tremble on the floorboards and his slippers slapped against the wood. The chair itself was rattling and banging and moving across the floor. Jack and his sisters looked on, incredulous. From the very edge of death their father was returning to a frightening abundance of life, uncontrollable life.

A look of surprise visited Mr Nettleton's leathery face, temporarily smoothing his wrinkled features. He sucked his cheeks in, and his clay pipe fell from between his pursed lips. His eyebrows lifted higher and higher. Eyes wide, mouth hanging open. All of a sudden, however, he crumpled, collapsed inwards. His mouth drooped, his eyes hooded over, his eyebrows sank to their normal position and his body was racked with violent sobs. His lungs filled to the brim with air in great gasps followed by juddering exhalations that propelled the old man forward from the chest. His eyes filled with water. Tears sprang from his blinking eyes, and as a gigantic sob strained his frail body, wringing a terrifying wail from his shuddering lungs, his teeth flew out of his mouth and landed on the floor at Jack's feet. His daughters looked on in speechless amazement. His son bent down and put the porcelain dentures in his pocket.

Through the dawn traffic of market gardeners and cattle drovers, milk-criers and farmers. Past the Fleet, past the Marshalsea. Newgate already far behind. The houses passed intermittently, interspersed with flashes of green as the city gave way to the countryside and the darkness to light. Then the houses were gone altogether and there was nothing but the fields and the horizon. Trees, cows, horses, sheep, pigs. The sights and smells of the garden of England.

Jack pulled down the blind. His body still ached from the beatings and batterings of the previous week. Every jolt brought fresh reminders of his narrow escape from death and jangled the money in his pocket. The sound of the money almost compensated for the pain in his ribs and the fear of losing his money displaced all other fears. He was not afraid of death when confronted with the possibility of robbery. In truth he would rather be dead than broke again.

Like the prodigal, he had returned and instead of slaughtering the fatted calf he had taken it (in the form of a bag of hair and a set of false teeth) to the pawnbrokers. He had a second chance and this time he would not waste his freedom.

Even freedom, though, seemed sour. Soon it would be eight o'clock. He was glad he had not stayed until the very end. But he was glad he had plucked up the courage to visit. He had been lucky to arrive when that clergyman, Wilson, did. He would never have got in otherwise.

When Wilson had gone they held their breath for a few seconds but both men found it impossible not to laugh.

'You shouldn't have come,' said Bellingham when he had recovered. Jack smiled. He did not know why he had come. He only knew that he had to, that he could not leave without saying goodbye. 'I thought I was ready to face up to it, Jack. But talking to the reverend, I'm not so sure. Who can be sure? What troubles me now, the thing I think about most, is that

I could have escaped. Nobody knew what was going on. There was terrible confusion. I could have slipped away. The only man who saw me shoot – he paid me no attention. He was not even called as a witness at the trial. But I didn't escape. I sat back down. I just sat down and waited for someone to arrest me. Why did I do that, Jack?' He paused as if expecting a reply when none was possible. 'I sat on a bench and watched the blood pump from the wound in Perceval's chest and spread out slowly beneath his shirt. And as I sat there an unaccountable urge gripped me. I wanted desperately to walk over to the convulsing man and plug the small perforation with my finger. Not because I wished to save his life, but because I wished to show that I could reverse the consequences of my action if I so desired, to prove that I had control over the situation, when the truth was I had none and instantly regretted what I had done.'

He looked tired. The weight of his fetters dragged him down, made movement difficult. His eyes were less alert. He seemed to be gazing inwards, blind to his surroundings. Nettleton saw him as Bellingham saw himself. A living dead man. In less than twelve hours he would be lying on a surgeon's slab, naked and oozing from a score of incisions. His vital organs would be removed and weighed and in a week or less the flesh and muscle would be boiled from his skeleton and John Bellingham the man would disappear forever while his bones adorned a doctor's study or a students' lecture hall and plaster casts of his skull would be advertised for sale in gentlemen's magazines to part-time phrenologists, criminologists or collectors of the macabre. And the transformation from human being to infamous, lunatic murderer would be complete. Nobody would complain, for those closest to him would only wish to forget – and why should anybody else care at all?

Nettleton understood that his role in bringing this unfortunate man to his unfortunate fate was far from insignificant. He had betrayed him, right to the end. He could have stopped him. He could have warned somebody. He could have tried. He had persuaded himself that Bellingham's fate was in his own hands, but that was just an abdication of responsibility, a rationalization of failure, the product of guilt. Nettleton was convinced that he had done a terrible thing, and the urge to seek redemption and absolution grew strong within him as he watched his friend sit in silence (except for the jangling of the chains, iron upon iron).

'Aren't you scared?' asked Nettleton. Bellingham was so calm, so placid.

'My heart's pounding. My stomach is aching. Muscles in my arms and legs, my abdomen too, are in spasm. My back hurts. I am not comfortable in any position. I am restless. But, despite that, I am calm because there is no escape. There will be no last-minute reprieve. The sentence will not be commuted. There will be no delay. At eight o'clock tomorrow morning I will be hanged.

'I have lost interest in myself, Jack. In a sense I am no longer John Bellingham. He disappeared in a puff of gun smoke. In that instant he was free. Free of all the details that bound him to the earth. His anger vanished. His desire for vengeance waned. His hopes for compensation? To be honest, he never really had any hope of compensation. In a single act of inhumanity he cut himself loose from the world and slipped free of its moral knots and social coils. I could have struggled to return. I could have clawed and howled and battled my way back, but I chose not to return, and in a few more hours I will have left all laws far behind.'

Nettleton left him before midnight. He was lying

on his bed, reading his prayerbook. His eyes were sunk deep into their sockets, the skin around them the colour of a bruise. A cut on his forehead was scabbing over; another across his nose still wept occasionally. His clothes were crumpled and torn, though a clean shirt lay neatly folded on one of the chairs with a pair of carefully darned stockings. His ankles and feet were swollen beneath the shackles. As Nettleton said goodbye Bellingham rose to his feet. He took Jack's hand and held it for a long time. Nettleton was ashamed of himself but he began to feel uncomfortable. 'Goodbye, Jack,' Bellingham said as he dropped Nettleton's hand. Nettleton walked away accompanied by a turnkey. He heard Bellingham ask for pen and paper.

The stagecoach trundled onwards. The journey to Southampton would take a day and a half at least. He could have travelled from London docks on a coastal boat, but he wanted to get out of the city as soon as possible. He did not want to be there when they hanged him. He tried to think of the future. He attempted to consign Bellingham to the past.

He took an envelope from his pocket. It was tied with ribbon. From it he pulled out a piece of paper. He unfolded it on the seat beside him. It was a map of New York and Manhattan Island. The map was already ten years old. He imagined the city expanding at its edges. The blocks marked out with string and white poles. A house or institution developed here and there, the rest virgin and waiting for him. He had just enough money for the passage. He had always dreamed of arriving in style, but he bowed to pragmatism. He had a trade to ply, a good trade. People would always need books, they would always need printers.

He thought of his father. They had believed him to be weeping, but as it turned out he was laughing.

At what? That they could not decipher. He thought of Thistlewood. And hoped he was dead. He thought of the tall man in black. He did not know who he was. He thought of Bellingham. It was five past eight.

SEVENTEEN

SMITHFIELD

Newgate Gaol
May 17th 1812

My blessed Mary Ann,

It rejoiced me beyond measure to hear you are likely to be well provided for. I am sure the public at large will participate in, and mitigate, your sorrows. I assure you, my love, my sincerest endeavours have ever been directed to your welfare. As we shall not meet anymore in this world, I sincerely hope we shall do so in the world to come.

My blessing to the boys, with kind remembrance to Miss Stevens, for whom I have the greatest regard, in consequence of her uniform affection for them.

With the purest of intentions, it has always been my misfortune to be thwarted, misrepresented and ill-used in life; but, however, we feel a happy prospect of compensation in a speedy translation to life eternal. It is not possible to feel more calm or placid than I feel; and nine hours more will waft me to those happy shores where bliss is without alloy. Yours, ever affectionately, John Bellingham.

Sunday Night, 11 o'Clock

Dr Ford will forward you my watch, prayerbook, with a guinea and a note. Once more, God be with you, my sweet Mary. The public sympathize much for me, but I have been called upon to play an anxious card in life.

Mary Ann, as I lie awake on my bed (a very hard bed that has done wonders for my back in the few nights I have spent upon it) and outside it begins to grow light, I think of my nativity and find it difficult to conceal my disappointment at its humdrum, homespun ordinariness. I can picture it with ease. I can hear my mother's screams and cries as my blood-drenched body emerges from between her stirruped legs and is clasped tight in the midwife's warty embrace. But what is revealed as the muck and mess are wiped away is the face of a tired and beaten middle-aged man and not the wrinkled, squashed-up features of a new-born child. And the cries I hear are the songs of the birds.

Did choirs of angels sing? I doubt it. Did the heavens open and a dove descend? Again, no. Did a comet glide gracefully across the night sky? Not that I know of.

It cannot be long now until Dr Ford urges me, as he has incessantly for the last three days, to seek absolution. I have not decided yet if I shall accept the Chaplain's offer or reject it again. I have no need of his forgiveness. I don't want the pity in his eyes. What use have I for pity? And I am not dead yet. Not quite, though it won't be long now. I would rather spend what time I have left in contemplation and reflection than floundering in a mire of shame and recrimination.

It would seem that my dreary birth was followed by a dreary youth. A childhood singularly lacking in earth-shaking, life-shaping, fate-forming events. An average sort of a childhood. I am, however, convinced that there must be something there somewhere. An overlooked incident. A forgotten moment.

So, I battle through the haze that envelops all recollection to find some remembrance of joy. I struggle to conjure up the image of some long-lost, dreamy summer. One of those summers that everyone experiences as a child when it was hotter and brighter than it has ever been before or since. A season when the months of July and August stretched on and on forever. A summer packed with momentous events and unrivalled feats of daring, strange discoveries, great mysteries. The memory is elusive. Surging forward one moment and receding the next until finally it drains away as if someone had pulled out the plug in the sea.

That childhood summer seems more like a collective delusion than a real event. It tempts us and taunts us with the sense of its loss: lost comforts, lost hopes, frustrated desires, dulled senses. (Perhaps God has planted this idea in all of us, an illusion of Eden; a race memory of innocence before the Fall.) Even if I could pinpoint the exact time and nature of this tantalizing event, which I cannot, what would it reveal? Only this, that I am the same as everybody else. That there is nothing special about myself, no fatal flaw. On the other hand perhaps my hubris is my dullness.

These past days I have found it increasingly difficult to hold on to my memories. Recollections bubble to the surface, carried on the wind by a smell, awakened by a half-remembered physical sensation or stirred by something in a gentle face, but constantly they elude my mental grasp. Memories, like moths attracted to the light of my burning need, flutter momentarily before my eyes, only to vanish, as if some unscrupulous collector were catching them with a shrimp net and imprisoning them in jamjars with pierced lids, ready to pass on intact to another; someone (I imagine them dirty and confused) who is lost, who wanders around in a daze of distant forgetfulness until he stumbles upon a tiny alleyway that wasn't there the week before and finds at the end a prosperous street-seller hawking my memories at a knock-down price.

Mostly, though, I think of you, Mary Ann, and the boys. I am glad you are not here to see me like this.

I believe that I must remain callous with regard to my own life in order to emerge from this ordeal with any semblance of dignity. They will do their best to strip me of dignity – that, after all, is the function of a State execution. It is the nature of a deterrent that the victim and the manner of his dying are as great a part of the process as the threat of death itself. The hanged as much as the hanging. They do not wish to furnish the mob with a martyr but rather to present to them a pitiful, simpering, cowed fool screaming for forgiveness from Almighty God. If I remain hardened, then they cannot achieve this aim until I am dead. They may do whatever they like with my soiled, blue-tinged corpse. By then it will no longer matter. Not really. Then I shall just be a slab of meat, offal.

There is a knot tightening in my stomach. Sweat is flowing under my armpits, down my neck, across my lip. It is becoming harder to control myself. My right leg is jigging up and down continuously. My hands shake. The knowledge that all of this can only end in death is curiously comforting. In Russia the fear was different, more desperate. I never knew if it would end or when. Every day was a hopeless submergence of personality in a routine filled with violence and fantasy. Second-guessing a sadistic gaoler: if I do this, if I don't do this, will he hit me? Will he hit me anyway? How far will he go? Does he want me to scream? Should I scream? In Russia, desperation, but always, too, a glimmer of light. If I could just survive another day, tomorrow they may release me. Straw-and-shit-strewn, the tang of iron. At least in Newgate the small dignity of a bucket. At least here the outcome is certain and the waiting is almost at an end. How much is ever certain? This is a rare moment in my life.

In the meantime I take comfort in the corporeality of my body. I run my fingers through my greasy hair and trace a line from my forehead to my navel. I sense that beneath my clothing my limbs still function and assure myself that my organs remain intact. And when time presses or memories crowd I can disappear into my body and travel through my arteries and veins. I can listen to my heartbeat and feel it pump the waves of blood to every corner of my body. I can travel the mysteries of my nervous system by pinching and prodding, distracting from or adding to the pain in my legs and ankles. I would do more if the chains did not restrict me so. My last refuge is the bucket where I can discharge my bowels or bladder.

I feel already the cool morning air on my face. If I stand on tiptoe I can see through the window, see the drizzle and hear the crowd gathering with their hampers and picnic baskets. Breakfast at the execution? What sort of food do you think they would bring to a hanging? Chops? Cold meat? Or something sweet to disguise the bitterness of the moment? What is their fascination with executions? Isn't death already a big enough part of their lives? It cannot be an entirely pleasurable experience, especially for those at the front.

I lie down again – my favourite position. The chains clink and clank, the manacles chaff. Incredibly, I feel sleepy. I close my eyes and search for those elusive memories for the last time.

But when I close my eyes and grope for innocence all I find is guilt and a wretched desire for justification. It is best then that I keep my eyes open.

Why? Of course I ask myself why. Eyes open or closed, it doesn't really make that much difference. I went there to meet my fate. Destiny commanded and I obeyed.

That's one way of looking at it, certainly. I went there to take my place on the relentless March of History. Another way of looking at my presence there, in the Commons, and here, in a condemned cell, is more practical, less excusable but more comforting in its intimations of posterity. If you will, I am a self-appointed punctuation mark in time. A full stop. You will reach my name and shortly afterwards a new chapter will begin. I will be an historical first. My actions may be celebrated or denigrated, examined fully or largely ignored, but whatever happens our names will always be linked, bound together in the public consciousness; as lovers' names carved into a tree trunk – Spencer Perceval & John Bellingham together forever.

However, both these ideas presuppose some sort of forward thinking. A dash for infamy or some ideological, long-term strategy. While I must confess there is some truth in both, neither is the bulk nor the heart of the matter. (Neither really explains how and why I find myself here at this particular point in time, for this particular reason.)

All of which brings me back to that hard wooden bench and the chaos of MPs and lobbyists who bustled around me. None of them showed me the slightest attention. In this world you have to grab people, as it were, by the trouser leg and cling on for dear life until they notice you. Sitting quietly and patiently on a bench will get you nowhere. Noise and movement, this is all that anyone understands. If you are still, you will be left behind, unheeded, unwept for. I was happy to go unseen. It had always been that way with me, until recently. I haven't made much of a mark on life. When I'm gone only my family will miss me. Maybe Jack Nettleton, too, maybe Jack. Who will remember John

Bellingham? Who will remember his story when it is reduced, refined, defined, distilled to its essence. Who will remember him except as a catalyst to events that touched other, more important, more memorable lives? Who will remember him except as that notorious murderer whose actions provoked a major Government reshuffle?

When I looked up from my seat in the lobby and saw Perceval walking towards me I realized I had reached the apex of my life – the narrowest point of its focus. It was like staring down a narrow corridor or a tunnel. Darkness closed in on all sides. I saw nothing but him and he saw only the pistol in my hand. I do not remember the shot. The actual moment of the killing is lost. One minute I am there pressing the gun against his chest, the next I am back on my bench watching him stagger and fall. I hear the thump of his body, I see the blood spreading beneath his shirt like a rose opening, the sepals reaching out further and further.

It was not pleasant to see all that. I take no pleasure in what I did. Indeed, I deeply regret killing him. Not because it means that I must forfeit my own life. That is not the reason. It's that he lay there twitching like a dog, or a chicken, or a man. He died. His life poured out of him For some reason, and I cannot explain it, I thought he would simply disappear. Turn into a wisp of smoke and vanish. I never believed that he or I had a single ounce of humanity left to lose. I was wrong.

Mary Ann, have you lain awake all night? Have you held a vigil for me? Are you thinking of me? I cannot bear to imagine you Mary Ann, it distresses me too much. I should have let you visit. I have been in need of your presence, your touch, your voice. But perhaps you would not have come, perhaps you have already put me from your mind. Are you laying out your widow's weeds or drinking a toast to new beginnings and happier times. Why do I think these things? Has betrayal been so much a part of my life that I cannot even trust you?

I made a wooden boat with my father when I was five years old. I launched it on to a pond in front of all my friends. The boat sank. I sailed for China when I was seventeen years old. That ship sank too. I lived and worked in Russia; I was imprisoned and half-killed in Russia. I returned to my native land; England humiliated and mocked me.

It occurs to me now that the wooden boat is my significant moment, the elusive memory. It occurs to me also that I should have given up when I was five years old.

I always wanted to go on the stage. No, that is not true. As lies go it could have been a good one, provoking mirth or derision, only to be overturned at the last minute and a small victory attained. I killed it at birth.

Wooden steps, grass pushing up between the unpainted boards. A shadow of the gallows falling even in childhood?

It is late spring, almost summer. The cherry blossom is in bloom. It covers the street and floats and rots in the gutter. I stare out of the window into the street covered in blossom. Half remembered. My memories are clouded. I remember moods and sensations not faces or places. I used to love to lie on my back in the long grass and see the brightness of the sun through my closed eyelids and the coloured dots dance across my retina. I love the night drawing in and the days growing longer. I feed on the sensations of the past longing for them to repeat, season after season, year after year.

*　　*　　*

314

As an apprentice I could watch the workings of a watch for hours on end, letting time slip, but I never understood how it worked or how something so small and intricate could be made by a hand that size.

Jingle-jangle. Here they come. Here they come. Turn-key, turn key. I always thought that's what it meant. The key scrapes in the lock.

I thought she was the most beautiful woman I had ever seen. That was from a distance. Close up, that illusion was dispelled. Her complexion was not perfect, her proportion not as I had guessed from my first fleeting glimpse of her in the park. She was five feet one inch tall and eighteen years old. She wore a canary-yellow dress, opaque white stockings, shoes of white silk and a yellow bonnet tied with lace in a bow beneath her round chin. I revealed nothing of my disappointment (which in any case was very slight) when, at last, we were introduced. I am a practical man. I know that perfection does not walk the earth.

Mary Ann Neville, a slender young Irish woman with a giggly laugh, tiny hands and burnished hair (hennaed, I later discovered, but such intimate details are never exposed on first meeting). I was struck by her unaffected manner, her plain speaking, her modesty. I fell in love.

I would say that everything I have ever done – the trip to Russia, the fight to clear my name, my struggle for compensation, the act for which I am justly infamous – I have done because of her. For Mary Ann and the boys. But that would not be fair. I destroyed Spencer Perceval's existence in an attempt to keep a grip on my own crumbling life. I only wished to hold on to that which I held most dear: my children, the dear infant Henry, the unfortunate John; my wife, my sweet Mary Ann. I have forsaken sound advice and followed my own course, and in so doing I have utterly destroyed everything that was most precious, that gave my life meaning. I have, in the final instant, lost all that I have striven to keep. I am utterly ruined.

The door swings open on creaky hinges.

Here they are.

They all seemed to stand there staring at each other for a long time. It was the rum-fortified chaplain, Dr Ford, who broke the silence with a discreet belch.

Bellingham offered no resistance as they led him from his cell. The chaplain trotted alongside him, puffing out his final offer of absolution. Bellingham smiled cheerily at him.

The walk was a short one. The party entered the Press Yard shortly before eight o'clock. Gathered around a small anvil was a group of twenty sober men, each dressed in an impressive black suit. Bellingham noted the rain. He was led up to the anvil and his leg irons were struck off. He winced involuntarily as the rivets were hammered out of his fetters. The entire party then removed to a small room off the yard. Bellingham observed that the whitewash rubbed off on the sleeves of their suits as they brushed against the walls. A sheriff approached him and quietly asked, 'You were completely alone in your actions?' Bellingham nodded. 'You did not act with the knowledge or cooperation of any other individuals?'

'No,' replied Bellingham.

'Is there anything further you wish to add to your previous statements?'

'No.'

'Do you wish to make a final confession?' asked Dr Ford.

'I would like you to deliver this to my wife.'

Bellingham took the letter from his snuff-coloured jacket and handed it to the chaplain. He took his prayerbook, his watch and money and gave him them also. 'Please make sure she receives these items too.' Ford nodded.

The executioner bound Bellingham's arms behind his back. Bellingham tried moving his hands up and down. 'Tighten them a little. I wish not to have the power of offering any resistance. And please, when you have finished, turn down my sleeves to cover the cords.' The turnkey led the hanging party out to the scaffold. They ascended it quickly to the cheers of the large crowd. The streets seemed to be paved with umbrellas. Bellingham surveyed the crowd as Ford prayed loudly and fervently by his side. The clock struck eight, the supports were struck away and Bellingham dropped.

The two young men pulled hard at his heels. Pulled several times. They tugged and tugged to make sure his neck was broken.

Joshua and Samuel had a few problems trying to cut the body down. The light drizzle had made the rope slippery.

The body flopped heavily on to Samuel's shoulders. He buckled a little under the dead weight. Joshua climbed down to help, and between them they man-handled the corpse on to their crude cart. Those nearby strained to glimpse the cadaver's bulging eyes, its gruesome grimace and what was left of a tongue lolling, swollen and black, between the yellowed teeth.

'Hurry up, Joshua. It's bloody disgusting looking at his face,' said Samuel as Joshua rifled through the pockets. 'Anything?'

'Nothing. Jacket's nice. Looks like silk. Bit torn, bit dirty. Good quality, though.'

The crowd closed in. A woman yelled out, 'Let us have something. Go on, a stocking or something. Go on.'

'What do you think, Joshua?'

'How much you got?'

'Shilling?' the woman called back tentatively.

'You'll be lucky. Anybody else? Who'll give me two shillings for a stocking. Guinea for the coat. Famous murderer. Notorious. Killed the Prime Minister. Hero of the people, this man.' A mixture of subdued boos and cheers from the crowd. 'Come on, it's got to be worth something.'

The cart trundled round the corner of Newgate toward Smithfield, pushing slowly through the crowd, and in a matter of minutes turned into the courtyard of St Bartholomew's Hospital. Sammy and Joshua unloaded and made their way through the back corridors to the dissection room. An officious young man in shirt sleeves slouched on one of the tables waiting for them. He raised his arm languidly and indicated to them to place the corpse on the table. The young man lifted the makeshift shroud and nodded.

'Where are the clothes?' he asked absently while examining the pupils and injuries to the neck. Joshua and Samuel shrugged. The bored student did not see them. 'Well?'

'Er, don't know,' said Joshua.

'What do you mean? Did they hang him in his long johns?' Samuel smirked. Joshua sniggered. 'Oh, all right. Get out of here.' The student consulted his paperwork before yelling for an orderly. 'Strip him, clean him. Class tomorrow.'

The orderly set to work removing the undergarments. He dipped a cloth in a bowl of alcohol and rubbed down the cadaver. He grasped the jaw, not yet seized with rigor mortis, and shoved the tongue back inside. He looked for a moment at the open eyes, searching as he always did for a picture burned on to the eyeball – the last image the dying saw. As always, he found only darkness and his own reflection. He closed the eyelids and laid out the hands to cover the genitals, because, he thought to himself, even a corpse deserved some measure of dignity.

A SELECTED LIST OF FINE WRITING
AVAILABLE FROM BLACK SWAN

99618	1	BEHIND THE SCENES AT THE MUSEUM	Kate Atkinson	£6.99
99531	2	AFTER THE HOLE	Guy Burt	£5.99
99628	9	THE KNIGHT OF THE FLAMING HEART	Michael Carson	£6.99
99692	0	THE PRINCE OF TIDES	Pat Conroy	£6.99
99602	5	THE LAST GIRL	Penelope Evans	£5.99
99599	1	SEPARATION	Dan Franck	£5.99
99616	5	SIMPLE PRAYERS	Michael Golding	£5.99
99668	8	MYSTERIOUS SKIN	Scott Heim	£6.99
99169	4	GOD KNOWS	Joseph Heller	£7.99
99605	X	A SON OF THE CIRCUS	John Irving	£7.99
99567	3	SAILOR SONG	Ken Kesey	£6.99
99542	8	SWEET THAMES	Matthew Kneale	£6.99
99660	2	STEPS	Jerzy Kosinski	£5.99
99595	9	LITTLE FOLLIES	Eric Kraft	£5.99
99580	0	CAIRO TRILOGY I: PALACE WALK	Naguib Mahfouz	£7.99
99384	0	TALES OF THE CITY	Armistead Maupin	£5.99
99502	9	THE LAST WORD	Paul Micou	£5.99
99597	5	COYOTE BLUE	Christopher Moore	£5.99
99577	0	CONFESSIONS OF AUBREY BEARDSLEY	Donald S. Olsen	£7.99
99536	3	IN THE PLACE OF FALLEN LEAVES	Tim Pears	£5.99
99667	X	GHOSTING	John Preston	£6.99
99664	5	YELLOWHEART	Tracy Reed	£5.99
99607	6	THE DARKENING LEAF	Caroline Stickland	£5.99
99636	X	KNOWLEDGE OF ANGELS	Jill Paton Walsh	£5.99
99673	4	DINA'S BOOK	Herbjørg Wassmo	£6.99
99500	2	THE RUINS OF TIME	Ben Woolfenden	£4.99